Montpelier Tomorrow

A Novel

Marylee MacDonald

ALL THINGS
THAT MATTER
PRESS

Montpelier Tomorrow

Copyright © 2014 by Marylee MacDonald

ISBN 13: 9780990715818

Library of Congress Control Number: 2014948822

Cover design by: *the*BookDesigners
Published in 2014 by All Things That Matter Press

Acknowledgments

In writing this book I wanted to capture the immediate, lived experience of a family struggling to cope with the challenges of ALS. This book could not have been written without the support of writers in Evanston and Tempe. In the early stages of the book's creation, Fred Shafer encouraged me to move forward. That early validation made me think there was, indeed, a story here. Writers who read multiple chapters and even whole drafts of the book include Chicago writers Lynn Sloan, Jan Leary, Jan Deal, Lee Strickland, Katie Shonk, Jackie Keer, and Vivian DeGraff. My Tempe and online writers group helped me enormously in the later stages: Jim Clark, Alex Kroll, Jerome Long, Neil McCabe, Paul Bennett, Bhira Backhaus, Kathy Hughes, Pat Hayes, Polly Baughman, Bridget O'Gara, Ann Bergin, and most especially Deborah Bauer and Greg Williams. For looking at the first chapter and sharing his own family's journey with ALS, I sincerely thank Robert Boswell. For early publication in *StoryQuarterly*, thank you to its editor Marie Hayes. Writer and writing coach Kevin McIlvoy read the manuscript twice in its entirety, and gave me invaluable suggestions for places the story could be expanded. Writing this book would not have been possible without the support of my husband, Bruce Rittmann. His astute comments and desire for me to have this book speak for all the families whose lives are touched by ALS gave me the courage to find its deeper truths. And lastly, thank you to my daughter and her family for allowing me to share their journey.

For Elliott and Jonathan

Is there another life? Shall I awake and find all this a dream? There must be, we cannot be created for this sort of suffering.

—John Keats, letter to Charles Brown, September 30, 1830

CHAPTER 1

Time robs us of chances for reconciliation. Time makes us liars. I wanted to save my daughter, and even now, I don't know what made me think I could keep her from going through what I had gone through, widowed and pregnant, all at the same time. The scars from her father's death had never fully healed, but if not for Tony's illness, Sandy would have sailed into her future and I would have gone on trying to save the world, one kindergartner at a time.

That June, when I closed up my classroom and headed off to Washington, D.C., I teetered on the brink of an exciting transition. For the past few years, aging parents had kept me in Chicago. Not that I begrudged them: This was the natural progression of a woman's life, or so it seemed, even though women of my generation thought we had liberated ourselves from traditional roles. You can't really free yourself from love though, nor from the surprise that middle-age doesn't mean you have more time for yourself. Children leave the nest about the time parents grow frail. One minute you're changing babies' diapers and the next you're tugging up Depends. My mother had died. I missed her terribly, but her death had freed me. Finally, with an unencumbered heart, I could see my daughter's new house and help when the second grandchild arrived. The birth would give me a chance to make amends for the baby showers and birthdays I had missed.

Standing on the sidewalk in Glover Park, a neighborhood in the capital's northwest quadrant, I looked from my day-timer to the rusted numbers above a set of tilted concrete steps. In the upstairs windows, the blinds had yellowed. Brown paint, like shaved chocolate, curled back from the porch-beams. Next to the door, plastic recycling bins overflowed with newsprint. The grass looked brittle and the azaleas dead. Hoping I'd written down the wrong address and ignoring the clues that something disastrous might have happened, I prepared a smile I might have brought with a casserole or condolence flowers.

An envelope poked from the mail slot. Surreptitiously, I slid it out. A letter for Tony Dimasio. Yep, I had the right address. Tony, my son-in-law, was a good-looking punster with scads of friends—lacrosse friends, college and law school buddies, environmental activists, reporters—and he had pursued Sandy as if she were the hottest babe on the planet. Which to him, she was. Her savings had paid for their first house.

Sighing at the mountain of work that awaited them, I cupped my hand against the glare and pressed my nose to the door's glass panel. Sandy had no idea what it really took to fix up a place, even though she had seen me do it a dozen times, and I feared she'd taken on too much. Before I could even catch a glimpse of the interior, the clomp of footsteps made me back away.

Sandy's face appeared. A nutmeg of summer freckles. A smile. The door flew open. "Mom!"

Like her father, Sandy had deep-set eyes. In bright light, they looked blue, but in the shadows of the porch, her eyes reminded me of clouds before a storm. In the years since her teenage rebellion had come at me like projectile vomit, I'd learned to watch for the early warning signs of her bad moods. I saw none now. Since Christmas, her belly had inflated to the size of my exercise ball. She was nine months pregnant and the baby had dropped. A flowered jumper hung from her bare, hunched shoulders. Sandy had never been much of a hugger, but this time she threw her arms around me, a drowning person lunging for the life preserver. Which was my neck.

"Don't choke me," I said, disentangling her arms.

"Thank God you're here," she said.

Reflexively, I tucked in her bra strap. "I can't believe the pregnancy's almost done."

Sandy looked sideways at my hand, and then brushed it aside to massage her shoulder. "I hate my bony arms. Even eating for two, I can't seem to put on weight."

"You look fabulous, honey."

"I must look better than I feel," Sandy said. A taut grin flipped up like a mask. "Well, you're here, at least, but I expected you an hour ago."

Maybe we could rewind this to the knock, I thought. Had I said something or done something to deserve this tiny flash of anger? I'd tucked in her strap. That was it, and I should have known not to. She could not stand to be touched or drawn into an embrace. At that moment, however, her brief hug had left me wanting more: a longer and less desperate hug, the downy softness of her cheek against mine, or a map crumpled to bring Chicago and Washington, D.C. closer together.

"I really should have pulled over and called you," I said, still searching for what had made her say she hated her bony arms and why she was angry because I had arrived an hour late. "I thought about calling, but then I thought it'd just make me later and anyway, I had a map so I wasn't *lost*, just playing pin the tail on the donkey."

Exhaling, she reared back.

"Sandy, please," I said. "I came to help, not get in your way."

She must have had a long day, but so had I. Weary from the drive and the demands of the last few months, I needed a refuge. "Can I come in?"

"Sure. I don't know why we're standing outside in this heat." Backing into the living room she looked around. "The place is a pigsty, but, oh well, you can't do everything."

The inside looked better than the exterior. No books on the end tables, no out-of-place couch cushions, and, surprisingly, no toys on the floor.

"The place is definitely not a pigsty," I said.

She shook her head. "I try to keep it picked up, but it's hard because Josh doesn't have a playroom. We have a basement, but it's so dingy I can hardly bear to go down there."

She had planted a hook in my mouth. I felt the barb, but let her reel me in. "Maybe I can do a little painting while I'm here."

"Oh, would you, Mom?" Sandy said. "That would just be amazing."

"Sure," I said, though on the two-day drive out, painting Sandy's basement had been the last thing on my mind.

"I'm trying to get the house organized, baby clothes washed and in drawers, and work's crazy. Some cases I can't delegate because I'm the lead attorney." Sandy checked her watch. "Oh, no. I'm late."

I'm late, I'm late, for a very important date. "Where are you going?" I said.

"A doctor's appointment." Sandy grabbed her purse. "They're squeezing us in at the end of the day, and I didn't find out about it until a couple of hours ago. Can you watch Josh? He's upstairs in his crib."

"Sure." I followed her to the porch.

Holding her watermelon belly, she jogged to the car. Just like the White Rabbit. *No time to say hello, good-bye, I'm late, I'm late, I'm late.* In the parking strip Sandy opened the car door.

"Should I wake Josh at a certain time?" I called.

"Let him sleep. His teacher said he didn't nap."

"How long will you be gone?"

"An hour or so." Sandy slid back the seat of her Toyota Tercel. The car had scratched bumpers and a caved-in passenger door, an almost new car turning into a junker. She roared out of the parking space. Sandy's brothers joked that she'd never learned to tell time, but that didn't matter because she had lots of other skills. She'd never find herself in my situation, *Broke With Children.* My life would have made a good sitcom.

Back in the house I knelt on the couch and tried to raise the front windows: painted shut and no curtains. A stroller stood in the corner. I could have taken Josh out for a walk, but Sandy hadn't left a key. I opened the TV hutch. On the shelves below the boob tube sat wooden puzzles and LEGO blocks. Good for fine-motor skills. Grabbing blunt-nosed scissors from the dining room table, I returned to the porch and eased into a plastic chair. From the recycling bin, I separated out two pages of the *Washington Post*, folding and refolding the newsprint until I held a rectangle the size of a book. The key to making paper-dolls, paper-houses, or paper anything was to start with the right shape, fold in the same direction, and leave part of the fold uncut. In my classroom, I always had something like this on the windows—leaves in fall, pumpkins in October, and snowmen at Christmas. Across the street the houses had twisted, licorice porch railings, attics with small, winking windows, and chimney pots smack in the center of tiny slate roofs. A neighborhood of Hobbit houses. And here was Sandy's. Dead azaleas and recycling bins.

Inside, I threw the paper houses on the couch. Until I could get curtains made, I'd tape up the cityscape to provide privacy. Sandy must have tape on her desk. Upstairs, the door to the right opened to the master bedroom—the room with the yellowed shades. On Sandy's desk, next to a wicker basket of unpaid bills, sat a roll of American-flag stamps. No tape. Maybe Josh had used it up. When my kids were little, I could never find a roll of tape to save my soul. I looked at the indent in the chenille spread, the pillows propped against the wall, and a novel she'd tossed on the bed. I picked it up. *How Stella Got Her Groove Back*. I sniff-laughed. That book had inspired me to dip into the barrel and see if I could pull out an edible apple. I hadn't found the young hunk Stella found, only some bruised bananas.

In the room across the hall, Josh lay spread-eagled. Small for three, he had Tony's black curls and Sandy's fair skin. His pink neck felt hot to the touch. The nursery school teacher had forgotten to hit it with sun block. Three-to-six was my favorite age. They were little philosophers, as I had seen last Christmas, when Josh said he thought dolphins had a secret language and someday he would learn to speak it. The Spiderman shirt, one of my presents, had faded. An inch of skin showed above his shorts. I hated these big gaps between visits, and I hoped the creak of stairs as I descended would wake him.

The paper houses had dropped like a slinky from the couch. I should tape-up the diorama before Josh needed attention, but where had Sandy put the tape? A drawer to the left of the sink held silverware, and below it, the drawer my mother always called the "Fibber McGee and Molly" drawer: string, screwdrivers, thumbtacks, birthday candles, white glue, and the odd button. Whether women wanted to or not, we took on our mother's patterns: spices in the cabinet to the left of the microwave, cookie sheets in the oven drawer. I could be blind and cook a meal here.

A pen-mug sat on the counter. Next to a stack of unopened bills sat a roll of tape. Twirling it around my finger, I whistled softly, trying to fill a silence broken only by the bark of a neighbor's dog and a motorcycle's distant cough. Kneeling on the denim couch, I taped the paper houses to the windows. The silhouette reminded me of the skyline at the Adler Planetarium. Newsprint blocked the view of parked cars, but that was good. If I couldn't see out, no one could see in. Breastfeeding Josh, Sandy had always thrown a receiving blanket over her shoulder. A private person, she wouldn't want every Tom, Dick, and Harry looking through her windows.

With no more self-assigned tasks, I thought about taking a look at the basement, but the heat punctured my balloon of good intentions. I can picture myself innocently walking through the house, curious about the life my daughter had begun to construct for herself. It was the last moment of tranquility before fate blindsided me. Blindsided me again, I should say, because my husband's death had come at me in much the same way, on a day so ordinary that such an alteration of circumstances seemed unimaginable.

The screen door wheezed open, and I stood on the porch. The rooflines' spiked shadows had advanced across the small, square lawns. Across the street, a paper skeleton hung on the door, a relic of last year's Halloween. When I heard a hubcap scrape the curb, I turned.

Their Toyota sedan was backing into a parking space. Tony sat in the passenger seat. Usually, he drove. Sandy, on the driver's side, turned off the engine. Then she leaned on the steering wheel and stared straight ahead, the way people do when they're having a fight and trying to decide whether to finish it or go in. I leaned on the porch rail, fearing that Tony had crossed her in some way. Better him than me. Finally, she opened her door. One hand at the crook of her back, the other on the hood, she went around to Tony's door and opened it. Tony started to get out but fell to his knees and curled up in a ball.

I stood. My mouth went dry. "Tony, are you all right?"

"I'm okay," he called.

"I've got him, Mom," Sandy said.

To keep myself from dashing down the stairs, I grabbed the railing and prayed that Sandy wouldn't injure herself. Holding him under the elbow, she lifted him to his feet and brushed grass from his pants. He swiped an arm across his forehead. His cheeks looked flushed. At work he glad-handed so many people he'd probably picked up a bug. When he felt better I'd tease him and ask if the halls of Congress needed an Elvis impersonator: Since Christmas, he'd grown muttonchops shaped like the boot of Italy.

Sandy unlocked the trunk and took out his sport coat. Letting her carry it and shuffling his feet, he came up the walk. I held the screen.

Inside, Tony flopped down on the sofa, the one beneath my paper silhouette. Stretched out full length, he put one foot up on the sofa's arm and left the other on the floor. His shoelace had come undone, and though tempted to kneel down and tie it, I didn't want him to feel like he'd gone back to kindergarten.

"You look like you had a terrible day," I said.

"The longest day of my life," he said.

I put my palm on his forehead. It felt clammy, not hot. He drew his hands to his chin. His chest heaved, but no sound came out. Elbowing me aside, Sandy bent over Tony and put her arms around him.

He pushed her away. "Too hot."

Sandy went to the kitchen. Water splashed. When she returned, her bangs dripped. "Where's Josh?" she said.

"Asleep," I said.

"He won't sleep tonight, but then, I guess that's all right because I won't either." Sandy sank down onto the other sofa and bumped a framed poster from the National Zoo, a mother panda with a protective paw curled around her baby. My legs shook, and I backed toward the rocking chair.

"Hey, Colleen, do you happen to have a handkerchief?" Tony said. Beads of moisture dotted his upper lip.

I always carried packages of tissue to wipe runny noses. Reaching out, I handed one over.

He blew his nose. "So, did Sandy tell you what this was all about?"

"I didn't want to worry her," Sandy said.

"What should I be worried about?"

"My finger." Tony held up the index finger of his right hand. It moved like the second-hand of a clock: tick, tick, tick. Not a smooth motion.

"What's wrong with it?" I said.

"Since March, we've been thinking he had a pinched nerve," Sandy said.

This was June. "What do you have, carpal tunnel?"

"I wish." Tony propped himself on an elbow, opened his mouth, and pointed to his tongue.

"He was testifying a month ago on Capitol Hill—" Sandy said.

"A swine farm bill was coming up—" Tony said.

"And he got so tongue-tied—"

"I couldn't speak," Tony said.

"You?" Driving through Ohio, I'd heard him interviewed on public radio. There'd been a call-in program on factory farms. The stench. The animals' living conditions. It wasn't an issue I'd ever thought twice about, but Tony had been so eloquent, I'd actually begun to think the animal-rights folks had a point.

Tony pulled up his shirt. The dark, curly hair, once thick on his chest, had been shaved clean, leaving only the stubble. Dozens of white circles the size of bottle caps dotted his chest. He looked like he'd been stood against a wall and used for dart-gun target practice.

"I saw this neurologist—"

"Two, actually," Sandy said.

"The second doctor was a mom from our nursery school," Tony said. "She saw Sandy coming down the elevator, just losing it."

"So she brought him back upstairs and ran the tests again," Sandy said.

"I had a hundred electrodes on my body."

"Nipples and everything," Sandy said.

Tony looked down at his chest. He shuddered. "They shocked me over and over again. I felt like a rat in an experiment."

"After the second battery of nerve tests," Sandy said, "the doctor told him he has ALS."

Through the open screen came the hum of tires and the urgent ring of a tinny bell. Riding a purple bicycle with training wheels, a curly-headed girl, biting her tongue, stood on the pedals. Her mother jogged behind, close enough to grab the seat. The ring echoed long after they'd passed.

Tony pulled down his shirt. "The doc said I have Lou Gehrig's Disease." He shook his head from side to side, moaned, and put a hand over his eyes and the other on his heart. "I thought I had it right from the start. I mean, that was what the HMO doc told me back in March, that I had ALS, and I thought if I did, I could be brave and suck it up, but it's different when neurologists tell you for sure."

Sandy reached over and massaged Tony's foot and with her other hand pressed her belly. "The baby's quiet."

"Probably sleeping," I said. One domino-disaster tipping another. That's what she feared.

Tony blew his nose and wiped his eyes with a corner of his shirt. "I'd better start dinner."

"You can't be in a mood to cook," I said. "Let's order pizza."

Tony stood up. "I have stuff for spaghetti."

I followed him to the kitchen. The doctors had to be wrong. Tony was in the prime of life, a lacrosse player, a runner, and lately, a vegetarian. He took an onion from the refrigerator. After peeling off the dry outer layers, he used the flat of his hand to force down the blade.

"After Christmas, when Sandy saw her brothers in the kitchen, she said I had to learn to cook. I actually like it, and I want to cook while I can."

"While you can . . ." I wanted to draw out this moment, the moment when I couldn't yet see around the corner. "Can what?"

"Cook, of course." Tony stared at me. "My muscles will atrophy."

"I don't know much about ALS."

"Actually, I don't either," Tony said, "except I've got it."

Trying to have a normal conversation and accept this news as if Tony were telling me about a raise or a promotion, I found myself feeling increasingly upset. I thought of the Chinese woman who lived two doors down from my new house and how she'd stand on the porch in the bitterest weather, going through her *tai chi* exercises. Balance in slow motion. I opened the silverware drawer and took out knives and forks.

"What, exactly, did the doctor say?"

"A lot of men get it."

"So what are they going to do?"

"Nothing they *can* do," he said.

"Nothing?" I said. "But there's something they can do for everything."

He shook his head like it was a *fait accompli* and dumped onions in a cast-iron skillet, one that had belonged to my mother. I wondered how I could possibly deal with this loss when I'd barely absorbed her death, and immediately felt ashamed that the first thought that bubbled up was whether I had space inside my skin for another grief this big. This was Sandy's tragedy, not mine.

"Have you got another kleenex?" Sandy called from the living room

"She can have this." Tony handed me the rest of the packet.

I took it, returned to the living room, and sat down next to Sandy, who leaned against me. Like a kitten on a tree, she dug her nails into my shoulders. Tears soaked my blouse.

"Your daughter's upset," Tony called from the kitchen.

"I can see that."

On the second floor, the toilet flushed.

Sandy lifted her head. "Josh is awake." She blew her nose and crumpled the kleenex in her fist.

"Do you want me to throw that away?" I said.

Sandy held out the damp wad. "My body feels all numb, like it went to the body dentist."

Mine did, too. "Where's your trash?"

"Under the sink."

"Sandy, could you open this can?" Tony said.

Letting out a silent scream, Sandy flung her head back, bumping the panda poster.

I leapt up. "Let me help him."

"Thanks so much, Mom. I've had Braxton-Hicks all day."

"I've heard the word, but what is it?"

"Contractions," Sandy said.

"But they stop if she sits," Tony said.

"In my day, we called that going into labor."

Sandy put her hands on her stomach. "I don't think it's true labor. I hope not, anyway. My due date's not for another ten days."

"Mom," a little voice called from upstairs.

I helped Sandy to her feet, but I had to lean back and counterbalance her weight, or she would have pulled me down.

"I'm coming," Sandy said.

The voice said, "I need you to wipe me."

"Could someone open this can?" Tony said.

I went into the kitchen. "What do you need?"

A can of pomodoro tomatoes sat on the counter. Tony held out a can opener. "My fingers don't have the strength."

I picked up the tomatoes and squeezed the can opener's handles. Air hissed.

"One thing I don't quite get," I said, "is what happens. I mean, what's the progression of the disease?"

"I have a year to live," Tony said. "Maybe less."

"No way!" The can dropped on the counter. The lid sprang open. "Are you sure?"

"I'm just going by what the doctor said." Tears streaming, he looked over his shoulder. "Fifty-five's the average age."

"But you're only thirty-four."

"I was young, she said."

I put my arms around him, but he pushed me away. "I need to finish dinner."

Tony broke spaghetti into the pot, stirring the pasta with a wooden spoon. He wiped his forehead with the back of his arm. "Shit, it's hot," he said.

"That's because the back side of the house faces east, and you're getting the late afternoon sun."

"Sandy said you'd have known that and not let us buy it. It's the one thing about the house she hates."

"Unless I'd come by at the end of the day, I wouldn't have flagged that as a problem. I told her to hire a home inspector."

"Well, she's over it so you can relax."

"Over what?"

"Over being angry because you didn't fly out."

Eyes down, I laid out silverware and napkins. "My mother was dying."

"Yeah, well. Sandy needed you and you didn't come."

"A home inspector looks at homes full time. Most of them are engineers or former contractors. I doubt I could have told her anything more than what they wrote up in their report."

"You don't have to sound so defensive," he said.

"But … oh, never mind," I said.

The last three weeks of mother's life had passed in a blur. I had to make decisions about a feeding tube or comfort measures. Sips of water dwindled down to ice chips and spongy swabs of her tongue. I couldn't reconstruct when exactly, in that blur of days, Sandy had called. And, of course, my daughter had a right to feel let down. No one could understand what the inversion of roles meant, the child behaving as a parent, making end-of-life decisions for an emaciated, vacant-minded shell. Sandy had just started her journey. The first house. The second baby. And now this.

Tony bit into a noodle. "*Al dente.*" He looked at me. "Whole wheat. They turn mushy if you cook them too long."

Tony. The newbie in the kitchen. My boys would have found his sudden culinary interest hilarious. But then, no they wouldn't. Not now.

Sandy came down holding Josh by the hand. Smiling, she looked down at her son. "Do you remember Grandma?"

"You're Mommy's mommy." Josh's eyebrows looked like charcoal smudges and from beneath them shone two blue marbles. Rob's eyes and the eyes of Sandy's brothers.

"Remember last Christmas we went to an aquarium where they had dolphins?" I said.

"And jellyfish." Josh tugged his mother's hand.

She smiled.

"It's time for dinner, Josh," Tony said. "Get the stepstool and wash your hands."

"He washed upstairs," Sandy said.

"Could somebody dump the water out of the pan and put the sauce on the noodles?" Tony said.

I did as he asked and put food on the table. Josh climbed into his booster seat and buckled the strap.

"No salad?" Sandy said.

"I'm not in the mood," Tony said.

"I don't like tomato sauce," Josh said.

I wondered if the opening gambit of this negotiation were for my benefit or if they negotiated every meal. That kind of thing wore me out.

"Daddy made a nice dinner," I said. "Why don't you try one bite?"

"I already know I won't like it," Josh said. "It's red."

"He likes plain noodles with butter and cheese." Sandy went into the kitchen and rummaged in the refrigerator. She put a turkey roll on his plate. "He's fine with this."

I twirled my spaghetti. The sauce tasted burnt. Maybe I could bargain for a turkey roll.

"What's wrong?" Tony said, his dark eyes glaring at me from across the table. "Don't you like it, either?"

In my stomach, a gerbil raced madly on a wheel. "No, it's fine. Whole grain noodles. Very nutritious."

Standing behind Josh's chair, Sandy took a taste of spaghetti, frowned, and put her plate down on the counter, a pass-through between the narrow dining room and aisle kitchen. "The humidity takes away my appetite."

Tony looked up at her. He hadn't touched his dinner. We were pretending to be normal for as long as we could.

"Why don't you take Josh outside and let me do the dishes?" I said.

"I guess we could do that," Sandy said. "It's still light."

"Okay," Tony said. "Fresh air would feel good."

I cleared the dishes, listening to the tape that ran in my head whenever I wasted food. Think of the starving children in Armenia. The distant tragedy flashed up from my childhood, and it was the rare meal that found me leaving a bite of food on my plate. The spaghetti was really, really bad. I dumped it into the garbage.

On the dead grass that passed for a lawn, Sandy pitched a wiffle ball. Tony wrapped his arms around Josh's shoulders, showing him how to swing a plastic bat. Josh connected. The ball bounced across two neighbors' lawns into a clump of ice plant. He gave a whoop, then raced, his arms pumping. All elbows and knobby knees, he looked like a cricket.

"Did you see that one?" Josh held up the ball. "Wasn't that a great one?"

"That was good, Josh." Tony looked over at me, sitting on the porch. "I always dreamed of taking my kids to Yankees' games. Josh won't remember this."

I leaned over the railing. "Why don't I take Josh to the park and give you some time to decompress?"

"No, that's okay," Sandy said.

Tony wiped his brow. His face turned sullen and Sandy looked at him.

"Then again," Sandy said, "maybe that's a good idea."

"He'd better run off some energy or he'll never go to sleep tonight," I said.

"I want to play baseball," Josh said.

"Grandma knows how to play baseball." Sandy handed me the bat.

"Not as good as your dad," I said.

"I'll carry the ball."

"Sure," I said. "But don't drop it."

From the sidewalk, Josh looked back at Sandy and Tony entering the house. The screen slammed. "What's wrong?"

"Your dad just found out he's sick," I said.

Josh looked up, his eyebrows in a squiggle. "But the doctor can make him better. Right?"

"I hope so."

"The doctor makes *me* better."

"Doctors can do a lot."

I didn't want to be the first to tell him his father was going to die. That job belonged to his parents, and maybe they could shield him by breaking the news gradually.

Sandy had found out the worst way possible. Rob's mom had invited us for dinner. It was Friday. We lived in Schaumburg then. I fought traffic on the Stevenson to get to his parents' house on the South Side, and Rob planned to drive straight there from work. By the time I arrived, Jean had a pot roast on the stove, and the smell of onions and gravy made me instantly sick. Three months pregnant, I threw up and came out of the bathroom to find Kevin pulling open the cupboards. I apologized for him getting into things, but she said that was nothing. Her kids got into a lot worse mischief. Having a smoke and scraping cookie dough from a spoon, she sat at the kitchen table. Across from her, Sandy, five, a little girl with lopsided pigtails and a dishtowel apron, knelt on a kitchen chair and waited for permission to lick the bowl. Jean launched into a story about the time she came back from the grocery store to find all ten kids standing on the garage roof. A phone call interrupted her story. I took the call.

"I'd like to speak to Mrs. Gallagher," a police officer said. "Her husband has been in an accident."

Oh, my God, Rob's father, I thought, then covered the receiver and looked at Jean, tapping an ash into her cupped hand. Her gray hair caught back in a bun made her look like one of those impoverished women from the dust bowl. Rob had three brothers in high school. Who would pay for their college? Jean took another drag of her cigarette, waiting to tell me how she got the kids off the roof and what punishment she'd devised. I put the receiver to my ear. "Are you sure you've got the right Gallagher?" I said. "There's lots of us here on the South Side."

"Robert Gallagher," he said. "Age twenty-six. His driver's license lists this as his permanent address."

Feeling the earth turn to sand beneath my feet, I steadied myself against the table. "That's my husband."

"Mrs. Gallagher," the man said, "I'm sorry to tell you, your husband's dead."

"My husband's dead?" I screamed. "What do you mean, dead?"

Jean stubbed out her cigarette on the Formica and stood, leaning across the table to take the phone.

Sandy jumped off the chair. She looked up at me, her face white. "My daddy's dead?"

"Yes," I said. The room spun and, knees weak, I fell back against the wall. My teeth chattered. Sandy tore down the hall, running upstairs to her uncles' room. "My daddy's dead. My daddy's dead." Her screams barely penetrated the roaring in my ears. The baby I carried would never know his father. Sandy would never see him again. Death meant not coming back. Not ever.

***

Strolling down the streets of Glover Park, pretending everything was all right, I watched Josh, his arms extended, walk the tightrope of a brick retaining wall. He might remember this day as his last hour of unencumbered happiness, or he might let the hour submerge into the sea of similar, carefree days, not realizing he should treasure this moment of innocence, along with the speckled stones he picked up and slipped into his pockets.

In the effort to fit one more, he let go of the ball. It rolled slowly into the street. Josh sprang after it. A brown UPS truck bore down on him. With a hand up to shield his eyes, the driver dodged and squinted against the glare.

"Watch out," I screamed. Dashing into the street, I jerked Josh off his feet.

The truck rumbled past.

I dragged Josh to the sidewalk and looked him straight in the eye. "Don't you ever, ever do that again."

His mouth quivered. "Yes, Grandma."

"What were you doing, anyway?" I said. "You know you're not allowed to go in the street."

"I was trying to help." He shivered.

I turned him under my wing. "Here's what we'll do next time. If it's necessary to get a ball, I will get it. Understand?"

He looked down at his feet. None too gently, I lifted his chin. "Is that clear?"

His eyes flicked up and caught me in their blue glare. Just as quickly, he looked down again.

Maybe we should go back home. If we did, though, he'd find out what was wrong.

"All right, Josh. Show me the school."

***

Surrounded by lawn, the two-story brick building with its tall, white windows reminded me of Evanston's Lincolnwood, the school I'd taught at long enough to see my former students return with their offspring. I wondered if Tony would live to see Josh's first day here at Stoddert. But maybe he'd got it wrong about how long he had to live. Recently, I'd watched an interview with the astrophysicist, Stephen Hawking. He'd lived a long time with ALS; crippled up, sure, but still alive.

Josh pointed to the playground. "The tot-lot's over there."

"I thought you wanted to practice hitting."

He looked down at his shoes. "I'm only good when my dad helps me."

"I can help you," I said.

"That's okay. It's kind of hot."

That scare sure had taken the stuffing out. As I walked to a bench, the two gold bands suspended from a chain around my neck jingled and bounced against my breasts. Josh, kneeling in the shadows of the slide, dug down and unearthed a toy car. Even if he didn't remember this moment, I would remember him clawing a road through the damp, dark sand. A road to where, though? My daughter, a new mother, would have to deal with childcare and work demands and face the impending death of her soul mate. She'd lost a father. That had been trauma enough. She didn't deserve this.

By the time I brushed off Josh's hands and emptied his shoes, a tangerine sun hung above the canopy of trees. Between the bird songs and the cacophony of cicadas, the neighborhood echoed with a happy, buzzing undercurrent of life: fathers greeted at the door, screens slamming, the smell of curry from a house where a sign on the window said BLOCK PARENT. Josh sprinted ahead to the corner. A white-haired man, his thumb on a garden hose, stood watering new sod.

"Hi, Mr. Jaffee," Josh said.

"Hi, Josh," the man said in a gruff voice. The armpits of Mr. Jaffee's undershirt were brown, and he wore a straw hat to which he'd attached fishing lures. His pants were baggy, held up by rainbow suspenders. Before retirement, he must have been a large man, but now he had started on that journey of regression I witnessed my father make: the work life gone, the circle of friends dropping one by one, the life outside the self growing distant until the only thing left to talk about was bowel movements and prunes at breakfast.

"Has your mom had that baby yet?" Mr. Jaffee said.

"Not yet," Josh said.

By way of introduction, I offered my hand. "I'm Sandy's mom, Colleen Gallagher."

His palm had the velvety feel of old skin.

"Call me Lowell," he said. "You're a State Farm customer, I see."

"How'd you know that?"

"Bumper sticker on your car."

"You're very observant," I said.

"Nah. I used to be an agent. Let me know if you need anything. I look out for folks."

"I will." For the life of me—not then, not now—I couldn't figure out how to hand off any of what shimmered in the heat waves of our future: death's sharp blade cleaving years from Tony's life, the terrible loss for my daughter, the loss for Josh. I felt as if I were standing in a hurricane, boards blowing past me, rain pelting my face, the whistling of a terrible wind in my ears. I didn't want to believe it.

Josh ran down the block and hopped up the front steps. I followed.

Before going in he turned to me. "Mr. Jaffee has butterscotch candy in his pockets, but I'm not supposed to ask."

"He seems like a nice man."

"I'm only allowed to if my mom says it's okay."

"That's a good rule," I said.

Through the screen, I saw Sandy and Tony huddled on the couch, their arms around each other. "We're home. And we're thirsty," I said.

Josh pressed the screen's thumb-latch.

Their faces streaked with tears, Sandy and Tony sprang apart. An empty box of tissue sat on the couch. Like white carnations, used ones lay scattered on the floor. They had been sitting there the whole time, locked together. Death was something Tony and Sandy had plenty of time to deal with, figuring out how to tell Josh after absorbing the news themselves. I brushed sand from my shoes and left them on the porch. Like Rob, Tony was irreplaceable, a guy with a big, big heart. His death would be devastating for Sandy, doubly so because she'd lost her father. Rob had adored her, his first-born, and I had never found a way to make up for that loss. Nor did I know until much later that on the day I got the phone call from the police, Sandy believed she had lost me, too.

CHAPTER 2

In the morning I poured a bowl of raisin bran and took it to the dining room table. Through the rectangular pass-through, I watched Sandy unload the dishwasher and fought down the urge to tell her I'd do it if she gave me a minute to eat. A navy blue dress, shrink-wrapped around her belly, made me think she had not anticipated getting so big or else didn't want to spend money on a maternity dress she would only wear for another month. That was probably it. Sandy, ever practical. Or maybe thinking if she just made it through the delivery, she could go back to her regular clothes and regular life. She put a hand on the counter, braced herself, and closed her eyes.

"Are you having contractions?" I said.

Sandy nodded and scrunched up her face. "They're not much worse than yesterday, but my doctor wants me to come in." She straightened and took a deep breath. "That was a long one."

Gulping two bites of cereal on my way to the sink, I dumped my breakfast down the drain.

"Tony, we'd better go," Sandy called.

"Josh is almost dressed," he hollered, the cool-as-cucumber, second-child father. "My mom and dad are on their way."

I hadn't spent much time with Tony's folks, but if this really was ALS and not some weird misdiagnosis, we would need to put our heads together.

"So has Tony thought about the Mayo Clinic?" I asked.

"I don't think that'd do any good." Sandy closed her eyes and grabbed my hand, crushing my fingers. The labor pain passed. "Oh, Mom, I don't know how I'm going to get through this."

"You will."

"I keep telling myself, you did."

"Your dad's death was more of an amputation," I said. "Easy, compared to this."

"Do you have to be so brutally honest all the time?" Sandy put a hand on the counter, grimaced, and then looked down at the floor.

A puddle of water spread across the linoleum.

"I'll clean that up," I said. "You get going."

She waddled toward the door. "Tony!"

Watching her pick up her overnight case, I thought about telling her I hadn't meant to be brutal, or honest, or brutally honest. I was merely stating a fact. I didn't know how I knew what I knew, only that I did. What she faced would be bad, maybe even unendurable.

Holding Josh's hand, I stood on the front porch and called, "Good luck."

Tony made a U-turn. Sandy dropped her seat back and that made me wonder if she was further into labor than she thought. The old protective instinct that had started at Sandy's birth—that umbilical tug that persisted—leapt from my gut and dried my throat. My hand felt sweaty. Josh pried his fingers loose. Down the block, the white-haired neighbor—What was his name? Lovell? Lloyd? God, I was getting Alzheimer's like my mom—carried his recycling to the curb.

"Hi, Mr. Jaffee." Josh waved.

"Hi, Josh." Lowell, that was his name, wore the same stained undershirt and straw hat he'd worn yesterday. His retirement uniform. I recognized the type. My dad, a carpenter, his face weathered by years of Chicago winters, had dressed in holey overalls he'd bought decades before at Farm and Fleet. "No point in buying new clothes," he'd said. "Waste of money."

Mr. Jaffee went down the alley and returned with an appliance box. He put it on the parking strip, then looked toward us, shading his eyes against the sun. "What's happening in your house?"

"My mom's having our baby," Josh said.

Mr. Jaffee straightened up. "Well, well. A new baby."

Josh pointed. "What's that?"

"I bought a new stove," Mr. Jaffee said. "This is the box it came in."

I looked from the box to Josh. "Can we have it?"

"Help yourself."

"What's it for?" Josh said.

"A playhouse," I said. "Let's build one."

"Yippee! Can I help?"

"Of course you can."

With Josh holding the flaps, I dragged the box into the living room. In the kitchen's Fibber McGee and Molly drawer, I found a ruler, markers, and a knife. I drew windows and flowerboxes and cut the cardboard. Josh folded back the shutters. I asked if he wanted a Dutch door so he could close the bottom half to keep out burglars. He did. Then I drew bricks and he colored them.

"What about the inside?" he said.

"You can decorate it however you want." I pushed the box next to the stairs, and, with a scrap of leftover cardboard, made a low table for Josh to eat his peanut-butter graham crackers. In the playhouse he sat on the floor cross-legged, having a tea party with his stuffed bear.

You could never tell what a child would do with a toy. Once I'd been putting toys away in the little-boys' room—my little boys, Kevin and Sean. Sandy had trailed along, repeating my commands. *Pick up all your*

Matchbox cars. Put the Tinker Toys away. "You're not the boss of me," Kevin had said. Even a year after Rob's death his favorite game had been car crash; but that day, he'd pulled over a toy telephone, picked up the receiver and dialed. "Hello, Daddy? Did it hurt when you died?"

I put a hand on my heart and joined him on the floor. Baby Sean had just started to pull himself up. In his yellow terry-cloth suit and with his Easter-chick hair, he stood gumming the bar of his crib.

Sandy closed the toy box. "What did Daddy say?"

"It hurt," Kevin said, "like when I broke my arm."

"I want to talk," Sandy said. He handed her the receiver. A little bell rang as she pulled the phone. "When are you coming home?" With a serious face, she appeared to listen to his answer.

The cord of that silly phone tangled as the three of us huddled and cried.

I should call the boys and let them know. Then again, maybe it would be better to have a face-to-face. I looked over at the playhouse. Josh had finished his snack. "How about a story, Josh?"

"I don't want to take a nap."

"Who said anything about a nap?" I said. "Pick out a book."

He ducked under the playhouse door and chose a dictionary illustrated by Richard Scary, a kindergarten favorite. I opened the book to a cutaway drawing of a house. On the top floor, rabbit children took naps. In the dining room, rabbits set the table. In the kitchen, the rabbit mommy, wearing an apron, cooked dinner.

"Mommies have to do everything," I said.

Josh leaned against my arm and pointed to a rabbit in the basement. "What's that one doing?"

A rabbit in overalls stood at a workbench.

"That's a daddy rabbit," I said, "and that one's a ..."

Josh's eyes closed and I carried him upstairs. While he slept, I could take a nap. Sleep-deprived, I couldn't function. Too many years of late nights during my years as a single mom and, more recently, the night sweats that came from the final blast of menopause, made me hoard sleep the way squirrels tucked away nuts. Still feeling guilty about blowing my stack when the ball rolled into the street, I plugged in the baby monitor, took it to my room, and flopped down on the futon. Jerking a kid's arm like that. Geez. At fifty-three, I sure didn't have the patience I'd had at twenty-four. Or the energy.

***

I woke up, grabbed the baby monitor, and went to check on Josh. In his crib, fingers splayed, wavy hair flattened by the padded bumper, he still slept. Might as well let him. Halfway downstairs, I saw a man's gray slacks and cordovan dress shoes. "Who's there?"

"Tony's father."

"Oh, Aldo." I put a hand on my heart and continued down.

A youthful seventy-two, Aldo had sharp features, and the darting movements of the eyes behind his glasses showed that he was thinking, even as he sat on the couch and leafed through the *Washington Post*.

"Didn't mean to startle you. I rang the doorbell, but no one answered." He held up a key. "I let myself in."

The doorbell must not work. Another thing to fix besides the stuck-tight windows. "How'd you get here so fast?" I said.

He nodded to the big suitcase in a corner by the playhouse. "We had the pilot on alert. Lillian's had our bag packed for weeks."

"You mean Southwest held your plane?" I said.

"No. I took the corporate jet." Aldo ran the East Coast branch of a St. Louis brewery. The Dimasios lived in New Jersey. Tony and Sandy had eloped to Las Vegas, but the Dimasios had insisted on a wedding reception. At their country club, I'd seen enough minks to stock a Chicago furrier's.

"When we arrived," Aldo said, "I called Tony to check in and find out what he wanted us to do." He smiled. "Sandy had another boy. Benjamin. *Benjamino* in Italian."

"You're kidding," I said.

He shook his head. "Nope. They barely made it."

"And the baby's okay?"

"Yes. Full term."

"That's one bit of good news," I said. "Where's Lillian?"

He nodded at the giant black purse between the two couches. "Down at Kinko's xeroxing his test results. She's ready to contact all the neurologists between Florida and Nova Scotia."

"How long have you known about this?" I said.

"She first heard about it in March."

"Three months ago," I said.

"Actually, the middle of February, come to think of it."

That long. Gosh. I sure had been out of the loop.

Aldo touched the back of his neck. "One doc thought Tony had a pinched nerve and told him to take Advil."

"Oh, yeah. 'Take two aspirin.'"

"At the March appointment they started tossing out other ideas," he said. "That was the first time Tony heard ALS mentioned, but the doctors back then thought it might be MS."

"What's the difference?"

"With MS, he could live a more or less normal life," Aldo said. "There are periods of remission. With ALS, there's no remission."

"Tony said he has a year to live. I can't believe it."

"Believe it." Aldo crossed his legs and pulled an ankle onto his knee. "Not only does he have ALS, he has the fast-acting kind. Bulbar onset. For months, we've been hoping the diagnosis would be different. Tony's mom is beside herself." He snapped open the paper and held it in front of his face.

I could take a hint. "I think I'll make a run to the hardware store. It's sweltering upstairs. I need to buy a fan."

"Have fun," he said.

"By any chance, do you know what hospital they went to?"

"Shady Grove Adventist."

***

The hospital was all the way out in Maryland. No wonder Sandy had barely made it. Standing at the door of her room I saw that she was asleep. Her eyebrows, a touch of brown, matched her tangled, ash-brown hair. Even if labor went fast, the final minutes had put her through a workout.

A clear bassinet held the new arrival with his ivory stocking cap. *Benjamino*. The dark-haired little Italian with olive complexion looked a lot more like a *Benjamino* than pale-complected baby Josh, whose legal name was actually *Giuseppe*.

"And who do we have here?" I whispered.

"Don't wake him," Sandy said, her eyes suddenly open.

"I'll be careful." I gathered him up and put the baby on my shoulder. Patting his back and listening to him snuffle, I felt the rhythm of his breathing and his knees against my chest. He squirmed and stretched and a shudder passed through him. Holding him on my forearm, the position Rob called the football carry, I watched him dream. His eyelashes stuck out like little combs.

Sandy pressed the control to raise the head of the bed, rolled to one side, and winced.

"Stitches," she said.

"Oh, yeah," I said.

"Did you ever have them?"

"An episiotomy?" I nodded. "With Kevin. His head was big."

"Ben's was, too," Sandy said, "but even so, his features didn't get all smashed up. Isn't he beautiful?"

"Yes." One romance a woman never forgets, newborn love. Before Sandy's birth, not sure if we'd have a boy or a girl, I'd painted the bars of a garage-sale crib pink and blue, but when she arrived, so healthy and compact, the crib dwarfed her, and I'd sent Rob out to splurge on a bassinet.

Sandy leaned forward and pulled the baby's hand from the blanket. "His nails are so small."

I straightened his fingers. "They're pearls."

"Did Tony tell you what happened?"

"I haven't seen him."

"He left a while ago," Sandy said. "He told me he was going home to take a nap. I bet he went for a run instead. He was upset."

"What happened?"

"He couldn't cut the cord."

"No."

"He had to use both hands on the scissors. With Josh, he could do it one-handed."

"I wish I could have been here."

"Oh, that's all right," Sandy said. "It wouldn't have helped."

"My friend Maureen was right there in the labor room when her daughter had a baby," I said. "There were so many aunts and sisters that her daughter's labor coach said she felt like she ought to pour champagne and serve wedding cake."

Sandy smiled. "That was one of the options here, having the whole family around, but when I'm in pain, I'm like an animal."

"What, howling at the moon?"

"No." Sandy laughed. "More the other way. I want to curl up in my den alone." Sandy settled back onto her pillows and lowered the head of the bed. She smiled, wiped her face with a damp washcloth, and yawned. "I hope you don't mind if I conk out."

"Not at all."

Sandy's eyes were already closing. Her cheeks went slack and her head fell to one side. Mouth open, she began to snore. How easily she fell asleep then. How hard it would prove later on to grab hold of that single antidote to exhaustion.

I hugged the baby against my shoulder, smelling his sweet, lotiony scent and rubbing alcohol. Some must have spilled on his blanket when Sandy dabbed the umbilical cord. Adjusting the baby's knit hat, I remembered the soft center of the head that, when Sandy was born, I had been terrified to brush, and as a result, she'd had a mean case of cradle cap. I placed Ben, or was it going to be *Benjamino*, in his bassinet.

Pausing at the door, I looked back at Sandy. The neon lights faded her freckles, and she had no color in her cheeks. The birth had gone quickly, but she looked spent.

"Well, Rob," I whispered, slipping a finger through the rings around my neck. "What on earth are we going to do?" Not that I believed he'd actually hear me, though I had felt that once, a tap on the shoulder followed by a moment of extraordinary comfort. Holding my breath and hoping for a message telegraphed along the space-time continuum, I waited and then went about my errands.

CHAPTER 3

On the corner, Lowell Jaffee pulled weeds from a large cedar planter. Wire garden-cones supported the overburdened branches of three tomato plants.

"Are those beefsteaks?" I said.

"No, Paul Robesons," he said. "Ever had 'em?"

"Nope," I said.

"I'll bring some down when they're ripe."

What a nice guy. Maybe Sandy had lucked out after all. There was plenty of time to plan for the future. Neighbors would provide support. Tony's family would get involved. It wouldn't all fall on my shoulders.

"How's that baby?" Lowell said.

"Fine," I said. "Should be home any minute."

"Make sure they get their parking sticker renewed."

"You mean their vehicle registration?"

"No, the neighborhood sticker."

"Where is it?"

"On the driver's side window. Theirs expired two months ago."

Busybody. "I'll remind them."

"You need one for your car, too."

"Okay, okay." I held up my hands.

"Or, tell Tony to pick up some visitors' permits."

"I will."

"Want me to spray you?" He picked up the hose.

"Sure, why not?" Drops arced like a rainbow over the alley and water spattered on my outstretched arms. "Okay, that's enough. I don't want to get totally soaked."

"You got it," Lowell said, redirecting the water to his tomatoes while I walked home.

Home. The word alone made me cast a glance at my Jetta, its windshield bug-spattered from I-80. Rob had not come to comfort me with his sheltering presence, though some part of me wanted to believe this crisis would bring him back, that I would feel him perched on my shoulder like Jiminy Cricket, urging truth and caution and patience. Sandy needed two parents on her side, not just one.

Cooled by the spray, feet propped on the front-porch railing, I wished I could motivate myself. I'd bought a fan. That was my big accomplishment for the previous day. My shoulders felt tense, as if I were dragging an anvil, and I watched Tony fight the Tercel's steering wheel. Backing into a parking space, he nudged the bumpers of cars in front of and behind him. Dual car alarms rocketed through the insect-humming air.

Sandy threw open the passenger door. "What a scorcher."

I touched the brick wall behind my chair. Yesterday's heat, baked in.

With the infant seat swinging from his good hand, Tony carried the newborn, wrapped in a flannel receiving blanket. Inside, Tony stood at the bottom of the stairs, and I hunkered down to get a closer look.

Sandy ran her finger across the baby's cheek. "Look, Mom. He's got zits."

I laughed. "He's a teenager already."

"I know he's going to be horrible." Sandy laughed. "Just like me."

"You weren't that horrible," I said.

"At least I didn't do drugs."

"No. Thank goodness." Sandy had always been such a Girl Scout. A little angry at times, but that was normal. If Rob had been alive, her outbursts wouldn't have been any big deal. He and I could have laughed. We could have cried. We could have driven her to college and set up her dorm room. Alone, I didn't do any of that. I was so glad to be rid of her that I put her on a Greyhound down to Champaign-Urbana. Now, here she was, a lovely young woman.

Sandy grabbed the banister and began dragging herself to the second floor. "I'm exhausted," she said. "I wish this house had air conditioning."

"Waste of energy." Tony took the stairs two-at-a-time. The baby seat, swinging out of control, bumped the wall, and the baby's hands flew up.

Sandy gasped and took the baby carrier. She looked down at the rug. "Mom, watch the dust."

"What dust?" I said.

"There are footprints on the rug." Sandy's voice trailed off as she went into her bedroom. "And either put that box in the basement or the backyard."

"You mean Josh's playhouse?"

"It takes up too much room."

"What if it rains?"

"Mom," Sandy shouted. "This house is small. I don't want it cluttered up."

Tony called down from the landing. "Oh, and my folks called. They have Josh. If they need help, could you watch him? I want to go for a run."

My forehead bunched up. Trying to douse the match-flame of anger, I looked at the playhouse and its shutters. Josh had colored one blue and the other purple. In half an hour, I would think of what I should have said: something kind, but definite. I'd made the playhouse for Josh. Let him have fun.

Still in his street clothes, Tony came back down and stood hands on hips. "Well?"

"Where did your folks go?" I said.

"Out shopping. I can wait if it's inconvenient."

"No, I can do it," I said. "Where's the vacuum?"

Tony nodded to the coat closet at the foot of the stairs.

Like footprints in freshly mown grass, the indentations in Sandy's shag rug gave it a trampled look. I carried the box around to the back of the house and unlocked the basement door. The basement had two rooms: one small and one slightly larger, but both full of moving boxes. Someone had painted the textured walls the shiny aqua of a swimming pool. White paint would brighten it up. Then, maybe Josh could spread out his toys. One problem, though: Dirt clogged the window screens, leaving the air still and humid. Painting this room in the heat of summer would be an awful project, and I wished I had kept my mouth shut. If I started early, it might be doable. Just not today.

I returned to the porch. Out front, Aldo was trolling for a parking space. He stopped and let Lillian out. Her swept-back hair and tight chignon reminded me of an Italian movie star's, one whose cheekbones remained high, drawing attention from the fine lines on her upper lip.

Huffing, Lillian hauled herself up to the porch. "This house is an oven. Don't you wish we could buy them a big house in the suburbs?"

"I hadn't thought of that," I said.

Buying my own house had drained my bank account. I'd never had the money to do what Aldo did: buy his kids' cars and put them through college without student loans.

Lillian looked down the block. "What's taking Aldo so long?"

"There's no place to park in this neighborhood."

"But it's the weekend."

"Everybody's home," I said.

"I'm so upset. I hardly know where to turn."

From the direction of Mr. Jaffe's house, Josh ran towards us. Behind him slogged Aldo, shoulders bent, his fingers straining under the weight of grocery bags.

"Don't let me forget. Tony needs to renew his parking permit." I held the door, and Josh ran under my arm.

"Oh, Josh, darling." Lillian followed him in. "Come see what Grandma Lillian bought. Come see. Come see!"

Josh took a quick look in the living room, and then ran into the kitchen. "Where's my house?"

"In the basement, sweetie," I said.

"I'm not allowed to play down there."

"Why not?"

"There's bad things in the paint."

Great, the place was a dump and it needed lead abatement, too. That should have been on the disclosure form. Sandy must not have read the fine print. Either that, or she'd been too distracted to give it her attention.

After putting bags of groceries by the door, Aldo said, "I'm going down the block to buy a paper."

"What's wrong with the *Post*?" I said, looking at yesterday's paper. He'd left it on the couch.

"I prefer my paper," Aldo said.

"We're addicted to the *New York Times, bella*," Lillian said, picking up the sacks. "We're outraged about William Kristol's latest shenanigans."

"Billy Crystal, the comedian?" I said.

"No, the guy who's killing Clinton's health care plan," Lillian said. "Do those Harry and Louise commercials run in Chicago?"

"I don't know," I said. "My TV's on the fritz."

Lillian cocked her head.

"I know some people the President should call," Aldo said. "They'd fit those bozos with cement overshoes."

"Don't say that," Lillian said. "Even as a joke."

"It's not a joke," Aldo said.

"Well, it sounds criminal."

"You kidding? Half of Congress is on the take," Aldo said.

Like a child spying on her parents, Sandy, in a nightshirt, her legs bare, looked down through the balusters. "Would everyone please keep their voices down? I was up every two hours last night."

"Oh, sure, *bella*," Lillian said. "I'll go in the kitchen."

Holding the newel post, Aldo called upstairs. "Tony, don't get on your mother's case. I told you this place had cardboard walls. It's cheap construction and hot as a Brooklyn tenement."

Tony came to the top of the stairs. "Dad, it's done."

Lillian touched Aldo's arm. "Your blood pressure."

He looked down at her hand. "Okay, I'll shut up." On his way out the door, Aldo let the screen slam.

I wheeled the vacuum to a corner by Sandy's old piano. The piano, shipped out when she and Tony rented their first apartment down near Foggy Bottom, stood to the left of the arch between the living and dining rooms. Despite the years of music lessons and her being a better than average pianist, I had never seen her play. Even Josh never got up on the piano bench to bang on the keys. So what was the piano doing here but taking up space? Oh, well. Not my problem.

Lillian needed help putting away the groceries. I'd do that first, finish the vacuuming, and then, maybe take a second look at my painting project.

Coming downstairs, Tony, a running singlet covering his shaved chest, said, "I'll be back in a few."

"Tony, the guy down the street says your parking permit expired."

"Yeah, yeah. I know. Don't nag me about it."

I saluted. He left by the front door.

In the kitchen, Lillian stood on a stepstool to make room in the food cabinet. "If you could hand me—"

"Sure," I said, looking in a bag. Tortilla chips and pretzels. "Sandy and Tony don't eat junk food."

"I always buy the things I like," Lillian said. "Like that pound cake." She pointed at a cellophane-wrapped cake on the counter. "It's got five hundred calories a slice, almost pure butter. Nothing could be worse." Lillian, descending the stepstool, had been on a diet, and her arms looked like baggy nylons.

"Why do you buy it?" I said.

"Oh, I always buy things I'm dying for . . . oops! I said that word again. Salty snacks, pretzels—yummy, yummy—and donuts. Saturated fat calms me down. I'm dying for chocolate." Stricken, she looked at me. "Ever since Tony got sick, 'dying' pops out of my mouth and food pops in. I can't help it."

"But you're thin," I said.

"No. Fat," Lillian insisted. "Gross. I talked to my fella about liposuction, but he says I'll have to do a tummy tuck if I do that. Oh, well. It's only money. That's what I tell Aldo."

I heard the clang of footsteps on metal. The kitchen door flew open and Tony burst in, his tank top soaked. Pushing me aside, he bent down, drank from the faucet, and then wiped the stubble on his chin with the back of his hand.

"Too hot," he said. "I had to call it quits."

I found an electric can opener in one of Lillian's grocery sacks. "Hey, Tony, where do you want this?"

He stared at it. His mouth opened. "I've spent my whole life fighting for a sustainable environment. Why are you bringing that thing in?"

Lillian backed against the refrigerator. "You told me the other day you were having trouble—"

"I don't want it."

Josh tugged on his father's shorts.

Tony looked down.

"What's wrong, Daddy?" Josh said.

Fuming, Tony stared at his mother, whose hand covered her mouth. Then he looked at Josh. "Nothing," he said, tousling Josh's hair.

"Oh, Josh." Lillian clapped. "I completely forgot your present."

What cow pie would Lillian step in next? I followed her to the living room. From her black, leather purse, Lillian brought out a pink child's tape recorder. Popping in a tape, she cranked up the volume. Mexican trumpets began to play, soon joined by violins and guitars. Tony leaned against the archway, one hand on his waist. When he was in preschool, his mother had dragged him to the Romper Room studio. He'd been one of the regulars, and it was easy to picture him as an eager, curly-headed boy, shaking bells on red sticks—a real "do bee."

"It's the *merengue*," Lillian cried. "Come on, Josh. Let's dance."

In her tight pants and heels, prancing with the beats, she swung Josh into the middle of the room. Josh looked up at her round, silver belt-buckle, mesmerized.

"Let's all do the *merengue*," Lillian called out. "Clap everyone!"

Sandy peeked over the handrail again. She pointed to Tony and crooked her finger. He stopped clapping.

"Oh, I forgot, Sandy wanted us to be quiet," Lillian said, turning off the music. "My voice carries so anyway. I just wanted to bring a little levity into the house."

"You'd make a great kindergarten teacher," I said.

"I never could have managed to hold a job outside the home," Lillian said. "Not with two children."

That's what I'd thought, too, but then, a couple of months after Sean's birth, I'd snapped out of the fog. The insurance money wouldn't last forever. I'd been lucky though, having that cushion. There were women who had it a lot worse.

I took out Josh's wooden puzzles and told him to play quietly. Lillian sat on the couch beneath the window. Her toes moved in and out. Upstairs a high voice cried and a deeper one mumbled. Aldo came in from his quest to find a *New York Times* and took a seat next to Lillian. He folded the newspaper to make a writing surface and took out his pen.

"Get this," he said, "a five-letter word for 'overdone toast.'"

"Crisp," I said.

"That's 'bacon,'" Aldo said. "I'd go with 'burnt.' The guy they got doing the Monday puzzle makes them way too easy."

Five minutes later, Tony marched downstairs. He carried his parents' suitcase with both hands and dropped it by the piano. Then with an artery pulsing in his temple, he stood knee to knee with his father.

"Get out!"

I placed a hand on Tony's shoulder. "Wait a sec."

"No," he shouted, wriggling away. "My wife asked my mom to be quiet once already, and she didn't listen." He turned to Lillian. "You came here to help, and you're not, so get out."

"All right." Aldo shrugged. "I've got stuff to do at home anyway." The phone sat on the buffet in the dining room, and although Aldo turned and plugged an ear, making him think, perhaps, that this was a private conversation, I heard him say, "Pick us up at Landmark."

"Are you flying out of Baltimore?" I said.

"No, Dulles."

"What's Landmark then?"

After a hesitation, he said, "It's for private jets."

"Maybe you could go to a hotel."

Aldo looked at Lillian, still sitting on the couch. Curled over her knees, face buried in her hands, she rocked back and forth. "Not under the circumstances," he said.

People had all kinds of ways of showing their upsetness. Sandy, for instance, hiding in her cave. Aldo had to be feeling pretty bad. Tony was his only son. The two of them talked about the Yankees, politics, beer and breweries, not about Tony's job or animal rights; but even so, Aldo leaned as far left as any rich guy I'd ever met. And who cared how much money he had? He would have donated bone marrow if that would have made a difference in Tony's prognosis.

While Aldo dragged the suitcase from the corner, knocking over the vacuum, Josh stood among the adults, a child lost in a train station. Tony took his hand and led him upstairs. I followed Lillian to the porch.

"Sandy's under so much stress," Lillian whispered.

"But Tony needs you," I said.

"Tony is handling everything magnificently. He's the comeback kid, isn't he? Like Rocky Balboa. Oh!" Her heel caught and she grabbed the handrail. With the other hand, she clung to my arm. Fingernails dug in. I took her the rest of the way so she wouldn't trip. Aldo unlocked the trunk. Lillian threw her giant purse in back, and Aldo slammed the lid.

"What about the can opener?" Lillian said.

"Leave it," I said.

"Do you think?" Lillian's chin quivered.

"We have to get him to a good neurologist," I said.

"They're like ostriches," Lillian said. "I have a list of the top people, but he won't even look."

"Have you talked to them?"

"Tony won't listen to me. Maybe he'll listen to you."

"I doubt it."

"What can you do?" Aldo shrugged. "If he doesn't want help, he doesn't want help." He got in the car and told Lillian to get in and shut the door. She did, throwing herself forward and covering her face.

Poor Lillian. The dike that held back her feelings was about to cave in.

At the corner, the brake lights flashed red and Aldo stopped, leaning over to pat Lillian's shoulder. Even then, I could have run after them. Instead, when the Dimasios swung out onto Benton, I folded my arms and took a deep breath, determined to stand my ground and see what I could do to make a difference.

Inside, I picked up Aldo's discarded crossword and decided he'd been right to go with "burnt" instead of "crisp." Time to tidy up so I didn't get thrown out, too. The black finger holds of the vacuum reminded me of Lillian's death-grip. With the vacuum making more noise than either Lillian or the tape recorder, I crisscrossed the rug, erasing Aldo's and Lillian's footprints and trying not to feel angry at Sandy, who was perfectly within her rights to be annoyed by Lillian's incessant chatter. Still, it was rude to make them leave.

I turned off the vacuum and heard footsteps on the stairs. Sandy, in a beige skirt, its waistband fastened by a diaper pin, lowered the baby carrier gently to the floor. Ben, wrapped tight in his blanket, had a blister on his bottom lip. Must be sucking pretty hard.

"Could you watch Ben for a few minutes?" Sandy said.

"You mean, as in, babysit?"

"We promised Josh we'd take him for ice cream."

"You just gave birth."

"It's Tony's idea."

"You should be resting."

Sandy tucked the newspaper into a stack of magazines on an end table. "If you want to tell us how to live our lives, you can go home, too."

"Look, Sandy, I'm going to tell you what I think, and you can kick me out if you want to, but good luck, because I don't like being pushed around, and I'm not going to skulk out of here like Lillian."

Ben was only a day old. His hands curled like kittens' paws. Besides, Sandy needed a nap.

Sandy's eyes turned to the front windows. "What on earth is that?"

I had forgotten the newsprint diorama.

"Paper houses," I said. "To keep people from looking in."

Sandy ripped them down. "Between you and Lillian . . ."

"What did I do?"

Sandy shook her head. "I don't want my house turned into a kindergarten."

"It's only temporary. Until I make curtains."

"I'm sorry, Mom, I'm not in a very good mood. Tony invited his sister down, and she'll be here for dinner."

I thought about the food I'd helped Lillian unload. Chicken breasts. Salmon. "Isn't Lisa vegetarian?"

"Yes." Sandy grimaced. "And she's going to be here tomorrow, too."

"Is Tony cooking?"

"I told him you would."

"What am I? Chief cook and bottle washer?"

"Mom, you said you'd come out to help. This is the help we need."

I couldn't just thaw the fish, boil rice, and make a salad. "I have to go to the store, then."

"You can go shopping after we get back."

"The thing is, I don't have a lot of vegetarian recipes in my repertoire."

"If it's too much trouble, I'll cook something."

"No, Sandy. I'll do it."

***

At Safeway, checking the price of bagged salad versus lettuce, I wondered if Sandy would reimburse me. Groceries were a third higher than in Chicago. The expense wouldn't have bugged me so much if Sandy and Tony had been a little nicer. I'd come to help with the baby, not be their lackey, and I couldn't believe I was letting my daughter push me around. But it wasn't Sandy so much as who I was cooking for. Bottom line, Lisa annoyed the heck out of me. Two years older than Tony, his sister loved liberal causes and political arguments. At Tony's and Sandy's wedding reception, she'd pointed to the wedding cake with the plaster figures of the bride and groom. "The happy couple. The wedding princess. How long's that going to last?"

"Do you think Tony and Sandy shouldn't get married?" I said.

"They should just live together," she said. "It's simpler and easier to untangle if it goes south."

"What about children?"

She rolled her eyes and shook her head. "Breeding's a dead end."

There didn't seem to be any way to budge her from her soapbox. "Where are you coming from on this?"

"Let me draw a picture." She outlined an imaginary chalkboard. "A woman comes in. Her jaw's wired shut. We get a no-contact order, but the instant she's feeling better, she boomerangs back to the abuser."

"Yeah?" I said.

"Because of the kids."

"Weren't you a psych major?" I said.

"What's that got to do with it?"

"I think women vacillate because of an intermittent reward phenomenon." I tried to persuade her that abusive behavior followed by fake contrition made it hard for women to know when to leave. It was the love that trapped them. The hope that a woman could flip a coin and make her man be nice.

Lisa worked in a battered women's shelter and that skewed her view of reality. All the problems of the world she attributed to patriarchy. Patriarchy my foot, though. Lisa had gone to Brown on her father's dime, as much in debt to one particular patriarch, Aldo, as any woman who leaned on a male provider.

At home, I put away the groceries and propped the fan in the dining room window. On the pass-through counter, I shook out lasagna noodles, cracked an egg into a mixing bowl, broke apart a box of frozen spinach, and, with a spatula, scraped fresh ricotta from its plastic tub. Squishing the ingredients together felt good on my hands—cool, soothing. I tried not to spatter on the pile of mail that Tony, opposite and on the dining room side, sliced with a letter opener.

He saw me layering the uncooked noodles. "That's not how I do it."

"You do it your way. I'll do it mine."

"Have it your way."

"I will," I said.

"Look at this." He tossed some pages at me. "I told my doctor not to bother sending this."

I picked up a letter and a product insert. His doctor had mailed him a prescription. I glanced at the big print. "What's riluzole?"

"It's medicine for ALS."

"I thought you said there wasn't any treatment."

"There's not," he said. "Riluzole slows down the progress of the disease. I guess it's supposed to keep me walking longer."

"But that's a good thing. Maybe they'll find a cure."

"Don't get your hopes up."

"I'm not," I said. "I'm trying to fix dinner."

It was insane to cook on such a hot day. When the alarm on the oven buzzed that it had reached four hundred degrees, I slid in the lasagna. The kitchen and dining room felt ten degrees warmer than when I'd begun.

Tony opened the door for his sister. A nimbus of black hair contrasted with the pallor of Lisa's face. She had her father's coloring. Leaning a cheek for her brother to kiss, Lisa looked around at the fan in the dining room window. "It's beastly here."

Beastly. What was this, a Katherine Hepburn movie?

"I'm opposed, on moral grounds, to air-conditioners," Tony said.

"How's it going?" Lisa asked me.

"Fine," I said. Ben had slept the whole time I was babysitting, so I didn't get to hold him, Tony and Sandy were ordering me around, but apart from that, everything was swell. With dinner in the oven, I sat down in the rocking chair. Lisa stood beneath the arch, her body blocking the fan.

"Could you move?" I said.

"I'm standing here on purpose, to stay cool." Lisa turned to her brother. "I brought you something, Tony. A price sheet for a computer that doubles as a voice synthesizer. Stephen Hawking uses one."

"I don't want it," Tony said.

"Fine." Lisa pinned up her hair with a barrette. "When you're ready." She moved to the couch, and the fan's breeze swept over me. It was the first time I'd felt comfortable all day.

"My doctor wants to run more tests," Tony said.

"Why?" Lisa said.

"To check my breathing."

"Do you want that?" Lisa said.

"She's already told me all I need to know," Tony said, clenching his fists. "I'm not going back."

"Perfectly understandable," Lisa said. "You need to feel in control."

"Exactly," Tony said. "I refuse to be treated like a human guinea pig. I'm glad you were able to come down. I have an important announcement to make later."

Maybe he'd bought a gun and planned to blow himself away. He didn't seem suicidal, though, just angry.

"What's up, Tony?" Lisa said.

"A surprise for Dr. Gallagher, here." Tony winked. "She never lets up."

My face felt warm. Not a hot flash. I was still trying to take it in, this attack on my family. Tony wasn't being fair.

Lisa leaned toward Tony in the posture I remembered from my time with a grief counselor, the body language of active listening.

"So how does that make you feel?" Lisa said.

I laughed.

Tony looked at me. "I resent everybody knowing my business. I'm literally suffocating in here." He hopped up, opened the front door, and went outside. Through the window, I could see him on the lawn. Hands at his waist, he leaned back and looked up at the sky.

Lisa drew her feet up under her and sat in a yoga posture. "Tony wants you to back off."

I had been rocking. I stopped. "I don't know what he told you, but I'm not pressuring him."

"Whatever it is, he wants you to stop."

Maybe it was the way I looked at him. You couldn't help but look at Tony without thinking, *That man is going to die.*

"Look, Lisa, I've been stuck in the house with two people who've just had the world cave in on them. I don't even really understand the trajectory of the disease."

"Maybe you should talk to someone who's got it, then."

"Who?"

"I have a friend. It's his mom. His sister's the caretaker."

"Have you talked to her?"

"No," Lisa said. "But if you feel the need . . ." She took a piece of paper from her pocket and held it out.

I took it. "The need to what?"

"Educate yourself." Lisa, legs crossed like a sitting Buddha, put the backs of her hands on her knees and pinched her thumbs and forefingers together. She closed her eyes. When she opened them, she said, "Now I feel centered."

"Good for you," I said. "If you'll excuse me. It's hotter than Hades. I need to take a shower before dinner."

"Enjoy," she said.

By the time I came up from the basement, lasagna and a salad sat on the counter. I'd meant for the lasagna to cool before we dug in, but Tony and Lisa had served themselves. "Where's Sandy?" I said.

Tony looked up from his chair at the head of the table. "Feeding the baby."

"Why don't we wait till she's done?"

"Lisa's starving." Tony took a seat at the head of the table. "Sandy told us to go ahead."

"Thanks for making dinner," Lisa said.

"You're welcome," I said.

"Are there any animal products in this?"

"Is ricotta cheese an animal product?"

Lisa lifted the top layer of pasta and moved it aside. She bent over to examine the filling. "Anything else?"

"I mixed an egg in with the spinach and the ricotta."

Tony frowned. "Lisa's a vegetarian."

"That's why I didn't use ground round," I said.

"I'm a vegan," Lisa said.

At the wedding reception seven years ago she'd chowed down on *spanikopita*. "I guess you've gotten stricter than you used to be."

"I don't eat milk or eggs," she said.

"If you tell me what you can eat, I'll whip something up."

"I'll be fine." Lisa pushed her plate away and picked up the drug company's brochure.

Tony pointed with his fork. "That riluzole is worthless."

Lisa held the paper close to her face. "I should have brought my reading glasses. This print is tiny."

"Drug companies are just out to make a buck," Tony said.

Lisa put the pages down. "What does your doctor say?"

I reached across the table. Even with bifocals, the print was hard to read.

"Then, why'd your doctor send you info on the drug?" I said.

"To waste her time and mine," Tony said.

Sandy came downstairs with Josh and the baby. "Dr. Stevanovic called today," she said. "She wants you to come in for that breathing test."

"No way," Tony said.

"What, exactly, is the breathing test for?" I said.

"Your doctor calls you at home?" Lisa's eyebrows shot up.

"Oh, she wants to get some kind of baseline measurement of my lung capacity." Tony shook his head and then ripped a page from the brochure. "I wish she and everyone else would just go away."

Awkwardly folding a paper airplane with his defective hand, Tony sailed it onto the junk-mail pile. "I should have gone to work today. There's a big congressional hearing on a swine-farm bill."

"You're entitled to parental leave." Sandy put Ben's baby carrier on the floor and lifted Josh into his booster seat.

"Should you be lifting him?" I said.

"I feel fine," Sandy said. "Just sleep deprived." Before sitting down, she warmed a bowl of macaroni for Josh and handed him a baby fork. He started eating.

Like a lot of my kindergarteners, Josh was on the white diet: macaroni, string cheese, chicken nuggets, white bread, and milk. If I'd lived closer, I would have introduced new foods, but I couldn't very well do that in two weeks.

Tony turned to Lisa. "Did you know that pigs are cannibals? On commercial pig farms, the workers crop the pigs' tails, but if the tail doesn't heal, the big pigs eat the sick ones. They eat from the rear until all that's left is skin, snout, and hooves."

Lisa had started on her salad, but she put down her fork. "Is the pig still alive?"

"Yes, alive," Tony said. "It's alive until the cannibals reach the vital organs."

"That's why I'm a vegetarian," Lisa said.

"Please, Tony, not at the table," Sandy said.

Josh put down his fork.

"On a swine farm, they call what's left a 'rug,'" Tony said. "The other pigs curl up on it."

"Hey, Tony," I said. "You've slacked off on the baby videos. Where's your camera?"

"The battery's dead," Tony said.

"Are pigs mean, Daddy?" Josh said.

Tony looked down the table at his son, and his expression softened. "Not most pigs. Most pigs are roly-poly." He began to snort, then threw back his head.

His laugh sounded more like a caw. The sound reminded me of the crazy lady parked in the hall of my mom's nursing home. Whenever I showed up, she'd cackle and reach out a skeletal hand. Poor Josh.

"Eat your macaroni, Josh." Sandy picked up Josh's fork and aimed a bite of macaroni. "Talk about something else, can't you? It's not amusing."

"All right, all right." Leaning back, Tony spread his fingers on the table. "I have an important announcement." His eyes, dark lanterns, beamed around the table. "I've decided to go on a respirator."

Sandy dropped the fork. "What?"

"Yes," he said. "So all of you who've been so concerned about me dying can stop. I've decided I can put up with the inconvenience. I want to see my children grow up." He blinked, teary-eyed.

"Grow up?" I gulped. "You mean, as in, graduate from college?"

"Why not?" he said. "The doctor said for me to think about whether I want to go on a respirator. I can live a more or less normal life on one, so I've decided to do it."

"What is a respirator?" I said.

"It's a breathing apparatus," Tony said. "For when I can't breathe on my own."

Josh looked across the table at Lisa. "My dad is really, really sick."

"I know, honey, but now, he's decided he's going to live until you grow up." Lisa reached for Tony's hand. "You don't know how relieved I am."

"I need to see how Sandy feels." Tony leaned back, his right hand twitching on the armrest. "But if Sandy leaves it up to me, I think I'll go ahead."

A candlestick sat next to the wilted flowers on the table. Wax spilled over its lip and ran down the sides. Stiff tears. I flaked some off, molding the wax and gouging it with my thumbnail. This was the first I'd heard about a respirator. I knew that Christopher Reeve had used one. Stephen Hawking, too. It might not be a bad idea. I looked over at Sandy, who dabbed her thin lips with a napkin. Her frown told me she harbored doubts. Maybe she knew something I didn't.

CHAPTER 4

At Denny's out in Silver Spring where Sean suggested we rendezvous, the smell of bacon made my stomach growl. Pigs weren't all bad. You could eat them for breakfast. But the stiffness in my neck told me the delay in breaking the news to the boys had more to do with a desire to straight-arm the situation than to protect them. The situation. What to call it? Tony's death? But he wasn't dead. Maybe impending death. Maybe "undertoad," what Kevin used to call the undertow at the beach.

A hostess led the way to a booth. I hadn't wanted to break the news about Tony in a phone call, and just seeing my sons' faces brought me comfort. Once Sean had scooted in and they were seated across from me, Kevin said, "So what's the big deal?" He had Rob's black hair and blue eyes—black Irish, as Rob used to say—but Kevin was taller than his father by six inches and left-handed like me.

Sean elbowed him. "Is there a problem with the baby?" Sean had crows' feet from smiling, but he wasn't smiling now. "Tell us, Mom. The baby's not developmentally delayed, is it?"

"No," I said, thinking that under the circumstances, a healthy child was a blessing.

Kevin had driven up from Chapel Hill. A high school math teacher, he took summers off, except for the Special Olympics' Mid-Summer Classic which he and Sean had coached for the last several years. This year Sean, who'd just finished his master's in social work, had a job and wouldn't be volunteering.

"Tony has ALS," I said.

"What?" Kevin said. "Since when?"

After ordering, Sean fell silent, and Kevin asked all the questions I'd had when I'd first found out a week ago. When he finished, he frowned and began cracking his knuckles. "We have to fight this."

"Fight it?" I said. "What are we going to do, put on boxing gloves?"

"You know what he means," Sean said. "There's gotta be some kind of treatment."

"It sounds like there's not much the doctors can do," I said.

There were a couple of medications out there—Baclofen that would help the muscle twitching and Riluzole that would slow down the muscle deterioration—but, as far as I'd been able to find out, no one had found a cure.

Like a winded horse, Kevin blew out a stream of air and ran his fingers through his hair. "Wow, this sucks big time. I wish I lived closer."

"There's probably not a lot we can do until they ask," I said, "although Sean, I'm guessing Sandy could use a babysitter once in a while."

"Sure," he said. "No problem."

"Diapers," Kevin said. In high school his lip had been split by a fall during a basketball game, and where the split had been, I could see a thin, white scar. Because the faulty repair had exposed two bottom teeth, he thought he looked like a teething baby, and more often than not, he smiled through his eyes.

"Diapers don't bother me," Sean said. "And, anyway, I owe Sandy. Whenever I babysit for Josh, she reminds me who she learned on." He pointed to his chest, a finger that might as well have pointed at me. I had overloaded Sandy, delegating my new baby Sean to her watchful eye.

Three plates of pancakes landed on the table. Sean tucked a napkin into the neck of his polo shirt. "Sandy told me a couple months ago some major shit was going down."

"You've known for that long?" I said.

"She made me promise not to tell."

"Why would she tell you and not me?"

"She was hoping it would turn out to be nothing."

I spooned up an ice cube from the water glass. Sean was a family counselor, but still. I crunched the ice and felt a pain shoot down a molar. It wasn't like I was some kind of worrywart. Not like Lillian.

Kevin picked up a strip of bacon with his fingers. "Why does this shit happen?"

"Right." That was the big question. "Anyway, Tony's not planning on dying."

"I thought Gehrig died of it." Kevin reached for syrup and spilled on his pants. He stood up and looked down at himself with disgust. "Damn, I just got these back from the cleaners, and I have to go straight to the gym."

"Is it a basketball game?"

"No, volleyball."

"You have shorts in the car?" I said.

"I do," he said.

"Change and wash off your khakis in the bathroom sink."

"I don't want to wear wet pants."

"Put them in the back of your car. By the time we finish, they'll be dry."

"Okay," he said. "Be right back."

Stabbing at his pancakes, Sean looked pensive. "So how are you?" I said.

"Busy." He looked directly at me, then, lids lowered, turned his eyes to the window. "Trying to figure out how to give people twice my age advice." When I looked outdoors to see what he was looking at, I saw a pretty blonde unlocking her car.

"Is there some piece of therapist wisdom you'd like to enlighten me with?" I said.

"Not when you put it that way," he said.

"Speaking of counseling," I said, "you know Tony's sister?"

"The bitch?"

"Don't use that word."

"Well, she is."

Kevin came back, waving to us as he carried a gym bag to the restroom. Moments later, he returned, wearing shorts and holding wet pants.

"Don't squeeze them," I called. "Lay them out flat. Put them right in the window, not on your seat."

He gave me a thumbs-up, and left.

"I don't know about these people," I said.

"What people?" Sean said.

"Tony's family."

"Yeah," Sean said. "His mother's a nutcase."

"Lillian's just in denial."

"Mom, she's a nutcase," Sean said. "Lisa hates her guts."

"You know that?"

"Yeah," he said. "From some things Tony said."

Kevin slid into the booth. "Move over, bro. Give me some room." He elbowed Sean, who moved closer to the wall.

"Hey, Kev," I said, "you want the waitress to stick your plate in the microwave?"

He forked up a bite. "No, it's fine."

Sean winced. "Mom, he's a big boy."

"I know. I'm sorry."

Sean unrolled his silverware and spread his napkin. "Mom was just saying Tony's family's being a little weird."

"I think they've been lobbying for him to go on a respirator," I said. "A week ago, he said he was going to. After breakfast, I'm heading over to talk to this woman whose mom is on one. Joan Calabrese. She's the caretaker."

"Care-*giver*," Sean said. "I think a care-*taker's* like a gardener."

"Going on a respirator is not a rational decision," Kevin said.

"Stephen Hawking has been on one for a long time. He's pretty rational."

"He holds the chair at Cambridge that used to be Isaac Newton's," Kevin said, "but that doesn't mean he's rational when it comes to his own health."

"So what's your point?"

"He has an amazing brain," Kevin said. "If Princeton could have kept Einstein's brain alive in a jar, they would have found the resources. I wonder what they pay him. Hawking, I mean. No one is going to pay Tony to keep his brain alive."

"His mother might," I said.

"For Sandy's sake, we can't let that happen," Kevin said.

"Why not?"

"There's this dad, father of one of my Down's kids. Spinal cord injury," Kevin said. "He can't breathe on his own. Gets bedsores. Everything in that family revolves around him, and they had to move into a mobile home out in Carrboro because his care was costing an arm and a leg. Mom, a respirator is an expensive, huge hassle, and it takes the focus right off the children. Kids need to be the center of their parents' universe. Isn't that right?" He turned to Sean.

"You're talking normal development or special needs?"

"Special needs, for sure," Kevin said, "but any kid."

"I guess that's pretty much true."

"If it was bad for Josh," I said, "I'm sure Tony wouldn't do it."

"You might be surprised," Sean said. "Tony wasn't raised the way we were."

"What do you mean?" I said.

"He's a great guy," Kevin said. "We love him."

Sean nodded. "But he doesn't always think of other people."

"We always thought Sandy should have shopped around a little more," Kevin said.

"Did you?" I said.

"The guy who worked for us summers?" Kevin said. "He would have been perfect for her."

Charles Gaudreau? God, they remembered him. Charles Gaudreau lived in Vermont. Montpelier, I recalled. Handsome, eleven years younger than me, he'd been closer to me than many of my girlfriends. Charles was the sort of person who wound up knowing all my secrets.

"I can stay a couple of weeks after the tournament," Kevin said. "For that matter, I could stay till the school year starts."

"If you stay, stay with me," Sean said.

"I guess I'm the point guard for the moment," I said. The main thing was, they had to inform themselves, and then, if they thought it appropriate, talk to Tony and Sandy. We needed to tackle this problem together and not be on opposite sides of the fence.

"Hey, Mom," Kevin said, "You know why sharks circle you before attacking?"

"No, why?" I said.

This was the way it always was with the boys. Jokes. Stories.

"Two great white sharks swimming in the ocean spied the survivors of a sunken ship." Kevin put down his fork. "'Follow me, son,' the father shark said to the son shark, and they swam to the mass of people. 'First we swim around them a few times with just the tip of our fins showing.' And they did. 'Well done, son,' the father said. 'Now we swim around them a few times with all of our fins showing.' And they did. 'Now we eat everybody.' And they did. When they were both gorged, the son asked, 'Dad, why didn't we just eat them all at first? Why did we swim around and around them?' His wise father replied, 'Because they taste better without the shit inside.'"

I laughed. Sean didn't. Maybe he'd heard it. Before school ended, a teacher had told a joke that cracked up everyone in the teachers' lounge, and I had promised to remember it so that I could tell the boys. Now, I had brain freeze. For a week, I'd done nothing but cook and clean; plus, I couldn't really believe this was happening.

I said, "Do you guys have any questions for the woman I'm about to go see?"

They did. A lot of questions. I wrote them on a napkin.

I could get Sandy through this. Arm myself with information. Find the best doctors. Maybe persuade Tony to enroll in a drug trial. The support Sandy needed could come from her brothers. I lived a thousand miles away. She couldn't expect me to come back here all the time. I stabbed hungrily at my pancakes, trying to get rid of the gnawing sensation.

After breakfast, I drove over to Takoma Park. The Calabreses' red-brick ranch house had a picture window that stared like Cyclops's eye. I walked up a buckled, plywood ramp and rang the bell. Stringy-haired, in a flowered caftan and with a wattle of chins, Joan Calabrese opened the door. I introduced myself.

"It was good of you to drive all the way out here." She held open the screen, and I wondered why she didn't just invite me in. "But didn't you say you were coming from Glover Park? I used to live there. Garden apartment, right across from the school."

"Small world," I said.

She nodded and turned to the inside. "I'm going out back to have a cigarette. Give a holler if you need me."

I stood aside and listened to Joan Calabrese's open-backed slippers flop down the ramp. She opened a gate, and I found myself in the backyard. A chestnut oak shaded the deck. Mushrooms grew from the corrugated bark. I looked at a fungus, a stack of small and large pitas, either an artist's conk, *Ganoderma applanatum*, or a mustard yellow polypore, *Phellinus gillis*. I wasn't up on my mushrooms, even though the docent from my local nature preserve had tried to teach me the botanical names; but, even so, I could see that the combination of shade, moisture, wood, and neglect was making the deck fall to pieces.

Joan sank into a chair, the plastic legs bowing beneath her weight.

"So, what can I do ya for?" Joan said.

"My son-in-law has ALS," I said. "His sister said I should talk to you. Apparently, your brother is a friend of hers."

"My brother." She stuck out her tongue and made a raspberry. "He's worthless."

"Why do you say that?"

"He lives in Boston and deigns to grace us with a visit once a year."

"Who is it has ALS?"

"My mother." Joan tapped out a cigarette. "She's had it five years."

Joan looked to be fifty-five or sixty. Perhaps because Lisa was young, I had expected a younger woman. I took out the napkin. "Uh, how do you cover the cost of your mother's care?"

They'd had one of the old insurance policies, Joan said, the kind that was supposed to cover the patient twenty-four-hours a day. Sometime back, the company had sent a rider saying the policy had changed, and they would no longer provide custodial care. "But who reads the fine print, right?" Joan had hired a lawyer to enforce the terms of the original policy, and after a five-year battle, she'd won. "That's what makes it possible for mother to stay on a respirator and not go in a nursing home."

"Wouldn't Hillary's plan change that?"

"I don't think it's supposed to cover custodial care. It would be good if it did."

"Let's back up." I consulted my notes. "Your mother's on a respirator."

"Yes," Joan said. "Otherwise, she'd be dead."

"Did she take riluzole?"

"For the first couple years," Joan said. "It might have helped her walking."

In the second year, her mother's breathing had become compromised. If Joan hadn't been her caregiver, the sick woman would have had to go in a nursing home, if they could find one—very few took people on respirators—and they would have had to be broke so Medicaid would pick up the cost. Finding a nursing home with a Medicaid bed that would *also* take a person on a respirator was nigh on impossible.

My throat felt dry. I wished the woman would offer a glass of water.

"So you must hire private duty nurses," I said.

Joan tapped off her ash and lit another cigarette. She had gone through three agencies and dozens of nurses. Salaries for the nursing staff alone ran $270,000 a year. "But money's the least of it."

"The least of what?" I said.

Joan walked over to sliding door, opened it a crack, and shouted, "I'm right here, Mom. Don't panic."

I looked at the napkin. Kevin wanted to know if Medicaid paid for the mother's care and what portion Medicare covered. The questions didn't seem pertinent.

"Had you always wanted to do this, or what?" I said.

Sitting down again, Joan reared back laughing. "Taking care of Mother wasn't something I chose to do. I had to do it. Mom went into respiratory failure. The EMTs intubated her. I had a job back then." At first, she'd monitored the nurses, popping in on them several times a day to make sure they were doing a good job. "My employer didn't like me leaving work."

"I can imagine."

"You might know the guy I worked for. Had a State Farm office. Lowell Jaffee."

"He sprayed me."

Joan raised her eyebrows. "He sprayed you?"

"With his hose. He's raising tomatoes."

Joan shrugged. "More power to him. If you see him, tell him to go fuck himself." Joan coughed and switched the position of her feet. Her bloated ankles were spider-webbed. She checked her watch and stood up again, rapping on the door until it opened. "After you suction her, check for a bm." Before the door closed, I heard a blow-dryer sound.

Joan sat down and fished in her bra for a lighter. "The person doing the caregiving has to realize that the patient knows what's going on. The nurse has to continue talking to a person who basically looks like they're not there. That's hard, but if you don't do it, the patient becomes depressed and lonely. My mom can accept the disease, but it gets tiring not being able to communicate."

"Tony's sister found a special computer," I said, "the kind used by Stephen Hawking."

Joan wrinkled her nose. "We tried that, but after Mom's muscles atrophied, she couldn't activate the switch. She's almost at the lock down stage."

"Lock down stage?" I said.

"Where they can't move anything."

"Nothing?"

"They can't even blink," Joan said.

I looked down at my notes. My face felt like I'd had a tooth extracted: numb, but with pain starting to throb around my eyeball.

"Don't worry," Joan said. "They die eventually."

I swallowed. "So, do you have an RN?"

Joan stubbed her cigarette out on the arm of her chair, tossed the butt in the bushes, and lit up again. "Nooooo," she said. "Not *an* RN. A *brigade* of RNs." It took two people to get her mother out of bed and dressed in the morning, so Joan had to be in the house; otherwise, there had to be two nurses on duty. Her mom sat in a wheelchair all day. If left lying down, she was more vulnerable to pneumonia. "Your son-in-law will lose his cough reflex. He won't be able to swallow. My mother has to be suctioned five to ten times a day and the same at night. That's what you need the RNs for."

The door opened. Joan waddled over. "Bedsore," she said when she came back. "Right on her ass. You can't leave her sitting in shit for more than thirty seconds."

A pencil point of pain stabbed right through my iris. I'd had too much coffee at breakfast, or maybe it was a migraine. "How about nourishment?"

Joan made a brush-off gesture. "Piece of cake." They'd had a feeding tube inserted in her stomach. "That's how she takes her meds, too. But, before that, God, she liked to eat. Their brains go haywire. Eating's a compulsion. Six, seven hours a day that woman could eat. Slowly, with me or someone feeding her, tiny bite by tiny bite. Eventually, Mom wasted away, and I got fat." Beneath the caftan, a pillow of blubber shifted like a squirming baby. "The feeding," she said. "That's what one of the nurses called it. The nurses can't take it. Actually, that's why most of them quit."

As I wrote down "look into getting a feeding tube for Tony," I wondered if Lisa had actually talked to this woman. Probably not. Joan Calabrese was just a phone number e-mailed to Lisa by Joan's brother. Lisa must have thought Joan would be all rah-rah about the respirator. I looked at my cheat-sheet on the napkin.

"Can we go back to expense?" I said. "How much equipment do you need, and what does it cost if insurance won't cover it?"

Medical equipment and accessories cost a lot, especially over the long haul, Joan said. As far as equipment went, you needed two respirators, one for bedside and one for the wheelchair. "You have ten hours of electricity on one respirator and ten on another, in case of electrical outage. Longer than that, and you have to take them to a hospital." The room had to be set up like a mini-emergency room, with tracheotomy-care kits, suction kits, boxes of gloves, jars of saline solution, and jars of distilled water. There had to be two suction kits and a Hoyer Lift.

I asked about dimensions.

"The trach-care kit will fit on a bookshelf." Pointing to her windpipe, Joan said, "They'll punch a hole in here, but the kit itself is yeah-big." She formed her hands around an imaginary shoebox. The Hoyer Lift was a big piece of equipment, maybe half a porch swing. Her back was shot from lifting her mother, and although the lift took up a lot of space, they'd had to get the Hoyer, or the dead-weight transfers from bed to wheelchair would have put them all in traction.

I nodded. At Sandy's house, the basement was the only place this much stuff would fit.

Joan stuck a hand down between her cassava-melon bosoms and scratched. "I don't see how your daughter can possibly hold a job, take care of two children, and Tony. She's going to need help."

"How much help?"

"Three shifts a day, eight or nine nurses total." Each nurse had to work three or four days a week. The nurses needed breaks to go to the bathroom or eat a meal. Once Tony went on a respirator, someone had to be at his side, alert, every minute of the day. "You can't have a person staring at a TV all day. If a tube pops off, he'll die."

"What about live-ins?"

"Maybe four live-ins could do most of his daily care," Joan said, "but you'll still need a good RN to teach you how to listen for wheezing and check fluid buildup. The respirator is the easy part."

I stopped writing. The respirator was the easy part. "So what is the hard part?"

"Lately," Joan said, "my mother has been depressed. Everyone's talking around her."

"How do you know?"

Joan tapped her temple. "We communicate telepathically."

The woman had gone round the bend.

"How much longer do you think she'll live?" I said.

"She's been hospitalized more than ten times, but she's always pulled through," Joan said.

"What's 'pull through' mean?" I said.

"Ha!" Joan slammed the arm of her chair. "Excuse me. Let me light this baby. There. 'Pull through' means get off antibiotics. It's the pneumonia that kills them. Either that, or choking."

Joan had small eyes, outlined in red, and when she closed them, they disappeared into the dough of her face. Tony would deteriorate, she said, but once on a respirator, with the will to live, he could probably survive ten years. A lot of it was mental.

My chair shifted. I moved my feet, trying to find solid footing on the shaky deck. The conversation reminded me of an underwater swim, lungs about to explode until I touched the side and surfaced. I couldn't wait to get out of here.

"What's your life like?" I said.

"Oh, what is my life like?" Joan tipped her head back and blew a puff of smoke at the sky. "I'm totally housebound. It's hell."

Heaving her body from the chair, she said her mother didn't have many visitors, and now that I was here, wouldn't I like to meet her? After opening the door, she turned back and beckoned. Unable to move my legs, I stayed seated.

"She won't bite," Joan said. Her breasts shook with merriment. "She can't."

I managed to stand. My teeth ached. Inside, a crystal chandelier hung from a doubled-up chain. A young Filipina nurse changed the sheets on a hospital bed. Bookcases with rubber gloves and medical equipment lined one wall, and the stench of a bowel movement made me cover my nose. Beyond, in the living room, I saw a contraption that looked like a construction crane, except it had pulleys and a winch. A wheelchair faced the window. In it sat a small person with narrow shoulders and limp white hair. Held in place with a Velcro band, the person's head was strapped to a chrome pole. An orange pennant hung from its top. I heard a sound like a bellows and saw more equipment under the chair's padded seat. Car batteries. The room had no sofa, only twin, black recliners. In the corner, a portable TV rested on a maple coffee table.

"Come on." Joan's cold, puffy hand dragged me forward. "Mom can't turn her head."

Then I stared down at Mrs. Calabrese's powdered face. A plaster cast of dental work—gums, teeth, pointy incisors—telegraphed through the sunken skin. Snaking from beneath the chair, a hose disappeared into an ascot at the woman's neck. Two peeled grapes compelled me to look at them. Mrs. Calabrese's eyes: veined, quivering, gelid.

Not having the least idea what might come out, I opened my mouth and heard myself mouthing phrases that would eventually constitute the *Cliffs Notes* version of the illness. Prior to getting sick, Tony had been a lacrosse player and his biggest vice was drinking beer. A minor problem with his index finger sent him to the doctor, who took months to confirm the diagnosis. He had bulbar onset, the fast-acting form of ALS, and he favored the respirator idea. "Thank you for letting me visit," I said.

Joan Calabrese picked up a stack of flashcards on the fireplace mantel. Turning them slowly, she watched her mother's face. Finally, she held one up for me to read. It said, *Thank you for coming. I know this is hard for you.*

"You're welcome," I said.

Promising to visit again, I left by the front door and felt the mushy wood of the ramp beneath my feet. I waved toward the plate-glass window, shimmering with the reflections of passing traffic, and stabbed at the car's lock with my key. Entirely disoriented, I drove a block, pulled to the curb, banged my head on the steering wheel, and screamed. I would never, not in a million, billion years, go back to that house again.

CHAPTER 5

Exhausted from nights waking up to change Ben's diapers and days painting Sandy's basement, I didn't sleep well for two months, and it would be like this every time I returned to Sandy's house, the exhaustion just piling up and piling up until I felt like a prisoner in a North Korean labor camp. On the drive west, truck-stop coffee soured in my stomach. Swept along in the wakes of semis, the Jetta veered over the centerline, and it took the thump of lane dividers to jolt me awake. Having a radio would have helped, but a vandal walking down Calvert had snapped off my car's antenna. The problems we confronted as a family should have conferred immunity against random mischief: traffic tickets, overdue bills, and grocery carts rolling across a parking lot to dent Sandy's car. But fate didn't care. Without me there to help, Sandy would have to handle it all. When I looked at the orange and white barrels lined up along the highway, forcing drivers into a single lane, I thought about Joan Calabrese, trapped not by someone physically chaining her to her mother, but by love.

Home, finally, I drove down the alley. Next to the coach house, which was what the realtor called my garage, the yard waste container overflowed with empty beer bottles. Y-A-R-D W-A-S-T-E. Couldn't Northwestern students read? My garbage cans overflowed with trash bags and soggy couch cushions, and to get through the back gate, I had to push aside the overgrown branches of *Vanhoutte spirea*. The backyard grass stood a foot high, and my home, with its pagoda-like dormers, rose up from this undulating sea. Stairs zigzagged to the third floor where the students lived, and I could hear the whir of the air conditioner popped out through the rental apartment's kitchen window. The pain in my throat was either thirst or a scream because, for some reason, I wanted to crawl in bed, pull up the covers, and listen to nothing but the sound of blood drumming in my ears. I didn't want to hear a baby cry or listen the creak of Tony's footsteps in the hall or ache at the sound of my daughter's tears.

I unlocked the mudroom door and went in the kitchen. A legion of dead flies lay on the windowsill. I turned on the kitchen faucet and drank from the tap. Earthy-musty, the taste of Lake Michigan water. In my downstairs office, I hoisted my suitcase to the spare bed. The smell of desitin and baby powder and diaper pail leapt out. I'd have to do laundry because I didn't want to bring any part of Sandy's house with me, not even its smells; but, first, a shower.

Then I heard one of my tenants coming down the stairs.

"Knock, knock," a girl's voice called. "Have you got a moment?"

"If you need to use the washing machine, you're supposed to use the outside stairs. Remember?"

"I know, but I need to talk to you about something else."

Tenants. Their rent covered my mortgage, but I would have preferred to have the house to myself. Especially today.

Standing at the foot of the stairs, I looked up at a pair of ankles tattooed with flames. Then I saw denim shorts. Next to the shorts' zipper swam an IZOD alligator, its jaw open. The girl coming down had black hair that looked chewed, rather than cut. Like a white, upside down flame, her tapered bangs touched one ear. Her nose was long and might have been prominent if I could have seen her in profile, but looking up at the face from below, what horrified me were the two silver rings in her bottom lip.

"Uh, are you the owner?" the girl said.

"Yes," I said. "And who might you be?"

"Uh, Brittany said I should talk to you and see if I could stay till school starts."

"I don't think so," I said. "How did you get into my house?"

"I'm, uh, Brittany's little sister."

The brown-haired, blue-eyed Brittany, one of the summer sublets, did not resemble this girl in the slightest.

"Where is Brittany?" I said. "I thought she'd enrolled in the ten-week summer session, not the eight-week."

"Uh, she, like, moved in with her boyfriend."

"And she let you have the key?"

"She wasn't using the place, and my dad was fed up with me, so he said I could stay over here until he decided if he was going to let me move home or not."

After Rob's death I had spent summers rehabbing two and three flats, flipping the properties until I had a nest egg for the kids' college tuitions; but in all my years of dealing with tenants, this was a new wrinkle.

"How old are you?"

"Seventeen."

Sixteen, more likely. The proportions of the girl's face were still those of a student in junior high: a small chin and disproportionately large eyes. Like Nefertiti, she had outlined each eye and blackened the lids from corner to corner.

"I'm sorry, no. I signed a lease with your sister. It's nontransferable."

"But my dog likes it here."

"Your dog?"

As if on cue, three yaps came from the third floor. Doggie toenails clicked downstairs, and a puppy that looked like a miniature polar bear stood stiff-legged next to the girl. The dog had black eyes, a sharp black nose, and a shiny coat that looked like cotton.

"He loves to play hide-and-seek in the grass," the girl said.

The dog looked up at her in a trusting, anticipatory way.

"Speaking of the grass," I said, "did Brittany happen to mention that I cut her a deal on rent so that I could come home and not find *that*?" I opened the front door and pointed to the foot-high lawn.

The girl bit her lip and looked up at her eyebrows. "Brittany told me I could make a good impression by doing the lawn, but all I could find was that old push mower in the garage."

"The blades are sharp, and you can adjust the height," I said.

"The one I normally use is gas," the girl said.

"I'm sorry. I don't have a gas mower."

The girl's head bobbed side to side. "Okay. I'll use the rust bucket. If the grass isn't super-wet, it'll work."

"You don't look all that strong."

"I mow the lawn where my dad lives," she said.

"Your dad, you say?"

"My mom died when I was ten."

I sighed. When a kid looked like this, there was always a situation at home.

"Where are the other girls?"

"They moved out yesterday. They burned some stuff in the oven, but Brittany left me some oven cleaner and rubber gloves. Also, I got the rust spot in the bathtub down to the size of a penny and defrosted the freezer." She looked upstairs toward the third-floor apartment.

I checked the date on my watch. "You better be gone before the new crop of tenants moves in."

"My dad's trying to find a place that takes dogs."

I looked at the dog again. He had expressive black eyes. Like the girl's, one was hidden by his bangs. He looked from his owner to me, and back again. "What kind of dog is that?"

"They told me he's a Coton de Tuléar," the girl said.

"Who's 'they?'"

"The Humane Society. I found him wandering in Harms Woods. I took the bus over to the animal shelter, and they said they'd try to find the owner, but they never did, and then they said I could leave him if I wanted, but if no one picked him up, in three weeks he'd be dead. My dad said it was 'him or me,' and I said, 'In that case, it's him.'" She picked up the dog, held him to her chest, and he licked her face.

"What's your name?" I said.

"Esmeralda."

"Really?" I said. "What a beautiful name."

"Everyone calls me Esmé."

"In all my years teaching," I said, "I've never met a single Esmeralda. Did you ever see *The Hunchback of Notre Dame*?"

"Yes, but I'm not beautiful like her."

"Your name doesn't mean 'beautiful,'" I said. "It means 'esteemed.'"

"Oh, you mean like self-esteem?"

"Yeah."

"I'm bad at that, too."

"That's funny," I said, "because already I have quite a high opinion of you. Look at how you cleaned the bathtub and the oven and how you saved your dog from the gas chamber."

Esmeralda nodded. "People like me because I make myself useful. I'll get started on the lawn, and I won't bother you. If you need anything, just ask." With the dog tucked under her arm, the girl trotted upstairs. "Come on, Bear. We get to go outside and play."

"The square key unlocks the side door of the garage."

"I know. It unlocks the basement, too."

Esmeralda had made herself at home, but I hoped she didn't plan on making herself too much at home. And what about that dog? I didn't like dogs and had never allowed my children to have one. The trip to Sandy's must have weakened my ability to say no.

I took a load of laundry downstairs. When I came back up, through the window came the whackety-whack of the push mower. It sounded like Esmeralda was having a hard time, but she had volunteered. Too tired to take a shower, I sat down and put my feet up on the desk. Making a tent of my fingers, I massaged the knotted cords in my neck. The phone rang. Probably Sandy.

"Don't worry," I said. "I made it back okay."

"Hi, girlfriend," a woman said.

"Maureen," I gasped.

Maureen was the sixth-grade teacher who was moving down to join the second-grade team. She was a fluffy-haired blonde with big hands and a gangly walk. At school, the kids called her "Big Bird" and the teachers, "Big B."

"So do you know what tomorrow is?" Maureen said.

I stopped before saying *my birthday*. "No. Should I?"

"The Kane County Flea Market," Maureen said. "Want to go? One of the dealers I like is having a special preview day."

"I just walked in the door. My place is a mess."

"How about a swing by the North Shore garage sales?"

"Oh, all right," I said.

***

The next morning, bright and early, when I could have slept in and wanted to, I heard Maureen's horn honking at me. For the past two months, Ben's insistent cries had woken me, but at least those weren't rude awakenings. I pulled on my jeans, grabbed my purse, and ran out to her brown Lexus sports coupe, a car with tan leather seats that felt as luxurious as a limo's. It was perfectly proportioned for its owner, whose plump hands commanded the leather-wrapped wheel. The car smelled like a funeral bouquet. I sniffed. "What's the fragrance?"

"Nina," Maureen said. "Like it?"

I unrolled the window. "It's overpowering."

"I can turn on the a/c."

"No, that's okay. The lake air smells good."

"So," Maureen said, "catch me up."

"It's a long story."

"We've got time."

"It's hard to be back in the chaos of family."

"I hear you," Maureen said. "So what else is new? Did you lose any weight?"

"No. I was stuck in the kitchen." At the beginning of the summer, we'd promised each other to be good and go on diets, but looking at Maureen's double chins and the way her breasts thrust out, it looked like she'd fallen off the wagon, too. Active in the Illinois Federation of Teachers, she'd got herself nominated for statewide office and that took up most of her psychic energy.

"How are politics?" I said.

"My campaign or the state's?"

"The state's, I guess." I didn't care a fig about the legislature, though they had made noises about not putting in their matching half of the public employees' pension—again.

"I can't wait till the legislature's back in session," Maureen said. "We're going to get this thing turned around."

"Oh, sure. Down in Springfield, they love teachers." I looked over at the Grosse Point Lighthouse and the Evanston Art Center, a slate-roofed, Tudor mansion where I'd always thought about taking a class. My plan had been to go to Sandy's for a couple of weeks, spend the summer finishing my house, and when the school year began, sign up for painting or ceramics.

"I'm so tired of sixth," Maureen said. "All those surging hormones. I haven't taught second for fifteen years. And, of course, if I win the election, it'll be easier if I drop down a level."

"Don't count on it," I said.

"I've taught second before."

"A long time ago." Of course, Maureen could teach second, but I'd meant she shouldn't count on winning the election. She might not make the best union representative, negotiation not being her strength. If Sean thought I was too direct, he should get to know Maureen. When her prairie wind blew at you, you'd better hang onto your hat.

"I need to do something to stay excited about this career," Maureen said. "It's hard to even know what kids are learning. I mean the tests measure something, but what, besides facts, are we trying to cram into their resistant little heads?"

"You should try kindergarten."

"I'd love to," Maureen said.

"Yeah, right." The upper-grade teachers thought kindergarten was supervised play, but to my mind, it was the great leveler, the place where the grand experiment of American public education began. A kindergarten teacher's job was to get children ready to learn: the kids who came in being able to read, those whose families spoke other languages, and the children addicted to video games and television. At Sandy's I'd been thinking my emotional center was back there, but that wasn't entirely true. Doors would open if a child were properly educated. If Rob hadn't died, I never would have known I had a gift to inspire young minds, and though it had been a bitter tradeoff, now I was glad I had a career.

"I totally forgot to ask you how the birth went?" Maureen said.

"The *birth* went fine," I said.

"Isn't it just amazing that they let you watch the delivery?"

"Yeah, pretty amazing." Sandy, in her cave alone.

Maureen took her eyes off the road and looked at me. "I mean, in our day, the husbands weren't even allowed."

True. Especially if they were dead.

A bower of maples shaded bicycle riders hugging the curb. The lacey, ribbed dome of the Baha'i temple came into view. I'd never known this beautiful building existed until Rob's work took him past it, and he came home saying he'd seen the Taj Mahal. The Taj Mahal! Against a blue backdrop of sky, the temple and its flower gardens stood on a knoll above the Wilmette harbor. Pushing strollers, two young mothers stopped on the bridge to look down at the sailboats. Ah, to be young again, to return to that state of obliviousness where you think life's going to go on the same way forever. Rob's death—the result of a ten-car pileup on Lakeshore Drive—disabused me of that notion. I hadn't spent twenty-nine years mired in the past, but Sandy's situation had certainly made me think hard about the vulnerability of young mothers. After the accident, it had taken me a couple of years to find a path forward.

"All right, keep an eye out," Maureen said. "We're within striking distance."

Just past Gillson Park, where I caught a glimpse of water through the trees, Maureen veered down a street that jogged left and became Michigan Avenue. The Lexus cruised slowly past a brick bungalow with a green tile roof. There were coat racks. Kids clothes on hangers. An assortment of wagons and tricycles.

"Playskool toys." Maureen stuck her finger down her throat. "Yuck."

"We are so done with that," I said. Then I thought of Josh. In the basement, which I'd cleaned out and painted, Josh had his cardboard playhouse, wooden blocks, and the kids' old Lincoln Logs, not a lot compared to some kids. I could buy some toys and ship them back, but it would cost less to scour the garage sales in Glover Park.

Maureen continued on Sheridan Road until it turned past the back gate of Ravinia and onto Lake Cook Road. "Did you get up here this summer?" I said.

"Just once," Maureen said.

"Who'd you hear?"

"The Captain & Tennille."

"You are kidding me," I said. "Did they sing 'Muskrat Love?'"

"Sure did," Maureen said. "And they sound better than ever."

"They never sounded that good in the first place."

"You cynic," she said.

Rob said cynics were nothing more than failed idealists, but having ideals suited me better than having no ideals at all. We were all just bumbling along, trying to bring the vision of who we'd like to be a little closer to the flawed human beings we actually were.

"Hey, stop." I pointed to the number on a stone pillar.

Maureen swerved into a half-circle drive and parked.

Holding the hand grip I said, "Is this another garage sale?"

"Honey," Maureen said, "we are in Lake Bluff. Call it an *estate* sale."

A collector of Depression glass and California-ware, Maureen never bought anything large; and in fact, her husband Bill had put his foot down on her buying anything at all, claiming their house was full of bric-a-brac. Maureen hopped out of the car, slammed the door, and went over to the tables of sale items. Maureen wasn't a deep person, but she was good-hearted. I got out. My limbs felt heavy. I needed to plunge into the sale's distractions.

Maureen pulled a tablecloth from a plastic sack. "What do you think?"

I held the corners and, together, we shook it out. There were smudges at the folds, but nothing that wouldn't wash out.

"Whose was it?" I said.

"I don't know." A white-haired woman in a rose pantsuit motioned to a box behind her folding chair. "If I had to guess, I'd say it's hers."

I saw two portraits in oval frames: a young woman with curly bangs and a black, high-necked dress and a bald man with a handlebar mustache and bow tie. The painter had done a good job on the eyes. The highlights shone like little windows to their soul. I moved from side to side. The eyes followed.

"How much do you want for the tablecloth?" Maureen asked.

"A hundred twenty," the woman said. "It's bobbin lace."

"We know," Maureen giggled. "We're what used to be called 'lace curtain' Irish."

"I doubt my ancestors could have afforded lace," I said. "Mine were the 'mop-bucket' Irish. Are you selling the portraits?"

"Everything goes."

The humble couple sat with hands folded in their laps. I didn't absolutely need these. I turned away. Lost souls, their mild approving eyes would not let me go.

"Would you take five each for those?" I said.

A gust of wind blew some of the lighter weight things from the table. "If you want them, just take them." The woman handed me the box. The oval frames flopped against my breasts. Imagine putting your relatives in a garage sale. These people, for instance, the young woman with the clear eyes and pale skin, and the young man, slightly older, who were they? Most likely, a house wife and her husband dressed up in their Sunday best.

"I am such a compulsive rescuer," I said.

"They had your number," Maureen said. "Where are you going to put them?"

"Over my mantel."

Maureen counted out twenties. "I need this tablecloth like I need a hole in the head," she said, "but I just can't see it going to someone who wouldn't appreciate it."

"When's the last time you gave a dinner party?"

Maureen laughed. "Easter. My mom can't do it anymore, so I have all the nieces and nephews over for the egg hunt and the sacrificial lamb."

With our purchases safely stowed in the trunk, Maureen fell into the driver's seat and slammed the door. "The next big holiday will be Thanksgiving." She backed out the driveway and headed south. "Every year I swear I'm not going to get roped into hosting, but then my mom pleads and once again I have the whole entourage: brothers, sisters, aunts, uncles, first and second cousins, wives and exes, the whole nine yards."

Being around Maureen was like bouncing on an exercise ball. Eventually, fatigue set in. It was my birthday, and I was spending it going to garage sales. At a stoplight, I looked west toward the Edens. That would be a faster way home. Then I noticed cars turning into the Chicago Botanic Garden.

"Hey," I said, "why don't we go for lunch at the garden?"

Maureen waggled her hand. "I'm not much of a garden person. Besides, there's one more place I want to stop."

"If it's up here, why don't we—"

"No, it's back in Evanston," Maureen said.

The feelers I had put out to the universe had put the Botanic Garden in our path, but now Maureen was driving on. I leaned against the window.

Maureen looked over. "You can go there anytime."

"But I don't."

"Why not?"

"Inertia." Sitting on a park bench alone was about as much fun as eating in a restaurant with a book. Not that that was bad. Sometimes, it was fine. Just not today, when I would have preferred to be with someone.

The car sped up, then braked, then sped up again. Light and shade flashed across my eyelids. When Sandy was little, she was convinced she could see through her eyelids. Rob humored her, holding up two fingers and asking how many. "Two," she'd say, and Rob would say, "Right," even when it wasn't. With Maureen talking about teachers' pensions, I could just about fall asleep.

"Oh, look at the balloons," Maureen said.

We were back in Evanston. Maureen slowed down to keep from hitting picnickers jaywalking across Sheridan. Passing Dawes Park, I saw a brick building that housed restrooms and a concession stand.

"Would you mind letting me out?" I said. "I have to buy my beach pass."

"Sure, I'll let you out." Maureen honked and rolled down her window. "Woo-hoo! We're here!" She swerved to make a U-turn and squealed into an empty space. "I wanted a Mazda RX-7, not this friggin' boat. Oh, look, there's Bill."

Bill Flaherty, tanned and lean, wore jeans and a bright orange tee-shirt the color of his company's panel truck. A silver Uncle Sam's hat, probably a leftover from the 4th of July parade, made him look ridiculous.

"Hey, Colleen, like my new tee-shirt?" He pointed at his chest.

SHIT FLOWS DOWNHILL

At a 2 percent grade.
CALL FLAHERTY PLUMBING

I gave him a thumbs-up.

"Happy happy you-know-what," Maureen said.

Was this for me? A surprise party?

"I'm stunned," I said.

"Good stunned or bad stunned?"

"I don't know," I said. "Give me a moment." Maureen hopped out. From the car, it looked like fifteen or twenty teachers had shown up. I had wanted to be with someone. Well, here they were. I sat there, chest heaving, trying to psych myself into a more social mood.

At the picnic table, Maureen mustered the troops to set out what they'd brought to the potluck. By the time I'd received hugs and birthday wishes, she had sliced tomatoes and arranged them on a sheet of foil.

"We know how much you like cream cheese frosting," Maureen said, "so we sent Linda over to one of those Jewish bakeries in Skokie that has carrot cake to die for."

To die for. I thought about Lillian and her pound cake. Linda would never touch pound cake. My co-teacher felt about sugar the way Tony did about pork.

"That's funny you sent Linda, of all people," I said.

"Why?"

"Because she's on this raw food regimen," I said. "She's not just vegetarian. She doesn't eat anything cooked."

"She didn't object," Maureen said.

"Of course not," I said. "She's a team player."

"Well, she eats donuts."

"I don't think so."

"It'll be okay. It's *carrot* cake."

Linda's concern for school nutrition was well known; it seemed baffling that Maureen would forget this important fact, especially if she wanted Linda's vote. If they ever had to teach together, Maureen would bowl Linda over.

Despite Maureen's calls to "Come and load your plate," no one seemed in a hurry to eat. Someone had tied a badminton net between two trees. Short-haired, athletic Marsha Philips, who'd just completed her first year, had persuaded Ann Street to play *takraw,* a game of foot-volleyball Marsha had learned in the Peace Corps. Ann Street coached soccer and she caught on quickly, but Neil Tanner, who had the sixth-grade class across the hall from Maureen's, kept kicking the air. A white-haired and white-bearded grandfather, he had not grown up playing sports that required foot agility. Laura Rider, the school secretary, took off her heels. Chubby and cheerful, she dropped her glasses and shrieked. "I just can't do this."

"Everybody," Maureen clapped. "Listen up. You're going to line up on the left and work your way down the table. Birthday girl first."

"Oh, no," I said. "You should—"

"Don't argue with me," Maureen said. "Set an example."

I picked up a plate. Someone said, "That's my potato salad. I put bacon in it. I hope that won't offend anyone." Someone else said it looked dangerous with all that mayo. Those in line offered opinions about how long mayo could sit outside the refrigerator without causing food poisoning, and the woman who'd brought the salad said she didn't think fat-free mayo had the same problem because it didn't have eggs. "Oh, in that case," I said, digging in the spoon.

By the time I reached the end of the line my plate wobbled. Bill Flaherty, whom I thought of as the brother I'd never had, looked at the open bun. "Sure you don't want to get another plate to put under that one?"

"It's fine."

"I told Mo these plates looked flimsy." Bill slipped a patty onto my bun, and with his tongs made an arrow through his head. "But, you know, in one ear and out the other."

When everyone was served and sitting cross-legged on the grass, Maureen proposed a toast. "To our colleague, Colleen Gallagher." She made a little speech about how teaching had changed in the many years we'd taught at Lincolnwood. The district office was caught up with metrics and test scores. In the old days, no one questioned what went on in the classroom. Now, too many people told us what to do. Our Principal, Dr. Angela Hidalgo, in a navy pantsuit with white piping, had seated herself at a nearby picnic table. Her back was turned, but she waved a hand like the Queen of England.

"We know who the *real* teachers are." Maureen's voice faltered. "They're the ones who care."

I waited to see if Maureen would pass out union flyers, but when she didn't, I stood up. "Thank you all for giving up your Saturday. Especially when there's no alcohol allowed in the park."

Several teachers laughed. The younger teachers liked to go to happy hour at Tommy Nevins' Grill.

I went over to see Dr. Hidalgo.

"Think Maureen will win?" she said.

"If she doesn't become too strident," I said. Teachers said they wanted a union, but when it came right down to it, most of us preferred to mind our own business.

Dr. Hidalgo licked her plastic fork in a contemplative way. "Someone must have made the coleslaw from scratch. I can taste the caraway."

"I was looking for your seven-layer salad."

"I didn't bring it," she said. "Today's not one of my better days."

"Your knees?"

"My hands." Dr. Hidalgo flexed her fingers. "Pretty soon I'm not going to be able to get this ring off."

She held up a gold school ring with a blue gemstone. I adjusted my bifocals. University of California Los Angeles.

"I didn't know you went to UCLA."

"Yes, I'm a Bruin," Dr. Hidalgo said. "In 1984, the only year the Illini and UCLA went *mano a mano* in the Rose Bowl, I was getting my doctorate."

"Who won?"

"UCLA prevailed," she said. "Forty-five to nine. No contest."

Besides Sean and Kevin—oh, and Tony, too—Dr. Hidalgo was the only person I knew who had a genuine interest in sports, even though she wasn't athletic. I'd seen her in her office with a heating pad wrapped around her shoulder and asked if she'd injured it doing water aerobics. "No, it's the rheumatoid arthritis again," she'd told me. To combat a flare-up, her doctor had put her on steroids. "There's a reason they say doctors 'practice medicine.' I just wish they didn't practice on me."

"I should help Mo with the cleanup," I said.

"Better you than me," she said. "I'm going to sit here and enjoy my view of the lake."

Everyone had eaten. Maureen was putting tops on the Tupperware bowls.

Bill Flaherty was scraping the grill with a wire brush. "I don't care what she says," he muttered, pulling loose the chinstrap of his party hat. "I'm going to take this stupid thing off."

"Bill," Maureen said. "You need to wear it till we light the candles and sing."

"It's choking me." He threw the hat in the trash and strode quickly across the grass. "Anyway, the cake's here."

Beyond him, I saw a car double-park. In Bermuda shorts and a white polo shirt, sunglasses pushed up on her head, my co-teacher, Linda Farrell, took a pink cake box from the trunk. Unlike me with my braid long enough to sit on and my few extra pounds, she wore her hair clipped short and dressed in a way my mom called "tailored." While Bill carried the cake like a ring-bearer at a wedding, Linda drove off to find a parking place. He put the box on the table, cut the string with his pocketknife, and folded back the flaps. The bakery had decorated the cake with Bugs Bunny chewing a carrot. A giant number four—an inedible, plaster-hard 4—decorated the cake.

"Four years old." Bill put his arm around me. "You hide your age well."

"Leave her alone, Bill." Maureen rolled her eyes. "I thought I told them it was for an adult."

"I don't mind if they shave a few years," I said.

"I forgot the candles," Maureen said.

"The wind would blow them out anyway." I looked up at the leaves. Like ballerinas' skirts, they were turned inside out by the wind. Plates blew off the table and cups tipped over.

Arms pumping, Linda Farrell hurried toward the tables. "Sorry the cake's late," she said. "The stupid bakery gave yours to someone else. I told them we had to have a carrot cake, so this is what we got."

I laughed and said that's always the way it was. Best laid plans and so forth.

Linda elbowed me and whispered, "It's all about the election. Don't you just *hate* this?"

"Yes," I said automatically. But wait. Maybe I didn't *hate* it.

Maureen was being misunderstood. Motives imputed.

"What are you two talking about?" Maureen said.

"We were saying it's time to cut the cake." I picked up a spatula and cut a corner piece with Bugs' foot. It was fun to be in a park on a summer's day, to just join in and let life be celebrated. Whether it was my life or someone else's didn't matter.

"I'll be back in a minute," Linda said. She walked back to her car and returned with a leash around her wrist and a miniature poodle. The brown-eyed dog looked docile and stupid, like a sheared sheep with cotton anklets. Linda trained guide dogs, was a board member at PAWS, the no-kill humane society, and occasionally took a rescue dog.

I wanted to tell her about my new tenants, Esmeralda and Bear, but Linda would have been incensed that the animal shelter would kill a quality pet. For all of Linda's do-gooder intentions, she could be instantly bummed out on two fronts: cruelty to pets and bad nutrition.

"Want some cake?" I said.

Linda patted her stomach. "Still doing the raw food thing."

"Thanks for picking it up," I said. "Especially since I can't imagine an eating event having any appeal for you."

"That's true."

Pregnant Rickey Michener in her tent dress and Deborah Tanner, the other first-grade teacher, broke into our conversation. If it looked like all the hyperactive kids were going to be together, there was still time to switch them around. What did we think? Licking frosting off my fork, I gave evasive answers. Even children who couldn't sit still could have their energy channeled. Laura Rider, the secretary, agreed with me on this. It was hard enough to meet the district's education requirements without playing musical chairs.

Linda looked toward the street.

"Here comes Phoenix," Linda said, "barreling along as per usual."

A late arrival, Phoenix Patton, an adoptive mom who had been a pro tennis player in a former life, gave me a birthday card on behalf of the PTA. Like Linda, she spent her days at the gym and had turned into an ally in Linda's efforts to reduce childhood obesity. Linda had been lobbying the PTA to influence the district's policies on school snacks, and just recently, she'd won a victory. Finally, the district had published a list of healthy snacks. Parents, and the cafeteria, too, had to offer oranges, carrots, and celery sticks instead of cookies and cupcakes. And here we were celebrating my birthday with carrot cake. A thousand calories a slice. How funny was that.

Over on her bench, Dr. Hidalgo turned around and motioned. "Bill, Neil, could you boys give me a hand back to my car?"

White-haired Neil Tanner smiled. "Sure. *No problema.*"

Bill put down his cake plate. The men took Dr. Hidalgo's elbows and lifted her from the bench.

"She is just an amazing person," Maureen said.

"That she is," I said, newly aware of the courage it took to live with a disability.

Dr. Hidalgo had recently moved her mother up from Pilsen. They shared a townhouse near Evanston Township High, and because she knew of my reputation for rehabbing houses, Dr. Hidalgo had come to me for advice on grab bars. She hadn't asked about wider doors or getting up and down to the second floor, but now that I saw her struggling to walk across the lawn, I wondered how long before illness confined the two women to the first floor. Tony would face that problem, too.

"We should call it a day," I said.

Returning from carrying a box to his orange panel truck, Bill brought back an extra-large tee-shirt. "Here's your present from me."

"Extra large?" I said. "I don't think I've gained that much weight."

"You're big-boned," he said. "Like my wife."

"I'm not big-boned," Maureen said. "I'm five-eleven."

"Well, you big gals look better every year, if you ask me." He winked at me. "The shirt's cotton. It'll shrink."

Dumbfounded, I stood there holding the tee-shirt and watching Maureen's eyes narrow into a look of hatred. Bill turned away. Full of good intentions, the people who loved you most could plunge an ice pick in your ribs.

CHAPTER 6

"I went over to Sandy's a couple days ago," Sean said, his voice raspy from a cold. "Tony wants me to babysit every Friday night."

With the phone cradled on my shoulder, I pushed back the pans I'd left upended on a kitchen towel. "Sean, I'm in Illinois. What am I supposed to do about it?"

"I don't know," he said. "But something."

I found a shish-kebab skewer in a drawer and dug out the dried goop from a blue caulking gun. My house looked more chaotic than before I'd left. A strange girl lived upstairs—a dog, too. The rental apartment needed a ton of work. I hadn't even had coffee.

"You still there?" he said.

"They belong to a babysitting co-op," I said.

"Why can't they trade with other parents?"

"I assume that's a rhetorical question."

Sandy hadn't been in touch, not even to thank me for painting the basement. But that didn't surprise me. I was bad about writing thank-you notes, too, and my mother would have been ashamed to know I didn't have a box of note cards in my desk.

"Kevin was asking, did you ever talk to her about that respirator thing?" Sean said.

The visit to the shrunken woman with the big eyes. "No," I said.

"You need to do that, Mom."

"What, long distance?"

"I'm not kidding, Mom," Sean said. "They're all lovey-dovey. It makes me want to puke. Sandy should know what's in her future. Even I can see the headlights of the train."

"I'll type up something."

"Soon, Mom," Sean said. "You won't believe how far Tony's gone downhill since you left."

"I've only been gone two-and-a-half weeks."

"I know," he said. "That's what I mean. The progression is really bad."

His own life wasn't so great either. An auditing team from Maryland's Department of Human Resources had swept in for a site visit and found some problems with the way records were being kept. Not his, thank God, but a couple of his colleagues had gotten their hands slapped. Yesterday he'd spent all day in court with one of his clients, a fourteen-year-old foster child in dreadlocks and a sock hat. The boy had been picked up after curfew, and the court ordered Sean to find another placement. A group home was the only option. Thinking of Esmeralda, I made sympathetic noises. Suddenly, Sean, my youngest, faced the juggling act of adult life: How much should you step outside your comfort zone to help other people? When I was back at Sandy's place, he'd had thirty kids added to his caseload. Despite that, he had helped me carry the futon down to the basement. He'd promised to fix the roof leak on Sandy's porch, and now it looked like he'd have to babysit.

"Hey, honey," I said, "I need to get some breakfast."

"All right," he said, "but don't keep procrastinating."

"I won't," I said. "I'll do it now."

"Did you ever get signed up for CompuServe?"

"Yeah, I did."

"If you can't get her attention on the phone, just e-mail her."

After good-byes the line went dead. Turning, I punched Sandy's number into the black wall phone. Through the glass panel in the kitchen door, I saw the mudroom where I'd lined up my down boots and the leather Redwings I wore in the garden. A fall clean up—shrubs pruned, bulbs put in—that's all I'd have time for. A five-gallon garbage pail held rock salt. I needed to refill it. Last December I'd learned it wasn't safe for students to go up and down the back stairs, and I didn't want them tromping through the house.

After I talked to Sandy, I'd go down to the Unicorn for breakfast. Give myself a half hour to not feel frantic. I waited for the answering machine. *Hello. This is the home of Tony Dimasio, Sandy Gallagher and Josh Gallagher-Dimasio*, a little voice would say. *Please leave a message and my mom or dad will call you back.*

"What do you want?" Sandy said, interrupting the spiel.

"Nothing special," I said. "Just to see how you are."

"I'm trying to feed the kids and get them off to the babysitter's," Sandy said. "I wish you wouldn't phone this early."

"Okay," I said, "but—"

"I can't talk now. Good-bye."

Stunned, I looked at the receiver and slammed it into the cradle. I'd planned to fly out to Sandy's for Labor Day, but I wasn't going to make another trip if she spoke to me in that tone. It wasn't as if I had nothing to do here. I needed to clean the rental unit, paint it, and replace a faulty circuit breaker. That morning Esmeralda had come down to report that the air conditioner didn't work, she couldn't turn on the lights, and the fridge didn't keep things cold. I looked at my watch. Eight o'clock. It was nine back East. What was making Sandy so irritable? It had been years since she'd snapped at me for no reason.

Since I was already standing by the phone, I called Illinois Power. Sure enough, the girls who'd moved out had cut off the electricity as of

August 31. I told the woman on the phone to put the account in my name and went upstairs to give Esmeralda the news. She came to the door in the same shorts she'd worn yesterday and stood with her arms crossed over her almost flat chest.

"You'll have power soon," I said.

"I don't want you paying for me to live here."

"That's okay," I said. "I need light or I won't be able to see to paint."

"Can I help you do that?" she said. "Sort of, like, trade, or something?"

"Sure," I said. "I'll buy paint today. We'll start bright and early tomorrow."

"Why not today?"

"I've got to pay bills."

"I'll just start cleaning if you don't mind."

"Feel free."

Now I was glad I hadn't told Sandy about dropping in on Labor Day. I could put some labor into my own place for a change.

***

But first, a walk downtown for breakfast. If I brought my laptop, I could kill two birds with one stone: eat and jot down details about my visit to the Calabreses'. I threw on a jacket and set out, reveling in the freedom to come and go as I pleased.

Two houses to the south the Chinese woman who did *tai chi* had already finished her porch exercises. One of these days, I would knock on their door and bring them a loaf of zucchini bread. Tony's diagnosis had blown a hole in the way I normally conducted my life, but I was home and didn't have to think about the future. Through the overarching maples blazed the sky, and on each block I felt the welcome tug of familiar strings: the children's park with its old fire engine, the senior care center where my mother spent her last two years, my tax accountant's. I felt a certain pride in living right next to a university where the student concerts and plays provided a constant stream of low cost entertainment, where the Block Gallery, with its rotating exhibits, was a ten minute walk from my front door.

Downtown, I was surprised to see the camera store on the corner of Sherman and Clark with a closed sign on the door. I had taken my dad's old Argus down there, and the owner had promised to sell it on consignment. I'd planned to go in after breakfast and find out if he'd had any luck. When I looked through the door, I saw everything just as it had been back in June. The cases still had cameras in them. The wall behind the counter had cubbies of Tri-X and Ektachrome. A note on the door gave a phone number to call. I wrote it down but forgot to call, and it wasn't till months later, when a bagel shop opened, that I remembered my dad's camera. By then I had lost the phone number, and the loss of a few bucks was the least of my problems.

A few doors further on Sherman, smokers filled the Unicorn's outdoor tables. I thought about sitting at a counter that faced the front window so I could watch people scurry in and out of Starbucks across the street, but I didn't want to perch on a stool. I usually sat in the back corner at one of four marble tables; however each table was occupied by a student with a laptop and a stack of books. Two church pews against the wall were free. I dropped my computer on one and unwound the cord, once again, preparing to attend the Church of Coffee. As I approached the counter, I saw that the chalkboard menu had something new: *Panini*, either ham and cheese or roasted pepper and eggplant. Sean's least favorite vegetable. I ordered a latte.

Behind the cash register, a young woman with a wandering eye smiled urgently. "Hi, Mrs. Gallagher. Remember me?"

The face didn't look familiar, but when I focused on the girl's eyes, I remembered a family that had fled Ceausescu's regime in Romania. Thirty years ago, parents told their kids, "Don't cross your eyes or they'll get stuck that way." This girl had a stuck right eye. Surgery was beyond the parents' means. The father, a doctor in his home country, had treated the girl himself. All year she'd worn a patch on her good, left eye. The bad eye compensated. Now, in the place of a girl who'd come to school in what the parents surely thought was proper clothing—a starched white blouse and, on alternating days, a brown skirt and a black one—I saw before me a poised young woman in a sleeveless, tangerine top. Below were hip-hugger jeans and red cowboy boots. Her hair, parted down the middle and tucked behind her ears, was held in place by rhinestone clips. She no longer wore a patch, but one eye still roamed.

"Sonya," I said. "How are your folks? Did your dad ever get his license?"

"Yes," the girl said, pumping the espresso machine's handle to pack down the grounds. "I knew you'd remember."

"Of course," I said, relaxing as I recalled the feisty little pirate girl. "Sonya Iliescu. You must have been in my first or second class."

"I am an artist now," the girl said, pointing behind me to the paintings above the pews. "Those are mine."

I glanced at one of the oils. The white paint still looked wet. A slash of orange made a diagonal. She had dripped splotches of navy blue in one corner. I liked modern art, big splashy colors and big canvases, but only in museums.

Sonya pointed to the wall behind me. "There's more over there."

I turned. Above the church pews hung another dozen paintings. On one, a red circle opened and dripped color toward the bottom of the canvas. On another, two tilted squares cracked against one another like broken eggs. The paintings looked unbalanced.

"I just finished my MFA at the Art Institute." She handed me a peach muffin. "On the house."

"Thanks," I said, "and congrats."

"Your class was where I decided I wanted to be an artist."

Yikes. "Children are born artists," I said, "until school beats it out of them. I'm glad that didn't happen to you."

"Me, too."

"I'll take a closer look after I eat." I took my latte and muffin. Sonya had made a tulip in the foam. An *artista-barrista*.

I hoped Sonya could figure some way to make a living besides working at a coffee shop. From the looks of the art, she'd have a hard time surviving as a painter; but then, no painter had it easy and parents could only be glad when their children found a career with some job security.

Kevin had been the most artistic of my children. From the moment he'd first picked up scissors he'd been ambidextrous, an asset in art and basketball. Those two passions had woven through his life. In Chapel Hill, basketball paid for his education, but he'd sat on the bench till the end of senior year. He probably had more innate talent for his other passion—art. Copying all the *Batman* cartoons, first by tracing and then drawing freehand, he'd done well enough to gain some recognition in his summer classes at the Art Institute. When he was a teenager, he and his friend Jeremy, whose parents owned an art store, had made claymation movies. Lately, Kevin had gotten into Japanese cartoons. Some *anime* thing.

I often heard friends talk about "following your bliss," but I hadn't been able to summon the courage to tell Kevin he could make a living doodling. In college, he'd been a good, solid student in his academic subjects, leaning more in Rob's direction: engineering. He'd tried that major for a semester but had not been able to stomach what he called "the roteness of it all." He'd majored in math and gone into teaching. Math teachers had good job security, better than if he'd tried to find a job in phys ed, but I still worried a little because he lacked seniority.

After squeezing around the table and sliding across the pew, I turned on my computer, a laptop that had been my Christmas present to myself. Originally, I thought I'd use it for recipes and accounts—Maureen kept telling me great things about TurboTax—but lately, I'd found that the boys liked to use e-mail.

Sean was undoubtedly right. Sandy needed the information. Trying to think how to begin, I nibbled my muffin and listened to the background chatter of half a dozen middle-aged men, rocked back in chairs, talking sports. I recognized a couple women from water aerobics at the Y and a student journalist from Medill who'd visited my class for background on a story about class size in the Evanston schools. The occasional roar of the blender made me feel less alone with the horror of Sandy's future, which was Tony's future, too. Not mine, though. I had done my time in purgatory and had no wish to go there again, even as a tourist. What I wanted most was to give Sandy the straight dope about what lay ahead. If she didn't have a clear picture of what this disease might require of her, she would not be able to make a plan for Tony's care or her own survival.

I wished I could capture Joan Calabrese's voice, Joan Calabrese's crazed laugh, and the way the woman had fished inside her bra for her cigarettes. It was impossible to imagine who she'd been before she became a caregiver. And what about the mother?

The elderly Mrs. Calabrese had giant eyes, open all the time. The eyes glowed in my memory. *Let me out!* Or maybe the message was just the opposite. *I'm still here!* It was tragic the way she was confined to her wheelchair, her head strapped to a pole.

Tony would evolve into such a being. Instead of growing fur and fangs, he would grow immobile. People would avoid him because it was awkward to make conversation. If visitors came once, they would not come back.

Dear Sandy,

Hi, how are things going? I'm sorry my phone call caught you at a busy time, so I thought I'd try to send you this missive about a subject I know you probably won't want to think about. I'm also sending it to your brothers who live a lot closer than I do and who, I'm sure, will offer you every bit of support they can. (Hint, hint, boys.)

When Lisa was down visiting, she gave me the name of a woman out in Takoma Park. Joan Calabrese. Joan is her mother's caregiver, and Lisa thought that visiting her would help me "educate myself." Knowing you don't have a lot of spare time to be running around educating yourself, I thought I would try to give you sort of a vicarious experience. This is what I learned from being with Joan and her mother.

Joan's mother has been on a respirator for five years.

CG: Why did your mother go on a respirator?

JC: Her breathing became compromised.

CG: When was that?

JC: In the second year.

CG: Did you consider having her live in a nursing home?

JC: It is very difficult to find a nursing home that will take a patient on a respirator.

Keeping the elderly Mrs. Calabrese alive requires teams of nurses and $250 to $300 thousand dollars a year, and the daughter had to sue her insurance company to get them to pay for the nursing help. She had an old policy, and she warned that modern policies do not pay for "custodial care," but when a person is on a respirator, someone has to be with them and vigilant 24 hours a day. The mother and daughter use note cards to communicate.

She was entombed in her body. She was almost at the lock down stage where she couldn't even blink.

In sum, this is what "going on a respirator" means. Maybe Tony's doctor has told him more about it since his initial visit, and my information will be redundant. I hope Tony will give this serious thought. Once the decision to go on a respirator is made, it might be difficult to reverse that decision without his signature. And, if he's on a respirator, there's little likelihood he'll be able to use his hands to sign. The decision will affect your life, not just his.

—Love, Mom

When I got home, I'd connect up my new 2400 baud modem and see if I could send. Sandy could look into the crystal ball of her own future. If Sandy felt like kicking me out, well, she didn't have to bother because I wasn't within kicking distance. I was sitting in a church pew licking foam from my lips.

CHAPTER 7

The upstairs apartment had three bedrooms, a kitchen with a four-foot counter and a bath with a claw-foot tub. Now that I had checked the Calabrese thing off the mental list, I needed to dig into getting the apartment ready for new tenants. Even though I'd given Esmeralda fair warning, I expected to find her in bed. Seventeen-year-olds were like lemurs, active and busy at night, sacked out during the day.

"Knock, knock," I said from the open door.

"You're in, so I won't say 'Come in,'" Esmeralda said.

"Smart ass," I said.

Esmeralda, holding an eyeliner brush, stood in the bathroom.

"Do you know Kelly Crawford, Cindy Dawkins, and Meghan Phillips?" I asked.

"How would I?" Esmeralda said.

"I thought they might have been in Brittany's class."

"Whose? No." Esmeralda dropped her eyeliner brush and bent to pick it up. "Damn, I just mopped the floor."

"I didn't mean to startle you," I said. "I was just wondering if they'd like to add you as a fourth. The front bedroom's large enough for two. That might make it affordable for all of you."

She stared at me in the mirror. "They're more like my sister's friends."

I looked around to see how much the apartment had gone downhill, but it was much cleaner than when Brittany and the other sublets had lived here. Not perfectly clean. Not move-in clean. At least there weren't any pizza boxes or kegs of beer. To address the former tenants' complaints that they had no place for a dish rack, I needed to make a shelf for the microwave. I went down to the basement and got my tools.

Watching me plug in a Skilsaw, Esmeralda asked, "Did you take shop when you were in school?"

"Girls couldn't take shop in my day. My father taught me." I finished the cut and bolted brackets to the wall. "He was a carpenter."

Esmeralda, in the same pair of jeans-shorts she'd worn every day, and, for that matter, probably slept in, scrubbed the grease off the wall behind the stove and painted the metal drawers of the kitchen cabinets. I spackled and rolled the walls. Bear stuck right with us, cocking his head to the side, dancing in a circle if one of us made a sudden movement toward the counter where a box of dog biscuits sat. We worked all day and didn't stop for lunch. It was five-thirty when I heard the doorbell ring downstairs. I lowered the roller into the paint tray.

"Want me to get it?" Esmeralda said.

"Sure," I said. "I'll finish up." While I listened to her footsteps on the stairs, I squeezed off the extra paint and made one more V-shaped swipe. Then I heard laughter. Only one person ever dropped in on me, Maureen, with her bouncing, optimistic patter. Her goal was to pull me out of my shell, I suppose, though over the years, my tolerance for being alone had far exceeded anything I'd imagined when I was young.

I rinsed the roller in the kitchen sink. By the time Maureen appeared, white sacks from Hecky's Barbecue in one hand, a thermos in the other, uttering exclamations about how much progress I'd made, I had poured the rest of the paint back in the can and tapped down the lid with my hammer. I pulled the drop cloth off the sofa and folded it up. My father used to say, "Good enough for who it's for," and I guessed that was true because Maureen wasn't going to let me keep on working.

"I didn't know you had company." Maureen smiled at Esmeralda, and the girl grimaced, as if she preferred to make herself invisible. I handed her the drop cloth and pointed to the paint can. She picked up the dog biscuits.

I gathered my tools. "Let's go downstairs."

"I thought I'd stop by with some dinner and margaritas," Maureen said, "to celebrate the start of school."

We made a little parade.

"I'll just take this stuff to the basement," Esmeralda said, "and I'll get out of your hair."

"No you won't," I said. "You've got to eat."

"There's plenty," Maureen said.

When we reached the first floor, Esmeralda continued on to the basement. I put my tools by the basement door, and, as I thought she might, she found them and put them away.

Maureen stage-whispered, "Who is that, for god's sakes?"

"A girl who took over from one of my sublets."

"She's a sight." Maureen opened a cabinet and took out two glasses. "Let me pour you a little drinkey pooh."

"Just an inch of that." I took a Diet Coke from the refrigerator and found a Coke for Esmeralda.

"Oh, come on. School starts tomorrow." Maureen took out ice cubes. Pouring from the thermos, she filled her glass.

I held up a hand and shook my head no. "Where's Bill?"

"He's on some sewer cleanout. Won't be home till midnight. I didn't feel like cooking, and I thought it'd be smart to pick up some dinner and hit the sack. I brought three chicken dinners, but he'll have eaten by the time he gets home, so if you want to feed that girl, go ahead."

Of course, I wanted to feed her. I was famished. She must be, too.

We sat at one end of the dining room table, pulling apart the chicken, dipping fries in ketchup, and licking our fingers. Maureen talked about establishing discipline on the first day. How she had to be on her game, or the class would be out of control. Esmeralda looked at me and rolled her eyes. She had been on the receiving end of first days at school.

"So what else do you have to do before the place is habitable?" Maureen twisted around toward the living room.

Before going to Sandy's I'd refinished the oak trim and painted the walls olive green. I'd opened up the pocket doors.

With a drumstick, I pointed to the plate rail. "Unpack my mom's china and put it up there."

"Ah, the baggage of the past," Maureen said. "I know it well."

She finished her dinner and went back to the kitchen for a refill on her drink. I heard the clank of the garbage can's lid. "Hey, Colleen," Maureen called out, "is it okay if I use your facilities?"

"Sure," I said. "I think there's a roll of toilet paper." I hoped she didn't intend to drink that entire thermos of margaritas by herself.

"Is she getting wasted?" Esmeralda said.

"I don't think so," I said. "She has a lot of body mass."

"Does she do this a lot?" Esmeralda said.

"What, stop by?"

Esmeralda nodded.

"She views me as a charity case," I said.

"What, you?" Esmeralda wiped her hands with a wet wipe.

"Yeah," I said. "It's funny. Then again, maybe she was just lonely tonight."

Standing, Esmeralda held out her plate. "What should I do with this?" She had picked apart her chicken, but there was still a lot left.

"Cover it with foil and put it in the fridge," I said.

The toilet flushed and water ran in the bathroom sink. Maureen, wiping her hands on her jeans, filled the door. "I think I'm going to head on home." A hand to her cheek, she fanned her face.

"Are you okay to drive?" I said.

Maureen looked at Esmeralda. "I'm fine." She collected her thermos and purse and cut through the dining room to reach the front hall. "See you in the teacher's room," she called.

"Thanks so much for the dinner," Esmeralda said. "The barbecue place is right near me, but I never had their food."

"You're welcome," Maureen called. The door slammed.

I looked down at Bear. He yapped. "Did she feed you?"

"No, I didn't," Esmeralda said. "I'm out of dog food."

I dug in my pocket for some change. "If you're done eating, why don't you go down to 7-Eleven and get him some liver dinner."

"I shouldn't take your money."

"You're not taking it. He is."

"Do you think I could leave him here so I could jog down?" Esmeralda said.

"I didn't picture you as a jogger," I said.

"I'm not, but after this big dinner, I feel like running."

"Sure, go ahead."

"Another thing." Esmeralda brushed back her flame-like bangs.

"What?"

"I know you told me I have to move out," Esmeralda looked down at Bear, "but I still don't have any place to bring him."

The dog, with his black, button eyes, looked at me and let out a yip. "Oh, all right." I pulled off a piece of chicken breast, one without any sauce, and balanced it on his nose. "Not yet," I said. Tail twitching, he looked cross-eyed, intent on the food. "All right," I said, making a circular motion with my hand. He tossed his head back and snapped. I reached over and stroked his head. Not that he needed additional reinforcement.

"I guess you could let him stay here," I said, "but you're going to have to come over after school and walk him."

Esmeralda's eyes widened. She put down her plate and leaned toward me. I prepared to receive a hug, but the girl's hands fell to her sides.

"Sure," she said. "Right."

"He needs his exercise," I said.

"It's kind of late tonight. By the time I get back from the store, it'll be—"

"I didn't mean tonight. I meant when you go back to school."

"I thought so," she said.

I carried my plate to the kitchen and scraped bones into the garbage. Esmeralda held out her plate. I found plastic wrap, covered the chicken and put it in the fridge. If she came home hungry, it would make a good snack. "What school do you go to?"

"ETHS."

Evanston Township High School. "What grade are you in?"

"I'm a junior."

Back when my kids went there I'd lived a few blocks from the school. My new house was a couple miles away. It would be a pain for her to come over just to walk the dog.

"Listen, there's a camping cot in my basement. I'll set it up in that back bedroom on the second floor. You can throw a sleeping bag down on top of it."

"Really?" Esmeralda said.

"Don't get too excited," I said. "It's not that comfortable."

"Would it be okay if Bear sleeps with me?"

"Might as well," I said. "Get going." I shooed Esmeralda toward the door. "And pick up something for yourself for breakfast while you're at it."

"I don't eat breakfast," Esmeralda said.

I looked her up and down. The skinny arms. The knees that looked like bulbs of garlic. She might be anorexic.

"This is just for tonight," I said.

"Oh, I understand. You don't want anyone in your space." The girl looped a beaded purse over her head and opened the back door. "I might need the house key to unlock the front door."

"Of course." I took a spare from my key chain. So she had discovered that I locked the stairs between the basement and the first floor. I couldn't lock the apartment door. In case of fire, the tenants needed a way to escape.

"Please don't wake me up when you come in," I said.

"Don't worry. I'll feed Bear and go right to bed."

As the door slammed, I felt a puff of air. Bear stiffened his legs and extended his neck, the way he did when Esmeralda attached him to his leash. "She'll be back in a minute," I said.

Bear looked up.

"She's not abandoning you."

He yipped. I took a dog biscuit from the box on the counter. Esmeralda wouldn't have approved. No trick, no biscuit. That was her rule.

How rigid I'd been with Sandy. Ease up on her, Rob had said, but I was anxious because I'd never had brothers or sisters and didn't know the first thing about young children. Rob's death—the instant shattering of so many of my assumptions about life—made all my admonitions about cleaning up toys and putting clothes in the laundry basket look arbitrary, even cruel. In truth, I'd been a better parent to the boys from the get-go, and it wasn't because I loved them more, but because I'd grown more confident.

CHAPTER 8

My co-teacher, Linda Farrell, had arrived half an hour early to scrub the desks. Maureen leaned in the door of the kindergarten room. "You shouldn't have made me drink that entire jug of margaritas all by myself." The back of a hand against her forehead, she rolled her eyes. "Oh, and also, that girl."

I looked up from the chair I was pushing under a table. "Esmeralda is none of your business."

She held up both hands and backed away. "Sor-ry, but she's just so …" She shook her head.

"Pathetic?" I said.

"I was going to say such a little tart."

"Listen, Big B, enough of that. I just saw security heading down the hall. You'd better get back to your room before the hordes descend."

Through the open door I could see a girl whose backpack hung rakishly from her shoulder. As she bounced down the hall, I heard the click of her beaded, cornrow braids. She was looking in the display cases at last year's class pictures.

"Hi Latisha," I called.

"Oh, hi, Miz Gallagher. How you doing?"

"I'm fine," I said.

"My baby sister be in your class."

"Really? I didn't see her name."

"Her last name be different."

"You could have walked her to school."

"No, my mama be coming."

Latisha's mom, a single parent who showed up for parent-teacher conferences in blue scrubs, worked at Evanston Hospital as a nurses' aide. Full-day kindergarten had been a godsend. One course at a time, she was working on her nursing degree at Oakton Community College.

Linda Farrell, who'd set out paste pots on the tables, untied the apron she used to protect her cotton slacks. "Will you do story time, or shall I?"

"I'll do it," I said.

And there, holding her father's hand and looking scared, came a curly-haired girl sucking her thumb. "Welcome," I said, moving out into the hall to let them pass. Linda, bending over to take the girl's backpack, showed her to a cubby. The father, dressed in a suit and carrying a briefcase, checked off his daughter's name on the clipboard by the door. I invited him to stand by the wall. "I've gotta run for the train," he said.

The Central Street Metra station, a block away, went straight south to the financial district.

Half an hour later, boys bumped shoulders and girls linked arms with play-date friends. Latisha's mother, a lanyard with her hospital ID hanging from her neck, came in last, hurrying her daughter through the door. "I'm sorry I can't stay," she said. I told her not to worry. The children would introduce themselves. Linda would remind parents to let the office know if someone else would be picking their child up. I would dismiss the parents and watch their fond, protective looks. Linda would pass out construction paper, and I would pass out scissors, watching to see which hand each child reached with, right or left. Dr. Hidalgo's voice would come over the intercom, and a fifth-grade boy, Kamesh Gupta, would recite the Pledge of Allegiance. The school year would begin.

***

Esmeralda took the leash down from a nail in the mudroom. She had cleaned the dog food bowl and put out fresh water. "Do you think I could spend one more night here?"

The first day of school had wiped me out, but one more night wouldn't kill me. "Oh, sure, why not. How'd your day go? Was it nice to see your friends?"

"It was fine," she said. "Like any other boring day."

Opening a bill, I sliced my finger. "Ouch. Paper cut."

"I hope you don't mind if I let the girls in."

"What girls?"

"Your tenants."

My tenants weren't supposed to show up until seven o'clock, but that's the way it was. You could never tell.

"Has your dad got any leads on a place?"

Esmeralda bit her lip. "Not yet."

"Now that school is starting, I won't be home till five or six o'clock, and—"

"I know, I know," Esmeralda said. "You want Bear gone."

"You've got to be consistent about coming over. You can't skip a day."

"You don't have to tell me."

Esmeralda had things going on in her life, too. Once high school started in earnest, she began to skip days, and two weeks later, when I asked her why she hadn't called, she claimed not to have a phone. Her father said they were too expensive. She gave me a number I could call if I needed to reach her, but I had the feeling it was a neighbor's.

Every day when I returned from school, Bear waited at the kitchen door. If I picked up the leash and clipped it to his collar, he yipped and clawed the door. "Don't like it here too much," I said. "You're not going to get a green card." Bear watched me climb the stepladder and arrange dishes on the dining room's plate rail. I talked to him about moving to a shelter, but when I looked down to see how he was taking this news, I saw that he had flattened himself on the floor. "I don't mean the bad kind of shelter," I told him. "Not all shelters are equal." Linda's rescue shelter might be an okay place for him to live out his doggie existence, even though by now, I thought he had accepted us as his people.

Evenings were short: bills, a cup of tea, a book. To fill the silence of the empty rooms, I put on music: the "1812 Overture" if I wanted to fill the house with thunder; Coltrane, if I was in a certain mood; *The White Album*, always; and, sometimes, just for nostalgia's sake, Rob's old Tony Bennett albums. Reading by the glow of a floor lamp, I'd pat my lap and Bear would trot over. I was alone, but not lonely. The oval portraits hung above the mantle, and when I looked up I saw the eyes of the humble couple looking down at me. Apart from these two, and the occasional sounds of my third floor tenants, the stillness began to make up for the frantic pace of summer. Even so, Sandy wasn't out of my mind a single moment.

Toward the end of September, the weather cooled. When Esmeralda appeared one day after many days not, I handed her the leash. Watching her from the front porch, I saw Bear look back at me, yipping as if he wanted me to come, too. As soon as her father found a pet-friendly apartment, she had to take ownership. I went inside and made hot cider to have ready for her return. It was fall—fifty degrees—and the girl still wore denim shorts.

The back door slammed and I heard her in the mudroom.

"That was a short walk," I said.

She shrugged. "Bear did his business."

"Aren't you cold?" I said.

She plunged her hands in her pockets. "Sometimes. But my dad says if I want something new, I have to get a job."

"Winter's going to be here before long," I said. "I can't see you walking to school in that outfit. I'm going to buy you some clothes."

"I don't want charity," Esmeralda said.

"It won't be charity," I said. "Besides, it would be fun. T.J.Maxx has clothes that aren't expensive."

"But they're new," Esmeralda said. "The place I like is the Junior League Thrift Shop. The Classy Closet is way too expensive. You might as well go buy new."

I hadn't realized that one used-clothing store could be more expensive than another. The thrift shops were in south Evanston, near Main Street, Esmeralda said, and on Wednesday afternoon, I found myself standing among the racks of resale clothing and watching Esmeralda examine the tops and jackets. The clothes were clean enough and the racks organized by size, but if a size 4 didn't fit, then Esmeralda couldn't ask for a 6. What she finally picked out was a purple satin blouse, red tights, and a black, lace bolero.

"Altogether, it comes to fourteen dollars," she said, looking up with soulful eyes. "If it's too much, I can put back the blouse."

In a concession to the cold weather, she had worn a denim skirt that came to mid-thigh. "Don't you want something that'll keep your legs warm?" I said.

"The tights'll be good."

Handing money to the cashier and watching the woman take a long look at Esmeralda's lip rings, straw-colored bangs, and ebony hair, I made a point of complimenting Esmeralda on her fashion sense. What she'd picked out would look ridiculous on anyone else, but on her, it actually looked chic.

"Do you want to come back to my house?" I said.

"Maybe it would be better if I go home," she said. "I promised my father I'd make some mac-and-cheese, the real kind, not out of a box."

"I didn't know you cooked."

"Just what's in my mom's recipe-box."

Esmeralda lived on the block behind Hecky's Barbecue, and I remembered her mentioning that fact when Maureen dropped over. Fumes from the restaurant curled down over the gray frame house. The grass in the front yard looked like her bangs, bleached one too many times. On the front porch sat an overstuffed couch. Someone had chained a three-speed man's bicycle to a porch column. At the end of parallel strips of concrete sat a small Airstream trailer, connected to the house by a hose and an orange electrical cord.

"Is this where you live?" I said.

"Yeah," Esmeralda said. "Is there something wrong with it?"

"It's fine."

Esmeralda got out of the car, but held the door open. "Tomorrow I have to go with my dad to the doctor's. Would you mind walking Bear?"

"I don't mind, long as I know."

"I'll pay you back," Esmeralda said. "Do you have any projects where you need an extra pair of hands?"

"As a matter of fact, I do." Every month, I shelled out $65 a month to Public Storage. "I have a lot of stuff in a storage locker."

"And you want to move it to the basement."

"Yep," I said.

"What is it, boxes or furniture?"

"Both," I said. "It's stuff from my parents' house."

"It'd probably be easier if you borrow a hand truck."

"A hand truck?"

"You know. A dolly." Esmeralda made a pushing motion. "For the boxes."

"I want to move the furniture," I said. "The rooms on the second floor are empty, and I'm tired of the echo."

"When do you want to do it?"

"Would you be free a week from now? It's November 10. The next day you don't have school."

"I'm okay with that," Esmeralda said.

"Four o'clock?" I said.

"Sure," she said. "Well, see you." Carrying her sack of clothes, she leapt over a puddle, went up on the porch, and stood holding the screen until I pulled away.

***

The storage lockers sat in a triangle of land bordered by Green Bay Road and the railroad tracks, close to where Esmeralda lived. While I stood fiddling with the key ring, trying to remember which of two dozen silver, round-headed keys would open this particular door, I looked up to see her coming around the U-Haul. She was dressed in gray sweat pants and a flannel shirt. It was the first time I had ever seen her in clothing that wasn't punk. Only when she drew near did I notice the yellow radio in her hand.

"Is that a Walkman?" I said.

"Yes, it's a radio *and* a tape player," Esmeralda said. "I bought it with your money."

"It's not my money. It's yours. Without your help I never would have finished the apartment."

Esmeralda looked at the Walkman. "I guess you're right."

"What's that you're listening to?" I said.

"Smashing Pumpkins," Esmeralda said, taking out an ear bud.

"Are they a local band?"

"Yeah," she said. "Brand new. This is from *Siamese Dream*. Take a listen." She pushed the earpiece in my ear.

The music reminded me of the early Beatles, with a peppy drum-push and a hummable melody.

"They're actually good."

"Here, you take it." She took out her other ear-bud and offered me the Walkman.

"That's okay." I rolled up the door. Boxes were stacked five high. "I'd better get to work."

"Wow, you sure got a lot of stuff here." Esmeralda offered me a piece of spearmint gum.

"No thanks."

"Is it okay if I have some?" she said. "I have to quit smoking, and this helps."

"I didn't know you smoked."

"My dad doesn't either."

"When did you start?"

"When I was eleven."

"Was it related to your mother's death?"

"I never thought about that, but, yeah, probably." She flicked the light switch. "Where did all this crap come from?"

"My parents' place," I said. "My mom died nine months ago."

Esmeralda counted on her fingers. "In February?"

"Yeah," I said. "On the seventh."

"Mine died on the fourth."

"I'm sorry," I said.

"Yeah, well." She shrugged. "She's better off."

"People say that, but I'm not sure it's true. *We're* not better off, that's for sure."

"You got that right," she said, staring at the boxes collapsing under their own weight. There had to be fifty or sixty—stuff from my parents' house stacked on top of the kids' college notes, baseball gloves, art projects, sheet music, and old guitars. Small, blue notebooks poked from one of the boxes. I grabbed three. The 4x5 size would fit in my purse. For Josh's and Ben's sakes, I had to start keeping a journal. Soon, ALS would rob Tony of his speech, and I wanted my grandsons to know their father when he could walk and talk and joke around. I also wanted to keep a journal for Sandy's sake. Because of Rob's death, I remembered very little of Sean's first two years. My original notion was to write things down as they happened and to try to make sense of them later.

"My dad says there are hoarders and thrower-outers," Esmeralda said. "Everything I own fits in a duffel bag."

"Have you always lived that way?"

"When Mom was alive, it was different. We didn't move all the time. That's why I'm good at this." The girl rolled up her sleeve and flexed a muscle. "Let's do it."

"Let's move the bedroom furniture first."

"I'll take out the dresser drawers to make it lighter." She pulled out two drawers and carried them up the truck's ramp. "Before he hurt his back, my dad worked as a custodian."

"For a school?"

"No, an apartment building."

I handed up the other four drawers, and she stacked them.

Standing in the truck bed and looking down at the locker, she said, "The best way to move that bed is if we walk it over to the truck and slide it."

"You've done this before."

"Many times."

The footboard of the bed weighed less than the headboard. I took one end, Esmeralda the other. "Take the weight with your thighs," I said.

Esmeralda squatted. "I know how to lift."

Loading the bed was easier than I'd expected. The dresser was another matter. I could get a hand in the empty spaces for the drawers, but the back had no handholds. Esmeralda managed her end by lifting it, then dropping it, lifting it, then dropping it. She couldn't weigh more than a hundred pounds. I pushed the dresser up the ramp.

When we had the dresser in, I looked at the boxes. "I think I'll leave these for another time."

"Are you sure?" Esmeralda said.

The sun had started to set. I wanted to get the furniture unloaded before it got dark.

"I have to fly out to D.C. tomorrow. My daughter's got some kind of conference, and she needs me to babysit." Two weeks ago she'd sent me an e-mail asking me to save the date. I couldn't show up cranky and tired.

Climbing up on the running board, I felt my back tighten. Nothing a little Advil couldn't fix. Esmeralda hopped in the passenger side, we drove home, and while I backed the U-Haul into a parking space, she jumped out and ran inside to get Bear. With Esmeralda walking backwards and Bear yipping at her ankles, we managed to get the dresser onto the porch.

I leaned against a pillar and exhaled.

"Maybe you could get one of the paint tarps from the basement. I want to cover the furniture in case it rains while I'm gone."

Esmeralda took out her gum, wrapped it in foil, and put it in her pocket. "Is your back bothering you?"

"No, I'm fine." With my hip, I pushed the dresser against the plate glass window.

Esmeralda returned with the plastic. "Shall I cover it or do you want to bring the other stuff in first?"

"Other stuff," I said, barely able to gasp. The jaws of a giant clamp squeezed my lower back.

Esmeralda looked up and down the block. "Maybe I should get a neighbor."

"I can do it." Going down the steps, I put my hand on Esmeralda's shoulder. She slid the headboard down the U-Haul's ramp. Then, with me pushing and Esmeralda dragging, we got it to the steps.

"I'll take the bottom," Esmeralda said. "That's the heaviest part."

"I don't think I can bend over," I said.

"In that case, I'll get the top."

Hugging the headboard, Esmeralda backed up two steps. I pushed. Esmeralda rested. Then, she went up another step. Shooting pains started at the back of my thighs. By the time we muscled the headboard to the porch, I was in more pain than I wanted to admit.

Esmeralda picked up Bear and gave him a kiss. "Now what?"

"By any chance do you have a driver's license?"

"Sure," the girl said, hugging Bear. "I've been driving ever since my dad went on disability. I can even drive stick."

"Do you think you could take the U-Haul back? I can give you money for a cab."

"I can walk home from there."

"It's past closing time."

"They usually have a drop box for keys." Esmeralda looked me up and down. "You should be on a heating pad."

"There's one upstairs in the linen closet." Catching my breath, I tried to straighten up. Asking her to come back here would be an imposition, but I didn't want to be alone. "Do you eat beef?"

"Sure," Esmeralda said. "Are you going to feed me?"

"I put a crock pot on this morning. Beef stew."

"That's great," Esmeralda said. "The last beef stew I had came from a Dinty Moore can."

"You're going to like this better and if you eat here, you might as well sleep over, too."

"Sure," she said.

All the times the girl had come and gone, I had never thought to offer her a meal apart from the one Maureen brought over. I sat in a dining room chair and waited. I should have invited her before. When she returned, I had her bring me the cordless phone. My voice was shaking when I called Sandy and asked if there was any way I could possibly get out of the trip. "No," she said. "You have to come. I'm counting on you." After we ate, I crashed on the bed in my office. My back would feel better if I didn't baby myself.

CHAPTER 9

A white, Ford van had parked in front of Sandy's house, and after the taxi driver helped me out, I leaned against the van's hood and caught my breath. Spasms rippled from my shoulder blades to my hips. My thighs shook. Sandy flew out the door, a folded walker clutched to her chest. A walker. That might help.

"Does Tony need that?" I said.

"He's been falling." Sandy leaned the walker against the van.

"Could I use it for a sec?"

"I have to pack it," she said.

Sighing and taking it slow, I hobbled up the walk, and using the handrail, dragged myself up the porch and sat down.

From inside the house came a shrill cry. "Oh, Colleen, you're so brave to show up with a bad back." Lillian, breathy, her voice an octave higher than normal, shouted, "I could easily have babysat during Sandy's conference."

"I wish you'd told me that last night," I called over to Sandy. "My back feels like shit."

Sotto voce from the parking strip, Sandy said, "I couldn't have stood it. She's down here too much as it is."

Sandy slid open the van's panel door. The opening was blocked by a mesh grate. She folded the grate down, pressed a button, and lowered the platform. The van had no middle seat.

"Where'd the vehicle come from?" I said.

"Lillian," Sandy said.

"I scoured six states looking for a used van with a wheelchair lift," Lillian shouted, "and finally found one in Connecticut for only $6,000."

"Sounds like a bargain," I said.

"I've got the wheelchair on order," Lillian called. "Just say when."

Sandy put her hands over her ears, then rolled her eyes, and yelled, "Tony doesn't need it yet."

Poking her head out, Lillian said, "Can I make you instant coffee?"

"That would be lovely," I said.

Inside the house, the phone rang. A moment later, Lillian's arm reached around the door and passed me the handset.

"It's me," Esmeralda said. "I just wanted to see if you're okay."

"I'm okay," I said.

"I have to tell you something." Esmeralda sniffed.

"What?" I said.

"Two weeks ago I got a call from the humane society. They found Bear's owners and they want him back."

"But that's wonderful," I said.

"But he's mine, now," Esmeralda said. "Sort of mine. I mean he's yours, too."

"If he's got real owners who want him, I think you have to return him," I said. "Or, what did you think the options were?"

"I thought he could stay with you, like, permanently. My dad says we can't afford a dog. You know. Like, that liver dinner. And he thinks we'd be better off with the reward."

I pictured Bear's alert black eyes and the way he'd jerk his head and snap a biscuit. The mystery owners had taught him that trick. "How much are they offering to get him back?"

"Five hundred dollars."

"Wow, that's a lot," I said.

"It's because he's a show dog."

"He is?"

"I talked to the woman again a couple days ago, but I didn't tell her yes or no. Maybe we can talk about it when you get back. I mean, like, he belongs in your house."

Lillian brought out a steaming mug. I saw two people turn the corner, a woman pushing a stroller and a man walking like a clown in big shoes. "There's Tony," Lillian said. Behind the adults, Josh, absorbed in his own little world, hopped and turned. To allow Sandy time to pack, the coordinator of the Glover Park babysitting co-op, Alice Deukmejian, had volunteered to take Tony and the children to the park. Every Sunday, she and Sandy walked together. Alice needed the exercise, I saw. Her jeans looked a size too small. Also, she had a mustache a teenage boy would have shaved by now. On my previous trip I had met her at a potluck supper and thought she might be the sort of neighbor Sandy could call on for help.

"Listen, Esmeralda," I said. "I need to go, but I think you have to bring Bear back and collect your reward."

"Really?"

"Yes, really."

"Do you want to split it?"

"No," I said. "The money is for you."

"See you, then," Esmeralda said.

"When I get back, you'll come over for dinner." I felt Lillian's hand on my shoulder.

"Should I leave the key under your mat?" Esmeralda said.

"That's the first place burglars would look. No, keep the key. You might need a place to stay in the future."

"All right," Esmeralda said. "Thanks a lot. Especially for the dinner. I bragged about you to my dad."

I pressed my eyes. "It's okay, honey. You helped me a lot, too."

Tony, emaciated hands at his sides, stood on the front walk. Black as onyx marbles, his eyes challenged and pleaded. His hair looked like an unpruned bush. He needed to go to the barbershop.

"Colleen's so courageous," Lillian said. "Her back is bothering her, and here she is."

"If your back feels bad," Tony said, "you should have blown off the trip."

"I tried to," I said.

"Sandy thinks I need a babysitter at all times." Tony sounded like a harmonica. Words wheezed out. The ALS was affecting his vocal chords. Tuning my ear, I replayed what he'd said.

"I'm not a babysitter," I said. "I'm your mother-in-law."

"Even worse," he said.

Usually, a remark like that would have been followed by a smile. I waited. It wasn't. He sat next to me on the porch, while Sandy raced back and forth with suitcases.

***

Tony had mapped out a scenic route to Koolfont, the West Virginia resort where Sandy had her conference. As I drove, Tony dozed, his withered hands dangling from the armrests. Sandy fell asleep in the back seat, her cheek resting on Ben's head. Tony and the kids would have sapped most women's energy, but Sandy pressed forward with her career as a litigator in the enforcement division of the Environmental Protection Agency. With expenses mounting, she couldn't afford to plateau on the mommy track.

Rain changed to sun, and the van roller-coastered over gullies and hills. I glanced in the mirror.

Josh, wide awake, looked ashen. "My stomach hurts," he said.

Sandy sat up. "What's wrong?"

Josh looked at her and hiccupped. Cheesy vomit shot from his mouth. "Stop," Josh cried.

The two-lane road had no shoulder, but I spotted a driveway where a small bridge crossed a drainage culvert. I pulled over and let them out. Crying, his chin globbed with puke, Josh crawled off the lift-gate and looked down at himself in disgust. Sandy took apart Josh's car seat, swished the velour padding in the culvert's clear water, and changed him into a clean outfit.

I got underway again. The road began to wind.

"It's not far," Tony said, his hands resting like rocks on the map spread across his knees.

"My stomach hurts," Josh cried, and then again, blagh, all over himself, the back seat, and Sandy. The road forked at a gas station. Veering into a parking lot, I accidentally threw Tony against the door.

"Why are we stopping?" he said.

I stifled a giggle and cut the engine. "Your son barfed."

"Don't stop now," he said. "We're almost there."

While Ben slept, Sandy unclipped Josh and helped me to the bathroom. From inside the stall, I said, "Sandy, the state should put up warning signs: two-barf road."

"Yeah, like the little man who jumps up to clap if the movie's good," Sandy said.

Josh took off his clothes, and Sandy rinsed them in the sink. I decided to wait outside. She had left the van's panel door open.

"Sa-aa-ndy, Sa-aa-ndy," Tony called.

I went to see what his problem was.

Inside the van, the stench of vomit overpowered me. Horseflies swarmed the interior.

Tony lifted his elbows, dodging in slow motion. "Flies on me."

"Poor you." I dragged myself back into the driver's seat to swat them.

"Can we go?" Tony pleaded. "It's not far."

Through the windshield, I saw Sandy come from the convenience mart with soap, a bucket, and brush. Attached to a spigot next to the women's room sat a coiled hose with a spray nozzle. Sandy pointed. I started the engine.

"Thank you," Tony said.

"We're not going far." I drove ten feet and stopped. The hose would reach. I got out and leaned against the car. The warm engine felt good on my back.

Still laughing about the road, Sandy pulled the carpet from the van and soaped it.

"Just so you know," she murmured, "about that woman, Joan what's-her-face, I can't believe it will ever come to that."

"Why not?"

"He'll die first."

"Oh?" I said. "You know that for a fact?"

"The doctor said he's going downhill fast," Sandy said. "He hates how he is right now, so I don't think he could stand being like Joan's mother."

"Did you show him the interview?"

"I told him about it, but he said it would make him too depressed."

"Okay. Well, thanks for taking a look." Relieved she'd at least read my e-mail, I was dismayed she didn't think the information applied to her. But I understood. There was just so much you could take in.

When Rob died, the police wanted me to identify the body. Identify the body? They had his driver's license. Our car was totaled. What else did they want? They insisted I come down to the morgue.

Someone drove me. I don't know who. Like a butterfly in a chrysalis, the shock wrapped me in a thousand spun threads. There was a ringing in my ears. Tintinnabulation. I remember thinking that word — tintinnabulation, tintinnabulation — as if crowding my mind with syllables would cancel out the sight of him, lying naked in the chilly room. From the chest down a green sheet covered him. He did not look dead. Cold, yes, but the room made me shiver, too. I crossed my arms. His were crossed, one wrist covering the other. Tufts of black hair softened the stiffness of his hands. His eyeballs looked flat; the lids pasted shut. His jaw canted to one side, as if the impact had caught him in mid-thought. The position of that jaw was so familiar that I stared at it and the dried blood that leaked from a corner of his mouth. Not much more than a shaving cut. I took out a handkerchief, spit on it, and started to wipe it off. Someone said not to bother. They would clean him up. I remember feeling distant from myself, as if I were a spirit hovering above his corpse, looking down at myself, a young woman with a hand on her abdomen and a baby within.

***

The conference center assigned us a two-story house with a wheelchair ramp. Josh scampered upstairs, and I gave my suitcase a kick and watched it bump down to the basement. Sandy opened the blinds. "Look at the beautiful woods."

I did. The maples had turned yellow, orange, and brown, and I regretted that I hadn't brought crayons. Tony hummed "The Sound of Music."

"You're a downer, you know it?" Sandy said.

"I don't do hills," he said.

"You have the walker," Sandy said.

"Slopes make me fall. I'll be stuck in the house with your mom."

Sandy opened her mouth to respond, but seeing Josh come downstairs, closed it, and picked up her briefcase. "I'm late for my meeting." She gave the children kisses.

"Don't I get one?" Tony said.

"No." She slammed the door.

Tony stared at it for a moment and then walked down the hall to their bedroom, pausing by the bath. "Look. A Jacuzzi." Spinning around and falling against the wall, he said, "I'm going to get her in that if it kills me."

"Tony." I made a *T* with my hands. "Too much information."

Josh ran down to the basement and came up with ping-pong paddles. "Let's play a game, Grandma."

Great. Ping-pong. "I can't, Josh. My back's killing me."

Tony gave me a look. Ben, in his stroller, began to fuss.

"Let's get lunch," Tony said.

As the restaurant's hostess led Tony, feet flopping, to a table by the window, heads turned. People lined up at two long buffets. Josh could select his usual white diet of bread and macaroni. Ben would be happy with Gerber's. Tony could serve himself. This should be easy.

The window by our table overlooked a muddy lake. Kneeling on a chair, Josh pounded the glass. Just outside, hanging feeders attracted hyperactive birds. A bird ricocheted against its reflection, and Josh stopped banging long enough to stare down at the unconscious creature on the ground.

Sandy had left me a paper bag labeled "Tony's eating things," and I opened it and held up a Velcro strap with a spoon-sized slot. "What's this?" I said.

"The eating gizmo," Tony said.

"Do you need it?"

His face grew red. "Yes." He nodded toward the buffet. "You're going to have to serve me because I can't carry."

I loaded him up with spaghetti and lasagna and baked beans. Using the eating gizmo, he shoved blobs of food against a plastic ring that clipped to his plate. He sent me back for seconds. Josh ate little, and back at the house, with rain drenching the woods, he stared out the window and said, "I'm bored."

For three meals a day, I shuttled Tony and kids from house to restaurant, and I began counting the hours until Sandy's conference ended. My back was not getting better.

***

On the third night, while Sandy dined with the other lawyers, Tony finished his custard pie and said he wanted tapioca pudding. I bent down to pick up Ben's pacifier. My back tore, and I screamed. Ben stopped crying.

"Get over it," Tony said.

"That's it. You're finished." I removed the eating ring and ripped open the Velcro straps of his eating gizmo.

"But my tapioca," Tony said.

"Too bad." I pushed back my chair and cried out again.

"Grandma, what's wrong?" Josh asked.

"My back."

Josh picked up his coat from the floor and put it on.

A young waiter with an acned face buckled the kids in their car seats and helped Tony climb in the van. It was raining.

When I had everyone back in the cabin I told Tony, "We have to skip the kids' bath."

"I promised Josh I'd let him go in the Jacuzzi," Tony said.

"Please, Tony."

Josh threw down his coat and stomped his feet. "Daddy said I could."

"I'll help," Tony said.

His offer was undoubtedly the straightest path between this moment and the moment I could fall into bed. The muscles next to my spine felt like andirons.

"All right," I said.

Smiling, Tony ordered Josh to run upstairs and find pajamas. I pushed a chair toward the bathroom and wheeled in the stroller. Sitting in the chair, I lifted Ben onto the vanity and unsnapped his terrycloth suit. Tony balanced on the Jacuzzi's rim, his hands tweezing the faucet. "Turn on the water," he said.

I did. While Josh shrugged out of his clothes, I scooted to the side of the tub with Ben on my lap.

"Wait!" Tony sprinkled drops of water on his forearm, then he nodded for me to go ahead and put the baby in. Josh grabbed Ben around the waist.

As long as I kept my back straight, I was in only moderate agony. Any bending brought another spasm. "Between us," I said, "we just about make a whole person."

"I'm sorry I've been in a bad mood," Tony said. "I'm happy when other people are in pain. Then they know how I feel."

"Are you in pain?"

"Not physical."

Thighs shaking, Tony asked Josh to tuck a washcloth into his pincer-like fingers. I prepared to grab Ben, who was slipping underwater. "Take him out," Tony said. I did and scooted my chair to the vanity, where I placed Ben lengthwise on a towel. He made faces in the mirror.

Tony beamed at his son's reflection."Where's Daddy? Where's Daddy?"

"He's such a happy baby." I dried Ben's arms. "He has your disposition."

"But you never got to know me," Tony said.

How was I supposed to get to know him when he and Sandy lived a thousand miles away? Besides, I had him pretty well figured out: a rich kid, thumbing his nose at his parents' values while taking money under the table. Unquestionably, he loved Sandy. That and his sense of humor were the best things about him. I held Ben's legs like a Thanksgiving turkey's and untaped a diaper.

"We always use desitin and baby powder," Tony said.

How many diapers had I changed in my lifetime? Ben tried to flip over. Catching him, I twisted. Scissors of pain cut across my lower back.

"Josh, you're clean enough," I said. "Get out of the tub and put your pajamas on."

"My mom's paying for a room addition," Tony said.

"What on earth for?"

"To make our house bigger. It'll give us a bathroom on the main floor and an extra bedroom."

"I'm glad you're letting her help."

"She's all for me going on a respirator."

"Do what you want," I said.

"Stop pressuring Sandy."

"I've barely talked to her since August. Every time I call, she's too busy."

"She tells me that, too, how oppressed she is, how her life is so hard."

"Tony!"

"She could find the time if she wanted to."

"What, to talk to me?" I said.

"No, me," he said.

"Could we table this?"

"Okay," he said. "There's a game on anyway. Could you turn on the TV?"

"Sure," I said, glad for a truce. A room addition. That would cost a fortune and was just what Sandy didn't need: dust and construction chaos. But, Tony was dying. Tony was more important. If I'd only known Tony better, I'd place his needs at the center of the target. That's what he was getting at.

After I tucked the kids in bed, I finally had a moment for myself. I climbed in the Jacuzzi. Water bubbled up around my shoulders, reminding me of the bath I'd taken the afternoon of Rob's accident. Kevin had taken a long nap and Sandy was playing quietly with her dolls. Morning sickness had made me quite ill, as it always did, and about the only thing that helped was to take a bubble bath. Giving myself permission to take ten or fifteen minutes before heading over to Jean's, I was in the tub, bubbles to my neck, my eyes closed. The tap of a finger on my left shoulder startled me, and I sat up, covering my breasts. The bathroom was as empty as it was now, with the jets shooting bee-bees against my skin. To this day I have no rational explanation for what happened, only a belief that we are connected through time and space in ways we can't quite fathom.

***

After lunch Tony and I sat outside the double doors of the conference center and waited. At five o'clock, Sandy emerged. Middle-aged men in gray suits smiled benevolently as they watched her kneel and open her arms for Josh. Ben, rocking, demanded to be released from his stroller. Sandy picked him up, and he slid a hand inside her blouse.

"Is anyone besides Ben hungry?" she said.

Tony nodded. "I am."

He had finished eating half an hour ago. Tony ate three times what any normal man his size, 145 pounds, needed.

The restaurant's hostess, looking down the stair-steps of the family to Ben, headed for the table by the window where the staff had put down a drop cloth, knowing we'd return. The acne-faced busboy brought a carpet sweeper. I thought of Joan Calabrese's description of "the feeding." Their brains go haywire, she'd said. Here we were in the dining room again.

Josh knelt on his chair and wanted Sandy to look at the birdfeeder.

"Sit down, Josh," Tony said, "before you fall."

Josh jumped off his chair and crawled under the table.

"Josh, sit like a good boy," Sandy said.

I felt Josh crawling on my feet. A house remodel pushed normal people over the edge. No way could Sandy load a room addition on top of a job, a sick husband, and two kids. "Oh," I groaned.

"What's the matter, Mom?" Sandy put a cool palm on my forehead. "Do you have a fever? Is it your back?"

"No," I said, flipping through plausible excuses. "I just realized you have a birthday next month. I wish I could fly back for it."

Sandy made a dismissive gesture. "Lillian's flying down so Tony and I can go out for a romantic dinner."

"Do you have plans for Christmas?" I looked at Tony. Usually, they went up to Camden.

"I want to go somewhere snowy," Tony said.

"Chicago's snowy," I said.

"I've always wanted to see Nova Scotia," Tony said.

"Nova Scotia is not going to happen," I said.

"But it's my last Christmas," Tony said, "unless Sandy lets me try the respirator."

"I'm still thinking about it," Sandy said.

"I hate to tell you, Tony," I said, "but you're not going to Nova Scotia or the North Pole, either, even to see Santy Claus and all his little reindeer."

Another bird smacked the window.

"Is that bird okay?" Sandy stood up and pressed her nose to the glass, her smirk captured in the reflection. The sight of her shoulders shaking made me turn to Ben before I burst out laughing, too. "Hey, little baby." I banged his tray. His Cheerios jumped, and he giggled. Making a joke at Tony's expense was a cheap shot, but he could barely handle the hills in West Virginia. His desire to go to Nova Scotia struck me as absurd.

He wanted snow. "Where can we go for snow?" I said.

"I know." Sandy snapped her fingers. "Doesn't that old carpenter friend of yours live in Vermont?"

"Vermont." Tony smiled.

"Montpelier is the capital of Vermont," Josh said.

"Charles Gaudreau, you mean?" I knew very well whom she meant. The Pierce Brosnan look-alike. The object of every woman's desire.

Beaming, Tony sent Sandy off for banana cream pie. I watched the lithe young woman, not with my broad shoulders, but still, with a strong athletic walk. A woman hit her stride in her thirties, became easy with her body. Babies spread the pelvic bones. Nursing provided an everyday warm-fuzzy. And the sex drive went up, too.

Charles Gaudreau. We had talked on the phone from time to time, but I hadn't seen him in years. I put my fingers to my neck and felt my pulse. The eleven-year difference in our ages was huge when I was thirty-four and he was twenty-three. Now, it would be nothing. He might not be good for a committed relationship, but I could definitely see a Christmas fling.

I watched Sandy reach for chocolate pudding. She looked up. "Want anything, Mom?"

"No thanks," I said. There was one thing I wanted and that I had denied myself back then. Charles was like a dessert I could have enjoyed if I'd just told him, Come over after the kids are in bed. It wouldn't hurt to lose fifteen pounds before Christmas. Charles liked his women on the lean side.

"Amtrak runs a ski train to Vermont," Tony said.

"It's a long train ride with two kids," I said. "Why don't you fly?"

"It's my last Christmas," Tony said, with bright, excited eyes. "I haven't taken a long train ride in years."

Popping out from his hiding place, Josh said, "Are we going on a train?"

Sandy returned to the table and pushed Tony's pie across to him.

"The only problem is, it's already October," I said. "Cheap places will be booked."

"I bet Charles can find a place," Sandy said.

"Sean and Kevin can take the train up with us," Tony said.

"All right," I said. "I'll see what I can do."

***

I awoke to a buzzing sound, like a hedge-trimmer. I heard a faint cry and rolled over, groping for the lamp.

The house was quiet. It was dark. Maybe the cry had been a dream.

"Come quick, Mom. Help!"

I threw off the covers and crawled up the stairs. The stroller stood in the living room, outlined by a rectangle of moonlight.

"Damn. Oh damn." Sandy's muffled voice came from the bathroom. "Where are you?"

"In the tub. Come in quick! No never mind."

"Are you sure?" I said.

"Oh, God. I'm about to drop him."

I opened the door to see Sandy and Tony standing naked in the bubbling Jacuzzi. Holding him from behind, Sandy had locked her hands around his waist. Tony's chin rested on his collarbone. Mouth open, eyes rolling, his face had turned yellow. Water streamed down his hairy chest and dripped from his purple penis, all but the tip shrunk back into his balls.

I covered my eyes, then took a deep breath and looked at Sandy. "What do you want me to do?"

"Turn this damn thing off," Sandy said.

I flipped the switch and the bubbles collapsed. Beneath the surface, Tony's stiff, arched feet slid toward the drain.

"Let's get him out," Sandy said.

I knelt and made a karate chop at the back of Tony's knee and grabbed the hairy rock of his calf.

"Step back, Sandy. His legs are rigid."

Sandy, pale and naked, her breasts flattening as Tony slipped down her body, braced herself against the wall. One at a time, I lifted his feet out.

"Can you get your end?" Sandy said.

I gripped his ankles. "Yes."

Cupping Tony's armpits and with the unconscious man sagging like a rolled up carpet, Sandy and I carried him to the bedroom and alley-ooped him onto the bed. Sandy threw the bedspread over Tony, and, blushing, dashed into the bathroom. When she returned, she was wrapped in a towel.

Tony began to pant. His eyes opened. "What happened?"

"You passed out," Sandy said. Leaning over him another minute, Sandy assured herself that he was going to be okay, then grabbed my wrist and pulled me to the bathroom. She sat on the edge of the tub, face in her hands. "Mom, he stopped breathing."

"He's breathing now," I said.

"Should we call 911?"

"No. I think he's okay."

Sandy looked up, hands like blinders. "What if he had really stopped?"

"You'd be forced to decide in the heat of the moment. Respirator or no respirator."

"I can't believe this," Sandy said. "I can't believe this is what I have to face."

"You do, Sandy. This is exactly what you have to face, and, if the EMTs hook him up, he'll be on one forever."

"I could never live like that woman," Sandy said.

"The mother or the daughter?"

"Joan what's-her-face. If it was just me, maybe, but how could I manage with the children?"

"Honey," I said.

"I hate this."

"I know. I hate it, too."

Sandy looked up. "How's your back?"

I had been leaning against the wall. I pushed away, wiggled my shoulders, and bent. No pain at all.

"Cured," I said. "I can't believe it."

CHAPTER 10

The house at Koolfont had been surrounded by trees from the eastern forest. That old saying about not being able to see the forest for the trees kept going through my mind, and I decided to assign myself a little project: learning the botanical names of trees. When I took walks with Josh or went to Sandy's conferences, I could hone my observation skills, and having a project for myself would help me combat the resentment that had begun to build. My new friend, Natalie Konigsberg, a docent at the Ladd Arboretum, would make the perfect tree-guide; plus, a planned activity would give me an excuse to hang out with Esmeralda. She came and went from my house at such irregular hours that I had the feeling she might drop out of my life entirely if I didn't make an effort to spend time with her.

Natalie dressed for cold weather: mittens, sock hat, parka. Esmeralda showed up ten minutes late in the baggy sweatshirt she'd worn the day we moved furniture.

Walking briskly, we headed south on the bike path that ran parallel to the canal. Twenty feet to our right, on busy McCormick Boulevard, commuters swished south toward Skokie.

Annoyed, Natalie glanced over at the traffic and said, "Let me know if I need to speak louder."

"You're fine," Esmeralda said, hugging herself.

Natalie picked up an acorn. "This is white oak, although the bark's not really white. More like ash gray. It's Latin name is *Quercus alba*."

"Is there some school that teaches you that stuff?" Esmeralda, shivering, needed a parka.

"I learned the names from field guides," Natalie said. "Whenever I go for a walk, I take a field guide with me. You have to look at the bark, the needles or leaves, any fruit pods, and the shape of the tree. Anyway, I felt stupid for the first three or four years I was doing this, but eventually, the information stuck."

Esmeralda frowned. "But why bother? I mean, it's a lot of work, all that memorizing."

"Because it makes me happy," Natalie said.

"That's cool." Esmeralda said. "I never thought about teaching stuff like that to myself, but it makes a lot of sense. What do you call the books again?"

"Field guides," Natalie said. "Libraries have them."

"I don't have a library card," Esmeralda said.

"I can take you to get one," I said.

"You need a permanent address," Esmeralda said.

"Use mine."

Five minutes later I thought maybe I shouldn't have offered. She might get the wrong idea. I had blurted that out because my mind was overloaded: buying tickets for Amtrak, finding a cheap flight, making arrangements with Charles to use his house. I looked at Natalie peeling the cap off an acorn and telling Esmeralda how the Indians removed toxins from the acorn meal. I could sense Esmeralda taking in the information. Behind her dyed hair and eyeliner lived an alert and intuitive consciousness such as I had not often seen in one so young.

***

And then it was Christmas. Because of a flight delay getting into Burlington, I found myself navigating the dark rural roads with a map of Vermont spread out on the van's steering wheel. I wished I had brought Esmeralda to help me navigate, though when I'd thought about dropping by her place to explain the invitation to her father, I'd hesitated, imagining that she might be embarrassed to have me see how she lived. Also, I'd pictured what Kevin might say: "Did we need a stranger in our midst on top of everything else?"

I was close now, just pulling into Montpelier's Amtrak station. Puddles in the parking lot had turned to ice, and there were great mounds of dirty snow. It was nearly midnight, but I could tell that the train had not yet arrived because drivers sat in their idling vehicles.

A thread of smoke rose from the chimney of the small, brick station. Just as I arrived on the platform, the locomotive's bright glass eye swept across a boy in boxing-glove mittens. The train shuddered and screeched. Passengers spilled from its doorways. Over the hubbub I heard, "Mom! Mom!" Sean, this time. I swam through skiers wielding long canvas sacks. Next to the caboose, a crowd circled someone on the ground: Tony, flat on his back. Sandy, kneeling beside him, stroked his cheek. "Sweetie, not again."

"Just let me die," Tony said.

"Walk it off," Kevin said, taking an elbow and placing Tony's Russian fur hat on his head.

Kevin and Sean stacked the luggage at the edge of the parking lot. With Tony suspended between them, they headed for the van. Sandy had Ben in a baby carrier. In a snowsuit, his face circled by a drawstring, he looked like an elf. Hard to believe he was already seven months old.

Sandy leaned over and whispered. "When Tony's feet hit the platform, his hand slipped off the grab bar."

Josh said, "Are we going to the emergency room again?"

"Again?" I said.

"Two weeks ago, he had a concussion," Sandy said. "Last Monday, he cut his chin."

"My socks slipped on the basement stairs," Tony called.

"Tony was going down to the bathroom," she said.

"It's easier to go down than up," Tony said. "They better step up the pace of construction and get a lot done while we're gone."

I stopped to wipe my glasses. "Are you really subjecting yourself to a remodel?"

"When we got back from Koolfont, I decided we had to make the house more accessible," Sandy said. "It's just a bedroom and a handicapped bathroom."

"They'll badger you with a thousand small decisions about paint color and light fixtures and who knows what else."

"I've already signed the contract," Sandy said. "We need someplace safe. I'm tired of him falling."

I unlocked the passenger door. Tony's teeth chattered like joke teeth, and he was wrapped up better than any of us. Even Josh, in a train engineer's cap, didn't seem cold. While Sean and Kevin went back for the luggage, I started the engine and turned on the heater. Sandy, in a voice of false cheer, said, "They promised to have the addition finished by Tony's birthday." Tony's birthday was six months off. The contractors weren't exactly rushing. I hoped she'd had the sense to put in a financial penalty clause. I always did.

The back of the van opened, and I heard the thunk of suitcases. Sandy turned. "Hand me the car seats, will you?"

"Say please," Kevin said.

"Pretty please with sugar on it," Sandy said.

Kevin passed them over. Ben and Josh were buckled in. Kevin and Sean took the middle seat. Snow came down in flakes the size of quarters.

In downtown Montpelier, Christmas lights were strung from the awnings. The town, so quaint with its tall arched windows, reminded me of a model train set. Through the wipers, I saw a domed building, floodlit, with a cupola on top.

"Dad?" Josh said. "Is that the Capitol?"

Tony took three labored breaths.

"Is it, Dad?" Josh said.

Using his forehead, Tony smudged a porthole in the steamed glass. "Yes." He turned to me. "He knows all his state capitals."

"That's good," I said.

"For this trip," Sandy said, "I told Tony I'm putting him back in charge of fun."

That was the way it had always been. Tony in charge of fun. Sandy was a lot like me, job first, then fun, if time permitted. As a single mom, I'd loaded a lot on her shoulders, telling myself this was normal in other cultures, the oldest taking more than her fair share. Now she was too responsible for her own good.

Tony lifted his forehead from the window. He'd planned a tour of the Capitol, a trip to Ben & Jerry's, a late afternoon coffee at the Trapp Family Lodge, and a romantic dinner for the two of them "if someone will babysit."

"It's midnight," Sean said. "Ask me in the morning."

"Mom will," Sandy said.

"Sure thing," I said. Snow flew toward the windshield, then melted.

"Tony hopes he can keep on working," Sandy said.

"Who said he had to stop?" I said.

"Stop talking about me like I'm dead," Tony said.

"Don't be a jerk," Kevin said from the back.

"He's tired," Sandy said.

"I am, too," Kevin said, "but I'm not copping an attitude."

"Kids, stop bickering." I looked in the rear view mirror at Sandy, buckled in between the car seats, and her brothers, scrunched into the small third seat. I wanted them all, but especially Tony, to have a happy Christmas.

The van slid into the driveway of a white Cape Cod style house. Charles had insisted we stay at his place. He'd left a key under the mat and with it, a note that I read by the yellow outdoor light. He'd banked the stove, but I should add more wood before we went to bed. No need to change the linens because he'd put on clean sheets and laid out towels. While I fiddled with the lock, Tony jammed his fingers in his armpits. His head jerked spastically.

"I'll help Sandy bring their stuff in," Sean said.

"Thanks for doing it before I asked." I had tried to train the boys to see what needed to be done, rather than waiting for me to give them a prompt. This Christmas would be a test of how well I'd done, and if they pitched in, then Sandy wouldn't have to be the bossy older sister. Upstairs, I heard her issuing instructions on who would sleep where. If she didn't stop soon, Kevin would get on her case.

He flicked on the kitchen light. "The house is freezing."

I touched the kitchen's green-and-cream woodstove. Cold to the touch. What had Charles meant about banking the stove?

"Hey, Mom. In here," Kevin said. At the back of the house, in a low-ceilinged room that must once have been a screened porch, sat a blue Swedish stove. With a knee down, Kevin looked in the stove's glass door. "No wonder it's freezing. The fire's almost gone."

"Let's throw some wood in," I said. "The woodpile's behind the garage."

Kevin jerked his thumb toward the door. Outside, he loaded my arms with logs.

"This reminds me of Boy Scouts," he said.

"I do sort of feel like a den mother."

"We should have come to your house."

"So was the train ride fun at least?"

"The trip from D.C. was a rolling circus," he said. "Tony couldn't walk down the aisle alone, and he wouldn't allow anyone but Sandy to help him in the bathroom. The motion of the train made him pee on his shoes. Between requests for food from the snack car, beverages, and trips to the head, Tony was a complete pain in the ass."

"Kevin, he's helpless," I said.

Since the trip to Koolfont when Tony had gorged in the dining room and passed out in the Jacuzzi, his speech had become harder to understand. There were so many real problems to worry about—Tony's ability to walk and feed himself, money and medical bills, Sandy's energy—that Kevin's gripes seemed petty. Dumping the logs beside the stove, I banked it and hoped the fire would last till morning. In a former pantry just off the kitchen, I threw myself down on a futon. Thank heavens Charles had offered to lay in groceries for Christmas day. I wouldn't have to go shopping.

***

When I woke up, I could see my breath. Stumbling out of the pantry with a comforter around my shoulders, I returned to the sunroom with its mismatched easy chairs and old couch. Someone had gotten the stove going. The flames reminded me of the Thanksgiving I woke up to find Sandy kneeling down blowing on the fire. She was five, a little young to be doing that. Rob had a hand on her back. He turned to me, proud as punch. "Our little Girl Scout."

As I looked at the lights blinking on the tree and Kevin and Sean handing presents to Josh, I felt grateful for the extra hour in bed.

"What time is it?" I said.

"Nine o'clock," Kevin said. "Sandy said we should let Josh unwrap his gifts."

Josh had opened LEGOs, a train set from Aldo and Lillian, and an ant farm, the present from Kevin. Without waiting for adult help, he poured sand into the ant farm's plastic sleeve.

Shuffling down the hall in bare feet, Tony stepped in the sand.

"Put that away and play with something else," he said.

"I want the ants to come out, like it shows on the box," Josh said.

Looking at Kevin, Tony said, "Did you have to?"

"Ant colonies teach a lot about social organization," Kevin said. "I thought observing the ant behavior would make a good father-son activity."

"Because I'm too gimpy to do anything else."

"Get over it, will you?" Kevin said. "The kids on my Special Olympics team don't have your good health, and there's nothing wrong with your mind."

"You don't understand because you don't have children," Tony said.

Kevin's mouth twisted and he looked out the windows. Snow had buried the picnic table.

"Where's Sandy?" I said.

"I'm in the kitchen," she called. "Kevin and I got the fire started, and we made pancakes for everyone. Yours are in the electric fry pan." Drying her hands on a dishtowel, Sandy came into the sunroom, smiled and gave me a kiss. "Merry Christmas, Mom. Thanks for getting this place. It's just great."

"Was it cold upstairs?"

"A little," she said, "but I put on layers." Sandy wore ragg-wool socks and black stirrup pants. From beneath the sleeves of her shirt poked the cuffs of pink long underwear. "Could I have the car keys? I need to run to the store for baby Tylenol."

"What about me?" Tony said. "You haven't given me a shower, and I want to see you open my presents."

"Ben has a fever," Sandy said.

"I always come last."

Josh brushed the spilled sand into a plastic sack and stood up. "I can unbutton Daddy's pajamas."

"I can wait," Tony said. "Colleen, what's for lunch?"

"Christmas dinner," I said.

"I'm hungry now," he said.

"You just ate breakfast." Sandy lifted a parka from a hook by the door.

I wondered if Esmeralda had opened her gift yet. I hoped a purple parka was her style. If not, she had the exchange receipt.

"Could someone feed me?" Tony said.

"You can wait." Sandy slammed the door.

I looked around for Sean and Kevin. "Boys, where are you?" They'd disappeared. A few minutes later I saw Sean in the yard. He and Kevin threw snowballs that disintegrated in midair. I zipped Josh into his snowsuit and sent him out to play.

"If you're still hungry," I told Tony, "you can have more pancakes." I patted my stomach. "I've been on a diet."

"You'd have to feed me."

"Where's your eating gizmo?"

"Sandy forgot it," Tony said.

"I can cut the pancakes and duct tape a fork to your wrist."

"I'll wait for my wife," Tony said.

"All right, then. I'll start dinner."

I took the turkey out of the refrigerator, peeled off the plastic, and pulled the gizzard bag from the cavity. Bloody water spread on the counter. In the cupboards, I found an aluminum baking pan. I put the bird in it and opened two packages of bread cubes. I had to chop onions and celery, make broth, and cook the heart, gizzards, and liver. If I made the traditional dinner, I'd be trapped in the kitchen all day, and yet I felt compelled, as if pushed by an invisible hand, to spend the morning on my feet because Christmas would not be Christmas without Mom's stuffing. My mother, born in Kansas City and transplanted to Chicago when her father took a job in the stockyards, celebrated Christmas with gizzard stuffing, three kinds of homemade pie, and two kinds of potatoes, mashed and sweet. Her example set the gold standard, and I would have given anything to ask her if she felt the same tension in her neck, if she felt at war with herself when she stood at the kitchen counter on Christmas Day.

Sighing, I took the lid off the electric fry pan, rolled a pancake, and stood there eating. This spread wasn't going to be the best dinner I'd ever made, but no one would starve. Ben, in a baby bouncer on the floor, began to whimper and kick. Sandy had left breast milk in the freezer, but chances were good she'd come right back. One time when Rob was still alive, I'd had to run down to the store for A & D ointment. I came back with breasts about to burst, only to find Rob looking up smugly from the baby in his arms. Kevin or Sandy? The babyhoods of my children had blended into a dreamlike blur. Even with a dinner to prepare, I had to make sure I wrote about the ant farm and Josh volunteering to help his father dress. I threw kindling into a compartment on the stove's side, and as heat circulated around the oven and exited the chimney, the top warmed enough for me to sauté the celery.

"Col-leen, my head is throbbing," Tony called.

"Want some Excedrin?" I grabbed a bottle from my purse and shook out two tablets.

"No," he said. "It's not advisable to mix medicines."

"What medicines would you be mixing?"

"Riluzole," he said, "and the doctor started me on a new thing to keep my legs from twitching."

"Last call." I shook the bottle.

"I'm fine," Tony said.

He might not need a pill, but I did. The oven had warmed. I put the turkey in. Ben, his head tilted sideways, went back to sleep. Tony padded into the kitchen and, after watching me peel potatoes, wandered back out to the sunroom where he stood looking out the window. "They're taking over my son," he called.

I blew out a stream of air and went to see what he was talking about. Kevin, Sean, and Josh had built a snow cave. Outside, Josh screamed with glee and crawled in.

"Josh'll take a good nap," I said. "That'll give you and Sandy time together."

"She doesn't want to spend time with me," Tony said.

"Of course, she does," I said.

"No, I'm a bother," Tony said. "She'll dress the kids, but . . ."

Sandy opened the sunroom's door. "I found baby Tylenol." She dropped a white sack on the floor and pried off her boots. In the kitchen, I opened the oven and rubbed a stick of butter on the bird. Cholesterol be damned. Looking for a second potato peeler, I thought how I'd helped my mom make Christmas dinner and was about to ask Sandy if she'd lend a hand. Then, I saw her unstrap Ben and slide her fingers in his diaper. "Dry," she said. "I hope he's not dehydrated."

I put the second potato peeler back in the drawer and started on the pile of spuds, watching the peels curl like the paint on Sandy's porch.

"What's wrong with Ben?" I said.

"He woke up with a runny nose," Sandy said, but the second child is a lot easier than the first. With Josh, I would have panicked. I feel sorry for him. All my insecurities as a young mother will show up later in his life." She laughed.

"What on earth are you talking about?" I said. "You're a terrific mother."

"Josh still doesn't sleep through the night," she said, "and he didn't sit at the table and eat the way other children did. He'd hop up, walk around the table, and lean on Sandy's legs. His diet wasn't balanced, but, at least, he didn't eat sugar all day, she said. "I guess I can take credit for that."

"Josh seems pretty normal to me," I said.

"He doesn't eat much protein," Sandy said, "and he might turn out like me, always having to watch my iron. In fact," she said, "his personality is a lot like mine. He's a little worrier, and I don't know how to help him."

"Welcome to the club," I said.

"Sa-aan-dy, Sa-aan-dy, Sa-aan-dy," Tony moaned from the sunroom. "Can you please stop talking to your mother? I haven't had my shower."

Sandy slapped her cheek. "I completely forgot him."

How was that possible? Tony made himself the center of attention, no matter what.

"I'll watch the kids," I said. "You two have a romantic stroll through town."

"I'd rather stay inside where it's warm," Tony said.

"Let's have a shower, first," Sandy said. "Then we'll see."

After she had given Tony his shower, Sandy settled the children upstairs for a late morning nap. On the couch, I pretended to read the *New York Times*, but dots floated before my eyes. Codeine, codeine, if only I'd brought some. Now I was going to have to try my other remedy: a bag of frozen peas. Sighing, I went to the freezer. The sack of peas at the base of my neck reminded me of the time Rob came home to find me vomiting up green stuff that might have come from a cow's rumen. He'd driven me to the emergency room, a shot of morphine the only remedy for a three-day cluster migraine. I hadn't had a migraine all fall, but now, apparently one was coming. Through eye slits, I watched Sandy tug on Tony's snow pants and tie his boots. Rigid as a scarecrow, he held his arms out, and after Sandy snapped his parka, she embraced him and gave him a kiss that sounded like a plunger in a drain. After they'd gone, I pressed my eyelids. I couldn't decide whether I felt more like laughing or crying. If Rob had been here, it definitely would have been laughter. I missed having a partner interested in the petty ups-and-downs of daily life. I missed having a buffer.

Rob had picked up the slack when Kevin threw temper tantrums, which happened predictably between five and five thirty, even when he'd taken a good nap. An intense sort of boy, he would ball up his fists and scream until Rob wrapped his arms around him. Even at two, Kevin could not sit still. He'd smash his trucks into the baseboards and crayon the walls, and we were at a loss about what to do. Then my dad came up with a solution. One of the people my dad did handyman work for had given him a box of puppets. My dad made Kevin a masonite puppet theater and set it up in a corner of the living room. Sandy didn't know how to play with puppets—how to make a story come to life—but when Rob came home, he dropped his briefcase on the dining room table and loosened his tie.

"That is so cool," he said and crawled behind the puppet stage. "Did your dad make that?"

"Yeah," I said.

"This is better than anything you'd find in a store." He took Sandy behind the stage, a triptych where the wings hid the puppet-masters. I came out of the kitchen, where I was making dinner. Rob had Snow White on one hand and the Evil Stepmother with her poisoned apple on the other. Sandy did the dwarves, and Kevin sat cross-legged and enthralled.

How badly Sandy wanted to entertain Kevin, to make him laugh, because when he laughed, his disposition changed. He'd play dolls and sit through an entire game of Candy Land without overturning the board. Until Rob's death, that was our routine: a puppet show, followed by a board game, followed by dinner, baths, and bedtime stories. Rob liked to play more than I did, which was odd, considering I went on to teach kindergarten, but even after I started teaching, it was hard for me to let my hair down. Play was synonymous with lesson plans and structured activity and fifteen-minute increments called *playtime*. Supervising children was tiring. This so-called Vermont holiday reminded me of taking my class on a field trip. Each child needed a nametag, permission slip, jacket, hat, and gloves, and still things wound up falling through the cracks. Maybe I didn't need to provide so much support *for* my brood; I needed support *from* them. Support orchestrating these get-togethers.

The phone rang. Probably Charles. Swinging my legs off the couch, I went to the kitchen, picked up the receiver, and leaned against the wall.

"Hi, Mrs. Gallagher, it's me." Esmeralda's voice. "I'm calling to wish you Merry Christmas. Thanks so much for the parka. You didn't have to do that."

"You can exchange it if it's not right," I said.

"It's perfect," she said. "Warm."

"How's the temperature in Evanston?"

"I'm in Ohio," she said.

"Ohio?" I said. "I didn't know you were going to be away." I thought of my thermostat set at 68 and hoped the pipes wouldn't freeze.

"My dad took me to Akron. We're staying with my aunt."

"It's nice to be with family," I said, watching Kevin back through the door with an armload of wood. Sean was behind him with another armload.

"Hey, Mom," Sean said, "I'm going to take a nap."

I nodded and covered the mouthpiece. "I'm talking to someone."

"When's Charles coming over?" Kevin said.

"I don't know." I lowered my eyes to the floor and took my hand off the receiver.

"Am I interrupting your Christmas dinner?" Esmeralda said.

"We haven't gotten to that yet," I said. "I've actually got a migraine, and I should lie down before I throw up."

"You get stressed out a lot."

"Do I?"

"Yeah, you do," she said. "I noticed when I was staying there."

"It's all self-imposed," I said.

"Well, here's something else you're not going to like," Esmeralda said.

Kevin stood two feet away, making a winding-up motion with his finger. He mimed hanging up.

I slid down the wall and shielded my forehead. "Are you on drugs?"

She laughed. "No, it's not that bad. In fact, it's not bad at all, I don't think. I'm going to have a baby."

"You're pregnant?" My voice rose.

"Yep," she said.

"What about high school?"

"I passed my GED," Esmeralda said.

"Congratulations, but you're a smart girl. You can do better." A GED might get her a job flipping burgers, but how could a mother support a baby on that?

"My dad says I have to give up the baby," Esmeralda said.

I curled up, cuddling the receiver and talking into my knees. "It's a baby," I said. "It's not a dog."

"He says we could get money. Like, he saw some ad where the people were offering ten thousand dollars. He said he'd put that in a school account."

Kevin still had on his snow boots. Charles wanted us to leave them at the door. I looked up at him and pointed to the boots and the back door. A moment later he returned, whisper-screaming, "Get off the phone. I have something I need to say before Sandy comes back."

I shook my head *no*. The smell of roasting turkey filled the kitchen. "Baste the turkey," I said, covering the receiver.

"I already did," he said.

"Well, do it again, and don't bother me."

Glaring at me, he opened the oven door. The shelf scraped. I put my head down and pressed my eyelids. It didn't help.

"Have you talked to your aunt?" I said.

"She wants me to keep it."

"So, I'm the tie-breaker."

"Yes."

I heard the girl's ragged breathing. She'd started crying.

"Surround yourself with strong women," I said. "Be helpful."

"My dad says I'll see how much work it is, raising a kid."

"You don't have to give up your child to go to school."

"I was wondering if I could come live with you?" Esmeralda said. "I mean, I don't have Bear. It would just be me and the baby. And your house has all those extra rooms."

This was heartbreaking. There was so much about this girl I didn't know. "I'm very, very sorry," I said. "I have to say no, and I also have to get off the phone."

"Okay," Esmeralda said, her voice flat. "I wanted to at least ask, in case it was an option."

"Please send me a picture when the baby's born," I said. "And send me a birth announcement."

"I've already picked out a name."

"What is it?"

"Colleen."

She could pick out a better name. Consult a baby book. "I'm honored," I said.

"I'm glad. I thought you might think, who is this little bitch?"

"What? No. And don't call yourself that. Maybe I can help you brainstorm some ways to make this work."

A computer voice demanded money.

"I'm at a payphone. Gotta go," Esmeralda said.

"Call me back tomorrow," I said. "We need to have—"

The line clicked dead.

It had cost her a lot to make that call, a lot more than money. Lowering the barrier. Asking instead of giving. I wished I had blurted out, *Sure. Fine. We'll work it out.* The small sounds of the house—the drip of water from the eaves, the gaseous pops and crackles from the stove—brought a temporary calm, but a buckshot of new thoughts fanned out from my eyeball-pain. I was the mother. Indomitable. I had signed up for this a long time ago. Was my life really too crowded to welcome one more person into it?

"What the hell was that all about?" Kevin said.

"A girl who appeared out of nowhere." I lifted my hand and he pulled me to my feet.

"Was she one of your students?" he said.

"No, she was no one."

Kevin opened the stove to load firewood. "I thought you were never going to get off the phone. I want to finish our talk. Sean and I are worried."

"About what?" I staggered over to the couch and put the peas behind my neck. The cold, hard balls had softened.

"We're worried about the kids." Pulling over a chair, Kevin cracked his knuckles in the way I'd asked him a thousand times not to. "Josh and Ben aren't getting enough attention. Tony monopolizes Sandy's time."

I turned the bag of peas. "I have a migraine. I wonder if you could baste the turkey."

"Mom, the turkey's fine. I know Tony needs help, but when I had my training for Special Olympics, one thing they taught was that the kid with the problem couldn't get all the attention."

"He's not like this all the time."

"He was on the train. It's almost like that fire there," Kevin said, turning and pointing to the woodstove. "Tony's sucking all the oxygen from the room."

"He does act like a baby at times, but what can we do?"

"In basketball, we'd put a man on Tony," Kevin said.

"Are you volunteering to dive on the grenade?"

"I'm ready to strangle him." Kevin leaned forward, his big hands dropping between his knees.

"You could cut him some slack, don't you think?"

"He's not rational."

"Rationality's just a veneer," I said. "What's underneath are feelings. Fear, I should imagine. He must be terrified."

"Yeah, well . . ."

***

Rosy-cheeked, Sandy opened the door and stood aside for Tony. He held his arms out, and she undressed him. Pulling a chair next to Kevin's, she put Tony in it. "Sit there and thaw out."

Pale, he looked like he'd given blood. His teeth chattered.

"All the coffee shops were closed on account of Christmas," she said. "We walked for an hour with no place to warm up and no place for Tony to rest."

I heard the doorbell of Ben's cry. Sandy headed for the stairs.

"Want me to get the little guy?" Kevin said.

"That's all right," Sandy said.

I felt like telling him that Sandy didn't need help with Ben. She needed help with Tony. He could stop volunteering for Special Olympics and pitch in. I swung my feet off the couch, the bag of peas in my hand. "So, no tour of the Capitol, Tony?"

"It's closed for the holiday." Tony slumped forward, shaking his head. "I am so, so sad."

"What's making you sad?" I said.

"All morning I've been thinking about Rob."

A claw-hand squeezed down on my heart. The room felt airless. I stood up, intending to return the peas to the freezer before they thawed, but the headache made me dizzy, and I sat back down. Seeing Tony wipe his eyes, I couldn't help but ask, "What are you thinking about *him* for?"

"I wish I'd met him is all." He buried his face in his hands and began to cry. "I'm not having any fun, whatsoever. It's too cold."

"You originally wanted to go to Nova Scotia," I said.

"I can't breathe," he said.

"What do you mean?"

"Same as in the Jacuzzi." Tony wiped his nose on his sleeve.

"Do you need a tissue?" I said.

"No."

Someone knocked.

"Come in," I said.

The door opened.

As tall as Kevin, Charles strode in, axe in hand. "Your tool, madam. Looks like you're low on kindling."

"Oh, there's plenty of kindling," I said. "Got a match?"

"You haven't changed," he said.

"Nor have you." Deep-voiced, with stovepipe legs and hair like a chimney brush, he strode across the room to give me a hug and kiss on the lips. There'd always been the banter. Without marriage ever being on the table, we'd danced along the risky knife-blade of sex, never quite falling off and into bed.

Charles glanced at Tony. "You must be Sandy's husband. I've heard a lot about you." He held out his hand.

"I don't do hands," Tony said.

Charles looked back at me. "So where's the grandson?"

"The baby or the big one?" I said.

"The one who knows the state capitals."

"That's my boy." Tony smiled.

I pointed to the ceiling. Josh was sacked out upstairs.

"So what do people do to stay busy here in snow country?" Tony said.

One eyebrow shot up and Charles tipped his head, as if to identify a bird from its call. His eyes lit. "Well, me, I've been working on a novel."

Offered a job at *Rolling Stone* after a college internship, he'd turned down the offer and gone to graduate school, hoping to get a degree in English and write the Great American Novel. He'd taken time out to do construction, and that was how he'd been earning a living when I met him. A pinched nerve in his neck had closed off his construction career. He'd written manuals for software companies and made a killing on stock options. That bought him freedom. Finally, he'd finished the *magnum opus*.

"Can I read it?" Tony said.

"After it's published," Charles said. "You don't want friends staring at the runny yolk of your half-cooked egg." He flipped down the top of a writing desk, reached into a cubbyhole, and held a letter for Tony to read. An agent had agreed to represent him.

"I've always wanted to write the story of my life," Tony said, "or a story that's sort of like my life."

"A *roman á clef*," Charles said. "Fifteen hundred words a day."

"That's all it takes?" Tony said.

Charles nodded and turned toward the hall where Sandy stood with Ben. The baby was alert, squirming to look at everyone with his bright, black eyes.

"The youngest Dimasio," I said, "but he doesn't know his capitals yet."

"And I won't be around long enough to teach him," Tony muttered.

Sandy settled in the rocking chair and her fingers slid up Ben's back. A curtain of hair fell across one cheek.

Charles winked at me. "Well, well," he said. "The little pre-teen's all grown up."

"You look like Vermont agrees with you." Sandy gave him the once-over. "A few gray hairs make a man look distinguished."

"I need some gray hair, then," Tony said.

Sandy laughed, thumping Ben on the back. "My girlfriends always say gray hair is distinguished. But I never look at a man unless he's my husband."

"And you don't look that often," Tony said.

"You know that's not true." Sandy smiled gently.

Tony's eyes touched Sandy's. It was like watching the fingers of God and Adam on the Sistine Chapel.

Charles frowned and then looked at me. "Why do you have a sack of peas in your hand?"

"My mom gets migraines," Sandy said.

"I remember that," Charles said. "I used to give her head massages."

My scalp tingled. I held up the peas. "I meant to put these back in the freezer."

"Ben's almost out of diapers," Sandy said. "Could I ask you to move your truck?"

"I can do better than that." Charles stood up. "How much does the baby weigh?"

"Seventeen pounds," Sandy said.

"C'mon." Charles reached down and yanked me to my feet. I threw the peas in the refrigerator, grabbed a coat, and followed him to his truck, kicking coffee cups aside as I got in. Freezing air shot up my nostrils. Instant anesthetic.

Charles backed down the driveway. "Your daughter's a knockout."

I stiffened. "Is she?"

"What I remember was her shyness. She had her shoulders hunched in. But now." He whistled.

"Pay attention to your driving." The street looked black and slick.

"You were a knockout at her age," he said. "Weren't you about thirty-four, thirty-five when we hooked up?"

"Yes," I said.

"I sure had a crush on you."

"It was mutual."

He laughed. "I could stare at Sandy all day. She has an inner glow. I don't know how to describe it except to say that suddenly, you feel like she's discovered her warm center."

He pulled up to a 7-Eleven. I watched him run inside the store, pause, ponder, and pay. What an idiot though. He couldn't keep his mouth shut. Compared to most men—Rob, for instance, who never revealed his thoughts unless I pitched a fit—Charles was as transparent as Josh's ant farm, a cutaway of his psyche visible to the naked eye. He had a primitive side that was activated by the hunt, but after he landed a woman, he often became ambivalent.

Charles hopped back in and slammed the door. "Do you mind if I come by later for dessert?"

He'd bought the pies. "Of course, but why don't you just stay?"

"I'm staying with a friend."

"Of the female persuasion?"

"It's more like I'm the babysitter for her two boys."

I wondered about the woman he was with and whether he was half-in or halfway-out of the relationship. The way he talked, it sounded like he was in it for the kids, but that was strange because most guys I ever dated ran the other way when they learned I had three children. Certainly, Charles couldn't seriously be interested in Sandy, married to a dying man *and* with children, an infant, no less.

He pulled into the driveway and threw an arm across the seat behind me, massaging my neck. I closed my eyes and soaked up the pressure of his fingertips. The windows steamed. I placed my hand on Charles's knee and ran my fingers up his thigh. "I've missed you."

"She's nothing special," he said, his voice thick. "I wouldn't even have stayed at her place, except mine has only the one bathroom, plus that powder room off the kitchen."

"I didn't mean to put you out," I said.

"Hey, babe," he said, "ski lodges go for five thou a week."

"Yeah, but you're giving up your house."

"Think about how many times you fed me dinner," he said.

"Dinner's nothing," I said.

"So's letting you crash at my place." He transferred my hand back to my knee and gave my fingers a squeeze. "Is it working out?"

"Is what working out?"

"The house."

"It's perfect," I said. "Tony's moping around and Sandy's running herself ragged, but other than that, life's great."

"Maybe I'll throw a sleeping bag down in front of the fire."

"I'll throw one down beside you."

"Probably not a good idea," he said.

"Damn."

"I don't know if you heard the weather forecast."

"No, I didn't." I felt a lump in my throat. Swallowing my pride didn't go down well.

"The forecast calls for a heavy snow," he said. "Tomorrow I need to get up early and clean the eaves, or I'll have ice dams."

"We wouldn't want that, would we."

"That's Vermont for you," he said. "The predictable white Christmas."

I opened the door. "Since when is Christmas predictable?"

He smiled. "Never predictable, long's you're around."

Arms crossed, I stood in the driveway watching his truck with its big snow tires fishtail in the icy ruts. He leaned forward and waved and I read his lips. "I'll be back."

Disappointed but not entirely surprised, I went inside. Time to put dinner on the table.

***

I sat down to eat and feed Tony and then it was time for the cleanup. While I made room in the refrigerator and covered the turkey carcass in a foil tent, Sean and Kevin washed dishes.

Charles returned with a bag of bear claws. The smell of almonds filled the kitchen.

"Those must be loaded with marzipan," I said.

"Breakfast tomorrow," Charles said.

"I'm stuffed," Sean said, folding the dishtowel and hanging it over the stove's handle. "Who wants some exercise?"

"What kind?" Kevin said.

"Kickboxing," Sean said. "I brought three sets of practice gloves."

"Sounds good," Charles said.

"Think I'll pass," Tony added.

In West Virginia, heads had turned when Tony walked across the dining room. I hadn't noticed his feet flopping as much this time, but then, he'd hardly moved from a chair. His hair wet from the bath, Josh ran past in his pajamas, and Sean tied gloves on Kevin and Charles.

"I want to be a kick boxer when I grow up," Josh said.

"All right," Sean said, giving Josh a high five. I looked at Tony, sitting in a kitchen chair. He had tucked his crooked fingers beneath his arms, and his rhythmic rocking made me think of babies banging their heads on cribs. Tired, I wanted to lie on the couch and watch Charles dance and lunge, but I couldn't leave Tony looking wretched.

"I'm jealous of the next man," Tony said.

"What next man?" I said.

"How long did it take for you to start dating?"

"Tony, please." I squirted Joy on my greasy fingers.

"I need to know," Tony said.

"I don't remember."

"You never talk about Rob," Tony said. "He might just as well have never existed."

"Oh, he existed all right."

Rob had been my high school sweetheart at Marie Curie. In that part of my life where my "self" was clay, Rob's fingers had made deep imprints, diverting me from my proposed course of study: biology. Because of Rob, my focus had shifted to a liberal arts degree. He thought it would be a better fit with his engineering, and teaching could be my fallback profession. Like a little lap dog, I had followed along, jumping and barking, because the center of our world together would be the professional life he created. That and the children. And there, too, he showed me what to do. The oldest of ten, he taught me to swish diapers in the toilet before putting them in the diaper pail; he showed me how baking soda kept the diaper pail fresh; and he taught me about sibling rivalry, the "he saids" and "she saids" of the little perpetrator and supposed victim being not always as clear-cut as reported. What I wanted to tell Tony, but could not, was that he didn't have to worry. He and Sandy would be tied unto eternity. Sandy would find her happiness again, but she would never forget what Tony's hands felt like as they ran down her body, or the particular way he turned his head when they kissed. The illicit thrill of what, in my day, we called going all the way.

Rob and I had known it would happen. We didn't dare take off our clothes in the basement rec room, though he did slip his hand inside my bra. We didn't make love at the beach, even at night, when we could have wandered away from the youth group's bonfire. Other couples did. In the parking lot of an abandoned grain elevator, Rob folded down the back seat of the station wagon, but a police car coming slowly toward us scared us senseless for months. Maybe canoeing, we had thought. No one bothered to canoe in the marshes, where our paddles startled nesting egrets and sent herons skyward; but whatever slough we paddled down, we could see the Skyway or one of the rusting steel lift-bridges where a bridge-master sat in his conning tower. The time we came closest was the night we snuck into the South Shore Country Club, but the sprinklers on the golf course soaked us before we'd taken off our clothes.

I was just as glad because I was terrified of getting pregnant, and I wasn't exactly sure how the rhythm method was supposed to work. I mean, was the man supposed to pull out all the time, or just when you were ovulating? Rob had a book that explained the whole thing, but much as we pored over it, trying to understand the science, it didn't fit with what we'd learned at school.

We managed to hold out until we reached the University of Illinois. The single sex dorms had matrons who monitored the comings and goings of residents. We clung to the notion that our religion frowned on sex and that we should only do it if we were married. Rob proposed and we set a wedding date. Then he turned twenty-one, the age a motel would rent him a room. He checked in to the Lincoln Lodge, a family motel on University Avenue in Urbana, and I snuck through Leal Park and sidled up to his door. I thought we would go slow, but in the darkened room I ripped off my clothes and for the first time, saw him completely naked: his broad shoulders, an arrow of dark hair on his chest, the hip bones of his pelvis, and his penis, arcing up to greet me. With my heels propped on the headboard, my fingers digging into his buttocks, he drove into me with a satisfying, piston-like motion that matched my eager gasps.

***

I went to the door between the kitchen and sunroom and leaned against the jamb. The men had stopped their workout. Josh stood in front of the couch, kicking wildly and spinning around.

Charles wiped his forehead. "I'll find towels."

As he squeezed past, I kept my place, and his sweaty forearm brushed my breasts. A ripple went down to my groin.

"What could we do for fun tomorrow?" I said.

Charles looked to Tony, rocking in the kitchen chair.

"Ben & Jerry's," Tony said.

"No eating," Sean cried. "Today's feed will last a week."

"Sledding, then," Charles said.

"You can leave me at home if that's the plan," Tony said. "I don't intend to go out in the cold again."

"We can drive to the sledding hill," Charles said, "and leave the engine running."

"You don't understand." Tony put his hands on his knees and straightened up. "The cold makes it hard to catch my breath."

Maybe Sandy knew if the breathing problem was real or a ploy for sympathy. If so, I was going to tell Tony to stop with the gloom and doom. I went upstairs. Sandy had taken Charles's room, a room with gables that came down to the floor, a poster of Che Guevara thumbtacked to the ceiling, and a double bed. She lay on her side, nursing Ben.

"Tony says he can't breathe," I said. "Why's that?"

"It's too cold for him," Sandy said.

"How do you know it's the cold?"

"I called the doctor."

"And she said?"

"His lungs are compromised."

Back in June, Dr. Stevanovic said she wanted Tony to come in for some kind of breathing test. It was the day Lisa had made her visit, and Tony dropped the bomb about the respirator.

"So the Jacuzzi wasn't a one-time thing?" I said.

"Originally, the doctor thought Tony passed out because he'd eaten a big meal."

"He was eating a ton," I said. "Second and third helpings."

"Now, she thinks it wasn't the food."

"Damn," I said.

"It's not all bad news," Sandy said. "His doctor convinced him to join a clinical trial for human growth hormone. It's a little bit of a pain because I'll have to give him a daily shot and his folks will have to drive him to a clinic in Baltimore, but at this point it's our only hope."

"Don't clinical trials mean some patients get a placebo?"

"Yes, but if the medicine works, he'll be first in line for the real stuff."

"What's it supposed to do?"

"Stimulate nerve growth."

I held up my crossed fingers and for good measure made the sign of the cross.

Propping herself on the pillows, she put Ben on her shoulder and patted his back. "Oh, and if my life isn't complicated enough, here's the latest thing. His boss wants him to go on disability."

"Do you want that?"

"His salary covers the babysitter."

"Maybe Tony's folks can chip in."

"We'll get by." Sandy's face shone with love and her eyes sparkled with the inner warmth Charles had noticed. She held the baby in her arms. As Ben dreamed, his eyelids fluttered. That burden, Ben, would give Sandy strength.

"Is there something I can do?" I said. "I mean, I can't quit my job, but maybe I could deal with insurance claims."

"Remember those casseroles you used to make?" Sandy said. "When you came home from work, you'd put one in the oven. That's what I want."

"Consider it done." I could cook in Evanston and fill a giant suitcase with frozen casseroles. That would be my contribution, and I felt relieved to know Sandy thought that would be enough.

"The only thing is," she said, "the food has to be special."

"Special how?"

"Tony's started choking."

"What can he eat?"

"Anything in the ALS cookbook," Sandy said. "I'll tell Lillian to send you one."

I tried to imagine what ingredients would go into a casserole that Tony could swallow, Sandy would find palatable, and Josh would eat. White was probably the key.

***

Three feet of snow fell overnight, and even snowplows couldn't make it down the streets. I put on long underwear, slacks, and jeans. In the driveway Charles, on a ladder, had finished sweeping his eaves.

"Driving to the sledding hill is out of the question," he said, descending, "but the park's not far from here. You can walk."

Kevin and Sean had helped Tony dress, and when they brought him out, a neck scarf covered the earflaps of his Russian hat. They lowered him onto a toboggan. Charles handed the rope to Kevin and seized Tony's waist, propping him like a doll. They brought out quilts and tucked them behind his back and around his legs.

"Can you breathe?" Kevin said.

"Yes," Tony said, leaning back against the toboggan's curved front, "but you're smothering me."

"Sounds like you're warm enough." Kevin looped the toboggan rope over his chest and began to drag it.

Charles kicked snow from a Flexi-flyer at the back door and passed the rope to Sandy. "You'll love the hill."

In balloons of breath, she said, "You have to come with us. All work and no play make Charles a dull boy."

"Let me watch the baby." Charles reached for Ben, asleep in the baby carrier. "I saw the sacks of breast milk in the freezer, but I'll try to hold off until you get back."

"Okay," Sandy said.

Tony drew his knees up to his chest. "If Ben stays, I stay, too."

Charles, holding the baby carrier in one hand, ducked into the sunroom and emerged with an afghan. "Here's another blanket, buddy."

"Don't 'buddy' me," Tony said.

Kevin pulled the toboggan into the street, and I took a last look at the gabled house. I was no longer a thirty-some-year-old knock-out. I had weathered skin. As far as Charles was concerned, I had been, and always would be, the older woman. But so what, for god's sake? How good I felt, taking long, strong steps, hearing the snow crunch underfoot and the spill of powdered sugar off the black branches of the pines. Down the street the neighbors, in a mood of hilarity and community spirit, swung snow shovels to dig out stranded motorists. A Siberian Husky barked and jumped at the sprays of ice. The toboggan hissed over the snow and bumped across the tracks of cross-country skiers.

"This is the first minute of freedom I've had in months," Sandy whispered. She rubbed her neck. "The only time I relax is when I'm away."

The street turned uphill into a county park. Outcroppings of Vermont granite sparkled. Death was the bedrock, Plato said. Death was the human experience from which all other experience must be measured. Or, maybe, Rob had told me that. I smelled the woods, turpentine and cloves, and remembered looking over the back of a pew, an incense burner clanking against a chain. *Agnus Dei, qui tollis peccata mundi, miserere nobis.* Lamb of God, Who takest away the sins of the world, have mercy on us. Shafts of light burned down through the branches, and ahead, I heard the swish of the toboggan and Tony's nasal twang.

Kevin stopped at a clearing in the trees. "This is it."

A steep hill swarmed with happy children. Every possible conveyance took them down the slope: saucers, Flexi-flyers, and inner tubes. Sean, who pulled the sled, started for the top. The snow came to Josh's waist, and Sean picked him up and carried him with one arm. Kevin tucked the blankets around Tony's legs. "Want to come for a sled run?" he asked Sandy.

"Sure," she said.

"That's fine," Tony said. "Just go ahead without me."

"Don't lay a guilt trip on me." Sandy turned away. Steadily, she began to climb the hill, and when she was still within earshot, Tony called, "Enjoy yourself." Sandy looked back and kept walking.

"Tony," I said, "give her some space."

"Take me back to the house," he said. "I have frostbite."

"We're staying here," I said. "The problem is, you're in the shade." I dragged the toboggan into the sun and bent over to tuck him in.

"Call the others," Tony screamed. His teeth chattered. Squirming, he kicked the blankets off the sled. He sure could kick. If determination counted in the survival stats, Tony would outlive us all. I put two fingers in my mouth and whistled. Sean, who'd reached the crest, started back, walking in the crusty shadows next to the trees, while Kevin, Sandy, and Josh sailed down on the sled. The run ended feet from where Tony sat fuming on the toboggan.

Josh hopped up and down. "Let's go again."

Kevin looked at Tony. "It's your dad's turn now."

"Absolutely not," Tony said.

Sandy picked up his hands and blew in his mittens. "It'll get your blood moving."

"The ride through town damaged my coccyx," Tony said.

"Your what-ix?" said Kevin.

"His butt bone," I said.

"Get your ass up that mountain," Kevin said. "Come on. Have a little fun."

Kevin and Sean marched Tony, legs bicycling, up the mountain. When they reached the top, Sean held the sled while Kevin positioned Tony in front of him. Sean gave the sled a push. It picked up speed. Tony's head flew back against Kevin's shoulder and then Tony's eyes grew wide and a laugh burst and died. The sled shot toward a hummock of snow. Clearing the top, it launched into the air.

"Hold on to him," Sandy cried, already running like a deer.

The sled rammed a snow bank. I took off a glove and grabbed the toboggan rope. As I ran to the crash site, cold corkscrewed into my chest.

Tony had fallen off the sled. Curled on his side, he shivered. Tears streamed down his face. Kevin and Sean lifted him.

"Did you break anything?" Sandy said.

"I'm fine," Tony said. "That's the fastest I've traveled in months. It was a gas."

"You want to go again?" Kevin said.

"I think I'll skip it," Tony said. "The landing was a little rough."

Sandy wiped the tears from her cheeks. "The landing's been rough for months."

My fingers felt numb. I put my glove back on. If Tony had been injured, the toboggan would have turned into an ambulance, and the trip to Montpelier would have turned into a different sort of vacation. I couldn't believe our lives had come to this.

CHAPTER 11

Lying on the massage table, my face nested in the donut hole, I stared down at blurry, speckled tile. Percussive karate chops landed on my spine, and several *G*'s of gravity pulled at my cheeks. The masseuse, whom Maureen said had the best damned hands on the North Shore, warned me to drink plenty of water to flush out the toxins. Yeah, the toxins of Christmas. Three weeks later, they were still with me. A squirt of cold snaked down my back. Almond oil. Marzipan. The bag of bear claws Charles had shown up with and that I had eaten, despite telling myself they contained everything bad.

"I'm glad I'm Jewish," the woman said. "We don't do Christmas."

"Maybe I should convert," I said.

"This isn't to say we don't get uptight. You should see me when my mother comes."

Of course. Mothers were always to blame. Sandy was a mother, a young mother, and unless something changed, years from now, Josh or Ben would blame her for being too weary to respond to their needs. The demands on Sandy kept ratcheting up. The contractor building the room addition bombarded her with questions. Bills mounted. I could make a difference if I moved to D.C.—and I wanted to jump in for Sandy's sake—but maybe Sandy, with her infinite Tony-patience, could handle his mood swings with more compassion than I could muster. "You'd feel sorrier for him," Kevin said, "if he stopped that 'poor me' stuff." I agreed. I could feel a lot of sympathy for him a thousand miles away. I lifted my head and tried to turn it. Still tight. "Skip the spine and work on the shoulders, okay?" The masseuse plunged her fingers into my neck. For two weeks I had done nothing but cook casseroles. Now, I would get my first look at the room addition. With the blessings of my principal, Dr. Hidalgo, I had decided to take a family-leave day.

Waiting in the airport lounge, Tony wore a parka large enough for two of him. His glossy black mustache, new since the holidays, made him look like a Dimasio stepping off the steamer at Ellis Island.

"I can't believe you came all the way out here to meet me," I said.

He slipped his hands in his pockets. "I have a reason."

"What is it?" I said.

"You'll see."

At baggage claim, I unzipped my suitcase. Mushroom sauce had begun to squish from the chicken and rice casserole. "I have a suitcase full of frozen food," I said. "Well, it *was* frozen."

"You and my mom." Tony shuffled towards the Metro station. "She was down three days, and all she did was cook. She acts like there's a famine." When the train arrived, Tony took a handicapped seat. "We're stopping at Social Security on our way home."

"Why couldn't your mom have run this errand?"

"She's about to have a nervous breakdown. You'd think this was her tragedy, not mine."

"It *is* her tragedy," I said.

The train stopped. Tony stood up. "She's not dying."

"She is so," I said. "She's dying. I'm dying. You're dying. It's a matter of how fast."

"You really annoy me, you know?"

"You annoy me, too."

More than irritated by the change in plans, I followed Tony off the Metro, pulling my suitcase down the crowded sidewalk until we reached the Social Security building, a grimy concrete structure that blighted the urban landscape. Inside I took a plastic number, a form to fill out, and sat down in the U-shaped waiting room with two dozen other, mostly elderly or indigent, applicants. The form asked for Tony's entire work history, plus names and dates of employment.

"I don't see why they'd need that," Tony said. "They must have it on computer."

"You're right, of course." He hadn't come prepared, even though he knew about this errand. Typical Tony. All I wanted was to get home and put my casseroles in the freezer. Thinking out loud, Tony debated the pros and cons of privacy and freedom-of-information.

"Tony," I said. "We're here. If you know your employer information, give it to me."

"Of course I know it."

Tony had photographic recall. His memory wasn't affected by ALS.

Forty-five minutes later, an African-American woman in big spectacles popped up from a cubicle. "Ninety-eight."

"That's us," I said.

"This is a ridiculous waste of time," Tony said, not moving.

"Let's go." I grabbed his parka sleeve and dragged him through the office maze, then sat him down and found a chair for myself.

The woman read the application. I looked at the photos pinned up in the cubicle: a frail, white-haired woman in a wheelchair and a yellow bus that said Calvary Baptist.

The clerk handed back the form. "He's not eligible."

"Why not?" I said.

The woman smoothed her skirt. The shoulder pads of her blazer made her look trapezoidal. "He's employed."

"He's employed, but he can't do his job." I explained that Tony was a lobbyist. His job required public speaking. His voice gave out. His boss wanted him to go on disability. His disability ought to be obvious. Even I strained to decipher the mouth-organ wheeze of his twanged syllables.

"I can still speak fine," Tony sputtered. "My boss says people can't understand me, but he's full of it. Next week, a bill to increase the capacity of pig farms' holding ponds comes up. I have to be there."

"Can't somebody else do it?"

"No."

"Is Mr. Dimasio foreign-born?" the clerk asked.

"I was born in New Brunswick," he said. "New Jersey. Not the Maritime Province."

"We're not going to Nova Scotia," I said.

Tony smiled. "I thought I had you."

The woman looked at me. "I'm having difficulty following."

"His speech is impaired." I pointed to my tongue. "ALS affects the tongue and vocal chords."

The woman suggested a speech therapist, but I argued that it wasn't just the speech. Tony could barely make it to work. Boarding a bus posed dangers. He couldn't break a fall. The woman countered that the new D.C. buses could pick him up at home and an occupational therapist could modify his work environment. He could be assigned different tasks. "The Americans with Disabilities Act," she said, "was written for people like that."

"Like what?" Tony said.

"He can't keep working," I said. "End of discussion."

"I've got appointments with Ag Committee staffers all next week," Tony said. "The only reason I came down here was to get my wife off my back."

A picture of Sandy snapping a whip across the flank of a mule flashed through my mind.

The woman asked if Tony could drive. "No," I said.

"Can he dress himself?"

"No," I said.

"My wife does it, but she resents it," Tony said.

"What about eating? Can he feed himself?"

"No," I said.

"I f-f-feed myself," Tony sputtered.

"Not true," I said. "At Christmas, he couldn't lift his fork. We had to feed him."

"I can still do breakfast."

The stiffness in the woman's shoulders relaxed. "I see." Squinting, she looked at a letter from Tony's doctor. Then she made an X. "I just need his signature."

Tony scowled. He nodded to his breast pocket, and when I patted him down, I found a ballpoint with a blue foam sleeve that made his pen into a writing implement the size of a kindergartner's crayon. With his left hand, Tony positioned the pen between his thumb and index finger. As he wrote, wrinkling the application with the movement of his forearm, the pen wobbled and fell from his hand.

The woman looked at his signature. "This is illegible." Passing the paper to me, she said, "Just put your name and 'For Tony Dimasio.'"

"*Antonio,*" Tony said.

"Do you use your middle name for legal signatures?" the woman asked.

"No," Tony said. "I hate my middle name."

Remembering the time at Koolfont where Tony had said I'd never gotten to know him, I realized this was one of the things I didn't know. "What *is* your middle name?"

"*Pantaleone,*" he said.

"I can imagine what kids on the playground did with that."

"Exactly. That's why we call Josh 'Josh' and not *Giuseppe.*" He nodded to the signature line. "Also, Josh is easier to write."

I signed. Because Tony had only worked the minimum number of quarters to qualify for SSDI—Social Security Disability Insurance—his monthly checks would amount to $416 a month and $125 for each child, she explained. The checks wouldn't kick in for six months. In twelve months he'd qualify for Medicare.

"Would that cover home care?" I said.

"He'll only be eligible for home care if he's been hospitalized for three days."

He'd had concussions, I thought. Maybe after the next fall, his doctor would agree to a three-day stay.

As if reading my mind, the clerk said, "The maximum coverage is a hundred days a year."

"But during that time, wouldn't Medicare cover a home health aide?"

"If you want that, then your family has to spend down its assets and apply," she said.

"For Medicaid?" I said.

"Don't get your hopes up. He's only eligible if he's living in a nursing home."

"I'm not going to a nursing home," Tony said.

"Of course not." I thought of Joan Calabrese and her mother. So what she'd said was true: custodial care wouldn't be covered by the government.

"I can tell you," said the woman, straightening her skirt, "you're living in the worst place in the country if you hope to get any benefits from Medicaid." She pointed to the picture of the elderly woman on her desk. "We had to put Mother in a home out by my sister's place in Loudon County. You'd be a lot better off in Maryland."

"Why?" I said.

"Medicaid's a state program. Some states are more generous than others."

"I don't want to live in the suburbs," Tony said.

"Don't get all hot under the collar. Nobody's suggesting that." I thanked the woman for approving his application.

In the waiting room, Tony looked at the people holding plastic numbers, their worn shoes and shabby coats testifying to their circumstances. "I feel like an imposter," he said.

I picked up my suitcase. "Tony, the money's for your children."

Outside, he started for the bus stop. "No," I said, "we're taking a taxi."

"Waste of money," Tony said.

"So's this food going to be if I don't get it in the freezer."

In the taxi, balled up against the door, I tried to plug my ears against Tony's talk about pigs feeding at the trough of the defense industry while poor people suffered the indignities of food stamp cutbacks and welfare reform. He was outraged that Hillary's single-payer system was going down the tubes. Once again, in a nation as rich as the United States, poor people would have to make it on their own. What galled me was that Tony had never come close to poverty and had no idea of its indignities. To induce him to make calls home, his parents paid his phone bill. They provided a credit card for gas. All of which I was glad for now.

At home, I paid the driver, hopped out, and pulled my suitcase around through the alley to the garage, where the former owners had left a freezer. I stuffed in the casseroles, wiped sauce from my hands, and emerged from the garage to face the room addition. It looked like a sky-hook had dropped a doublewide manufactured home onto four concrete-block pillars. What an eyesore. I picked my way through the siding scraps and shingle cutoffs littering the yard and climbed the new backstairs which were wood, but still not anything Tony could easily walk up or down. I pushed open the door. The carpenter had already broken through the kitchen wall. Duct tape sealed plastic sheeting to the brick. I looked down at the floor. The new room sat three inches lower than the dining room. This was nuts. This was supposed to be a room for a guy in a wheelchair, and they couldn't figure out how to make the floors the same height?

Behind me, the door opened. A bearded carpenter in butt-hugging jeans thrust out a callused hand. "You must be Sandy's mother," he said. "I'm the builder."

"This floor's like a high dive," I said.

"Your daughter pulled the old switcheroo on finish flooring."

"What do you mean?"

"I framed for ceramic tile."

"What's she want now?"

"Linoleum."

"Don't bullshit me. That wouldn't account for a three-inch difference. You made a framing error."

He backed up. "Don't worry. I'll fix it."

"I don't see how." Summers, I'd worked with my dad. He'd taught me how to frame. This was pure carelessness.

"What's with the back steps?" I said. "They're made for a mountain goat."

"They're to code," he said. "Anyhow, your daughter said Tony's going to use the front way in."

"Not unless there's a ramp."

"I got one cut already," he said. "When you need it, I'll come back and put it together."

"Oh sure."

"No, I will," he said. "I promise."

Not wanting to untape the plastic but shaking with rage, I went back down the stairs and around through the alley, waving to Lowell Jaffe. Ever since my visit to the Calabreses', I'd kept my distance. Up on a ladder he worked on a plum tree with a long-handled saw that reminded me of the Grim Reaper's scythe.

"Back for a visit?" he said.

"Just for the weekend."

"Soon as the frost danger passes, I'm putting in tomatoes."

"The ones you brought over last summer were delicious."

"I'm putting in Black Krims and Red Brandywines this year." He climbed down from his ladder and came over, wiping his hands front and back on his baggy pants. "Josh told me his dad was sick. When I see them out for a walk it breaks my heart. I asked your daughter what we could do to help."

"What did she say?"

"She said they were doing fine for the moment."

"Probably for the moment, they are."

"I been thinking, it would be good if she got a permanent parking spot for that van. The city will put up a sign that says 'handicapped parking' and the car that parks there has to match the number on the sign."

"How do we go about getting that?"

"She'd need a permit." He went in the house and brought me the address. "It's downtown in the city building. They're closed on weekends."

"Thank you." As I looked at his shaky writing my eyes teared up. "You really do look out for people."

"I try." He cleared his throat. "By the way, you ought to watch the weight. Looks like you put on a few pounds. Maybe get your thyroid checked."

"It's none of your beeswax," I said.

He planted the pole of his tree saw. "You know you're going to have to move back one of these days. Either that or your daughter will have to stop working. One of my employee's mothers had the exact same thing as Tony."

Joan Calabrese. "It's not an option for me to relocate," I said.

"Their new room's ugly as sin. You better tell that carpenter of theirs to stop filling garbage cans with his debris. I've told him but he keeps doing it. If he doesn't stop, I'm going to call the city."

"Great," I said and turned away. "Thanks."

"The reason I held off is I don't want to cause problems," he called after me.

People who meant well often stepped on your toes. Maureen was like that, just kind of oblivious, whereas Esmeralda never said anything that made me feel bad about myself. I wondered how she was doing out in Ohio and if she'd ever forgive me.

Inside, Tony sat at the dining room table, the *Post* spread open before him. Glancing at me, he closed the paper. "You cursed at our carpenter."

"Did I?" Okay, so Tony had heard me being rude. Too bad. "The guy's building a room that's supposed to be handicapped accessible. I can't believe he couldn't make the floor heights match."

"I told Sandy the addition was a waste of money."

"Then why'd she go ahead with it?"

"She didn't want me trapped in the basement."

"It wouldn't have been a big deal to put a ramp out the back."

"Josh wouldn't have had a playroom."

"Oh, God, the playroom." The only way an addition like this made sense was if Tony still planned to go on a respirator. If he went on a respirator, he'd be dependent, not just on the machine but on his parents. The cost of the room addition would be a small down payment on years of nursing expense. Even Aldo, with his deep pockets, would eventually feel the strain. "Like that woman at Social Security said, Maryland would have been an altogether better option."

"I don't want to live in the suburbs," Tony said.

"All right, already."

The front door opened, and I turned to see Sandy stride across the living room and throw her briefcase on the counter. Tony's new bedroom would be Sandy's bedroom, too. The room opened into the narrow, galley kitchen, where the big, blue flowers of the vinyl wallpaper were enough to give you nightmares.

"Hi, Mom," Sandy said, offering me a Post-it. "Could I give you a list of things to do while you're here?"

"Oh, please do." I grabbed the list. "You've got me for the weekend."

"If you'll excuse me," Tony said. "I have to go to the bathroom."

"Don't fall," Sandy said.

"I'll be careful."

Sandy stood beneath the arch, a worried expression on her face as she listened to Tony climb the stairs. The dining room chandelier quivered as Tony thumped across the floor above.

Sandy looked up at the ceiling and then leaned closer. "I made a new friend, a woman at work whose husband has ALS."

"The same kind Tony has?" I said.

"Not bulbar onset," Sandy said. "He has the slow-acting kind. It started in his feet."

"Is he on a respirator?"

"Not yet. And you know what she said?" Sandy looked up again. "'I'm so stressed out, I can't wait until he dies.'"

I looked at Sandy's eyes. They were wide, waiting for me to be horrified. The poor woman.

"One day, you may feel like that," I said.

"Never," Sandy said. "Tony and I have an honest relationship."

"Never say never."

"You don't understand. Tony is my best friend. I can tell him anything, and he'll listen."

"I sure hope that makes a difference."

I turned my attention to the list: fix upstairs window that keeps crashing down; paint basement door; make drapes for dining room; file insurance claims; repair light switch on stairs; fix squeaky stairs; repair broken screens throughout house; repair dripping sinks, upstairs and down; fix basement deadbolt. Sandy stood with her arms folded.

"I can't move back here," I said.

"I'm not asking you to," Sandy said.

"At times like this, you wish you had a crystal ball, don't you?"

"If I only knew how long it was going to last, then maybe I could come up with a critical path."

"I'll give you as much help as I can," I said, "but I can't turn my class over to a substitute for the rest of the year. My retirement security depends on me socking away the maximum number of years. I pretty much drained my savings when you kids were in college, and before I knew this was going to happen, I bought my retirement house. Now, in a way, I wish I hadn't."

Sandy sighed. "I understand completely. It's my responsibility."

"It's not your responsibility, Sandy. Not yours alone."

"I promised, though."

"Promised who?"

"You know," she said. "In sickness and in health."

"Jesus, Sandy." I grasped her shoulders. "People say stuff on the day of their wedding they truly believe, but very few actually live up to those promises."

"You did," Sandy said.

"Not perfectly," I said. "I could have been a better wife."

"How?"

"I had a pretty bad temper."

"You don't now."

"Oh, I do," I said. "Pushed hard enough, I still explode. It just takes longer."

"Well, I don't see that," Sandy said. "You deal with Tony better than I do."

"I don't have to be around him every day." And besides, I didn't deal with him better than she did. His self-pity drove me nuts.

I put the Post-it in my pocket. Two days and I could go home to my normal life, but Sandy had to stick it out. A dead husband was definitely easier to deal with than a dying one. Tony had turned into a third child, a whiny one to boot.

CHAPTER 12

The night before I headed back to D.C. for the eight days of spring break, the girls in my third floor apartment clogged up the tub drain with hair, and I had to call Bill Flaherty's 24-hour plumber to rod it out. On the plane, as I looked at the shrinking balance in my checking account, I felt a rising panic that Tony's illness would jeopardize my future. By the time I turned sixty-five—a dozen years from now—I wanted a paid-off house. Every month I had been sending an extra payment to my mortgage lender to pay down the principal on my loan. If I had to fly back to D.C. every couple of months, plus shell out for food, I couldn't keep doing that. I wondered how much longer this would go on. For the second time in my life, I was living through a tragedy; but apart from making a small adjustment to the way I handled my house payment, I saw no way to shift the outcome. Tony would die. Me going broke wouldn't prevent it.

I ate at the airport, and by the time I arrived at the house, Sandy was reading the kids a bedtime story. I volunteered to help Tony brush his teeth. In the upstairs bathroom he leaned against the pedestal sink. It tilted forward, and I grabbed his belt. Tony moved a little slower when he walked, but at least he could still make it up the stairs. Despite his misgivings about the medicine, maybe the drugs were actually doing some good.

"Tony," I said, "you seem to have reached a plateau."

"Nah," he said, through bubbles of toothpaste.

"I don't think you've lost much muscle-function since the last time I was here."

He hooked his fingers, which had turned into talons, over a towel rack. Half-standing, he spit out the toothpaste and looked in the mirror. His eyes had grown more expressive. Brows lifted meant skepticism; head tilted sideways, fear. I dried his chin and walked him to the stairs. Positioning Tony next to the handrail, I waited for him to take the first step. The phone rang, and I made him promise to stand still while I grabbed the phone in Sandy's bedroom. It was Lisa, suggesting Tony fly up to Boston for the following weekend. She'd found an internet fare.

Lisa hadn't seen Tony in six or seven months and she was probably imagining him the way he was before, able to walk without assistance. She wanted an answer right now. Bringing Tony back from the top of the stairs, I settled him on his bed and opened Josh's door. Sandy sat on the floor with both kids in her lap.

"I'm reading the kids a story," she said.

"I know, but Lisa's offering to bring Tony up there for the weekend. You want to accept her offer?"

"He can't go alone," Sandy said.

"Why don't we go with him and take the kids?"

"Lisa's apartment's too small," Sandy said. "I have a better idea. He has a doctor's appointment Thursday and the nurse is going to drop by Friday, but we could fly up Saturday, leave Tony at Lisa's, and you and I could go out to Woods Hole for a night."

"Really?" I said. "Just the two of us?"

"I'm seeing a therapist at work," Sandy said. "He says I need to plan regular breaks or I'll get too worn out."

"One night isn't much of a break," I said.

"Anything will help."

"What about the kids?"

"Maybe Sean could babysit."

"For one night? I'm sure he could handle it."

Sandy would buy their tickets, and I would call Sean.

"I just need to totally put Tony and this situation out of my mind," she said.

How hard that was. Even in Evanston, I couldn't do it. But more power to her. Time off might give her a different perspective.

On Friday, Eugene Henderson, Tony's visiting nurse, stopped in for his biweekly visit. He wore a yellow tee-shirt and cutoffs. He always wore a baseball cap and half the time came with wet armpits, as if he'd just rushed over from a game. Eugene impressed me as a competent, but not caring, man. He reminded me of some teachers, not especially motivated, or maybe motivated for the wrong reasons. Dr. Stevanovic's secretary had phoned Eugene to say Tony seemed to be holding his own. Breathing tests showed his respiration had improved from the score two months ago.

"How can that be?" I said.

ALS, Eugene explained, hopped around the body from organ to organ. Sometimes, its progression mysteriously halted after taking out the function of several limbs.

This confirmed my observations. Tony must be rebounding from the dip he'd had at Christmas. Maybe there was a reason to hope the atrophying of Tony's muscles had reached a plateau. To stave off further muscle decline, Dr. Stevanovic urged Tony to move as much as possible.

"How much walking do you do during the day?" Eugene asked.

"Not much," Tony said.

"None," I said.

"I can speak for myself," Tony said.

"It's still none," I said.

Most of the day he sat at the dining table reading the *Post*. To avoid the trip to the bathroom, he drank nothing during the day.

"In that case," Eugene said, "you're facing a new risk. Thrombosis."

"What's that?" Tony said.

"A blood clot in your legs."

Eugene had scheduled a physical therapist, Roosevelt Washington, to begin a regular program of large and small muscle therapy; but, at the moment, the physical therapist had a full schedule.

Eugene slapped Tony's shoulder. "You're good to go."

He turned to me. "I don't know if you're aware, but Sandy's insurance just switched you guys over to a case manager. Before, your insurance would automatically reimburse you when you submitted a claim. Now, all decisions have to be pre-approved. Sandy needs to find out if insurance will cover the PT visits. I think they'll approve it, but I'm not a hundred percent certain."

"Tony, do you know anything about this?" I said.

"No." Tony shrugged. "Sandy handles the bills."

"When someone has a chronic illness, this is what happens," Eugene said. "After six months the insurance company moves you to a person who coordinates your care."

The wicker basket on Sandy's desk overflowed with window envelopes. Maybe having a case manager would help.

***

At Logan airport in Boston, I folded the walker and crammed our belongings into a compact car. When we arrived at Lisa's place in the suburbs, a twisting, pine-paneled stairway led up to the second floor. Lisa hadn't mentioned stairs. Tony took a deep breath and started up. At the top, Lisa stood aside to let him in.

"You made it," she said. "I rented all the Hitchcock movies. We can stay up all night and have our own movie festival."

"Thanks," Tony said.

I unfolded his walker and Tony leaned forward, bracing himself. While he stood, Sandy took a hypodermic and vial from a cooler in Tony's suitcase. With the efficiency of a nurse, she swabbed his arm with an alcohol wipe and jabbed him, and then she took the cooler to the kitchen. I heard the refrigerator open and close.

Lisa had turned pale and put a hand over her mouth.

"Is that your human growth hormone?" I asked Tony.

"Yeah," he said. "I think it might be doing some good."

"You didn't tell me I'd have to give him a shot," Lisa said.

"Don't worry," I told her. "You only have to give him his pills."

"But how will I know which ones?" she said.

"Tony can tell you."

"I'd better ask Sandy," Lisa said, hurrying to the kitchen.

Before Sandy and I left, I wanted to do a safety check to eliminate tripping hazards. I pushed the dining room table against the wall and, in the bathroom, draped a bathmat over the towel bar.

I heard a thud from the living room.

"What was that?" Lisa called from the kitchen.

"Oh, it's just Tony," I said, hurrying to see what had happened.

Tony had fallen backward like a log. His face turned white. Beads of sweat formed on his upper lip.

"He needs to sit up," Sandy said. "He's having trouble breathing."

"I think he should lie down," I said. "He may be going into shock."

"Put a pillow under his head then," Sandy said.

Lisa handed me a pillow.

Head elevated, Tony smiled. "Gravity is my enemy."

I held up two fingers. "How many?"

"Fifteen," he said.

"Tony," Sandy said, shaking her head. "Are you hurt?"

"My hands feel a little tingly," he said, "but I'm all right."

"Did the walker get caught in the carpet or was it your shoes?" Sandy asked.

"Shoes," Tony said.

Sandy took off his Birkenstocks and threw them in the corner.

When the color returned to Tony's face, I took one arm and Sandy the other. We slid him to the couch and lifted. Dazed, grinning, he looked like he'd just landed in Oz. Sandy made an ice pack and handed it to Lisa. "You can take over."

Her jaw set, face drained of color, Lisa looked at the dripping baggie. "But, I don't—"

"We're going." Sandy gave Tony a smooch.

"But, wait," Lisa said. "What do I do?"

"Don't worry," Sandy said. "This happens all the time. He's not bleeding."

We ran down to the car.

"Oh my God," I said, opening the door. "Lisa looked like she was about to pass out, too. I thought for sure we were going to get stuck there."

"So did I," Sandy started the engine, "and I need this weekend in the worst way."

"Me, too," I said.

While she drove I found a classical music station. The traffic on the interstate was thick, but soon she turned off I-93 and headed south on State Route 3 toward Cape Cod.

"This is really precious time, having a night with you," I said. "I don't want anything to spoil it."

"I pretty much had to bring you," she said, taking her eyes from the road to look at me. "Tony would have pitched a fit if I'd gone alone."

"He won't let you go away one night?"

"He's worried Lisa can't handle him if something goes wrong."

"Whereas you can."

"You got it." The smile disappeared from her face. "He's insecure when I'm not there."

I moved the seat to give myself legroom. A billboard for Bally's made me think about a gym membership. It would do me good to get out of my head. Maybe I wouldn't brood so much over things better let go: Sandy's comment that the only reason she'd brought me was because Tony wouldn't have let her leave. Didn't she want to get to know me? God, I sounded like Tony back at Koolfont. I'd never gotten to know him. Bullshit. Even Esmeralda I barely knew—not what made her tick or even the circumstances of her life—but with her, I felt a basic comfort despite the difference in our ages. A basic trust. Well, maybe not anymore. I hadn't heard from her since that call at Christmas. A raindrop in Ohio, she had fallen into Lake Erie and disappeared.

"I don't know if I told you, but the EPA offered me a promotion," Sandy said. "I turned it down."

"Thank heavens. You've got enough to deal with already."

"I've been thinking about going back to school for an MBA," Sandy said.

"Seriously?"

"No," Sandy said, laughing. "I'm teasing. My assistant told me today she was going back for one of those executive MBAs, and my first thought was that I'd rather have another kid than a useless degree."

"Could Tony *make* another kid?"

"Yes, but he doesn't want one. He says I'm certifiable."

"It would be another loss for him to absorb," I said. "He's told me several times he doesn't think the kids will remember him."

"I have very clear memories of my father."

"Yeah, but you were two years older than Josh. He might remember Tony for a while, but not all the way to adulthood." Kevin had been Josh's age, three, and he remembered only shadows.

"You know what Josh told me the other day?" Sandy said, taking her eyes off the traffic. "He told me he wants another baby, and when I explained that right now, my attention is divided between him and Ben and Daddy and that another baby would mean less attention for him, he thought about it, and a couple of days later came back to me, saying, 'By the time you have another baby, Daddy will be dead.' Then he wanted to know if, when Tony dies, he will be my husband, and I explained that no, sons and husbands were different things. 'But I could make a baby with you after Daddy dies,' he said. And I said, no, things didn't work that way."

"That's so Oedipal it's amazing."

Sandy laughed. "He loves his mommy a lot."

"That'll end."

"You know it."

Yes, I did. But that was part of the natural progression. If Rob had lived, Sandy would have had another parent to rebel against. He would have taken away the car keys and insisted she mind her tongue when she spoke to me. But her teenage rebellion was all in the past: those moments she'd confront me and scream, "Why do you have that look on your face?" It was petty of me to keep wondering what had derailed our relationship, especially now, when she'd given me this chance to spend time together.

I turned the radio down. "Why would you want to have a third child right now?" I said. "Don't you have enough to deal with?"

"I guess it's a form of insurance, in case Josh or Ben inherit ALS," Sandy said. "The woman who started the Boston support group, of which Lisa is now a member, had a brother die of ALS. A few years later, she came down with it. Later, one of her parents began to show symptoms. Doctors think Tony's ALS is the sporadic kind, not hereditary, but without DNA tests, they can't be sure. I don't think I could stand it if one of my children got sick."

"I know what you mean." As agonizing as Rob's death had been, it wouldn't compare to how I'd feel if anything happened to my children. Even so, I hoped Tony won this particular argument. I remembered how much I had wanted Sean—six weeks *in utero* when Rob died. I did fine during the pregnancy, sort of on autopilot, but after his birth, I overdrew my bank account and drove away from the grocery store without my bags of groceries. From what the grief counselor told me, distraction was common among the newly widowed. Sandy was only at the beginning of that long and painful process. There was so much I longed to share with her, not the day-to-day, but the deep knowledge, life's lessons learned. If I could find the words. After Tony's death would be soon enough.

When Sandy pulled into the Nautilus, a motel with gray, shiplap siding, I woke up. I rolled down my window and inhaled. The air had that damp, salty, North Atlantic smell, and from nearby came the gentle crash of waves. Sandy pointed to a parking space next to the office's weathered overhang. "The last time I was here, that's where the ambulance stopped. There was a big puddle of blood in the parking lot and everybody came out of their rooms and stared at us. Tony always seems to fall during those times of transition. We're so careful getting him to the destination, but the trip tires him out, and when we're unloading bags and not keeping an eye on him, that's when he loses his balance. Luckily, his folks arrived at the same time the ambulance did. They watched the kids while I went with Tony to the hospital."

"When was this?" I said.

"I don't remember exactly," Sandy said. "I'm so tired all the time, my memory's shot. Sometimes I think I'm getting Alzheimer's." She opened the car door. "Let's get dinner first. I know you're going to love this restaurant."

"I feel like I could fall asleep right now," I said.

"Me, too," Sandy said. "Although sometimes, I just lie awake and remember how it was before all this started."

After we checked in, Sandy led the way along a narrow sidewalk. On a cruise ship silhouetted against the sky, three tiers of lights, like the lights of the *Titanic*, moved slowly along the horizon. The sun pulsed like a ball of magma and threw rivers of orange across the sky. Two terns soared over the water and, feeding, dipped their bandit heads.

"That's so beautiful," Sandy said.

"Yes," I whispered. "I'm so glad we got away."

"The first time I came up here," Sandy said, "I was here for a meeting, and I was pregnant with Josh. I had horrible morning sickness. Tony carried all the luggage. I had to bring my business dresses and casual clothes because we were going to take advantage of having the weekend to ourselves. In one of my meetings a colleague said he saw Tony running down this road, which is the route of the Falmouth Road Race, one of the most famous seven-mile races in the country. That was always the thing Tony liked best, arriving someplace new and discovering its secrets. Afterwards, we took the ferry to Martha's Vineyard, and even though I was sick to my stomach, it was like being on a honeymoon. He was such a romantic, fun-loving guy, and I was the luckiest woman in the world."

The sidewalk widened. In the little harbor near the restaurant, sailboats rocked and tugged at their moorings. Sandy slowed her pace. In the distance, a ferry hooted, and a seagull, perched on the wooden piling, cried.

Sandy opened the door at Fishmonger's. The pine paneling reminded me of the stairway at Lisa's. Mounted on plaques around the room, fish looked down with glassy eyes. A waitress showed us to a table. I ordered a bottle of wine. The conversation continued. Sandy had made her getaway, but Tony had come with us.

CHAPTER 13

Snow days had kept me in Chicago an extra week, and the drive through Ohio was taking forever. I was anxious to get back to Sandy's in time for Tony's birthday party, but swaying semis, speed traps, lane closures, and orange-and-white-striped highway cones caused delays. I decided to stop for gas, a coffee refill, and some Ho Hos or Twinkies, anything with lard the main ingredient. When I stepped up to pay for my food, I noticed that the boy at the service station's counter had a ring in his lip. Maybe it was a style back here, to pierce yourself and get a job instead of going to college. Esmeralda said she'd gone to Akron. I should at least try to give her a call before I left the state.

"By any chance to do have an Akron phone book?" I said.

"Yeah," he said. "It's back in the office."

"Can you get it?"

"I guess." He slouched off with that waddle-walk of boys who don't wear belts. It made me feel old to notice things like this and to feel like the world was going to hell in a hand basket.

I opened the directory. Now, what was Esmeralda's last name? Hoping to jog my memory for Brittany's last name, I started with the a's, my finger moving down the page. Speed-reading, I made it to the g's. Nothing rang a bell.

"Well, dang," I said. I couldn't stand here all day reading the phone book.

Maybe Esmeralda wasn't really Brittany's sister. She probably wasn't Brittany's sister because the father of a girl who would go to Northwestern wouldn't have been living in a shack behind Hecky's. Or in the trailer next to the shack. The father of a girl who went to Northwestern wouldn't have let his daughter get lip rings or wear that garish eye makeup. He wouldn't have thought of a baby as a cash windfall. I felt stupid for not having seen this before.

I could have made a real difference in Esmeralda's life. If she had called me any other time but on Christmas Day when a migraine made my mind fuzzy, I would have at least talked her through her options. I would have asked for an address. I had been distracted and, admit it, reluctant to take on one more thing. To top it off, I'd been rude and cut the conversation short, and ever since Christmas, this pointless guilt had been eating at me. I mean, really, who knows where the turning points are, the moments you could have taken a different path. Turning points pass so quickly they seem ephemeral, and then you're where you don't want to be, looking back, wishing you'd been clairvoyant.

Pulling back onto the highway, I tried to believe Esmeralda would keep her head above water, and I would have given anything to reassure myself that it was so. When it came right down to it, I missed the girl, and knowing her for that short time taught me three things about myself: that I'm a person who loves for no apparent reason, who takes on other people's burdens and carries them as if they were my own, and who has great difficulty letting go.

***

I stopped in Wheeling for the night and hit the road early. Except for the heat and humidity that steamed my new bifocals, I felt glad to arrive at Sandy's with my own car and the tools I needed to tackle the items on her to-do list, although even at a distance, I had tried to do my part.

I hadn't been shy about letting the world know about Sandy's and Tony's plight. Anyone who made a trip to lobby Congress, visit museums, or attend a conference carried a suitcase of frozen casseroles. The tragedy had become not just my family's tragedy, but a horrifying reminder that an illness like this could strike any one. Sandy reported that the new people dropping by had lifted Tony's mood. The Illinois' "casserole schleppers" had breached the boundary that separated the world inside Sandy's house from the rest of the world, where life went on as usual.

Carrying my things up to the house, I looked at the tricycles and wading pools in the tiny yards. Summer had arrived. Sandy's newly shingled porch roof and the freshly painted green trim improved the property's street appeal; but lately, the market for real estate had softened, and I was worried about what might happen if Tony's illness forced Sandy to look for a larger place. Who would buy a house with that hideous trailer-appendage out back? Riluzole had kept Tony walking and today was his thirty-fifth birthday, his continued good health amazing for a patient with bulbar onset. Sandy had organized a party for fifty or sixty people, all of whom would be strangers to me.

I opened the front door. At the dining room table eating his breakfast, Tony sat in a black electric wheelchair with white, balloon tires. On the two batteries that powered it, I saw a red bow that reminded me of Lillian's lips. Tony looked up and smiled.

"Happy birthday," I stammered.

"Reports of my death have been greatly exaggerated," he said.

"Yes, Mr. Clemens."

He snorted and his eyes lit up. "That joke passed over Sandy's head. But then, she never gets my humor."

It was going to be one of those days.

"Where is everyone?" I said.

"My mom and Josh are scouting out ice cream," Tony said. "Ben's taking a nap. The brothers are in the basement with Sandy."

I had to think for a second before his words registered. His tongue kept him from pronouncing the first letter of every word. Vowels hummed like the struck keys of a piano. A person had to listen very carefully and look at the expression in his eyes. More and more, he was becoming the father the boys would later find when they entered the house and saw him facing his computer, less and less the father who'd changed diapers and pitched a Wiffle ball.

Down in the basement, Sean and Kevin hopped up from the indoor-outdoor carpet and pulled me into a rugby scrum. Kevin's cheek scratched mine, and when I pulled back, I saw he'd skipped his morning shave. Out of school for summer break, he had come up a week ago so Tony and Sandy could go to a B and B. The boys had taken over the cooking, reroofed the porch, and painted the exterior trim.

"Well done, guys," I said. "The porch looks great."

Sandy, in a tee-shirt that showed her bony arms, was picking up toys. "I don't know why I'm doing this."

"Could you be upset about something?" I said.

"Why would you think that?" Sandy said.

"When you were a little girl, you used to clean when you were upset."

She blinked and looked at her brothers. "I cleaned because the house was always a mess."

"Not everyone's as anal you are," Kevin said.

"Come on, guys," Sean said. "It's Tony's birthday."

"Be prepared, Mom." Kevin pointed to the ceiling. "He's throwing a hissy fit about it."

"He had a doctor's appointment yesterday," Sandy said.

"With Dr. Stevanovic?" I said.

"It wasn't good news," Sandy said. "Tony's breathing has gone downhill a lot faster than she anticipated. She doesn't think he'll be here at Christmas."

"No wonder he's bummed," I said.

"Also, he can't climb the stairs unless I drag him," Sandy said. "The addition's done. We'll move downstairs tonight. A store's supposed to deliver a trundle bed after the party. Oh, and I wondered if you'd mind putting up the party decorations."

"Happy to," I said.

"Don't worry, Mom," Sean said. "We'll help you."

Sandy gave me a brown bag. "Here are the balloons. Upstairs, there's a happy birthday sign you can tape under the arch, and Kevin, I need you and Sean to bring in a table from the garage. We're going to put drinks in the new room."

"The plastic's still up," he said.

"Rip it down."

I hadn't seen the boys since Vermont, and I thought of Kevin's remark about Tony sucking all the oxygen out of the room. Tony sat at the table reading and ignoring us, and I wondered if Sean, who carried in the stepladder and positioned it between the living and dining rooms, would have called Tony's behavior passive-aggressive.

"There's another thing for your list," Sandy said, pointing up at the arch.

"What?" I said.

"Josh used too much paper and the toilet overflowed."

Yes, I could see the dry, salty bubbles. After brushing away loose plaster, I bit off a piece of masking tape to hold the sign. "I'll take a look at the damage later. What time do your guests arrive?"

"Two," Sandy said.

It was 12:45. Tony was still dawdling over his cereal. Kevin tore down the plastic between the house and the addition. Finally, Tony could see into the peach-colored room.

"How do you like your new bedroom?" I asked.

Tony's head swiveled slowly, taking in the open door that looked like it had been made for giants and the three-inch drop-off, now bridged by a maple ramp. "The addition stinks. All it needs are Britney Spears' posters."

I laughed. The eyesore wouldn't be here if it weren't for him. I let one hand rest on his shoulder. "Finish up your breakfast. Your guests might arrive early."

"It takes me a long time to chew each bite."

"Maybe you should try something besides Grape-Nuts."

"I'll eat Grape-Nuts till I choke."

"Suit yourself."

Lillian came in with grocery bags. Josh dodged around her, ran through the living room ignoring the adults, and made straight for the basement.

I twisted crepe paper and attached it to the ceiling. Finished with the decorations and dripping sweat, I carried an armload of clean clothes down to the basement shower. Josh, Sean, and Kevin were sitting on the floor and had started building a Lincoln Log fort. "Put those away when you're done," I said, knowing Sandy would do it if they didn't. As I turned on the shower, children's feet pounded across the floor above me. The party had begun. I didn't feel like lifting the medicine ball of conversation and lingered under the hot water.

By the time I came upstairs, guests had emptied the bottles of soda. Seeing Lowell Jaffee dressed for the occasion in dark slacks and beret, I headed for the group standing around him. "Hey, here's Sandy's mom," he said, holding out a hand to include me in the circle. "Say, did you ever look into that permit?"

"One of these days." Since I'd last been out, Lowell had grown a short, white beard that reminded me of Colonel Sanders. "Very debonair," I said.

He stroked his chin. "I'm dating someone."

I hadn't even realized he was single. No wonder he'd spiffed himself up.

Lowell introduced me to Hoang, his left arm missing from the elbow down, and Sharon, both Vietnamese, who lived across the alley and had two children. "They grow phenomenal peppers." He measured an inch with his fingers. "Those things will eat a hole in your throat if you don't swallow fast."

Sharon, whose eyebrows pinched, said, "You have to take the seeds out. I hope you didn't eat the seeds."

Hoang elbowed his wife. "He's teasing."

"Oh," she said and covered her mouth.

"Where are your kids?" I said.

"My mother's watching them," Sharon said. "My parents live with us."

Hoang slid his half-arm in between two buttons. "Her parents come for six months. Then mine come."

"From Vietnam?" I said.

"No, they live in Shreveport."

"These other folks," Lowell said, pushing forward another couple, "are active in the neighborhood association." Christie Carney had an Irish accent, dark, neglected hair, and wide-set eyes. Her husband, Phil Krankauer, "not related to the writer who wrote the book on Everest," he hastened to add, was a reporter for the *Washington Post*. "I had the environmental beat," he said, "and because of that, I met Tony and found out he lived in our neighborhood." Phil had brought his own wine and poured liberally.

"If you want one of us to run interference about that permit," Lowell said, "just send up a smoke signal."

"It may not be necessary," I said, lowering my voice. "I guess the doctor's telling him he won't make it till Christmas."

Lowell looked toward the living room and shook his head. "Such a shame."

Tony's back was toward us. Under the happy birthday sign stood Charles Gaudreau, duded up in a cowboy hat, boots, and shirt. A pizza slice drooped from his hand.

"Hey, babe," he said, winking. "Surprised?"

Babe? Since when?

"Don't they have pizza delivery in Vermont?" I said.

"Wouldn't want to miss a party."

Lillian, on the couch, couldn't keep her eyes off Charles. And, lo and behold, right next to her sat Aldo, his hands clasped between his knees. Lillian and Aldo, the Bobbsey twins. Whenever Lillian came down, Aldo showed up, too. No, I had to take that back. Lillian had come down once on her own to help Sandy pack for Koolfont. She'd even driven the van down by herself. I was just jealous. Lillian had a husband for moral support.

Charles handed me a paper plate. "I came down to visit my sister."

"Speaking of which." I looked at the empty couch. No Lisa. No crowd. "Where is everybody?" I said.

Sandy shook her head. "I don't know. I advertised it as an open house from two to five. *Sans* presents."

"Waste of money," Tony said.

Sandy opened the door for Alice, the neighbor with the mustache who walked with Sandy on Sunday mornings. Her jeans whisked together as she made straight for the food. Sean and Kevin, stationed near Tony in case he needed help, made small talk about sports. Every ten minutes, Sandy opened the door and looked down the block.

"Is Rosemary coming?" I said, hoping Sandy's high school running friend would show up. Besides Charles, Rosemary was the only one I really knew.

"No, her kids are down with strep," Sandy said.

"What about Penny and Bill?"

"They're getting a divorce." Sandy looked over her shoulder at Tony. Holding up a hand, she whispered, "He wanted kids and she didn't."

I remembered that from a weekend I'd spent with them two years ago. "But Rosemary's okay?"

"Third child on the way," she said. "It was an accident."

"Oh, geez," I whispered. "They're Catholic."

Tony, immobile in his wheelchair, stared into space, indifferent to whether anyone showed or not. After Rob's death couple-friends had provided tons of support, and I had assumed that Sandy's and Tony's best couple-friends—Rosemary and Chandler and Penny and Bill— would not just vanish. I had thought they would rearrange their lives to be there; but, of course, everyone was busy these days. Other people had lives to lead, including me.

"Hey, more people are arriving." Sandy held the screen.

Frank Delaney, Tony's college roommate, was the kind of person who never removed his sports coat, even in humid weather. His only concession to informality was to loosen his tie. The pouches under his eyes made him looked prematurely old, like a man who'd had a mediocre career and struggled to maintain some semblance of success. At American University where Tony and Frank had earned their bachelors' degrees, Frank had been President of the Young Republicans and Tony, President of the Young Democrats. I had never understood how Tony, so casual, and Frank, so uptight, had managed to get along, unless Noah, who'd been their third roommate, was the reason. Noah Flanagan, with his blond, shoulder-length, thinning hair, shuffled in, not looking at anyone as he sat down on the couch and opened his battered guitar case. Listening to Noah tune his instrument, I wondered if he ever sang in the Metro for a buck.

"I'm taking requests," Noah said.

Sandy looked toward the second floor where Ben slept. His birthday had been my last week of school. Sandy raised her eyebrows at Tony.

"Put the guitar away," Tony said.

"You don't want me to play?" Noah said.

Tony shook his head, no. "Ben's taking a nap right now."

"I wrote a new song just for you," Noah said. "It's my present."

"Instead of a present," Tony said, "I would rather you help me with one of my projects."

"Anything," Noah said.

"Sure, buddy." Charles closed the pizza box. "I can help, too."

"You gave me the idea of writing a story for my kids," Tony said. "*Ramón on the Cliff.*"

Charles laughed. "Your *roman á clef*, is that it?"

Tony nodded. "But with a Hispanic character, set in New Brunswick." He looked at me and winked.

"Not Canada. New Jersey," I said. "But, Tony, I thought you grew up in Camden."

"I'm changing the setting to protect the innocent," he said.

"I like it," Charles said. "The adventures of a kid from the 'hood."

"Yeah, right," I said. More like the adventures of a kid from a gated community. Tony had always had such a longing to escape his family's affluence. Now, his Hispanic alter ego could do it.

"Do you think I could get it published?" Tony said.

"If you finish it, I'll surely try to make that happen," Charles said.

Tony's other projects included taping his favorite music and putting together photo albums of the wedding, honeymoon, and vacations.

Lillian leaned forward and raised her hand. I thought of kindergartners during show-and-tell.

"Yes?" Tony said.

"Can I help with that?" she said.

"If you restrain yourself." He looked from his mother to Noah.

"What kind of music?" Noah said.

"Blues. Have you got any Lightnin' Hopkins, Brownie McGhee, Elmore James, or Chester Burnett? " Tony said.

"I've pretty much got whatever there is," Noah said.

Tony lifted his hands. The atrophy had turned them into hens' feet. Staring at them, Noah looked shell-shocked. In college he had made two suicide attempts, and Frank and Tony had pulled him through, taking turns blowing off classes, playing records, and reading from joke books.

"Will it offend anyone if I take off my coat?" Frank said.

"Suit yourself," Tony said.

Frank hesitated, then folded the coat and placed it carefully on the piano bench. "When do you want to do the taping?"

"As soon as Sandy fixes the turntable," Tony said. "She needs to buy me a computer so I can start on *Ramón*. And she keeps saying she's going to buy me a computer table, but so far she hasn't."

Lillian raised her hand.

"No," Tony said.

"But—" Lillian said.

"Tony, it's not that I don't want to help you," Sandy said. "I haven't had time." She opened the door and looked down the street, then checked her watch. It was five o'clock. "I expected people from Tony's office and the carpenter who built our addition."

"He was probably scared I'd bite his head off," I said. Poor Sandy. Too bad the guests hadn't all come, tripping over each other. I went back to the group near the food table.

Hoang and Sharon looked at each other. "We'd better get going. Don't mind us. We'll use the back stairs."

"I guess I'll head on out, too," Lowell said. "The room addition looks better on the inside than it does on the outside. How much did it run them?"

"Too much," I said.

"They should have built it two feet wider."

"Too late," I said.

Drinking the last of his wine, he handed the bottle to Phil. The reporter snapped his fingers and looked behind him at the screen door that had just slammed. "I should have brought a camera to record this for the neighborhood newsletter." His wife, Christy Carney, made a slight motion toward the door with her head. To emphasize her point, she raised a pale eyebrow and pointed at the bottle. Phil handed it to me and slid sideways toward the exit. I held the bottle to the light. All gone.

"Cut the cake," Tony said.

"What was that, dear?" Lillian said.

"Cut the cake," I said. Her thoughts must be flying all over the place. Maybe that's why she couldn't pick up three simple words.

"First, your presents," Sandy said. "Kevin and Sean, would you bring them up from the basement?"

The boys leapt up and returned a moment later. Sean put down a mahogany computer table. Tony's wheelchair could slide under it. Kevin had been waiting in the kitchen. Tony, smiling, turned to look for him, and he came out bearing a computer. He placed it on the table, unpackaged a white croquet-ball-sized mouse, and connected it. The mouse reminded me of the planet Saturn. Tony leaned forward and clicked the ring with his thumb.

"Happy birthday." Sandy brushed her lips across Tony's forehead and looked upstairs. "I guess we should sing."

"It might wake the baby," Lillian said.

"He needs to wake up," Sandy said, "or he'll never sleep tonight."

Ben never slept anyway.

Lillian carried a sheet cake to the table: white frosting with thin, blue stripes and writing that said, "Lou Gehrig's #1 Fan."

Tony stared at it. "I wish you wouldn't use every occasion to remind me."

Looking at him and frowning, Lillian asked me to repeat what he'd said. When I did, she turned her back and hung her head, steadying her chin with her fist. A few stalwarts sang an off-key "Happy Birthday," and Josh blew out the candles. Tony wheeled over to the table, strapped on the eating gizmo, and tried a bite of cake. He stopped eating, stared at the rest of his piece, and switched to ice cream. I talked to Sean, who'd had a rough week with one of his clients, a sixteen-year-old boy in fifth grade, and Kevin sat with Tony. I overheard them talking about the ant farm. Tony said Sandy had vetoed the idea of ants in the house. "Better than in your pants," Kevin said. Tony laughed and laughed and people looked at each other, trying to carry on their conversations.

"I need to catch a train," Charles said. He bent and gave Tony a kiss on the forehead and put an arm around Sandy and told her to "Hang in there, babe."

There was that "babe" again. Charles was beginning to annoy me. He'd swooped down from Vermont without any warning, no warning to me, at least, and I wondered what he was doing here.

The tub of ice cream had melted. Lillian sat at the head of the table, clutching the scoop and swishing it through the mush. When Tony told her to stop fooling around, she put the scoop down and wiped her eyes with a napkin.

"Stop the self-pity," Tony said, "and throw the rest of the cake away unless you're trying to choke me."

I translated.

"But there's half a cake left," Lillian said.

"It sticks in my throat."

A silent communication passed between Tony and Sandy.

"One piece of cake is enough for Josh," she said, "and if cake's around, my mom won't be able to resist temptation."

"You're talking about me?" I said.

"You're the only mom I've got." Sandy smiled.

Funny, I didn't like cake. I could gorge on ice cream and had been known to stand at the freezer, spoon in hand, but cake? No. Sandy had a faulty memory.

Lillian stood, picking up the cake from the table. I took the trash can from under the sink. The cake slid off its tray. Lillian squeezed my wrist. "I'm about to collapse."

I tensed my arm just as Lillian's knees buckled. I had thought "about to collapse" was just a metaphor. In Lillian's case, it meant about to fold up like a deck chair. With an arm around Lillian's waist, I led her toward the living room.

Aldo looked up from his crossword. "Had enough?"

Lillian nodded. "I can't wait till this is over."

"Don't worry about the clean-up," I said.

"Oh, no," Lillian said. "I meant the appointment with Bronfman."

"Who's that?"

"The lawyer I found through my ALS support group," Lillian said. "Would you mind if I talked with you privately?"

"Sure." Relief washed through me. I had waited months to hear those words. Now, we would get on the same page. We would communicate. Together, we would help our children through this crisis. I opened the front door.

"We're going to sit outside for a minute and get some fresh air," Lillian told Aldo. "Do you think I should wear a sweater?"

"Why even ask me that?" Aldo said. "I'm not your father." He walked over to the phone and picked up the handset. "I'll call a cab."

I closed the door, wishing Aldo would come out here, too.

Lillian took the porch's only chair. The other one had cracked. I should buy a new one.

"I just need a minute," she said.

I parked myself on the porch rail. "So, what is it?"

"Bronfman is drawing up Tony's will," Lillian said, "but most important, he's putting Tony's wishes about the respirator into language that will stand up in court when Tony can't act for himself."

"The lock-down stage," I said.

"Yes. He won't even be able to blink. Can you imagine?"

"The appointment might be a waste of time," I said. "I don't think the kids have had time enough to work this out as a couple."

"Every time I ask them if they've made an appointment," Lillian said, "they say they're too busy."

"They are," I said. "Sandy has a full-time job, plus they have doctors' appointments, and they're trying to live a somewhat normal life."

"Sandy told me you thought it would cost $300,000 a year for nurses, but we can go to this agency in New York and hire three illegal aliens for less than $3,000 a month to do round-the-clock care. We could rent an apartment for them down here in D.C. Even if the insurance won't pay for it, that's still not too much."

"Lillian, can't you let Tony and Sandy make this decision?"

"We could try it for six months," Lillian said, "and see how it goes."

"And if Sandy can't manage to take care of Tony and the kids, what then? Are you going to pull the plug, you personally, or Aldo? Because I don't think Sandy could do it. She loves Tony too much. Besides which, do you really think three illegals are going to have the technical skills?"

"Oh yes," Lillian said, leaning forward, wringing her hands. "I talked to the respirator company and they said they can train anyone to take care of a person on a respirator, even a family member."

"Lillian, I've been out to visit a woman who's taking care of her mother, and that's not what she said. It takes specialized nurses, people with experience, to listen to the chest of a person on a respirator and know when to suction them. I did some back-of-the-envelope calculations. I figure we'll need five people minimum. Three people can work eight-hour shifts, five days a week, but we'd need two others to cover weekends and sick days."

"Oh, but the respirator company said anyone can be trained."

"People who don't speak English? People who aren't even nurses?"

"It's a lot easier than you think. Tony says the reason Sandy thinks he shouldn't do it is because you're influencing her against him."

I rolled my eyes. "It would be a miracle if I could influence Sandy in anything," I said. "Months ago, I wrote up my notes from my visit with Joan Calabrese and her mother, but I haven't so much as said peep since then. I don't think Tony has bothered to inform himself about what this respirator thing is all about. It's pie in the sky to him."

"One of the men in our ALS support group is on a respirator and he plays bridge all day and there are a lot of people on-line using respirators. I wish Tony would let me teach him to play contract bridge."

Lillian's mind flitted like a small, high-strung bird's. My fingers curled around the porch rail. I could rip it right out and use the steel pieces to beat Lillian about the head. "Lillian, what would Tony's quality of life would be like on a respirator?"

"Tony's always been able to entertain himself. We can rent videos, and I've been thinking about getting cable TV, only Sandy's so opposed to television. Don't you think we'll have to eventually get a TV for the bedroom, when Tony's in bed? The ALS chat group has people living ten or twenty years on a respirator."

"Without being able to move, to scratch, or even communicate?"

"Stephen Hawking communicates," Lillian said. "Now that Tony has the computer, he can start using the voice simulator. I told him I can't understand him, and he got really mad at me. He said I don't listen."

"The computer won't speak for him, Lillian. He'll have to type it in. It's not like spontaneous conversation."

"You understand him."

"From context. Also, I listen."

"Our house is so much more accessible. Even with the room addition, Tony has such a tiny space."

Aldo opened the door. "Lillian, the taxi's almost here. Come inside and say good-bye."

Lillian stood. "We'll both feel better when he signs the paper."

"Will we?" I said. "I doubt it."

I held the door, and Lillian went inside, staggering across the living room and catching a heel on the carpet. Until Tony made the decision about the respirator, and stuck to it, Lillian would not let up. But her nagging paralyzed him. It would have been better if he'd rebelled, like most kids did, but that was not Tony's way. His way was to make no choice, and as long as he put it off, Lillian would keep hammering away with unrealistic scenarios of his future. When Lillian reached the wheelchair, she put her hand on top of Tony's head and mussed his hair. Out on the street, the taxi honked.

Aldo put his hand on Tony's shoulder and squeezed. "Good-bye, son."

Aldo offered Lillian his arm, and she took it. He led her to the door. Lillian looked back at Tony, framed by the arch and the sparkly sign. "Bye-bye for now."

"Have a safe trip," I said.

"Thanks," Aldo said, averting his eyes.

The respirator decision hung over everyone: Tony's parents, Sandy, and Tony himself. It was so hard to discuss, and it exposed everyone's protective impulses, me for my daughter and the life she could still have if Tony were not alive, and Lillian for her son and the life she saw him being urged to end. Outside on the porch, I leaned back against the wall. A mosquito bit my cheek. Another one landed on my arm. I smashed it.

I had just about made up my mind to go inside when I saw a truck from a furniture store double-park in front of the house. "Right this way," I called.

Delivery men lugged in a trundle bed. Once assembled, it took up a third of the floor space in the room addition. With the bottom bed pulled out, two-thirds of the floor would be covered. The Hoyer Lift and stacks of briefs and the suction machine would have to go in the dining room, just as they had at the Calabreses'.

I carried paper plates to the kitchen.

Sandy handed the baby off to Sean and he and Kevin took Ben and Josh downstairs to the basement. Then Sandy brought Tony's clothes from their room and, standing barefoot on the bed, began stowing them in wall cabinets. "I hope the four drawers I've cleared upstairs will be enough for you," she said.

"I'm just here for a few weeks," I said.

"I know, but you need to make a more permanent arrangement for your things."

"My clothes can stay in a suitcase."

"Don't leave your dirty jeans on a hook downstairs."

"Fine." I pushed down the garbage, crushing Lillian's cake.

Sean, holding a diaper by his fingertips, came upstairs. "Don't get into it, you two."

"We're not," Sandy said.

"Mom, I'll finish the kitchen," Sean said. "Why don't you go upstairs and relax?"

A corner of his mouth turned up. I never worried about him, but he, apparently, worried about me. I hesitated before heading upstairs to put my clothes away. Sandy ought to be glad I was going to tackle the job list. This wasn't exactly the way I'd spend the summer if I had my druthers. I'd be biking along the lake and swimming and going to the Chicago Symphony's lawn concerts at Ravinia. I'd be taking the El to Taste of Chicago. I'd be trying to track down Esmeralda. She'd probably had her baby by now and there was no reason she couldn't live in my house, especially since I wasn't there. Oh, well. There was always next summer. Tony wasn't going to live forever.

Sandy's and Tony's bedroom, now my temporary bedroom, struck me as having all the warmth of a cheap motel: gray walls, no pictures, crackled window shades. Sandy had a knack for transforming even the dingiest rental into a place that carried the stamp of her personality. That she hadn't done so was evidence, not just that she'd only recently moved, but that her energy was being diverted.

The room had a desk and two-drawer filing cabinet. I opened it. Crammed with disorderly files. The wicker basket on top of the desk overflowed with bills. I might leave my clothes on a hook, but deep down, I was an organized person. Sandy tucked away her clutter.

I slid open the drawers beneath the bed. Two were empty and two still held Tony's sweaters. Sandy had said she'd cleared four. Maybe she'd meant drawers in a closet. I opened a door. Tony's suits and dress pants, athletic shoes, and lacrosse sticks had been crammed in willy-nilly. This, I'd expected. When he was in law school downstate, his bachelor apartment had been a disaster, and he'd brought his laundry up to Chicago and expected Sandy to make me do it. I gave him a roll of coins, a box of detergent, and two laundry bags: one white and one black.

Just as I finished emptying my suitcase, Sandy bounced down on the bed. "Wasn't it great to see Charles?"

"That was an expensive trip for a three-hour stopover."

"Sean watched the kids last night," she said, "and I ducked out for dinner."

"With Charles?" I said.

"Charles and his sister," Sandy said. "It's no big deal. You always said you had a lot of guy friends."

"Watch out for him."

"Enough of that topic," Sandy said. "I guess I don't have to ask your permission."

Squatting, I began to refold my shirts. I didn't want to look at Sandy's face and see the glow that might once have shone from my own. My knees cracked. Closing the drawer, I sighed and stood up. I stepped across Sandy's legs and sat down in the desk chair, my first sit all day.

"Now, about Ben," Sandy said. "He's been coming home with big, red welts in his diaper area."

"What!" I said.

"The babysitter's from Lebanon. She says he has strong urine."

"Fire her."

"I don't have anyone to watch the kids."

"I can watch him till you find someone."

"You'll have to screen phone calls," Sandy said.

"Put an ad in."

The second semester of my junior year at the University of Illinois Urbana-Champaign, Rob had returned from school the day before final exams to find Sandy in a loaded diaper. She'd sat in it all day, thanks to

Mrs. Hosni, the Egyptian babysitter, an upper-class woman who'd had servants until she moved to the United States. Rob fired Mrs. Hosni on the spot. We'd known all along that Rob would be the provider. I had taken incompletes without a second thought. It wasn't till Sean turned two that I finished my degree, and by then, Rob had been dead almost three years.

***

The next morning, Sandy placed an ad for a nanny in the *Washington Post*. Because she had offered room and board as part of the salary, it seemed that word had gone out on a grapevine of the homeless. Sixty-six phone calls came in on Wednesday, the ad's first day, and I began to jump when the phone rang. Joan Calabrese had warned about staff turnover. I tried to imagine doing this to find nurses.

A week into the ordeal Maria, a nanny from some African country I had never heard of, emerged from the heap of applicants. Sandy was on her way out the door when she looked back at Tony. "I'll be home at four so we can interview the babysitter." Looking at me, she said, "Could you take the kids out somewhere?"

"Sure," I said. "I need to buy groceries."

The door closed. As soon as Josh picked up his puzzles, we'd be off to school. Ben was pulling himself up on the stroller.

"I wish she had asked me before making that appointment," Tony said.

"Why's that?" I stood behind him and leaned over the back of his chair.

"Because I don't like people presuming I'm available," Tony said, motoring over to his computer. "Come here. I want to show you something."

Tony had software that was supposed to help him write his book. He clicked on the image of a log cabin and the screen zoomed in on the front door. Inside was a cartoon desk with a bookcase behind it. He clicked on the bookcase and showed me how the volumes in the cabin could contain pictures, music, and text. He was already working on an avatar, a cartoon figure that looked just like him, down to the mutton-chop sideburns and mustache. He'd created a bedroom for the avatar. It had wood paneling and college pennants on the walls and a lacrosse stick in the corner.

"I figure I'll need six months on a respirator to complete this."

"Maybe you can get it done before that."

"My doctor thinks I'll need to have a respirator by Christmas, and I won't be done with the memoir by then."

"How many words have you typed so far?"

"Fifteen hundred," he said.

He clicked on the outline. I read the chapter titles: "Ramón Learns about Bullies," "Ramón Visits the Three Little Pigs' Farm," "Ramón Rides a Bike," and "Ramón's Fort."

"My parents don't know half the things that happened to me in my life."

"No parents do." I kept an eye on the kids in the living room. Josh had a new puzzle, and Ben was playing with his stacking donuts.

"College was such a relief," Tony said. "When I got there, I thought, 'Thank God, I escaped her scrutiny.'"

He meant his mother. Lillian would have been mortified if she'd known he felt like that. Tony hadn't yet been a parent long enough to realize that even loving parents can never know the inside of a child's mind. One of the great mysteries of parenthood was the vulnerability that came with such excruciating love. You opened your heart. You hoped. You tried. You were always in pursuit. The relationship was one-sided.

***

I took the children to the grocery store to give Sandy and Tony time for an interview, but when I returned, Maria, forty, in dreadlocks and a lilac running suit, jumped off the couch, startling me. Josh backed away. Maria unbuckled Ben and took him from his stroller. She emptied a canvas bag of playthings on the floor.

Josh leaned over to look at the pull toys. "Those are for babies."

Maria, as if by magic, produced a toy *Tyrannosaurus rex*, holding it in her palm. "I heard a little boy in this house plays with these."

Sandy smiled. "Could that be you, Josh?"

Josh, pressed against my knees, held his hand out for the toy. Maria sat on the floor and played, but a second after she left, Tony said, "It's easy to buy kids off, and that's what the bag of toys was all about. I'm not sold on her." Sandy said she liked her. Tony asked Sandy to check references, but Maria's references came from Spanish Equatorial Guinea. The head-of-household traveled for his company. The mom had gone back to Africa for a visit. Tony refused to let Sandy make the hire. Listening to them argue—Tony powerless to call references because no one could understand him on the phone, and Sandy unwilling to break the logjam by overruling him—I thought I would lose my mind. I faced another week of multi-tasking: watching the kids and taking care of Tony. I had a lot of energy, but doing both jobs drained me. It was hard to believe I'd ever had another life. Maybe it was good I hadn't let Esmeralda move in. What I wanted most was to sit in my living room and listen to Coltrane or maybe sit out on my porch when it thundered.

Grabbing my phone, I stepped out on the porch, cupping my hand over the receiver. "Maureen, I'm afraid I'm going to be stuck here in the fall if my daughter can't make a decision about a babysitter."

"Reality check, girlfriend. You're not seriously thinking of quitting a teaching job to become a babysitter are you?"

"No, I'm not, but my feet are in quicksand, and I need you to throw me a rope."

"Make sure you give Sandy a definite cutoff date," Maureen said. "You need some recovery time before school starts."

"Do I ever." That's what summers were for. That, and to get crafts organized for the school year. The plastic bins where I stored pipe cleaners, plaster of Paris, and Elmer's glue needed to be replenished. The only egg cartons I had were plastic. I needed split peas for *papier-mâché* rattles.

When I came inside, Tony said, "I'm as unhappy as you that you're still here."

"Tony, I'm not unhappy," I said. "I'm just worried I'm going to have to keep taking care of you and the kids forever, and I can't do both jobs."

"I don't see what's so hard about taking care of me," he said.

"You spend five hours a day eating," I said. "I'm chained to a chair."

"Well, so am I," he said.

"If you wanted to you could still walk."

"Not very well," he said.

At last, Maria's former employer called back. The man had six children, teenagers now, and Maria had raised them from the time they were babies. He called her the "Mary Poppins of babysitters." And, yes, Maria had papers. Sandy wouldn't have the Zoë Baird problem.

"She's a con artist," Tony said. "Ask for more references."

"You're being unreasonable," Sandy said. "Maria will start tomorrow."

Finally, she was showing some gumption.

***

The next morning Maria came dressed in a purple sweatshirt, a garbage bag of clean clothes slung over her shoulder. During the week she would sleep in the basement's back room, and on the weekends, she'd return to her relatives'. Marching around the living room, she banged a pan with a wooden spoon.

"It's Purple Day," she proclaimed. "Everyone who wear purple can win."

Josh, pumping his fist, stopped eating his cereal and ran upstairs to find a purple tee-shirt. "I win! I win!"

I thought about how pleased Esmeralda had been with her purple satin blouse. There was something life-giving about the color. "How about a picnic to celebrate Purple Day?" I said.

Tony rolled his eyes.

"Come on," I said. "You haven't left the house in ages."

"Oh, all right," he said. "My purple tee-shirt is in the right-hand cabinet."

By the time everyone was ready to start their day, Ben wore purple socks and Sandy a purple business dress. Buoyed by Purple Day, I said, "So, Tony, shall we ditch the wheelchair?"

Tony reared back, opening his eyes.

"You can still walk," I said. "If not, I'll do a fireman's carry."

"What's that?" Tony said.

"A horsey-back ride."

He shook his head. "I'd rather go under my own steam."

At lunchtime, I parked in Georgetown library's handicapped space. Tony would have a short walk, Sandy said, and she could take the shuttle from Foggy Bottom. Across the street from the library, a path led down the sideline of a soccer field, and Maria, pushing Ben in the stroller, hurried after Josh who was already running toward the playground at the far end. With my arm around Tony's waist, I carried most of his weight while he lurched, step by step, across the hundred yards of grass. Glad to reach the picnic tables, I lifted his legs over the bench and gasped for breath, then straightened up, listening to my spine crackle like Rice Krispies. Not good.

"Tony, I'll be with you in a second." I walked over to the playground where Maria had kicked off her shoes. She had Ben in a baby swing. Josh scooted down a slide.

"Don't know if you've noticed, but there's a lot of tension in the house," I said. "Thanks so much for taking the job."

Maria took my hand and turned it over, tracing my lifeline in her palm. She smiled as if she saw a future happiness I didn't yet imagine.

"I thought the job might be too hard," Maria said, "but then I see your daughter, and I think, I can help her." She looked toward the yew hedge that bordered the park. Sandy, in her purple dress, walked through an opening in the shrubs.

"Tony is like a child sometimes," I said.

Maria grabbed Ben's swing, held it a moment, then released it. Ben laughed. "We make a tower," Maria said. "Tony sit on your shoulder, Sandy sit on top of him. I sit on her, and Josh and Ben on top of me. That how we do it."

"Like in a circus," I said, wondering which of the three rings we were performing in today.

Over at the table, I watched Sandy embrace Tony. They spoke for a moment, and then Sandy came toward the slide. Seeing his mother, Josh ran toward the jungle gym, and after climbing to the top stood, his shoes cupped over the bars. He threw his hands above his head.

"Look at me, Mom. Tony, look at me."

Tony? Not Dad?

Tony made a snuffling sound, half-laugh, half-cry.

Maria, barefoot in the sand, carried Ben to the monkey bars. A moment later, Sandy went to get him. He buried his face in Sandy's breast. Returning to eat her lunch and seated on the picnic bench, she unbuttoned. Tony smiled and she smiled back, and that look, the deep current of love that ran beneath the craziness of a working mother's life, gave me hope. This was a rare treat for Sandy, seeing her family in the middle of the day. I fixed Tony's plate, put the gizmo on his hand, and after Sandy had fed Ben, I followed her to the swings.

"I have a business trip coming up," Sandy said. "If you want to tag along, you can."

"To babysit?" I said.

"No. Just the two of us," Sandy said. "Lisa said she'd come down for Tony, Sean will take care of Ben, and Lillian will spoil Josh like she always does."

"Where is it?" I said.

"Cincinnati," Sandy said. "I know it's not exactly a tourist destination, but they're supposed to have a good art museum."

"When is it?"

"I have to look at my calendar." Sandy turned to go.

"Do you think Lisa can handle Tony?"

"Realistically?" Sandy sighed. "No. It was probably a stupid idea."

My heart sank to my stomach and I wondered why I hadn't immediately said, "What a great idea." Putting the food away, I thought about the pyramid. Probably Sandy thought that she herself stood at the bottom of the pyramid, the weight of all our needs and demands on her shoulders. But whether it was Sandy on the bottom or me, however you arranged the pyramid, the weight was a crushing burden, moreso all the time. We needed to work together, or the pyramid would collapse.

Sandy kissed Tony and the children good-bye. Josh ran back to the monkey bars. Maria asked Tony if she could bring the kids home later.

He smiled. "Okay, but make sure they take naps."

I gave Maria a thumbs-up and helped Tony to his feet. Squinting toward the far end of the park, Tony acted like a golfer approaching the green. Although his thighs were still the size of hams, he dithered about covering the distance a second time and nodded toward a spiky, iron fence that separated the park from a graveyard. "Let's walk over there."

"It's fifty yards further," I said.

"I know, but I can lean on the fence and rest."

I lifted his arm around my neck and encircled his waist. It really would have been easier to give him a horsey-back ride than have him lurch along, his weight throwing me off balance. Pain shot through my lower back. I stopped to rest beneath a magnolia with white, singed flowers. Tony panted.

"I had a dream that Sandy and I were canoeing," he said.

"Are you thinking about your past life today?" I said.

"My past life seems like an impossible dream. Doing laundry. Cooking dinner. Playing wiffle ball with Josh."

"You were happy then."

"I know," he said. "The happiest man in the kingdom."

"Let's get out more. Go to a movie."

Breathing hard, he let his head drop against my shoulder. I could smell his hair. Peppermint.

"You're a great comfort to me," he said.

"Thank you," I said.

"No, thank you," Tony said. "Thank you very, very much for a wonderful day."

I laughed and struggled on toward the car. I had felt like a thorn in his side, but I could see what he meant because really, who else could he talk to if he didn't have me.

CHAPTER 14

Before Tony's ALS he had, indeed, been the happiest man in the kingdom, as I had seen when I came out to spend a weekend with Tony, Sandy, and some friends at Lost River State Park. It was October, a year and a half after Josh's birth, and in the mountains of West Virginia a cold snap had already sucked the sap from the maples, leaving their canopies aflame. Skirting a field where a rusty green tractor plowed under the broken stalks of corn, I drove past the cedar-sided ranger station. For the past seven or eight years, Sandy had bragged about this park, a hidden gem, so close to D.C. and yet so far away. With stone fireplaces and hand-hewn logs, the park's cabins hadn't changed since the days of the Civilian Conservation Corps. The scent from pine trees wafted through the car's open window. Sandy, in shorts and a running singlet, pounded down the road. I flashed my lights and wigwagged an arm out the window.

She bent in, kissing my cheek. "Hooray, reinforcements."

"You need reinforcements?" I said.

"Not really," she laughed. "Tony's got it under control. He took Josh to the swings." She squeezed sweat from her running singlet. "I went out on a trail run. I'd better get going before I cool off."

By the time I'd parked the car she was far down the road, her ponytail swinging, her white singlet aglow in the fading light. Across from the ranger station, I saw a teeter-totter and swings with twenty-foot chains and wooden seats, wide enough for a person and a half. Tony sat in one with Josh, dressed warmly in a yellow moon suit and sitting on Tony's lap. I helloed and Tony helloed back. Next to Tony, a boy of nursery school age sat on a swing by himself. I recognized the stocky, bearded man behind him. "Chandler. I didn't expect to see you here."

"Hi, Mrs. Gallagher. Long time no see." He tipped his baseball cap.

Bald and a decade older than his wife Rosemary, a girl who'd been on Sandy's high school cross country team, Chandler taught at a private high school in D.C. I'd gone to their wedding, the last time I'd attended a Catholic mass. "How are you doing?" I said.

"How you doing?"

"Life's a little hectic," I said. "I just moved my mom into one of those retirement places. Boxes and boxes of stuff and three weekends of garage sales."

"Is she happy?" I said.

"Yes, she loves it," Chandler said. "Lots of people around. Activities 24/7. I haven't seen her smile so much in years."

"Well, good," I said, wondering what it would be like to live surrounded by people.

"Are you still teaching?" he said.

"Of course," I said. "Still kindergarten."

"This here's Taylor." He gave the swing a push. "He'll be starting school before long. Rosemary took Malcolm up to the cabin."

"And who's Malcolm?" I said.

"He's their baby," Tony said. "Nine months old. Did you have any trouble finding the place?"

"It was a pretty straightforward drive."

"We were hoping you'd get here earlier." Tony walked his swing back and lifted his feet.

The swing's pendulum made Josh slip. Tony hoisted him up.

"We took a hike up to the top of that ridge." Chandler pointed to the mountain behind him. "It was a bit much for Taylor." He gave his son another push. "Tuckered him out, didn't it buddy."

"Buddy". I don't why, but it bothered me when parents called their kids "buddy". There was time enough to be best friends later.

Plucking his red flannel shirt, Chandler said, "It's gonna be dark in half an hour. Did you bring a jacket?"

"I left it in the car."

"Chandler scored on the cabins," Tony said. "We got the old ones."

"My mom came last year, and she loved it," Chandler said. "Don't know if you remember her from the wedding, but she remembers you. We were going to bring her again so you'd have someone to hang out with, but she already had plans."

I didn't remember his mother from the wedding and wondered how she could possibly remember me. I wasn't that memorable. "I'm happy to hang out with you guys," I said. "I don't get to see Josh that often."

"Give us a push, will you?" Tony walked the swing back. I moved behind him. Josh squirmed around and stood on Tony's legs. Craning over Tony's shoulder, thumbnail dimples creasing his cheeks, he reared back and looked from his father's face to mine.

"That's your grandma," Tony said. "Say grandma. Graaand-ma."

"Am-maw," Josh said.

"He's talking?"

"Just a few words, but he's picking up steam."

"You'd better sit him down if you want a push," I said.

I grasped the swing seat and ran forward, ducking under it.

"Whoa! Hey! Next time give me some warning," Tony said.

"Is that too high?" Facing them, I stood in the damp grass, surrounded by a cloud of orbiting gnats. I shook my head, blew puffs of air, and batted my face. "I need to move."

Tony dragged his feet and stopped the swing. "I should get dinner organized."

The sun fell behind the pine-covered ridge. "What a beautiful place," I said.

Tony lifted Josh onto his shoulders. "The accommodations are a little primitive."

"Primitive's my middle name." I shivered and clapped my arms.

Inside the car I turned on the heat. Its headlights illuminated the silhouettes of the two men, one with a baby on his shoulders and the other holding Taylor's hand. Half a mile uphill Tony turned and pointed to a parking space. Beyond it, a dirt path led up to a log cabin. When they'd made it to the porch, I turned off the headlights.

Against a backdrop of black, the cabin's windows with their red-and-white checkered curtains hung like four suspended cafe tables. I groped toward the light and stumbled on the steps. A door to the right opened into another century: foot-wide logs and a soot-blackened fireplace tall enough for the syrup kettle hanging from a giant hook. Kerosene lanterns flickered on the mantle. Tony had put Josh down on a high double bed. After removing the moon suit, he taped a diaper. Sandy bent over a backpack, throwing children's sweaters, pajamas and tee-shirts onto the mattress.

"Damn it," Sandy said. "That's his last clean outfit."

Tony snapped the straps of Josh's overalls, tied his shoes, and put him on the floor.

"I packed five or six," Tony said.

"Let's hope he doesn't blow out a diaper."

From Sandy's profile, I could see the walnut of muscle just below her ear. I backed quietly out the door. Sandy turned. "Oh. Hi, Mom." She handed me the empty backpack and told me to put it outside.

Josh was crawling toward the hearth. I stepped across the stacking donuts and pull toys and grabbed him. "Hey, big guy, let Grandma get a good look at you."

"You can put him down," Sandy said.

"The floor doesn't look all that clean."

"We brought a Pack 'n Play." Tony pointed to the folded crib. "Why don't you set that up?"

"I'd rather have her start the fire," Sandy said. "Everybody's going to show up in a minute, and the cabin's freezing."

I looked from the fireplace to the folded crib. If I was supposed to start a fire, Josh couldn't be crawling on the floor. I pulled the crib apart and the bottom dropped into place. With a trestle table, two half-logs for benches, the bed, and an empty rocking chair, the only place for a crib was right in front of the fire.

"Where do you want this?" I said.

"In the corner next to the bed," Sandy said.

I carried it over and put Josh in it, along with some toys. He settled down to play. The crib reminded me of the gorilla enclosures at the Lincoln Park Zoo. Pretty soon Josh wasn't going to be too happy about being confined.

"Did you guys bring wood?" I said.

"They have some on the back porch," Tony said. "They provide everything."

Outside, I found a hatchet and a box of kindling. Kneeling on the hearth I made a tent of splintered pine and struck a match. I leaned down to blow.

"As soon as you finish that, can you help Tony with dinner?" Sandy said.

I brushed off my hands. "What are you going to do?"

"Take a shower," Sandy said, "as soon as whoever's in there comes out."

Besides the kitchen, I didn't see any other rooms. "Where is the shower?"

"In the breezeway," Sandy said. "The toilet's separate if you have to use it."

"I do."

When I returned I found Tony assembling a pan of *chilaquile*. A faulty hinge on the oven-door squealed. Shoe-sized holes had worn through the linoleum in front of the sink where I stood washing stacks of dishes. Two friends from the cabin up the road came in. Bill, a curly-haired lawyer in a pink cashmere sweater, worked for the Sierra Club. He and Tony had started out as law interns working for one of Ralph Nader's Public Interest Research Groups. Now, Bill worked for the Federal Trade Commission. His wife Penny, with hazel eyes magnified by owlish glasses, was also a lawyer. "Corporate," she said, looking at me as I stood in the doorway drying my hands.

"She works for the bad guys," Tony said, "but makes tons of money compared to the rest of us. She gives us intelligence."

"Oh, a mole," I said.

From across the breezeway came high-pitched shrieks. Penny turned.

"What on earth is that?" I said.

"That's Malcolm," Sandy said. "A tooth's coming in."

"It sounds like he's being dismembered," Bill said.

"Josh wakes up screaming almost every night," Tony said.

"Really?" Penny said, her eyes growing large behind her glasses. She looked at Bill. "Reality check, honey."

"It's getting warm in here." He pulled the sweater over his head.

Tony looked at Bill. "You can get used to anything if it's your own kid."

Sandy flipped the light switch. Kerosene lamps bathed the logs in amber light. The fire cast wavy shadows on the ceiling.

I looked at Sandy, putting folded clothes in a small dresser next to their bed. In shorts and a running singlet, she must be cold. "Do you still want to take a shower?"

"I'll do it after dinner," she said. "Taylor's in there and the water heater's small."

On the far side of the bed I heard the crash of a wooden puzzle. Josh's cowlick was just visible. On the mantel sat a pile of board books. If I took Josh out, we'd never get him back in confinement.

Chandler, droplets of moisture on his beard, knocked and opened the door. "All right if I come in?"

"Sure," Tony said. "Dinner's almost ready."

Looking at the fire, Chandler unbuttoned his flannel shirt, took off his baseball hat, and ran his hand across his scalp.

The three adults at the table insisted I take the straight-backed chair at the head. Rosemary, Sandy's high school friend, a girl with a beautiful spirit and a mother who second-guessed her daughter's every step, shut the door. "Hey, Colleen. Long time."

"It has been," I said, standing to give her a hug. Low on her cheek sat a mole that looked like a beauty mark. Despite disabling bunions on both feet, she'd run on the cross country team with Sandy; not the fastest runner but consistent, finishing in the top five no matter what the distance. Shin splints or muscle pulls had laid Sandy low. For weeks she'd have to practice in the pool. When she raced, she did better at longer distances, almost winning, but never quite. Not a runner myself, I had wondered about the psychology of the two girls: if Sandy thought she had to win, and thereby pushed herself beyond her limit, and if Rosemary might have won if she'd let herself believe she could. For a time, Rosemary and I had kept track of each other, and I had been invited to their wedding, though Sandy had to miss it because law school graduation fell on the same weekend. Rosemary, a stay-at-home mom, lived in Maryland, where Chandler taught high school chemistry. In touch for a little over a year, she and Sandy had picked up where they'd left off. Rosemary was one of those solid, Midwestern girls that I thought of as a friend of the heart.

I took salad and passed the bowl.

"Here's to a weekend away from the rat race," Bill, the lawyer with the pink sweater, said. He reached for the wine bottle and uncorked it with a pop. Plastic glasses were held out and he poured.

Tony looked toward the kitchen. "I can get the glass glasses."

"Last year they only had three," Sandy said. "That's why I brought plastic ones."

Tony picked up his. "We can always wash them."

"Sure." Bill swirled his wine. "Nader would approve."

"Is dinner ready?" Sandy said.

"Yeah, I'll bring it out."

Over in the corner I could see Josh, a tired prizefighter in the corner of his crib. He sucked the satin hem of his blanket.

Tony dropped the casserole on the table. Josh stood up and began to whimper.

"I'd better eat fast," Sandy said. She helped herself to the casserole and took three bites.

Josh let out a wail.

Bill and Penny looked at each other.

"Thank God for birth control," Penny said.

"Yeah," Bill said, half-heartedly. "I guess having kids is a lot of work."

"It's not that bad," Rosemary said.

"Yeah, but you stay home, don't you?" Penny said.

"I do," she said evenly, her eyes down on her plate. Even in high school, she'd been a slow eater. A peanut butter sandwich took an hour.

Sandy lifted Josh from the playpen and carried him to the table.

"Give him to me." Tony held out his arms.

"No, you eat," Sandy said. "I'll eat after I've nursed him."

When she lifted her singlet, Josh dove for her breast.

Bill and Penny looked at each other. Penny nudged her glasses up the bridge of her nose.

With the arms of his pink sweater draped across his shoulders, as if designating him to start the conversation, Bill of the curly hair mentioned his wife's brother, a reporter on assignment in Paris, and the latest projects of his wife's mother, a fine woodworker. She had made them a basswood dining table.

"Sounds fishy," Tony said.

Smiling, Sandy slapped Tony's arm. "Oh, stop it."

"I've never heard of basswood," I said.

"It's some exotic wood she found."

"Those come out of the rain forest, you know," Tony said.

I helped myself to the casserole and looked at Penny. "Is your mom a furniture designer?"

"Thank you." Penny took the serving spoon. "No, she has her PhD in Chemistry. She's also a medical doctor. On the side she does some research."

"On what?"

"On the electrochemical impulses that trigger Tourette's syndrome."

"That's impressive."

"They're all geniuses in her family," Bill said.

"She's got her fingers in a million pies," Penny said.

Bill turned to look at the skull of a deer mounted above the fireplace and sighed. "She made just one, small miscalculation. The table's about a foot too big in both directions. It looks great, but when we pull out our chairs, they scrape the wall."

"My mom says I should buy a bigger house," Penny said.

"For two people?" Tony said.

"She just wants us to buy a place that's swanky enough for *Fine Woodworking*."

"What does a magazine have to do you buying a bigger place?" I said.

"She wants them to come photograph her table," Bill said.

"That's crazy," I said.

With a twitch at the corner of her mouth, Sandy glanced at Tony. His mouth flattened. She switched Josh to her other breast.

Eyes glued to her nipple, Bill cleared his throat. "I, uh ..."

Penny wiped her mouth with a napkin. "Is RCRA funding going to make it through committee?"

"RCRA. Oh, RCRA's ridiculous. That's just a total disaster," Sandy said, livening up. "But you know who's got barrels of cash? Transportation. Have you heard about Iced Tea?"

"I have, but I thought that just went for IDOT projects," Penny said.

They went on flinging acronyms and I sat quietly, fascinated by the passion of these young lawyers. Bureaucratic gossip and insider mumbo jumbo about contract money and the end of the budget year: I wondered if this was how Sandy spent her days. I would have gone out of my mind.

"And what about your hobbies?" Penny looked at me.

"You gotta be kidding," I said. "I barely get done what I absolutely need to."

"Do you work?" Penny said.

"She's a kindergarten teacher," Sandy said.

"Oh," Penny said. "We need more teachers."

"My mom's the original hippie," Sandy said.

"I am not."

"It wasn't an insult," Sandy said. "It's just that you've always been such a free spirit."

Me? Not hardly. I folded my arms over my chest.

Josh had fallen asleep and Sandy handed him to Tony. "I'm done. Put him in bed."

Cradling Josh in his arms, Tony carried him to the corner.

Penny held the wine bottle over my plastic cup. "Want some more?"

"Don't mind if I do." I held up my hand at the halfway mark, and when I'd taken a sip, I said, "Not everyone who came of age when I did was a hippie. It would be more accurate to say I was a 'women's libber'."

"Oh, one of those bra burners," Chandler said. "I guess you used to march in parades. My dad told me all about it. My mom was the same way."

"No parades." I'd come in at the tail end of consciousness raising. Women owned their bodies. Okay, so I'd had the free love thing going for a while there, but I hadn't wanted it. Professional advancement, husbands who pitched in, deferred childbearing: all that came later. It was what we'd imagined might be possible for our daughters.

"Women's lib was just something I quietly believed," I said. "Mostly, I was trying to keep a roof over our heads."

"My mom worked the whole time I was growing up," Sandy said. "If we have another kid, I'm going to take six months off and be a proper mom."

"Can you do that?" Brow furrowed, Rosemary leaned forward.

"They just passed the Family Leave Act," Sandy said. "I'm going to see if it's for real."

"I'm always scared that if anything happened to Chandler, I'd be screwed," Rosemary said. "I wish I'd gone straight into nursing. Now I've forgotten every bit of science I ever knew."

"Isn't your mom a nurse?" Sandy said.

"She is," Rosemary sighed. "What I'd like is a job I could do part-time. I don't even know what that would be. I have no skills."

"I had this weird thing happen last night," I said, "and on the drive up here from the airport, it was on my mind. A homeless woman my age, fiftyish or thereabouts, gray hair in a bun, dressed in slacks and wool pants, unlike me," I said, sweeping a hand across my jeans and tee-shirt, "had been selling *Streetwise* in front of the Borders in downtown Evanston. I gave her a buck for a paper and told her to come in and we'd sit and have a cup of coffee. I asked her how she became homeless, thinking she was well-dressed, and probably it was divorce that had put her on the streets.

"Back in the day," I told her, "we always used to say women were one man away from poverty."

"I once had a husband who built robots," she said. "He moved to outer space."

Everyone laughed.

Sandy's lips narrowed.

"I'm not lying," I said.

I caught a smoldering look, then her eyes locked on mine. "New subject."

"Is the subject of homeless women off limits?" I said.

"You're dominating the conversation."

"No, she's not," Penny protested.

I looked at Penny. She had taken off her glasses to clean the lenses.

"The reason I even mention it," I said, "is that I don't even know why I asked a homeless person to have coffee. I think it was something in her face. She didn't look dangerous or threatening."

"Just because a person's poor doesn't mean they're dangerous," Tony said.

"Please, Tony." I held up my hands. "Do I have to be politically correct every minute of the day?" I looked at Penny's big eyes and at Rosemary's sweet, nonjudgmental smile. "You know how hard it is to sit down and talk to a stranger in the first place, and then if that person appears to be mentally ill, it's another barrier. That's why it sort of surprised me when it turned out she was."

"Mom," Sandy said. "Enough!"

There were other things about the woman I wanted to tell. She had grown up in Park Ridge, for instance. Married and had a daughter who worked downtown for the American Bar Association. The woman had joined her husband in the space ship for a while, but she had not found the food to her liking. "You know what frozen, chopped spinach looks like when it's just been thawed?" she'd asked. I did. What woman hadn't made spinach dip for at least one Super Bowl game? "That's what they eat every meal." She leaned across the table conspiratorially. "They take it without salt."

"Do they microwave it?" I said, barely able to keep a straight face.

"No. They take it cold."

I nodded. "I could see that would get boring."

The other custom she didn't approve of was that men and women could sleep with whomever they pleased. In the spaceship's pods, located around the perimeter of the vessel and into which she had to crawl on her hands and knees, sometimes you'd find three or four people already asleep, and you had to curl up next to them. She didn't like sharing a blanket. That was an additional reason she'd asked to leave. No privacy.

"I brought pumpkins to carve," Tony said. "We could do that after dessert."

"Oh, dessert." Penny patted her stomach. "I'm stuffed."

"Let's not do pumpkins," Sandy said, clearing plates. "That's a whole different activity and it'll make a mess."

Tony, holding the empty casserole, blocked the kitchen door. "When can we do it?"

"In the morning," Sandy said. "If breakfast doesn't take too long. We have to be out of here by ten."

Chandler returned with a pan of apple Betty. While they debated whether to heat it or eat it cold, the table was cleared and dessert plates clattered. Tony grabbed the dessert. "I'm going to heat it," he said. "Executive decision." The oven door shrieked. Josh stirred. I went over to the crib and stroked his back. The fire needed a couple of logs. With an andiron, I redistributed the coals. Flames leapt up. Sandy grabbed a towel and said not to wait. She was finally going to take a shower. Tony called out that the men might as well do dishes. In the kitchen, Chandler and Tony talked sports, and the cart of conversation shoved back and forth so it would appear to have momentum. Every so often, Bill said, "Where does this go?" and Tony answered, "Anywhere. It doesn't matter."

Rosemary undid her ponytail and shook her hair loose. Leaning forward she whispered, "This is the first break I've had all day."

"It's hard with a baby," I said.

"When Malcolm's not teething, he's pretty mellow."

"Time for dessert." Tony brought ice cream from the freezer and Rosemary took the pancake turner. There was twice as much food as we could eat. I thought of the woman selling *Streetwise*. In retrospect, what amazed me about our interaction was how easy it had been for me to slip into her frame of reference. If you accepted her premise that spaceships existed, then everything she said made complete sense.

CHAPTER 15

Tony needed attention, that was obvious, but I had stood in my daughter's shoes—kids tugging at me, a heavy workload—and Sandy was desperately in need of help, too. Sandy earned too much for Tony to qualify for Medicaid, and I could not see him in a nursing home with old folks in diapers. That left family. My ear became attuned to Tony's speech. Like learning a foreign language, I could almost always understand him. I don't know how that happened. Maybe just knowing him better or looking at the expression in his eyes. That took some of the pressure off Sandy, his sole translator.

Most nights I fell in bed wearing my clothes. In the morning, I came down in a tee-shirt and sweat-shorts, not really caring if I dressed or not. I opened the instant coffee and thought about my Braun grinder and the clove-like smell of fresh-roasted beans. Tony had vetoed a grinder and coffee maker so I was getting by with instant. In went the coffee crystals, clink went the spoon in the mug. I filled the mug with water. Another day, another fifty cents, or in my case, no cents.

Sandy picked up a shoe from beneath her bed, flexed the sole, and made a puppet. "My Mom has been so busy, she had to patch me with Odor Eaters." Sandy pitched the shoe into the kitchen. I caught it. The leather felt wet. Sandy lobbed another wet one, and I threw the shoes in the garbage. "I'll have to wear my tennies until I can manage to buy a new pair," she said.

Tony, in his eating place at the side of the dining room table—the head was reserved for the official "feeder"—looked up from his Grape-Nuts. His puppy-like gaze tracked his wife, holding her briefcase and springing along in her unlaced running shoes. Spoon dangling from the eating gizmo, he backed away from the table and motored towards her.

"Don't I get a kiss?" he said.

Sandy pecked him on the forehead, but he insisted on a full-mouth kiss. The first one didn't satisfy him, and he demanded a second.

"I'll miss my bus," Sandy said.

"Work," he said. "That's all you think about." Tony wheeled around, returned to the table, and grunted for me to turn the page in the sports section.

Josh came running downstairs. "I want you to walk me to school, Mommy."

After tying her shoes, Sandy stroked his cheek. "Mommy doesn't have time this morning," she said. "Maria or Grandma can take you."

"I can't leave Tony," I said.

Marylee MacDonald

Upstairs I heard Maria speaking Spanish to Ben, *"Tus zapatos nuevos son muy bonitos!"*

My high school Spanish flashed up from the deep freeze. New shoes.

"Why don't you buy shoes on your way home?" I told Sandy.

"I will," Sandy said, "if you can handle Tony and the kids."

"Catch a movie, too."

"That's not fair," Tony said.

"You want to see a movie?" I said. "We'll go this afternoon."

"It's not the same."

Sandy's grimace said, I've reached my limit. She pulled her bottom eyelid, her eyeball a glass of merlot. "Gross," I said. With the corner of her mouth an almost-smile, she picked up her briefcase. Maria took the kids downstairs, and I picked up Josh's discarded pajamas and Ben's puzzles.

"So, Tony, which movie are we going to?"

"I'm too busy," he said. "There's a game on TV."

"If it doesn't go too long, we could still squeeze one in," I said, "depending on what you want for lunch."

"Instead of always doing things for Sandy, maybe you could do some things for me for a change. Down in the basement should be some boxes of photographs," he said. His mom was buying albums, but she'd throw the pictures in any-which-way, and he wanted me to sort the pictures by year. And he wanted the turntable brought up, too. The old Garrard didn't work so I could put fixing that on my list. Noah said he'd help tape music, but he'd need the turntable hooked up to the tape deck, which I'd find tucked away in the dining room buffet. "Of course, if you're too busy doing things for Sandy—"

"I can do it," I said.

I asked if he had any idea where to look for photos.

"I don't have the faintest idea," Tony said. "I haven't been downstairs in months. Oh, I need you to find my albums, too."

Finding the photos and turntable, let alone the records, would take time. I had come here to help, not be an indentured servant. Tony expected me to function as his arms and hands, and suddenly, he had a raft of projects, things he could very well have completed before he became so incapacitated. I felt the weight of these cinderblocks on my shoulders and wondered if Tony had loaded me up because I'd given Sandy a night off. Sandy needed time away, but I did, too.

He finished the last of his Grape-Nuts and held out his hand for me to unsnap the eating gizmo.

Next, his socks. I went to the bedroom, climbed on the bed, and opened the cupboard. Tony motored over. Looking down at him in his navy shorts and with his bloated feet, I held up a pair of white tube-

166

socks. He shook me off like a pitcher not liking the catcher's call. I went through three dozen pair. My mug of instant coffee sat on the counter getting cold. I decided to play a trick on him and looped back to the beginning. On the third try he nodded. The ribbed ones.

Lillian lived for the privilege of standing and nervously turning to see if Tony approved of the socks she held up for him; and Sandy, who dressed him on weekends, was a pushover. We three found it hard to draw any kind of line with Tony. He always reminded you he was dying. Because of his swollen, spider-webbed feet, the skin purple from poor circulation, he could only wear open-backed shoes. I crammed on his Birkenstocks.

Finally, time for my instant coffee. I opened the microwave. Maybe I wasn't being fair. Tony had as much right as any man to choose his socks. Before he'd come down with ALS, he must have pulled out his bureau drawer, taken a quick glance, and reached in. From his wheelchair, he couldn't see his choices.

Now that I was up, I needed to justify my existence and fix that window in the bedroom. I could park Tony in front of the widescreen television his parents had recently purchased. I turned it on. The Yankees. In 1994 the team had outpaced the Orioles, but there were rumors of a players strike. A diversion would keep Tony from giving me more to do. Upstairs, sweating, I worked a screwdriver around the lower sash and removed the screws from the weight pockets. After tying a fishing sinker to a monofilament line, I dropped the lead weight over the pulley. Geez, D.C .was hot at the end of July. The ceiling radiated like an electric blanket. I wondered how Sandy had been able to tolerate the heat last June. It hardly seemed possible that a little over a year ago Ben had come home from the hospital. Tying new sash cord to the weights, I pushed them into the pockets and stood back, my legs against the bed, waiting to see if the window would slam down. It didn't.

My head felt as if it were bobbing. I wanted to take a nap. That rascal Ben. He would only settle down when Sandy nursed him to sleep, or when I sang my old Girl Scout song, "Dip, Dip, and Swing." It was either sing or sleep on the floor by his crib. If I let him cry for more than a minute, Sandy flew upstairs and nursed him. These frequent wake-ups were ridiculous. I felt like a wreck and couldn't imagine how Sandy could go to work and function.

Tony bleated that he wanted to talk about the movie schedule. "Just a minute," I called. I could hear the thunk of the ball. A pinch-hitter was taking batting practice. As long as I was up here, the wicker basket screamed overdue bills. I rolled over a desk chair and pulled out my checkbook. Downstairs, the doorbell rang. "What the . . . " I sighed and went to see who it could be. From the landing, I saw a bald, African-

American man holding a briefcase. In a dark suit and white shirt, the man stood whistling. Jehovah's Witness, probably. I went downstairs and opened the door.

"Mrs. Gallagher?" the man said, opening the screen and offering his hand.

"Yes?" I said, allowing my arm to be pumped. The stranger introduced himself as the physical therapist sent by Tony's visiting nurse, Eugene. Reaching in his pocket, he handed me a card that read "Roosevelt Washington."

"Come in," I said. Since Tony's birthday, Roosevelt Washington was the first non-family member, not counting Maria, to enter the house. With four, duck-footed steps, the physical therapist crossed the living room. "Say hey, man," he called out in a falsetto.

I went to the kitchen to make myself another instant coffee.

"Finally got some room in my schedule," Roosevelt said to Tony. He held out a fist. "Gimme five."

Tony grinned and made a weak effort to slap the physical therapist's hand.

"So what can you do, Tony?" Roosevelt said.

"Nothing," Tony said.

Roosevelt frowned and looked at me.

"Nothing," I said.

"Mr. Dimasio, you can do more than nothing," Roosevelt said. "Would you mind if I ask you a few questions before we get started?"

Tony nodded.

"What medications are you taking?"

"Baclofen and riluzole," Tony said. "Oh, and some experimental sugar water I take by shot."

The therapist looked at me. "What was that?"

"Baclofen," I said. "Two in the morning, two at night. And riluzole." I gave him the dose and told him about the growth hormone.

Sitting on the edge of the bed and with an envelope balanced on one knee, Roosevelt Washington scribbled notes in block letters. Kindergartners could print better.

"Anything other than meds?" he asked. "Herbs, vitamins, apricot pits?"

To make my presence less obvious, I began to fix Tony's lunch and minced onions to put in a quiche. "Four 1000 mg Vitamin E tablets."

"Oh, really?" the therapist said, his eyebrows shooting up. "That's a lot. Did the doctor prescribe that much?"

Tony shrugged and looked away.

"I think Tony's mother got that from the ALS Bulletin Board," I said. Tony nodded.

Roosevelt Washington excused himself to answer a beeper, and Tony went back to his computer. The call took a long time. I could almost hear Tony thinking, "another health-care rip-off." Roosevelt stayed on the phone fifteen minutes. He finished his call and washed his hands. He apologized for the length of the call, and I was pleased with that small courtesy. Mostly, Tony waited and waited. Scheduling screw-ups, late doctors, lost medical records. It was ridiculous.

"Would you mind wearing a belt?" the therapist asked. "I'm going to have you transfer to the bed, and since I haven't seen you before, I'd feel more secure if you'd wear it."

Good bedside manner. Lots of *I* messages.

"Okay," Tony said.

The therapist lowered the belt over Tony's head. "Have you lost weight?" he asked.

"Nah," Tony said.

"He's always been small," I said. "He used to weigh one forty-five, but that was when he was running and playing lacrosse. Now, he's down to one twenty-five."

"Oh, really," the therapist said, his eyes on Tony who was transferring slowly from his chair to the bed. "You're doing well at this, by the way. Taking your time."

"Not fast," said Tony, who was standing, one hand on the arm of the wheelchair, and one hip tilting toward the bed.

"Steady now." The therapist pulled up the slack in the belt as Tony let go of the chair and plunked down on the bed.

"Gravity is my enemy," Tony said.

"What's that?" the therapist said.

"Gravity is his enemy." I threw a handful of powdered garlic in the fry pan.

Roosevelt laughed. "You're transferring quite well, Mr. Dimasio. Now that you're sitting, I'm going to move your hands and arms. I'm looking for a range of motion."

The therapist moved Tony's arms in circles and checked Tony's chest the way tympani players test their instruments. He forced open the fingers of Tony's hand.

"Does that hurt?" Roosevelt said.

Tony nodded.

The therapist bent Tony's elbow and twisted his hand ninety degrees. "Does that hurt?"

Tony nodded.

"So how do you train for lacrosse? Do you run for conditioning?"

"Yes," Tony said. "It's mainly conditioning, but it's also hand-eye coordination."

The therapist bent the other elbow and twisted the hand. "How does that feel?"

"Not good," Tony said.

"Not good," Roosevelt said. "Okay. So do I understand that you run to improve endurance, but coordination is a matter of you have it or you don't?"

Tony nodded and raised his eyebrows, his mouth hanging open.

"Okay, now, can you lift your feet onto the bed and lie down?"

Tony leaned back and slowly moved his feet onto the bed.

"That's it. That's it. Good. You've still got quite a bit of control. It must be because you were athletic to begin with."

Tony smiled and crossed his hands on his chest. Under instruction, he raised and lowered his legs a few inches.

"It's easier in the supine position," Roosevelt said, nodding approval. "Okay, now Tony, I want you to do the Elvis."

Tony looked baffled.

The therapist bent over Tony's prostrate body.

"You don't know 'the Elvis?'" Roosevelt looked over at me.

Taking a mug from the microwave, I watched Roosevelt put his mouth to Tony's ear. Tony began to laugh.

"Okay, now, watch this, Mom," Roosevelt said. "I'm going to hold Tony's feet." Roosevelt moved to the foot of the bed, and Tony, arms folded across his stomach, lifted his pelvis off the bed.

Roosevelt grinned. "Do it again, Tony."

Tony lifted his hips again. Up down, up down.

"You know what 'the Elvis' is for, don't you, Tony?" Roosevelt cackled. "Ooooh, wheee. Look at you. You're doing your *thing*."

Tony bounced up and down until he wore himself out. After some leg lifts and arm lifts, Roosevelt transferred Tony back to the wheelchair. He knelt by Tony's legs and looked up at him. "What are your goals for PT?"

Tony shrugged and stared out the window. He'd had only one goal for a long time: dying.

"It could be walking around the living room or holding your children on your lap," Roosevelt said. "It could be anything, Tony, because we are going to get you better."

Tony looked at me, his eyes tearing up.

Roosevelt swiveled Tony's chin. "Don't look at her. Look at me. Listen to what I'm saying. We're going to set some goals, and you're going to get better."

A huge smile came over Tony's face. "I want to get out of this chair."

Roosevelt squeezed Tony's hand. "That's doable. We'll work on flexibility and conditioning. How does that sound?"

"Sounds good," Tony said.

"Okay, buddy." Roosevelt knocked Tony's arm with his knuckles and packed his paperwork. "See you in two days."

"Colleen, check my schedule," Tony said. "I want to make certain I'll be here."

"What schedule?" I said.

"My appointments are on the calendar. It's on the kitchen door."

Pushing the swinging door shut, I saw a calendar pinned by a red thumbtack. In two days Tony had an appointment with Bronfman, the lawyer. Lillian's birthday was coming up soon, too. That was it for the week.

I read him his schedule.

"I'm sorry," Tony said. "Two days from now, I'm booked."

"Okay, then," Roosevelt said. "We'll play it by ear."

I walked the therapist to the door. "Do you happen to know if the case manager approved your visits?"

"I assume so," he said.

"How would I find out?"

"Call the office," he said.

"This is the best thing that's happened to him all year."

Roosevelt gave me a thumbs up.

After he'd left, I said, "Maybe Roosevelt can light a stick of dynamite and blast you out of the house."

"I leave the house for movies."

"Yeah, but there are parks."

"Parks have birds."

"You're afraid a bird's going to crap on you?"

"I'm a sitting duck," Tony said, his shoulders shaking with glee. "Actually, the suitcase ramp scares me. I'm afraid it'll collapse under the weight of my chair."

I stood there, not quite knowing what to do with this information. Since Tony had moved into the wheelchair, I hadn't seen him leave the house except for Purple Day, and that day, he'd walked. I'd actually forgotten about the suitcase ramp, an aluminum contraption meant for getting a regular wheelchair into a restaurant. It folded to the size of a card table, but rattled and twisted under the weight of heavy-duty chairs with batteries and motors.

Tony might not want to go out, but I did. I felt like I was living in a hermetically sealed box and wasn't sure what would have helped: air conditioning, a walk around the block, or some intense, mindless sex. I was going to scream if I didn't see something besides these four walls.

Tony rolled over to his computer. "I had a super productive morning," Tony said. "I sent my list of tunes over to Noah. He can start getting the records together. And I finished the outline of *Ramón On The Cliff*. I want you to read it."

"Later," I said. "I need to buy groceries."

"Can you take me to the bathroom first?" Tony said.

"Okay." I opened the bathroom door. He maneuvered between the shower on his left and sink on his right. Parking his chair diagonally in front of the portable commode with its grab-bar arms, he moved his shoes slowly until the soles lay flat. Lifting him to a standing position, I curled his fingers around the commode's handles, tugged down his shorts, flipped up the seat, and aimed his penis.

"Why don't you just sit?" I said.

"Sitting is for girls." He glared at me and I backed out the door.

Folding my arms, I fell against the wall and closed my eyes. Nap. Maybe after a trip to the store.

Kaboom. I spun around and yanked open the door. Same deal as at his sister's. This time he'd wedged his head against the linen closet. The commode lay on top of him. I pushed it off and maneuvered the wheelchair out of the way. As he tried to clear his throat, phlegm rattled in his chest.

"Call 911," he said.

"You're okay," I said, though I wasn't sure. If Tony felt nauseated or his pupils dilated, I'd take him to the emergency room. Holding him like a crash dummy, I dragged him from the bathroom, picked him up, and flopped him on the bed. So much for letting him make the PT-approved transfer.

"Don't tell Sandy," he said. "She doesn't want me going on my own."

"What do you usually do?

"I save it for Sandy."

"I see." His shorts were still down around his knees. I pulled them up. He didn't mean urinating. He'd been trying to turn around and take a shit. His feet had twisted.

"What do you do when she's not here?" I said.

"I feel like I'm about to explode," he said.

"That would be a way to go."

"Yes."

"We'd have to call a hazmat team to clean it up."

"Sometimes they do that on pig farms," Tony said.

God, the pig farms. I made an ice pack with a zip-lock bag, wrapped it in a towel, and pressed the cold pack against the goose egg on Tony's head. "Do you still have to go?" I said.

"No." He started laughing. "The fall scared the shit out of me."

I shook my head. He must be okay.

"Listen, Tony," I said, "I know this is embarrassing, but why don't you let me take you to the toilet? It's better than exploding."

Tony let out a sigh. "You're my mother-in-law."

"Pretend this is a six-degrees-of-separation kind of thing."

"How so?"

"I'm not your wife, but I'm as close to her as it gets."

He sighed again.

"I'm not really lobbying to wipe your ass, but someone's got to do it."

"All right," he said. "But I hate it."

"Well, me, too," I said, feeling relieved and terrified at what lay in store for both of us. "Now that we've got that settled, why don't you close your eyes and rest?"

"I can't," Tony said.

"Can't what?" I said, examining his pupils. Both the same size.

"Can't close them." His eyelids closed partway and, like window shades, popped open.

I stood over him, hands on hips. Another muscle group atrophying. Pretty soon, he wouldn't be able to hold a pen or sign his name. Then, the respirator decision would be as good as made.

With Tony in bed, possibly with a concussion, I couldn't leave the house even for a walk around the block. Sandy had put a list of neighbors' phone numbers on the refrigerator. I called. No one answered, not even Lowell Jaffe. I'd go crazy unless I could get some fresh air. Fidgeting, I pulled a chair to Tony's bed. Breathing softly, he fell asleep.

Tony was right. The suitcase ramp was flimsy. It might be okay when they went to a restaurant, but at home, he should have a solid, permanent ramp like the one out front at Joan Calabrese's, only not rotting. Under a lemon magnet on the refrigerator I found the carpenter's card.

"Hey, there," I said, "this is Sandy's mom. I was wondering if you could build a ramp out front."

"Did Sandy change her mind?" he said.

"About what?" I said.

"It was included in the bid, but then she told me she didn't need it."

"Well, we need it now."

"I've got all the pieces cut," he said. "They're stacked underneath the room addition."

"That's great," I said. "Is there a chance you could do it today?"

"Sure," he said. "I could use the five hundred she was holding back."

"I'll pay you myself," I said. "Don't bother Sandy about it."

Upstairs, I worked on the unpaid bills. The carpenter, his armpits sweaty and his tools strewn about the remaining patch of lawn, assembled the precut pieces. By five he had the ramp put together.

"Can you paint it?" I said.

"Yeah, I think there's some leftover paint in the garage."

I sat on the porch and watched him slap paint over the pressure treated wood. In the heat, the paint dried quickly. I wrote a check and thanked him. One thing accomplished today. I could get Tony out of the house, maybe take him to a park, and get myself out, too.

Josh woke up from his nap, but looked groggy and lay down on the couch. Maria, carrying Ben, who pulled at the ruffles in her yellow top, went out to the porch.

Peering at me through the screen, she said, "Did you ask Sandy before you make that?"

"No," I said, joining her outside. "Should I have?"

"I don't know." With Ben on her hip, Maria frowned and sat down. "It stand out like this." Maria held up her thumb.

"I hope not." I sat on the rail. The carpenter had done a pretty good job, considering; but the ramp did resemble a green water slide, except that it wasn't wet. Unfortunately, it covered up most of the tiny front lawn that Lowell had coaxed back to life. But Sandy ought to realize there were two people in the house. Tony's opinion counted. I went in and got him up from his nap.

After taking him to the bathroom, I beckoned him to the door. "I have a surprise for you."

Still pale from his fall, he maneuvered his chair over the threshold and onto the porch. "Wow," he said, "that looks like an amusement ride."

"See if it feels solid."

"Solid," he said, smiling. "I can tell it's solid from here."

Inching his chair down he approached the first turn, then rolled faster down to the second turn and jerked around the bend. The instant he found himself on the sidewalk he took off for the corner, his head thrown back. "Woo-hoo!" At the corner he made a U-turn and came back, screeching to a stop. I went down to the sidewalk.

The screen door opened. It was Josh. "Is my mom going to like that, Grandma?"

"I hope so."

Josh seized a toy lawnmower and sent it careening down the ramp. It bumped over the curb of the first turn and crashed on the lawn. He thudded down the incline and jumped on the batteries of Tony's chair.

"Get down," Tony said. "You could fall."

Josh climbed down, but kept his hand on the handgrip. "I want a ride," he said.

Tony's eyes softened. "Okay, but just this once."

"Hold tight," I said.

Maria put Ben down on the porch. Gripping the railing, the baby stepped sideways toward the ramp.

"Mama Colleen, stand at the first turn," Maria said. "I want to show you what Ben can do."

I moved onto the lawn, but wanted to make sure Tony and Josh didn't go too far. Tony had fallen and probably shouldn't be getting himself too excited, but there he came, flying toward the house, Josh hanging onto the back of the chair, screaming with delight.

"Hold out your hands," Maria said.

I looked back at the porch.

At the top of the ramp, Maria held Ben's hands. He wore his new white shoes and pattered down.

I picked him up, my heavy little sack of sugar. "Ben, you're walking!"

Behind me, Tony said, "Did you see how fast I went?"

"Go again, go again," Josh screamed.

"It's an amusement ride," Tony grinned.

"I want an amusement ride," Josh screamed.

Carrying Ben to his father, I placed him on Tony's thighs. "Why don't you take him? Just go five or ten feet. I'll walk right beside you."

Ben sat absolutely still and held the arms of the chair.

"Take him. Take him," Josh said, jumping up and down.

"He'll just fall," Tony said. "Get him off."

I took Ben and he threw his arms around my neck, pressing his cheek against mine. Tony and Josh zoomed off down the block. Josh was the child of his healthy life, Ben the child from the life Tony didn't want to have. He felt different about them, and it made me sad.

Down the block came Sandy, her tennis shoes glowing in the dusk. I walked towards her, holding Ben. When we met, I said, "Stop right where you are. I want to show you something."

Sandy shook her head. "I need to deal with bills. A collection agency tracked me down at work."

"Wait one minute." I put Ben on the sidewalk and gave him a nudge. "Walk to Mommy."

Ben tottered forward and fell against Sandy's knees.

"Oh, Ben!" She scooped him up and hugged him. "I'm so relieved. Josh walked at eleven months. I thought there might be something wrong with Ben. He's almost fourteen and, with Tony's problems, I thought Ben might be delayed." Then her face clouded. "Did he take his first step for you?"

"No," I said. "Maria."

"Maria." Sandy turned around, clutching him. Tony and Josh were racing up to the corner by Lowell's house. Maria stood on the sidewalk with her turquoise and yellow outfit, arms folded.

Sandy kissed him. "I miss everything."

Ben made a face and pulled away.

Sandy looked at me. "They stop being babies when they start walking."

"Oh?" I said. Mine never had, not to me anyway. I was the only one left who, in the blink of an eye, could recall the continuum of each child's life: the night of passion, the crib selection, the miracle of labor, the black umbilical cord, the cradle cap, the baptism, the first words and first steps, the "everything" for which Sandy longed to be present. From the moment of conception, the vigilance of motherhood never switched off. That's why I was here.

Sandy picked up her briefcase and carried Ben away.

I hurried to catch up. "I thought you were going out tonight."

"Tony didn't want me to."

"How do you know?"

"He sent me an angry e-mail."

"Why don't you play with the kids for an hour, then leave?"

"Are you sure?"

"Very," I said. "I'll talk to Tony about not laying a guilt trip on you."

"Thanks so much, Mom. That's exactly what he does." Sandy stopped in front of the ramp, reeling back.

"What on earth is that?" she said.

"A handicapped ramp," I said.

"Where are the steps?"

"Underneath." I bent down and pointed.

Sandy stared at the green plywood snake and then looked up and down the block. Marigolds lined the neighbor's walk. A birdbath stood in the center of another neighbor's neatly manicured lawn. At the hook of her jaw, a walnut-sized muscle twitched. "I never know what I'm going to find at the end of the day."

"I can tell the carpenter to remove it," I said.

Tony roared up behind her. "Over my dead body."

Sandy looked at him with a look that said, "That could be arranged."

I didn't know how to explain to Sandy that what now looked like an impulsive decision to deface the front of her property had actually struck me as an improvement. But, I would make it up to her. I would talk to Tony and get him to lay off the guilt trips.

After dinner I bathed the children, took them to the basement, and told Josh to watch his brother. Then I sat on Tony's bed. "Tony, you have to stop the puppy-dog looks and the guilt-inducing e-mails."

Tony stared at his computer. His e-mail dinged an arriving message. Maybe one of the daily jokes he sent out to his contact list.

"Sandy's under a lot of pressure," I said.

"So she says."

"Show some empathy."

"I'm dying. I need support."

I put my hand on my heart as if I were reciting the Pledge of Allegiance. "I swear, Tony, demands for multiple kisses followed by hangdog looks are not going to get you what you want. Show even a modicum of appreciation, and Sandy will reciprocate."

Tony said nothing. I went down to the basement to corral the kids. My lecture had fallen on deaf ears.

Close to nine, having grabbed a sandwich at Subway, Sandy came home with new patent leather pumps and a new haircut. A stylist had feathered her hair into a bubble. She sat down on a corner of the bed.

Tony looked at me and took a deep breath. "Your hair looks beautiful and you look more relaxed. It's good to see you smiling." His shoulders sagged and he turned to Sandy, longingly.

She sighed and pushed off the bed. "I'd better finish putting the boys in bed."

That wasn't the response Tony needed.

I dealt with the third little boy, washing Tony's face and brushing his teeth. Sandy came down in flannel pajamas. Tony looked at her and waggled his eyebrows. "I wish you hadn't changed upstairs," he said. "I wanted to watch."

Sandy laughed. "There's not much to look at."

I took the bolsters and quilt off Tony's bed, pulled off his tee-shirt, and then stuck his limp arms through the sleeves of his pajama top, gripping his fingers to keep his nails from snagging on the cloth. I squatted, forking my hands under his armpits. As he stood, I felt his feet on top of mine. His cheek dropped onto my shoulder and I grabbed him around the waist.

"Didn't anyone tell you it's impolite to stand on your dance partner's feet?" I said, taking one, then two steps, sliding my feet as in a waltz. I spun him around.

He shook so hard with laughter that I thought I might drop him. Lowering his hips to the bed, I cradled his head, placing it on the pillow. He lay at an odd angle, his back curved, wrists twisted sideways, hands limp. I tried to straighten him out, but couldn't lift him.

"Sandy," I called toward the bathroom, "I think you need to hop on top." I sounded like Dr. Seuss.

"I'm good at that now," Sandy said, rolling up her sleeve. She flexed her biceps. "I can do thirty push-ups."

Climbing on the bed, she straddled Tony, and with her hands under his arms, scooted him up, then bounced up and down on him like a kid.

"I'm going to bed," I said.

"Thanks, Mom," Sandy said.

"You're welcome." I bent down to pick up Ben's shoes. On my way upstairs I heard Sandy say, "Let's have a third child."

"Elvis is back in the building," Tony said.

Entering the bedroom, I blinked back tears of exhaustion and joy. Finally, I was doing something right.

CHAPTER 16

A drawer slammed shut. I rubbed my eyes and saw Sandy parting the tightly packed clothes in her closet. "Damn it."

"What's the matter?"

"You put the clothes away, and I don't know where anything is." She pulled slacks off a hanger and turned around backwards to put on her bra. A gush of air came from her clenched teeth. "I hate not having a room of my own."

"I could sleep on the couch."

"You take everything so personally." Sandy threw a shirt over her head and slammed the closet door. "I'm about to explode."

The door-banging would wake the kids. Sure enough, Ben called, "Gamma, Gamma."

"Lillian has been on the phone nonstop," Sandy said. "We got another call this morning."

"I didn't hear it," I said.

"I turned off the ringer so it wouldn't wake you up," Sandy said. "I could tell you were tired."

"Thanks," I said. "But, what is it exactly she did to annoy you?"

"She's such a bundle of nervous energy. I feel like after Tony dies, I won't want to see her for six months."

"She makes me nervous, too," I said, "but she's his mother. She needs to be involved."

"You don't understand." Sandy stomped downstairs.

I probably didn't, but I certainly didn't need this nonsense first thing in the morning. I opened Josh's door. Lillian had bought him a bunk bed and Winnie the Pooh sheets. He slept on the bottom bunk, one hand around his bear, his sweaty face tilted to one side. I shook his feet and his eyes popped open. "Go give your mom a kiss before she leaves for work."

He smiled, hopped up, and ran downstairs.

Ben squirmed as I changed his diaper. He grabbed the desitin, reached for the toenail scissors, and smeared his fingers in the poop. Sandy was just venting. I needed to absorb these wayward comments and let them drift away like balloons. For now, I had to concentrate on the practical work of running the household: fixing Tony's lunch, the family's dinner, doing the shopping, and getting up when Ben cried. "She's just like Goldilocks, Ben."

Ben stopped rolling and looked at me.

"Who's been sitting in my chair? Who's been eating my porridge? Who's been sleeping in my bed?" I wiggled Ben's feet. "My mother!"

Ben clapped. I put on his tiny socks and stiff shoes. That "taking things personally" was a bad sign. I tried to pick up the slack and if I'd begun to get on Sandy's nerves, well, Sandy was getting on mine, too. Taking care of Tony had a few good moments, but not enough to keep me from feeling drained. I wondered how much longer this could possibly last.

While Tony worked on *Ramón*, I opened envelopes and sorted insurance claims, took a catnap, and woke up an hour later than Tony should have eaten. After making his lunch, I couldn't very well go back upstairs. He might choke. I sat down in the feeding chair. Tony ran out of steam with his eating gizmo, and I took it off and fed him.

"Do you know why Sandy was in such a bad mood this morning?" I said.

"Not really," he said, "except every day it's more and more obvious she can't cope with her grief."

I hoped he didn't expect Sandy to sit by his side, rending her clothing. "You can't grieve until a person dies."

"That's what I'd do," Tony said.

"Who'd take care of the children?"

"I'd send the children to my mother."

"Your mom could handle Josh maybe, but not Ben."

"I'd send Ben to you."

"Split up your kids?"

"That's what people did in the Old Country."

"This isn't Italy."

I heard the door open. It was Sandy.

"What're you doing back so early?" I said.

Sandy looked at her watch. "It's 3:30. Why isn't Tony dressed?"

"Just give me a second," he said.

"You'll have to go like that," Sandy said. "Your parents are paying Bronfman by the minute."

"What's this about Bronfman?" I said.

"The lawyer who's doing our wills," Sandy said. "Tony's known about it for weeks."

That's right. Lillian had mentioned it. I'd seen the appointment on the calendar.

Tony looked at me. "Next time remind me."

"Don't waste time blaming my mom," Sandy said.

"I can't go to a lawyer's office in shorts and a tee-shirt. Colleen, go upstairs and get my white shirt and dress pants."

Sandy clicked off the power on his chair and put it in manual mode. "You're fine as is." Steering him out the door and down the ramp, she called over her shoulder, "Is it okay if we go out to dinner?"

"Of course." It would be a treat to take care of the grandchildren.

It wasn't until Sandy had driven away that I realized how tired I felt, and this hadn't been a particularly tiring day, just the normal tortures of Ben's wakeups, Tony's sock selection, and the "feeding."

I made the kids an early dinner and watched Josh bound, like a paddle ball, from his chair to the couch. "Sit down, Josh," I said. "I mean it." He looked at me, lip quivering, and took a seat at the table. When Ben threw peas on the rug, I loosened his high chair tray and took him down. Lillian called and asked to speak to her son. What that usually amounted to was Lillian yammering and Tony listening with a long-suffering look.

"Tony hasn't come back yet," I said.

"The lawyer's office called me yesterday to remind Tony to bring the papers."

"What papers?"

"The ones I sent him to review last week."

"Where are they?"

"In the wire basket of his computer table. Didn't he bring them?"

"I'll go see." Sure enough, a brown envelope of legal papers sat in the basket: the will, the power of attorney, the living will, and a DNR order. The last page of the documents had two sample clauses, one saying Tony wanted to go on a respirator, and the other saying he didn't.

Ben grabbed a fork from the table and headed for an electrical outlet. "No, no, Ben." I picked him up and returned to the phone. "I found them."

"I knew I should have come down," Lillian said.

"Yes, you should, and not just to shop or go to the lawyer's," I said. "I need you guys to spell me once in a while."

"Oh, but I can't take care of Tony," Lillian said.

I felt a pain in the center of my forehead. "Why can't you?"

"I don't know how."

"You'd better learn how, starting real soon."

"I'm coming down for my birthday."

"Good. We can discuss it then."

Agitated, I carried Ben upstairs. Josh followed. I ran water for a bath. The mirror steamed, and I saw two words, "Lillian + Josh," written with a finger in the looping swipes of the Palmer method. I would be in trouble if Sandy saw the handwriting. Sandy couldn't stand toothpaste spatter, and she'd go ballistic if she saw this evidence of Lillian's presence materializing out of the steam. In the hall closet I found Windex. "Don't write on the mirror again," I said, rubbing at it with a rag.

"Grandma Lillian did it," Josh said.

"You told her to, didn't you?"

Josh submerged like an alligator and spread his fingers underwater. He raised his head.

"Didn't you?"

"Yes."

"Did you know your mom likes the house really, really clean, including the mirror?"

"Grandma Lillian says my mom is a neat freak."

"Let's not make extra work for the person who cleans."

"Who's that?" Josh said.

"Me."

"Oh."

"And tell Grandma Lillian not to write on the mirror, or I'll have to put her in a time-out."

"Grandma Lillian says you're mean," he said.

"Why'd she say that?"

"You don't want my dad to live."

"That's absurd," I said.

"I want him to live."

"Of course you do," I said. "We all do."

My hands shook as I helped Josh into his pajamas. It was time for a story, for several of them. I changed Ben's diapers, and we sat on Josh's rug and read all the board books in his room. I gave Ben a sippy cup of water and put him in his crib. After crying for a while, he settled down and went to sleep. Normally, Sandy nursed him. This was a first. I gave Josh a kiss and partially closed his door. He needed that triangle of light shining in or he'd be anxious.

The house filled with glorious silence.

Downstairs, I cleared the table, ran a carpet sweeper over the rug, and did the dishes. It was nine o'clock. I sat down on the living room couch, crossed my knees, and looked around. The couch cushions were tidy, the kids' books in a neat pile. Outside, through the windows, I heard the ding of wind chimes. I took apart my braid. I would rest a minute before going upstairs. Living here wiped me out.

***

Someone shook my shoulder.

"I was going to wake you last night," Sandy whispered, "but you looked exhausted."

"I was." I sat up, blinking. "What happened?"

"They had the papers all drawn up," Sandy said. "Wills. DNR orders. Power of attorney."

"Lillian called," I said, looking toward the closed bathroom door. Tony must be in there. It was safe to talk. "She asked if he'd remembered to bring the papers."

"They had duplicates, but even then, Tony couldn't make up his mind. We were in there three hours. The lawyers were really freaked out that he couldn't hold a pen. I had to move his hand."

I pictured Tony, his face stiff and frightened, sitting opposite the attorney. Formal documents in boiler-plate legal language—the deceased, the decedents—would be passed to him. He would stare at them, blinking slowly, and his jaw would stiffen. I could not visualize him actually picking up a pen and the pen shaking in his weak, emaciated hand. I could not picture Tony making a decision.

"Well?" I said.

"He said it would be better for me and the kids if he didn't go on the respirator. If it were just him, I think it's something he'd try."

"Thank God." I threw my head forward and buried my face in my hands. My body shook and I gulped down tears. I hadn't known how much I had riding on this decision, and now I did.

Sandy patted my arm. "You can stop worrying."

Dry-eyed, I straightened up. "No, I can't." Sandy had problems and so did Tony, and I couldn't let myself relax. Yesterday afternoon I'd tried to schedule an appointment with Roosevelt Washington. When the physical therapist finally responded to his pager, he said he wouldn't be able to come back. When I asked him why, he said the case manager wouldn't approve it, and when I asked why, he said, "You'll have to talk to my office. I don't handle the paperwork."

Another phone call to the bureaucrats. I was sick of phone calls. The indifference of the voicemail messages and instructions to punch one if I wanted to make an appointment, two if I were a new patient, three if I was calling from a pharmacy, or four if I needed to speak with accounting made me enraged. I could not break through. The person I was supposed to speak to would be out of the office or no longer employed or not the right person in the food chain of health-care providers. The shell game was maddening.

CHAPTER 17

Tony had decided not to go on the respirator, but everything around that—how tense Sandy had been and Tony's naïve notion that she could pre-grieve his death—would disappear if I didn't write it down. I had filled one notebook and today would start a second. For the moment, Tony was content to work on *Ramón* and I could sit quietly at Sandy's desk.

I flipped the notebook open. Green ink filled the page. I had thought the notebook empty, but this was my handwriting, slanted, with big, looping capital letters.

Momentous day in my insignificant life. To me it feels as if I had been elected President, gone to the moon, swum the Channel. This weekend I accidentally got to be alone the whole day! I crave solitude. I've had time to sleep, wake gently, fix coffee, wander the house. I need these times. I don't always want to have to go away to reclaim myself. Ironic. How I can enjoy Rob and the kids and bustle and then when they're gone, I feel emerging a whole separate self, the self I could become if I were alone. Like being given back "me." What loneliness that gift would mean—having to schedule friends. Find hugs. Now, I have such an abundance of affection that solitude feels good! I'm trying to find my own way, take time for myself, find my way back to myself.

With two fingers pressed to my neck, I felt my pulse thumping like a captive bird's. Where the heck had Rob taken the kids for a whole day? I had woken up alone, padded around the house … which house? Must have been that little ranch in Schaumburg, the place straight out of *Edward Scissorhands*: curved subdivision streets, dads backing out the drive at half past seven, every fifth house with an A-frame roof above the front door. Rob had seen the place, but I hadn't. His dad had co-signed, and he'd bought the house without telling me. "Surprise, honey. Our own place." I had stared in dismay at its ugliness. The ceiling and the smoke-stained corners of the room reminded me of a low-hanging cloud. Taupe shag carpet extended to the patio windows. The backyard lay in shadow. From the cracked patio to the warped fence staves, grass had failed to grow.

"I know it requires a little imagination." Rob put his arm around me and we both stared out at a tilted clothesline. He gave me an encouraging squeeze and kissed the top of my head. "Life's big adventure," he said.

Moving day from our apartment in Oak Park, Rob and his brothers carried boxes down three flights of stairs, and when the boys stripped off their sweaty shirts, the washer, churning away in the laundry room, felt essential on our list of things we could never again live without. The owner had left a hibachi in the garage. Rob fired it up. A badminton set came from his parents' basement. His mom brought wieners, my mom potato salad and a Jell-O mold, and we made lemonade from a lug of lemons. While I herded Kevin away from the charcoal's flames, my dad mounted a basketball rim over the garage. I remember the thunk, thunk of the basketball hitting the driveway. The hot dogs charred. We devoured the chips and pretzels. At dusk Rob's parents packed up the cooler and went home. Inside, my mom was still cutting shelf paper; she never knew when to quit. My dad, in a folding chair where he could keep an eye on Kevin, cooled off with a Schlitz. "You done good here." He motioned to the yard with its clothesline. "Plenty of space for the kids to run around."

I don't know whose idea it was, but one of us thought the A-frame entry would look better with some Swiss trim. Later, my father set up a work table in the garage and made gingerbread verge boards and matching planter boxes. With my red geraniums, the place looked like a cross between a World War II barracks and a mountain chalet. Reading the diary made me wonder if I had finally thrown a fit about the house and sent Rob off to the Field Museum. Kevin loved the dinosaurs and Sandy, the mummies. From out in Schaumburg, it was a haul. Maybe he'd stayed over at his parents' place. From South Kilpatrick, he could hop on the Stevenson and be at the Field in ten minutes. But overnight? His mom wouldn't have exactly welcomed that. Her own kids had not yet left the house.

I turned the page.

Why didn't I have the courage to go on with my own life instead of getting married? Why have I always feared loneliness so much, where now I long for it. Rob is a good man, but he doesn't know anything about the way I think and feel. In school, he used to read history and philosophy and literature, but now he never cracks a book unless it's one of those stupid business books. I'm bored with the relationship.

I'm bored out of my mind with our sex life. He won't try anything new. I've shown him what feels good, then thump, he's on me, and I have to stay very nonreactive or he gets distracted and can't get it off. Lots of things interrupt his mind—covers on his feet, the furnace coming on, the telephone, the sound of a child's footsteps in the hall, or God forbid, the door creaking open. How do I communicate to him that sexuality can be a far richer part of a relationship than it has been for us? How do I get him to imagine more than this way of being intimate, which hasn't changed since college, when we used to do it in the back seat of his old Ford? Maybe what I thought was great was that we were doing something forbidden. We were getting away with a mortal sin.

I feel that I am starting to make some internal preparations for this relationship not lasting. Fundamentally, I wonder if I am "in love" with him. Is it honest to live with a person out of economic need without that real strong drawing together that is love? It makes me not believe in love. Passion seems to have disappeared from all but my inner life. Right now, I only feel that kind of passionate attachment to my children. That kind of "go through fire" for them.

How did Jean do it with ten? Rob said he'd always wanted kids. I didn't think about whether I was together enough to have some core of myself left over to give them. Maybe my core wasn't sufficiently developed. Perhaps, it was embryonic in itself and gave and gave out of its own infantile need.

"What the hell," I shouted and threw the notebook across the room. The young woman I had been sounded wiser than the woman I was now, despite the crows' feet and gray hair. Wanting to be truthful with myself, I had not edited out the one thing I could never admit to my children. That my nature—the Colleen I faced when I looked in the conscience mirror—had a selfish streak. Even as a young woman I had bumped up against the limits of my own reserves.

Over the baby monitor I heard Tony. "Is everything okay?"

I went to the top of the stairs. "Everything's fine. I'm just venting."

I looked at the notebook in my hand. From wanting to record what happened in the run-up to Tony's respirator decision, I found myself diverted for a stroll down memory lane. And not a happy stroll, either. My arms trembled and I felt as if I'd caught a chill.

Who was this me? I sat down on the bed, cross-legged. Rifling through the third notebook, I saw handwriting in the blue of a fountain pen Rob had used to sign checks, and his words balanced carefully on the lines like a boy sitting astride a fence.

Well, it's happened again. I've spent most of the year working like hell at Motorola. I've made the switch from engineering to sales so I should get a big commission at the end of the year, but I don't know where I am. I've managed to isolate myself from Colleen and have almost lost her (not for good, I hope). It's an old story (for me), concentrate on work and forget about human relations and feelings. I don't know why I do it—it's not for love of engineering. I like my work. I don't love it.

This latest difficulty with Colleen has made me realize what I am (or rather what I am not). I need love and sympathy as much as the next person. The difference is, I've been too selfish to return the love and sympathy. (This is hard to write—keep getting interrupted by the kids—anyway, to continue). Colleen has supported me for eight years, but now I've managed to turn her off. And, all at once, I'm lost. My accomplishments cost too much, and now I'm stuck with them. The purpose of this book is to remind myself how I feel. Hopefully, by writing down what I feel periodically, I will keep myself from becoming isolated again. So to start, the problem with Colleen is she doesn't like sex anymore. At night she falls asleep with a book open on her chest. I understand that's the only time she has to read, but give me a break. She's always been a *good lay. I used to think she liked it even more than me, but goddamn, the frequency's down to twice a week. Even if I roll over with a hard on, she pushes my hand away.*

The journal ended there. Eyes blurring, I closed the book and pressed it to my heart. There was a lesson there, but it was all I could do to breathe. That day I began writing in earnest. The words spoken in the confusion of our lived lives would evaporate if I didn't get them down. On my next trip to the store, I bought new journals and saved these for the archive of what might have been.

CHAPTER 18

"That trip to Bronfman's was a pain in the ass," Tony said, "but let's move on." It was Sunday, July 24, and now that he could get out of the house easily with the new ramp, he wanted to start early for Great Falls, where the Potomac narrowed as it passed through Mather Canyon. "We can all wear purple in honor of Maria being gone." He cocked an eyebrow at me, as if Maria's absence made him happy. And, maybe it did, though I didn't see why. During the week, Maria slept in the basement on a futon, but on weekends, she went to her relatives'. She wasn't in Tony's way.

"Let's bring a picnic, like we did on our last family outing," Tony said.

"Oh, you're thinking about 'Purple Day,'" I said.

Now I got it. Tony wanted to be in charge of fun. Maria upstaged him. Maria was *more* fun, and especially more fun where Josh was concerned.

"I think a picnic's too much for one day," Sandy said. She needed to pay bills and file insurance claims. Besides, she couldn't do a picnic without going shopping, and by the time she finished giving Tony his shower, it would be ten o'clock and he'd have to eat breakfast and then lunch, which, she reminded him, took three hours. It made more sense to go to Great Falls after the children had their naps. "That would give me a chance to take a nap, too." Sandy stripped the sheets off Tony's bed, and I took them down to the washing machine. As I pushed them around the agitator, I noticed dry, irregular white spots. I was shocked that Tony could still do it, and even more shocked that Sandy would want to. The deprivation in my own life hit me like a water balloon. Physical intimacy. What a concept. When Tony died, Sandy was going to have to hunt for sex, possibly for the rest of her life.

As we pulled into the parking lot at Great Falls, I heard the sound of roaring water. Sandy, riding in the back of the van, unclipped the straps that held Tony's chair. With Josh standing on the batteries, Tony sailed off down an asphalt trail. Sandy stayed in the van to nurse Ben. In the distance, through the vegetation, I saw plumes of water and falls that stretched from shore to shore — not Niagara, more like water cascading over a spillway, and current strong enough to undermine trees along the banks and sweep away a child.

"Josh," I called.

Josh came running from the trees. His red tennis shoes were caked with mud.

"Those are new, aren't they?" I said.

Ignoring me, Josh pointed down the trail. "It's so fun down there. There's some old houses and everything. I was jumping on the rocks and I fell in the swamp."

"There could be quicksand in that swamp," I said.

"What's quicksand?" His shoes squished.

"A special sand that sucks at your feet." I made a slurping sound. "Where's your father?"

Josh pointed. "He went that way."

"I thought he was taking you with him."

"He said I could explore."

Only four, Josh had hopped off the wheelchair to explore the buildings. He'd run back to use the restroom. I hoped Tony wasn't in a ditch. Annoyed that he'd sped off, leaving Josh alone, I crossed my arms and tapped my foot, looking down the macadam path until I saw Tony's tiny figure in the shadow of the trees. I waited outside the restroom's block bunker and looked up to see Sandy, pushing the jog-stroller. When Josh came out, Sandy took a look at his muddy shoes and produced his old ones from her backpack. Josh changed into his faded blue tennies, and I knelt to tie them.

Sandy looked at the sky. "The sun's going down."

Tony braked to a halt, sending gravel flying. "This place is great," Tony said. "Get it? Great Falls."

"We should go home," Sandy said. "I need to throw Josh's shoes in the wash."

"I told him to stay out of the water," Tony said.

"It's late," Sandy said. "Let's not make a big deal of this." She started off with the jog-stroller, pushing Ben.

"But it is a big deal." Tony rolled over to Josh.

I finished tying bunny ears on Josh's shoes. "Why is it a big deal?"

"I specifically told him to keep his new shoes clean."

Josh stared down at his feet. The tips of his big toes poked through holes in the canvas. He took two small steps, rolling his feet to the outer edges. "My feet hurt."

"You never listen to me," Tony said. "This is what you get. Sore feet."

"You want to make a federal case of it?" I said.

"He needs to learn to listen." Tony turned his wheelchair in a circle. The chair's tires hissed, and Tony stared pointedly at Josh.

"Where'd my mom go?" Josh said.

"Back to the car," I said. "Tony, can Josh ride on the chair?"

"If he'd listened, his feet wouldn't hurt right now."

"You've made your point."

Tony did a loop. "He has to walk, but I'll walk with him."

Josh's eyes grew large and he looked at me.

"He just means he's not going to race ahead in the wheelchair." If Tony walked, we'd be there until midnight. Apparently, the excursion was ending before it had begun.

Back at the van, Sandy said, "I'll drive home."

"Be my guest," I said.

Squeezed between the kids' car seats, I listened to Josh make noises like a trapped squirrel. The moment we got home, I put Ben next to Tony's bed, hoping he'd haul himself up on the wheelchair and give Tony an impish smile, maybe put him in a better mood. Instead, Ben sprawled on the floor and found dust balls under the bed. I put a plastic container of leftovers in the microwave. Sandy walked past without making eye contact.

"Hey, don't be mad at me," I said.

"I've decided I'm entitled to a half-hour nap."

"I've decided I'm entitled to a movie," I said.

"This isn't your day off," Sandy said.

"When is my day off?" I said. "I haven't had one yet."

"Don't guilt-trip me," Sandy said.

"Take your nap," I said. "I'm going to a movie after dinner, and you can do the honors for your husband." I put Ben in his high chair and gave him a piece of raisin bread.

Ben picked out a raisin and held it up. "Talk-a-talk-a?"

I laughed. "Eat it, Ben. It tastes good."

He put it in his mouth and then pushed it out with his tongue. He rocked back and forth, pointing at the counter. "Na-na. Na-na."

"Sure, you can have a banana, but you better eat up, kiddo, because you're going to sleep through the night, starting tonight."

"Sandy spoils him," Tony said, from his position by the computer.

Ben looked up at me.

"Are you spoiled?" I said.

Ben wagged his head no.

"Josh was never spoiled," Tony said.

"No, but you are," I said.

After Ben finished eating, I put him in the living room where he dumped wooden puzzles on the rug. Sandy came down with Josh. Neither of them had been able to sleep. She lifted him to the sink to wash his hands.

Tony backed away from the computer. "I have to go pee."

"You knew we were about to eat," Sandy said. "Why didn't you ask me sooner?"

"I don't know why we're even surprised," I said. "Fifteen minutes before dinner, you should automatically take Tony to the bathroom."

"Why don't you?" Sandy said.

"If you're here," I said, "he won't let me."

Tony said, "Your mother's not my wife."

I slid into the kitchen. Duck and cover.

"Josh, sit down and start eating dinner," Sandy said. She followed Tony into the bathroom.

Kicking the chair, Josh stared at his plate. He got up from the table, stomped over to the couch, and plopped down. He felt the toes of his shoes. Wanting to console him or bring him back to eat, I abandoned my dinner and knelt by his feet, testing the fit of his shoes. Half an inch too small. No wonder his feet hurt. Sandy's and Tony's voices grew louder. The toilet flushed, the bathroom door opened and I returned to the table.

"Time for dinner, Josh," Sandy said. "You've got to eat something."

"I'm not hungry." Josh folded his arms.

"Low blood sugar," Sandy said.

"He barely ate lunch, as I recall," I said.

Sandy sat down next to Ben. Josh remained on the couch. "If you don't want to eat, go to your room and get ready for bed," Sandy said.

"I won't," Josh said.

Flying across the room, Sandy scooped him up. "Yes ... you ... will."

Face contorted, he pounded her chest. She pinned his arms. Her feet clomped upstairs. Josh screamed and cried, "No, no, no." Sandy raised her voice and ordered him back into his room. A toy clattered against a wall. Then the door slammed. Josh banged on it with his fists.

"Stop that," Sandy shouted. "Get control of yourself."

At the table, I looked at Tony. "What's going on?" he said.

"Want me to go see?" I said.

He nodded, his expression triumphant, and jerked his head toward the stairs. I tiptoed to the landing and peeked around the corner. In the upstairs hall, Sandy gripped the doorknob with both hands. She braced her feet against the jambs. Josh was trying to break out of his room. I heard his shoulder slam against the door. The rubber tip of his shoe appeared in the two-inch gap beneath the door, and he tried to kick Sandy's feet.

"Stop that," she screamed, "or I'll lock you in forever."

Crouching out of sight, scared and horrified, I slid silently downstairs. If I could get some time away from the house, maybe I could figure out what to do. It was getting harder and harder to keep a clear head. The disease was bad enough, but this was ridiculous.

***

The following day, Josh ran in, threw his lunch box on the couch, and went straight upstairs for his nap. I carried the sewing machine up from the basement, measured the dining room window, and chalked-lined the blue brocade Sandy had bought months ago. With one hand I fed Tony and with the other I folded and pinned, thinking that the expression my father had used, "busy as a one-armed paper hanger," applied to this day and others like it. When Josh came down from his nap, I pushed the sewing aside and made him a peanut-butter graham cracker. He took it to his seat at the end of the table, opposite the feeding chair. I wondered if he was thinking about last night, when he'd barricaded himself in his room.

"Hey, Mr. In-Charge-of-Fun," I said, "Josh looks like he could use some."

"I need to make some progress on *Ramón*," Tony said.

"What about that *Freddie the Fish* CD Sandy gave you for your birthday?" I wanted to finish the curtains.

"Of the two of us, I was always the better parent," Tony said.

"Sandy's a plenty good parent," I said.

"Sandy needs to learn patience."

I looked at Josh. He turned his cracker, nibbling the edge.

"She pretends I don't exist," Tony said.

That did it. "Put your coat on, Josh." I unplugged the sewing machine and tucked it under the buffet. "We're taking a walk."

"What am I supposed to do?" Tony said.

"If you're smart, you'll stay in your chair," I said. "Otherwise, you can chill on the floor."

Tony reared back from his computer. Josh hopped down, holding out his sticky hands. I wiped them with a kitchen sponge.

"Where are we going?" he said.

"I don't know."

It had to be somewhere special to get his mind off the fight he'd had with his mom.

I took a mental tour of the playgrounds in the neighborhood. As I walked down the ramp and begun to breathe the outdoor air, I thought of the craft store that had just opened. Josh could make a present for Lillian. That would shift his focus.

At a traffic light, the pedestrian signal flashed that we could go. I took Josh's hand, but he pulled away and ran out in the street. A blue sedan turning right screeched to a halt. Chin high, Josh straight-armed the driver, his eyes daring the car to run him over.

Catching up to him and dragging him the rest of the way, I said, "What are you trying to do, get yourself killed?"

"This is how I always cross with Tony." On the other side of the street, Josh stared glumly at the sidewalk.

"You're little," I said. "Drivers might not see you."

"He saw me. I saw him."

"I don't care if you think he saw you or not. Don't ever do that again, not even when you're with your father."

"He says it's okay."

"I know you're trying to help your dad, but your mom wouldn't like it if she knew you were doing that."

"I guess not."

Walking along the sidewalk, he scuffed his shoes. He was wearing the new ones.

"My feet hurt," he said.

"I know," I said, "but I think they'll feel better in a minute."

A steep hill, fortified by the walls of an overgrown forest, forced us to cross the street again. Looking up at this unlikely remnant of nature, I saw tons of native plants: Yellow Jewelweed, Elderberry, Wild Hydrangea, Loosestrife, and Panicled Phlox. The words had such good mouth-feel, like Ben & Jerry's ice cream, but without the calories. I would have loved to do a nature walk, but I hadn't brought my field guide and the hill looked too steep. At the top, surrounded by trees, I noticed the barely visible marble slabs of an old graveyard. I'd never seen it. No surprise though, because I never left the house.

Josh stooped to pick up a pink blossom that had blown onto the sidewalk: *Impatiens*, planted in someone's parking strip.

"Here, Grandma," he said. "Carry this home for my mom." Before I could stop him, he plucked a living blossom, taking the stem with it.

"Don't pick the live ones," I said.

"Why not?"

"Because the flower will die if you pull it away from the plant." I held out the blossom in my palm. "See? It's withering already."

He twirled his stem, scrutinizing the pink flower and its tiny, yellow heart. He walked a few more steps and picked up a maple leaf.

"Is this dead?"

"Yes, Josh."

Next, he picked up an oblong, polished stone. He spit on it and rubbed the dust with his thumb. "Is this dead?"

"Yes," I said. "It was never alive."

"Why not?" he said.

"Some things are alive and some are dead. That's nature."

"What's nature?" He put the stone in his pocket.

"Nature is the world we live in." I waved toward the vine-draped woods and thought of the day my friend Natalie taught Esmeralda to identify oaks. "The sun, trees, flowers, stones. We're part of nature, too."

"My daddy's going to die." Josh, with the look of a child expecting to be caught in a fib, cowered.

"Yes, he is," I said, tilting his chin up. "Everything living will die. Even the sun."

Shading his eyes, he looked at the sun and said in a sing-song voice, "Why?"

"Just because, honey. That's the way nature is." I took his hand.

We came to the pottery store, Bisque-It. The shelves sagged with fish-shaped plates, piggy banks, and mugs. Inside, I picked up a white, bisque mug that felt rough and chalky. I handed it to Josh and explained that he would paint on unfired clay, but when the people at the store baked the mug, the colors would turn bright. He stood attentively, thumbs linked behind his back.

"Wouldn't it be nice to make a special present for Grandma Lillian's birthday?" I said. "You could paint just like you do at school, with paints and a brush."

Josh nodded. "I can make her a card, too."

The young woman who came to help us wore a sleeveless red shirt and brown hiking shorts. She had brushed back the sides of her long, dark hair and captured it in a purple, beaded scrunchie. A widow's peak made her face heart-shaped, and her features reminded me of the Queen on a playing card. She showed Josh the thirty colors he could choose. His eyebrows shot up, but his bow-shaped mouth never opened. I told the woman I would bring him back the next day. At the coffee shop next door, MAMA JAVA, I told Josh he had to plan what he was going to paint.

"I already have a picture in my mind," he said. "I'm going to paint one of those big plates."

"I mean the design, Josh."

He nodded and tipped a juice bottle toward his lips, spilling a little on the table. "I'm going to paint a picture of a house with flowers and bees and a lake, and I want a rainbow in the sky."

"That sounds perfect, Josh. Grandma Lillian will love it."

"And I want to write my name on it—my whole name. Giuseppe Gallagher-Dimasio."

"How about, Happy Birthday Grandma Lillian?"

He nodded enthusiastically.

Sandy had stopped at the market and bought Josh's favorite dessert, bubble gum ice cream. At nine o'clock, maybe because of the sugar, Josh was still awake, hanging around downstairs while Sandy went upstairs to nurse Ben. After Josh went to bed, I'd have to finish the night routine, and then it would be late, and tomorrow, I'd be exhausted.

At night, Tony had to gulp down six pills: baclofen, the medicine that reduced the involuntary twitches in his muscles, and riluzole, his quality-of-life medication. Besides that, he had to down the Vitamin C and D horse tablets. Oddly, he never choked on them. I took a pill and put it far back on Tony's tongue. Tony's head rotated slowly, and he watched Josh watching him.

Josh winced. "Why do you give Tony medicine if the medicine doesn't help?"

Tony's eyes swiveled toward me.

"The medicine slows down his loss of strength," I said.

"But Tony's going to die anyway, isn't he?" Josh said.

"Yes, Josh, eventually he is, but while we still have him with us, let's make the most of it."

Josh began twisting one leg around the other.

Tony swallowed. "Do you have to go potty?"

"Yes," Josh said.

"You can use this bathroom," his dad said.

Normally, Josh wasn't allowed. Tony didn't like him moving the commode because Josh didn't put it back the right way. Josh closed the door, and I heard the rubber pads of the commode scrape the floor.

"Have you ever talked to him about death?" I said.

"I haven't the heart," Tony said.

Proud as if he'd won a blue ribbon, Josh came out, and through the open door, I could see the commode exactly where Tony liked it, centered over the toilet.

"How about some *Freddy the Fish*?" Tony said.

"Sure," Josh said.

I found the CD and put it in the computer. I turned down the bed and laid out Tony's pajamas. Josh climbed over a corner of the bed onto Tony's lap. His thumb touched the Saturn-like mouse, and he rested a cheek on Josh's hair. Josh clicked the icon of *Freddie the Fish*. A cartoon underwater landscape with shells, sand, and sea creatures sprang to life.

"Daddy, tomorrow after my nap, I'm going to make a present for Lillian."

"That's nice, son." Tony nuzzled Josh's neck. The game continued for half an hour until Sandy appeared.

"Ben wouldn't settle down," she said. "You could be in for a long night."

"Oh, great."

"If it's too much trouble for you to get up, I'll do it."

"I think the problem is you nurse him to sleep."

"He doesn't know how to self-satisfy," Tony chimed in.

"I can sing to him," I said.

"I don't want you substituting a new dependency for the old one," Sandy said.

"A new dependency?" I said. "It's a lullaby."

"I don't sing to him," Sandy said.

"Do you want me to let him cry?" I said.

"If he cries, I'll nurse him," Sandy said.

"Fine. I was just trying to help." Meanwhile, my eyeballs felt sandpapered. I couldn't wait to hit the sack. Josh and I had a big day ahead.

***

At the store, Josh put his hands around a chalky oval platter that was large enough to hold a turkey.

"Are you sure?" I said. "It's awfully big."

"This is the one I want."

Skeptical, I carried the plate to a table. Before coming to help, the friendly young woman with the heart-shaped face tied on a white baker's apron. She squatted down, a color chart on her knees. Josh pointed to several colors. She brought out a paint tray and squirted worms of color into eight concave bowls, warning him not to put one color on top of another. The colors would turn muddy.

Josh knelt on the chair, his arms crossed and cheeks sucked in. Half a dozen brushes stood upside down in a jar.

"You've painted before, haven't you?" I said.

"I'm not good at art," he said.

I picked up the biggest brush, its handle squared like a chopstick, and dragged the damp tip across the brown paper. "Hold the brush like this."

Hesitantly, he took the brush. His lower lip twitched as he made microscopic adjustments.

"Come on, Josh," I said. "You can do it."

Like wings, my arms enclosed his shoulders. I grasped his hand and plunged the brush in water. His hair smelled of baby shampoo, and his fingers shook as he moved the brush across the paper. I relaxed my grip. He freed himself.

"You're in charge," I said.

The top of a rainbow streaked across the platter. Below the rainbow, he painted a house and splashed on blue for a lake. Like a chalked sidewalk, the pale colors didn't look like much, but once fired, the pigments would pop.

"You can pick it up tomorrow," the young woman said.

"Oh, good." I couldn't wait for Josh to see what he'd created.

At the coffee shop, Josh looked at the Italian coffee mugs on display. He pointed to a mug decorated with blue-and-yellow stripes. "I could make that. It's just two colors."

While he'd been working on his plate, the sky had clouded over. We were a good twenty minutes from home, and I hadn't brought an umbrella. Across the street, I saw a stone wall and the cemetery I had glimpsed through the forest. Behind it, I was almost sure, a trail dropped into Glover Park. I lifted Josh to the top of the wall and climbed up after him. Brushing off my hands, I saw that the hill was steep and the graveyard long-abandoned. Knee-high grass grew around tombstones that leaned like old men on canes. I took Josh's hand and followed a gravel path that meandered through rows of headstones, each the small, arched door to a life.

Josh ran his fingers over a carved lamb with a weathered fleece. "Are animals buried here?"

"No," I said. "That's decoration." He was only four. He couldn't read the child's name.

Near the top of the hill, a row of mausoleums reminded me of Illinois' downstate banks. By a bronze door to one of these tombs lay a wool blanket and an amber bottle. Josh bent to pick it up. I tugged his hand. "We should get going."

A cross raised on a pedestal brought the boy to a stop. He took several steps back as if unwilling to lift his foot above the dark letter X thrown across the ground. "When my dad dies, my mom and I are going to bury him."

"What did you say?"

He turned in a circle and kicked at tufts of grass. "My mom and I are going to bury him."

"How do you picture that happening?"

"We'll use a shovel and dig a hole and put him in it."

"It doesn't happen like that," I said. "First of all, you and your mom won't have to bury your dad. People called undertakers do that."

He wandered over to one of a dozen graves lined up like dormitory beds with sagging mattresses. Looking down, he said, "But it's still in the ground, isn't it?"

"Yes," I said, standing beside him. "And the families were sad. Are you sad?"

"No," he said.

Never ask a child a direct question about feelings. After all my years teaching kindergarten, after umpteen years as a parent, I should have known better. I took his hand. Only a few more steps to the woods. "Do you remember before your dad got sick?"

"I remember me and my dad making muffins to bring to Mommy in bed."

"He is still the same person," I said. "Only the outside has changed."

I hitched him onto my hip. Tears made his eyes glassy. Wind plastered a leaf to his cheek. I picked it off and came to a trail where my feet began to slide in the mud. Reluctantly, I put Josh down. His hand felt hot and damp. I couldn't let go, even for a second.

***

After dinner it was time for the night routine. Tony opened his mouth and I popped a white Baclofen onto his fuzzy, green tongue. Tipping his head back, he thrust his chin forward, swallowed, and gagged. I reached for his water glass, but water made him choke now, too. Saliva flooded my mouth as I leaned forward, getting ready to pound his back. Until he finished swallowing his pills, I didn't dare talk about what Josh had told me in the graveyard, though I'd ached all day with the secret. Gulping like a pelican, Tony swallowed and nodded for me to open the bathroom door.

Here would be the place to tell him.

He turned his chair to face the sink. I cleaned his nostrils with a Q-tip, brushed his teeth, and squirted Dr. Bronner's peppermint soap on the washcloth. While I scrubbed his oily forehead, I waited for him to ask where Josh and I had gone. Tony's skinny ribs, arched like the bones of fish, were the very ones Josh had imagined underground.

It was after eleven. I put him on the toilet. Since his last fall, he'd been willing to sit. When he finished, I knelt on the floor in front of the commode and pulled off his pants. Pajamas went on next.

Then I rolled him to the side of the bed where I stood, reaching into the cupboards for socks. No. No. Too thick. Too thin. A hole in that one. Head shake, no. Finally, gray socks. Kneeling, I worked the socks over his feet and pushed on his shoes, which he'd wear until I'd made the transfer to bed. "Ready?" I said. He was ready. I held his wrists, and he sprang up, grinning at his ability to stand.

Idiot. Did he think he could stand on his own? I slid my arms beneath his armpits, swung him around, and felt his behind catch and drag against the sheets. I begged him to give me a little help by pushing with his heels. He did. Finally, I had him in the proper position.

Exhausted, I said, "Josh thinks he'll have to bury you when you die. Like with a shovel."

"What am I supposed to do about it?" Tony said.

"Talk to him."

"I don't have anything to say. He's got his whole life to live."

I pulled up the sheet and told him good night. Relying on the banister, I walked upstairs. I wished I had a shovel. I'd bury him myself.

***

Hands folded beneath her head, Sandy lay on my bed, talking to one of her girlfriends. The fax machine, a new purchase I hoped would help me sort out insurance claims and reimbursements, had replaced the phone. She said good-bye and handed me the receiver. After hanging up, I sat. Sandy's toes looked as long and narrow as fingers. I rubbed them. Her feet felt cold.

"Sandy, I have to tell you what Josh said."

"It's 11:30."

"I don't want to forget."

"All right. Go ahead."

I told her about the plate and our shortcut through the graveyard. Sandy picked at a tuft of the bedspread. "I want him to feel he can talk openly about his feelings, not keep them bottled up."

"Did you do that when your father died?"

"A lot."

"Then trust yourself," I said. "You know what he's going through better than anyone."

Sandy rubbed her temples. "I've had a headache all week. Tony always insists on his male privileges."

"What male privileges?" I said.

Sandy pursed her lips. "You know."

"Oh, *those* male privileges," I said. "There are female privileges, too."

"Not anymore," Sandy said.

"Pleasure's in short supply, is it?"

"Pleasure?" Sandy said. "That and sleep are things of the past, and when I do sleep, Tony's breathing keeps me awake. If Ben cries, even though you get up, I lay awake and worry. I haven't slept in two weeks." She shook her head. "Tony, Tony, Tony. The whole world revolves around him. Tony's illness has destroyed my trust in fate."

"I'm amazed you had any to begin with," I said.

"Well, I did. But now, I feel like I'm a bad luck magnet."

"Look what you're drawing to you, Sandy. All of us are here to help. What you're seeing is the counterweight to fate, a pendulum where one weight rises and the other falls."

Standing, Sandy went to the door. "There's a pollyannaish streak in you that reminds me of Lillian. Counterweight? If you're talking about you and Tony's parents, don't you think I'd rather have Tony healthy than have the universe cough up three poor substitutes?"

A fist punched my chest. Three poor substitutes? She lumped me in with Aldo and Lillian?

The door swung shut. I'd been trying to offer the hindsight of my own experience. When Rob's memorial service was over, the only thing that made an iota of difference was the support of my kin. I thought of my mother's Sunday dinners, the only time my kids ate anything but hamburger, beans, and rice. I thought of Rob's mother, Grandma Jean, with her flyaway bun. She had doubled up Rob's brothers and sisters and made room in an already crowded house for me, Sandy, and Kevin. Irreverent, bawdy, with her South Side "dese" and "dose," Jean had stood with an arm around my waist and assured those in the receiving line that, "Rob is in a better place where he can look out for us." The line at mass had gone half way around the block. I wondered how I could have endured the loss alone and why Sandy thought being alone might be better.

CHAPTER 19

Squirrels raced in the attic and I listened to them clawing about and building nests in the insulation above my bed. Ben fussed for his sippy cup until I padded in and found it on the floor. Sandy had a right to her opinion. There were two points of view on anything. I had thought our situations identical—children, dead husband—but obviously, my understanding only went so far. What did it feel like, watching a husband die, not even die so much as morph into a person you didn't recognize, a needy man? How fast the landscape of her life had changed. Three extra people—Ben, me, and Maria—jammed into a space where Tony, Sandy, and Josh fit perfectly.

In the morning, I stuck a cup of water in the microwave and watched Sandy slide her half of the trundle bed beneath the upper mattress. She went into the bathroom and left the door ajar. I tried not to be a voyeur, but couldn't help watching her toss down Tylenol. Two weeks without sleep. Two weeks *with* Tony doing the Elvis. He sat at the table with his drink and paper.

Sandy looked out from the bathroom. "Lillian's coming down this afternoon."

"Oh, good," I said. "While Josh is at school, I'll walk down and get the plate. I wanted to give it to her before her birthday."

"That's today," Tony said.

"While we're coordinating our calendars," I said, "I could use a night off."

"Lillian's coming down, but she's taking Tony to the Sleep Center." Sandy dabbed cover stick on the circles beneath her eyes.

"What Sleep Center?"

"A sleep lab at Georgetown Hospital. They have to keep Tony overnight. It's something Lillian's been promoting, so if it's her idea, I say, let her take the ball and run."

"Is this about your breathing?" I said to Tony's back.

"Sort of." Tony lifted his head. "But it's not the same as the breathing test they do in my doctor's office. That just takes a couple minutes."

"Why do you have to stay in the hospital?"

Tony turned around. "They want to see if I get a good night's sleep. My mom's going to stay overnight with me."

"She can't lift you," I said. "Besides, it's mean to make her spend her birthday in a hospital. Let me go."

"You do enough," Sandy said.

"That's true," I said. Sandy and I were the ones who needed sleep, not Tony. He slept fine, what with Sandy fluffing his pillows and scratching him when he itched. Several times a night he'd jerk awake on account of his fasciculations—spastic muscle movements. At night, his feet kicked uncontrollably. The one thing still intact, I'd learned from a trip to Kinko's and the ALS website, was his ability to get an erection. If he *thought* about moving a muscle, he couldn't do it. Thought meant motor neurons. Sex was part of an involuntary set of responses, and like his sensory nerves, his sexual function might very well remain intact until Tony lost control of his bladder. Eventually, he would have to be catheterized.

Grape-Nuts cascaded into a bowl. I carried Tony's cereal to the table and strapped on his eating gizmo.

"I was wondering if you could make something else for breakfast," Tony said.

"Like what?" I said.

"An omelet. Even if I let the Grape-Nuts get soggy, they're hard to swallow. And actually, it'd be simpler if you fed me."

I looked at him, head tilted, his brown eyes blinking. He held up his hand, a bird with a broken wing. Oh, my God, the feeding.

"I guess I could do that," I said.

While making his breakfast, I totaled up the number of hours I already spent feeding him. Lunch took two hours, dinner three. One meal blended into the next, like the townships in Metro D.C. I pictured myself in the chair at the head of the table, spooning food into Tony's mouth another two hours a day. An entire day of physical inactivity. I would go out of my mind. That phrase kept popping up, and I wondered what would push me to bail. One more feeding a day. That might do it. I needed Lillian and Aldo to do more than shop. They had to become at least minimally competent. In a couple of weeks, I had to go back to Evanston for the start of school, and I couldn't afford to be a basket-case. The omelet bubbled and curled.

By the time Sandy came home from work, I had picked up the plate from the store, cleaned the bathrooms, and thrown out the refrigerator leftovers. Maria had to run for her bus. She thrust Ben in my arms, and I put him on my hip so he wouldn't pull toys from the cupboard and cause Sandy to fly off the handle. Carrying him was like carrying a backpack of books. He kicked my hips. "Stop it, Ben," I said.

His solemn brown eyes fastened on mine. I whispered in his ear. "I'll put you down. Just sit tight, okay?" He had no idea what I was saying, but he stopped trying to escape. Sandy went upstairs and woke Josh. When he came down, I showed him the plate. It reminded me of the ceramic spoon holders my kindergartners made for holiday presents. An eye-popping rainbow of color arched over a gingerbread cabin.

"Wow," Josh said. "Do you think Grandma Lillian's going to like it?"

"How could she not?" While Josh made a card, I put Ben on the floor and wrapped the plate. Ben dumped out his wooden puzzles. Damn it. I'd just cleaned the place up.

Lillian let herself in, and Josh ran up to her with the gift. She pressed his cheeks, exclaiming, "For my birthday?" Beaming, Josh stood with his hands behind his back. I leaned against the stairs and watched Lillian undo the bow. Sandy's footsteps creaked in the upstairs hall. Had she gone upstairs to avoid us?

"That is the most beautiful plate I have ever seen," Lillian said. "And I know just where I'm going to put it. I'm going to hang it on the wall of our apartment."

"What apartment?" I said.

"Oh, look at this, Josh," Lillian said. "You made such a gorgeous rainbow. I can't thank you enough."

"Is Aldo retiring?"

"No, no." Lillian waved the idea away. "Last month we decided to rent a place a few blocks from here. It's a month-to-month lease."

"Is it for the illegals?" I said.

"No, for us, *bella*. We were spending a fortune on hotels." She held the plate at arms' distance, then hugged it to her bosom. "Birthdays. My goodness."

I didn't understand why they needed the apartment. Tony's folks didn't come down all that often. Maybe they wanted to get more involved. Even if Lillian couldn't lift Tony, she could feed him.

Sandy lugged a clothes basket downstairs. Buried by the sheer volume of laundry thrown on the floor of the linen closet, I had left a load of darks.

"There's two more loads in the basement." I took the basket from her hands. "I'll fold them after dinner."

"I wish you'd stop trying to put my clothes away," Sandy said.

"I'm trying to give you one less thing to do."

"Well, don't."

"Thank you, dear." Lillian held up the plate and looked at Sandy. "This is so thoughtful. I can't thank you enough."

"I didn't organize that," Sandy said. "My mom did."

"She did?" Lillian said, finally looking straight at me. "You did?" She looked up, as if trying to sort her thoughts. That look, not the "thank you" that should have been forthcoming, made me furious. Lillian had come out on the short end of the respirator decision, and she couldn't lose gracefully. Of course not. If Tony didn't go on a respirator, she'd lose her son. Feeling the weight of the clothes basket and its sharp plastic edges cutting into my palms, I said, "It's good you're moving down."

"We plan to come down two days, every other week," Lillian said.

"In a couple of weeks I have to be back to Chicago and start teaching."

"That soon?" Lillian looked around in panic. "I can take Josh off Sandy's hands and let Sandy concentrate on Tony. Of course, you'll take the baby."

"Like hell I will," I said. "I need time off, too, and I'm not going to be hauling a baby around. Plus, I'm going to be a thousand miles away."

"I can't believe you two," Sandy said. "I'd give anything to have more time with Ben. Most grandmothers would be thrilled."

"Oh, I'll be happy to take him," Lillian said. "It's just that Colleen is much more of a baby person. She's here every day, and he knows her better."

Having the apartment, she said, would allow her to fix dinners and have the family over in her space. She felt awkward cooking in her daughter-in-law's kitchen. It always made her nervous. She didn't know why, but it did. I laughed to myself. I knew why. I was living here.

Sandy glided back toward the stairs.

"Just a minute," I said.

"What?" Sandy said.

"I'm ready to collapse. From now on, Sandy, if you take a night off, get me some help. I can't handle the kids and Tony by myself."

"Why not?" Sandy said. "I can."

"I can't," I said. "Get one of his friends to come over."

"That's extra work to arrange," Sandy said.

"It's extra work to take care of Tony and the kids," I said. "I can't do it."

I wondered what Sandy was thinking. Well, I guessed I knew: the three poor substitutes. I carried the clothes basket to the basement, checked the front room to make sure Maria had picked up the LEGOs, and in the back room, toed open the bifold doors that hid the washer and dryer. During the week Maria slept in this tiny room with its round-topped refrigerator, gas range, and kitchen sink. The family didn't use her shower, which meant one less bathroom for me to clean. I moved the baskets of clean clothes to the floor, put the dirty ones in, and debated about where to do my folding. Tony had always folded laundry in the living room, but Sandy didn't like seeing clothes spread out on the couches. If I left folded clothes on top of the washer, the spin cycle would knock them off. I couldn't leave laundry baskets on the floor. No place to walk, plus, when the bus dropped Maria off at ten o'clock, she'd want to flop down in bed. Sandy didn't like me to leave laundry in the playroom—Josh's and Ben's sacred space—and I feared her reaction if I carried the heaping baskets upstairs and dumped them on my bed. Her bed, actually. Where would she want me to put these? But wait. She hadn't said not to fold them. She'd said don't put them away. She must want me to fold and sort to the best of my ability and then she would correct my errors before they wound up in the drawers.

Looking back, I can see how ridiculous this was, the whole charade of placating Sandy, of adjusting my behavior, or worrying about her state of mind and wondering what might set her off; but at the time, exhaustion clouded my judgment. Caught up in the day-to-day, I couldn't step back and see the big picture. I only knew that taking care of Tony wasn't at all like taking care of my parents. My dad had a stroke and wound up in a nursing home. Pretty bad, but still doable because I didn't have to do his day-to-day care, apart from a few times when he had a bathroom emergency and I had to put him on the toilet. My mom's Alzheimer's lasted seven years, and I did the things most kids do: handle the shopping and laundry, bring her to live with me and park her in adult day care, and then eventually move her to a nursing home. Taking care of Tony exhausted me because I didn't have power of attorney or even power of persuasion, and I couldn't step back without stepping out. When I look over the journals I kept and the Post-its with their snippets of dialogue, I can see the pressures on us all.

I folded the clothes and separated them into two baskets—grownups and kids. I would put the kids' clothes on the dresser in Josh's room and the adult clothes on Tony's bed. Carrying up the first basket I met Sandy, with Ben on her hip, and I backed down into the living room. Instead of the jeans or running shorts she usually changed into the moment she came home, she had put on a blue-silk blouse and tight black skirt, almost as short as the jeans-skirt Esmeralda wore. I put the laundry on the piano bench. "You look like a million bucks," I said.

She handed Ben to me. "I have to take Tony to the Sleep Center to check him in."

"I'll go get him ready, shall I?" Lillian said.

Lillian had never set foot in the bathroom. "Why don't you just do that?" I said. Maybe he'd take a big dump for her. Lillian disappeared into the back room.

I touched Sandy's shoulder and leaned in. "I'm dead serious about needing time off."

"I need time off, too," Sandy said. "I talked to Charles the other night, and he happens to be in town." In the back room, Tony was directing his mother about tee-shirts. I put a finger to my lips and looked his way. Sandy whispered, "After I drop Tony off, Charles and I are going out to dinner."

"Great," I said. "Just great."

Sandy touched my arm. "Don't worry. I'll get help for you."

That wasn't what I was worried about. I was worried about Sandy. Sandy had the combination that would turn Charles on. She was beautiful and strong, but he could see inside to the girl who longed for rescue. If Sandy revealed that part of her personality, the layer beneath the super competent lawyer and career woman, Charles would respond like her personal 911, the way he had with me, stepping in to rescue me from my building projects. Back in Vermont, Charles had a girlfriend with two kids. From what he'd said, he'd mainly been in it for the kids, but if he had formed a bond with those children, that would make it hard for him to walk away. The last thing Sandy needed was to be hurt by some guy who was ambivalent, not quite out of one relationship while beginning another. The signals were pretty clear.

***

The next morning, the chief poor substitute, Lillian, drove Tony home from the Sleep Center. Tony seemed eager to escape her company and work on *Ramón on the Cliff*. Instead, Lillian followed him into the bedroom and sat on the trundle bed, her back contorted as she strained, through reading glasses, to decipher the text on his computer. "Oh, Tony, this is wonderful. How marvelous. Who would have imagined you had such a creative streak." Tiptoeing into the kitchen to grab a yogurt, I eased open the refrigerator. At the gasp of the door, Lillian turned, her forehead a chevron of wrinkles.

"Have you read this? Isn't this just the most marvelous story?" Lillian's face was composed of two circles: an inner one, where the eyes, enlarged by her huge round glasses, flashed like a child's, and an outer face that showed every one of her sixty-eight summers at the beach. "I think we should call the nursing service about the BiPAP," she said.

"What's this about a BiPAP?" I said.

"Mo-om," Tony said, his hands suspended above the keyboard. "They said they'd send someone over."

She checked her watch. "Tsk-tsk. Whatever you say, dear."

From her oversized bag, Lillian extracted two photo albums. "Last night at the hospital I did this." She spread open the album on the bed. Before Josh's birth, Tony and Sandy had taken a bicycle trip along the Brittany coast. In one picture, Tony leaned against his bicycle, taut muscles ridging his thighs. He wore biking gloves. One hand gripped the brakes. Lillian turned a page, sighing and wondering aloud which album to do next.

"Do the wedding and honeymoon," I said. They had spent their honeymoon in Umbria, where Aldo's cousins lived.

"Oh, that would be fine, dear," Lillian said, "but where are the pictures?"

"They're in the basement or maybe the garage," Tony said.

I said I'd get them.

The completion of these scrapbooks would move Tony one step closer to tying up the loose ends of his life. I went down to the basement. On my way to the garage, I noticed a musty smell, like mildewed laundry. Sniffing, I opened the bifold doors and checked the washing machine. The clothes I'd washed last night smelled fine. I transferred them to the dryer. I sniffed. The musty smell came from somewhere close. I opened a second set of bifold doors. Behind them I saw the water heater, boiler, and dryer vent. The lint pile beneath the dryer vent felt wet. Water must have come in from outside. I opened the basement door. A downspout three stories tall carried rainwater from the roof to a terra cotta drain tile. I wiggled the downspout until a section came loose. A clot of leaves fell at my feet. The downspout was clogged with leaves. I looked up at the roof. It was flat, and at the top, leaves must have blocked the box gutter. With no extension ladder, I'd have to find a roof hatch in one of the bedroom closets.

One floor higher, Lillian opened the back door. "Colleen. Colleen!"

I shrank back in the shadow of the stairs and held my breath.

Above me, the dining room window slid open. Lillian looked down. "Oh, there you are. I thought you'd run off. Could you come up here?"

"Just a sec. I'm looking for Tony's pictures." In the garage I opened boxes and found only lacrosse trophies and law school notes. Finally, I found a shoebox of Walgreen's photo envelopes. I tucked the box under my arm.

"Collee-eenn," Lillian screamed from the dining room window. "We need you now!"

Why the big rush? Tony had sent me to get pictures. I'd found them.

I went up the back stairs and opened the door to the room addition. There stood Lillian with two men: a chubby man in a green baseball cap that said "Apria" and Eugene, the visiting nurse, in red shorts and a sweaty, Beltway Reds tee-shirt. He apologized to Tony for coming straight from a game. Apria had paged him.

"What's 'Apria?'" I said, making a little joke. "One of the teams you play?"

Eugene laughed. "No, it's a company that rents medical equipment."

"I guess you're the lady who needs to know about this," the Apria man said, looking at me. A white appliance the size of a bread machine sat on Tony's bed.

"What is that and why do I need to know about it?" I said.

"It's a BiPAP," Lillian said.

Eugene, the nurse, took a stethoscope out of his bag and said to Tony, "While I'm here, I might as well check you." He washed his hands in the bathroom. The man from Apria began his equipment rundown. Tony would use the BiPAP at night to give his lungs a rest. The machine had two settings, one for when Tony inhaled, the other for when he exhaled. The BiPAP would let him get more air in and out of his lungs without him having to use his respiratory muscles. Later, he could use it during the day.

"These people in my ALS chat group said they'd made a road trip to Florida and had the BiPAP plugged into the cigarette lighter the whole time," Lillian said. "They claim it's as good as a respirator."

"But it's not a respirator, is it?" I looked at Lillian.

Her eyes danced away.

"No, it's not," the man from Apria said. "A respirator's permanent. A respirator goes in here." He pointed to his Adam's apple.

Lillian shuddered and closed her eyes.

"I'm in the middle of something," I said. "Lillian, you arranged this. You figure out how it works."

I wasn't going to think about this. It wasn't my problem. It wasn't my business. Before deciding to spend my summer here, I'd told myself I'd draw a line, and this was the line. No respirators or things like respirators. If Tony went on a respirator, I was out of here. Of course, I was going to be out of here anyway. In a little over two weeks. I had never looked forward to the school year so much. I could have the class from hell, and the kids wouldn't drain me the way this did. If I could at least get Lillian to feed Tony, maybe I could duck out a couple of days early.

Upstairs I opened the closets. The hatch wasn't in Ben's, which would have been great because there wasn't a lot of junk on his shelf. In Ben's room, though, I found a brown stain right where the wall and ceiling joined. I poked my head out the window. Yep, the water had entered below the scupper. Rain threatened. I'd have to clean out the leaves immediately, or the plaster damage would equal the blistered spot over the first-floor arch where the happy birthday sign still hung. I should patch the plaster before I left.

"Colleen," Lillian trilled, "you might want to come down."

"You handle it," I called.

If Lillian truly wanted to make herself useful, she could start by learning about the BiPAP, which she'd made herself a pom-pom girl for. Hooking Tony up to it would become a new part of his bedtime routine, new on top of wiping his ass.

"Oh, darling," Lillian said, "I know you're busy, but I think you'd really better come down here."

"All right, all ready."

Downstairs, Eugene wrapped Tony's arm in a blood pressure cuff. The man from Apria showed Lillian the parts of the mask: a triangular, silicon contraption with a stiff, plastic piece that snapped into concealed grooves. Lillian ran to get a pencil and paper. I took hold of the headpiece and practiced snapping the plastic in place, then watched him demonstrate the correct alignment of the air hose, a one-inch version of the dryer vent. He opened a package and showed us a spandex cap with dangling straps.

"That looks like one of those things men wear." Lillian laughed nervously.

"No, it doesn't," Tony said.

"Well then, a brassiere," Lillian said. "We need a little levity. Isn't that right?" She looked at the man from Apria, but he had his back turned as he slid the mask over Tony's face. The plastic fogged with Tony's breath.

The man bent over. "How does that feel?"

Raising an eyebrow, his head cocked to one side, Tony blinked down at the machine.

"He wants to give it a try," I said.

The machine clicked on and the technician adjusted the air flow. I started back upstairs.

"Don't disappear just yet," Eugene said.

"Why? What's on your mind?" I said.

Eugene looked down at Tony. The mask covered all but his big, brown eyes. Tony thrashed his head and moaned.

"Take it off," I said.

The technician removed the mask.

"We got a call from Dr. Stevanovic," Eugene said. "The clinic that's giving you the human growth hormone called. They're stopping the trial. The good news is, no more shots."

"What? No. My nerves are growing back," Tony said. "I can feel them."

"Can't he keep taking it?" Lillian pushed aside the BiPAP's parts so that she could sit on the bed.

"That's why I signed the no-respirator agreement," Tony said. "I'm better and I know it."

Eugene removed the cuff.

I knelt eye-to-eye with Tony. Neither Eugene nor Lillian knew how to deal with him. "You must have believed the growth hormone would bring back some nerve function."

"Yes," Tony said. "It regenerates them."

Tony obviously had never taken biology. "The only regeneration I know about happens when lizards lose their tails," I said. "And you're not a lizard."

Tony blinked slowly, looking very much like one. He was about to explode.

"It was a joke. I'm sorry," I said.

"If I could fire you, I would," he said.

"But you can't, so you won't."

I told the assembled multitude I was going to bring the ladder up from the basement and that I would be on the roof for an hour or so.

"But who'll watch Tony?" Lillian said, pressing her palms together.

I pointed a finger. "You."

Eugene packed up his stethoscope. "Tony, you're only breathing in the top half of your lungs." He looked at me. "I'm going to write a prescription for some morphine. No biggie, but I'd probably fill it just in case."

"In case of what?" I said.

"You need to calm him."

"Morphine's a narcotic," Tony said.

Eugene thumped his own chest. His nostrils flared. "It'll help him take a deep breath."

Tony shook his head so hard his shoulders swayed. "There's no way I'm taking an opiate."

Eugene bent over the table, scribbling on his prescription pad, and tore off a sheet, giving it to me.

"That's a waste of money," Tony said. "Don't bother with it."

"I'll go right now." I could deal with the roof later.

Eugene packed up. "I've got to run back to my ball game."

"See if you can find me a relief pitcher," I told him. "I've got to get out of this house."

"Tony's entitled to a home health aide three hours a day," Eugene said.

"Even weekends?" I said.

"No, only weekdays."

"What would such a person do?" I said.

"Give Tony a shower. Feed him. Dress him."

"That'd give us a break," I said.

"I don't want some stranger touching my privates."

"Your insurance pays for it," Eugene said. "You might as well get some benefit."

"No way," Tony said. "No stranger is touching my privates."

"I'm leaving soon," I said. "Your mom can't lift you and Sandy works, so you're going to have to make some adjustments. Besides, Tony, frankly, it's not all about you."

Lillian put her face in her hands and began to cry.

Stupid ninny. I was losing patience with them all.

Driving to the pharmacy, I pictured Tony in his wheelchair, naked, a conga line of strangers waiting to touch his privates. Once he sank his teeth into a phrase like that, he'd never let it go. Strangers touching his privates. What a guy.

All these years later, I have so many words for him, and so few. Now, between the cookies I'm baking to mail Josh and the essay Ben has just asked me to read, I sit and write about one of the set of days we all lived through. Emotion recalled in tranquility. In the future, I plan on asking Josh and Ben to read this portrait of us all, our lives alone and together.

***

My low-grade headache and a problem that had developed with my close vision made the dashboard with its broken odometer look wavy: I was living in an aquarium. I needed an eye exam, but couldn't leave the house to get one. Overdue for a mammogram, too. While I waited for Tony's Roxanol prescription, I tried on granny glasses. The world up-close came into focus, but when I removed the glasses, I felt nauseated. I bought them, though, and a paperback. Maybe I could lose myself in a mystery.

Later that night in my bedroom, I changed into my nightshirt. Three able-bodied adults were downstairs: Sandy, Aldo, and Lillian should be able to get Tony in bed. I had completed one thing on my to-do list. To fix the leak in the basement, I had backtracked to the roof and, sure enough, found the scuppers blocked with leaves. The only access to the roof had been through a two-foot-square opening in the top of Josh's closet. I'd had to clear all his toys and put them on the floor, then hoist myself through the hatch. After cleaning the scuppers I'd stayed on the roof, smelling fresh air and watching the sky, thinking about the evening Sandy and I watched the sunset at Woods Hole and how the short-staffed EPA squeezed every drop of juice from the orange of Sandy's life. When I was her age, I had spent vacations remodeling houses. I'd felt the need to stay busy, even though I could have lived on my teacher's salary and taken summers off. For women of Sandy's generation, there was no time to catch a breath. Perhaps my refusal to come down looked infantile. I didn't care. It was self-preservation.

Lillian rapped on the door. "I'm sorry to bother you, dear, but would you mind coming down to show Sandy how the mask works?" I fake-snored, but Lillian tiptoed in and gave my foot a shake. I slopped downstairs in a nightshirt and saw a vial of growth hormone on the counter. Sandy was giving Tony his shot.

"What's that about?" I said.

"Tony wants to use up his supply," Lillian said.

"Why?" I said.

"I'm an outlier on the data set," he said.

"You're an outlier, all right," I said.

Hair wet from the comb and face pink, Tony waited in his chair. Aldo and Lillian stood back by the door: Aldo with his hands on his hips, one foot forward, as if he might spring into action and suddenly become effective, Lillian with her hands up by her chin where she could wring them. I showed Aldo the proper way to make the bed transfer. When I had Tony in bed, I adjusted the spandex cap. The machine started up.

"It's quieter than I expected," Sandy said.

"Will you be able to sleep?" I said.

"I have to make myself." Sandy folded her arms, a grim look on her face. "If I drop dead, who would take care of the children?"

CHAPTER 20

The mask pressed a red triangle in Tony's face and pinhead-sized pimples erupted. Eugene had never seen anything like it. Tony had sensitive skin. The nurse left a roll of hypoallergenic tape and told me to wrap the mask's rubber gasket. The BiPAP now lived on the half-wall at the head of Tony's bed, a reminder, during the day, that he faced a night of torment. I tried to get him in bed before ten, but his masterful delaying tactics, plus the difficulty of adjusting the mask to his satisfaction, pushed bed time later and later. Agitated and annoyed, I fell in bed at midnight and when Ben woke at five-thirty, I pulled the covers over my head and groaned. With a little over a week to go, I knew I could muster the energy to make this final push, but it dismayed me that Sandy hadn't yet made a plan to replace me. They're ostriches, Lillian once said. I changed Ben's diaper and brought him downstairs to start another day of grueling boredom.

"My therapist at work is encouraging me to get out more," Sandy said, talking to me over the divider between her room and the kitchen with its ghastly blue-flowered wallpaper. I'd meant to steam that off, but with only a week left, I didn't want to start a new project.

"I decided to join a women's movie group."

"Does this movie group meet the one night a week you take for yourself already?"

"No, it's on top of it."

"For god's sake, Sandy."

"Don't worry, Frank and Noah are coming over. I invited them for dinner."

"You didn't."

"I did," she said, rinsing the BiPAP's hose. "But it doesn't have to be elaborate."

At dinner time, Josh picked at his food and Ben threw peas on the floor. Maria had dispensed cheese sticks and crackers at five o'clock. I put on a video for Josh and brought up the farm set Ben liked to play with. Maybe the kids would stay out of my hair. The nights with Tony and the kids were killers. Josh felt abandoned and Tony ditched. Having Frank and Noah come over would probably be more trouble than it was worth, but at least they could help Tony tape his blues' favorites. Thanks to me, the Garrard turntable had a new belt and needle.

Listening to rain drum against the glass and smelling the clean, damp air wafting in through an inch of open window, I sat down to feed Tony. When I heard a knock and saw rain-bedraggled Frank Delaney standing at the door, I told Josh to unlock the door. A wobbly tower of records in his arms, his tan raincoat soaked, Tony's former roommate backed his way in. Blond-haired Noah, in loose jeans and a saturated windbreaker, followed him.

"Hey, Tony." With one thumb, Noah hoisted a plastic sack. "We managed to get these through the deluge." He slammed the door and Tony jerked, shivered, and smacked a bite of tortellini. On the couch, Josh sat with legs crossed, elbows on his knees, watching *Black Stallion*, a movie that looked like a movie about a horse, but turned out to be about the drowning death of a small boy's father. Josh was sitting stiffly, his eyes wide, and Ben had disappeared from view.

"Grandma, Ben's touching the VHS. No, no, Ben," Josh shouted.

"I've got to deal with the kids," I said, hopping up from the table. "Noah, please feed Tony the rest of his dinner."

Noah moved to the head of the table. I stopped the movie and turned on the cartoon channel. At Josh's end of the table, Frank lowered the records toward spilled apple juice, grains of rice, and peas.

"Wait," I said, running for a sponge.

"I don't want my buddies feeding me," Tony said.

"Why not?" I said.

"They won't do it right."

"Noah has a college education and he can't figure out how to feed you? Give me a break." Ben had a poopy diaper.

Noah stared at the spoon. "I've never done anything like this."

"The key is small bites," I said.

Noah aimed the spoon at Tony's mouth. Tony opened, began to swallow, and then choked. He choked and choked and Noah tried to thump him on the back. Josh climbed on the wheel of Tony's chair and stared, his eyes widening as Tony's face turned purple. The coughing fit subsided.

I carried Ben on my hip. "Let's move to the next course." With one hand I tried to make a milkshake. Tony could drink his dinner through a straw. I needed to throw Ben's diaper pad on the couch. I put the milkshake in front of Tony, who bent over the straw. Noah trembled, not because he was wet, but because Tony's coughing jag had shaken him. Having his own sort of meltdown, Frank jumped around the living room playing air guitar. Noah and Frank weren't going to be much use with Tony or the kids, but at least they'd brought the LPs: the cardboard sleeves fanned out over the dining room table.

After the diaper change, I uncorked a bottle of wine and put three glasses on the table. Cheese and crackers came next.

Noah cut off a hunk. "What kind of cheese is this?"

"*Morbier*," I said.

"What's that in the middle?"

"Volcanic ash."

Cracker snowed down Noah's shirt.

Frank held the wine up to the light, swirling it, and said, "You know how to live."

Tony looked up from his milkshake and cleared his throat. "But one of us is dying."

Frank and Noah looked at each other. Noah shivered.

"I'll feed him after I put the kids in bed," I said. "Maybe you can do some taping."

"Sure," Frank said.

Upstairs, I ran a bath and dunked Ben in and out of the tub. While Ben played with blocks, I lowered the crib's mattress. He'd taken to crawling over the top and coming into my room. Cross-legged on the floor, I scooped him into my lap and read *Good Night Moon*. He pointed to the Little Old Lady and the brush and the bowl of mush.

"Time for lights out," I said.

Ben pointed up at the ceiling fan. "Digh dout."

I carried him to the switch and he turned it off. I tucked him in, turned on a Raffi tape, and told him good night.

"Nigh nigh, Gramma," said a sleepy voice.

I was going to miss the little guy.

Leaning over the banister, I called down for Josh, who had decided he was too old to put up with his brother's occasional tub poop. Dragging his feet, he came upstairs, undressed, and climbed in the half-full tub. He pushed the moldy ducks and plastic boats aside.

"Why does my mom go out all the time?"

"She needs time with her friends," I said.

"But you never go out," Josh said.

"That's true," I said, "but I'm going out tomorrow."

"Will you be here after school?"

"Uncle Sean and Maria will."

That afternoon, Charles had called. "Can you meet me for coffee tomorrow afternoon?" he'd asked.

"Surely, you jest," I'd said. "I can't leave Tony by himself."

"That's why I'm giving you fair warning," he'd said. "Come on. Make time for an old friend."

"All right," I'd said. Reluctant to leave the house and not sure why I should bother, I'd called Sean and he'd promised to cover. Charles threatened my mission here, helping Sandy get through this ordeal without feeling any regrets. As horrible as Rob's death had been, I'd stepped into the afterlife of my marriage without anything to feel ashamed of. Rob and I had been faithful to one another. We had loved our children. He had supported me. I had supported him. Sandy was soon to make the same kind of transition. I didn't want her burdened by the "if onlys." Tony might not die for a few more months, but now that the respirator issue had been put to bed, I knew he wouldn't live twenty years.

***

The next afternoon Sean, in a suit, tie, and slacks, came straight from work. After I'd hugged him, he said, "This better be important because I'm taking half a vacation day."

"It's important," I said, annoyed at him daring to complain when I'd barely seen him the entire summer, or Kevin either, for that matter. "Sit in the living room and stay out of Tony's hair."

"I drove all the way over from Maryland to do nothing?" he said.

"She doesn't need to get a babysitter," Tony called from the back room where he sat, drinking water from a straw and pecking away at his computer. "I'm perfectly capable of looking after myself."

"Make sure you don't let him go to the bathroom by himself," I whispered.

Sean rolled his eyes. "Okay," he said, "but don't be gone too long."

"Sorry to impose."

"Mom, don't talk to me that way."

"I'm sorry, but I've hardly seen you. I'm leaving soon, and I don't even know what's going on in your life. Why don't you stay for dinner?"

He couldn't. He had something scheduled, but he'd take a rain check and come back Wednesday.

"Sounds good," I said. Sandy had her movie group. Sean could give me a hand with the kids.

To save time, I drove to the coffee shop next to Bisque-it. No sign of Charles. I looked at my watch. My body tensed. I looked at my watch again. In an hour, I'd have to head home. Sure, Charles had lent his house at Christmas. Very generous. He'd laid in groceries, for which I'd paid him. He'd shown up for Tony's birthday party and pitched in with the pizza, but that wasn't enough. In fact, his sporadic appearances did more harm than good. Sandy needed help. She was a mother with two kids, for god's sake, and she had a demanding job that she had to keep because the family's medical insurance depended on it. Right now, she was a heroine; but if she went down the slippery slope with Charles, she'd look back and wish she'd hung in there.

I looked up. Charles's hair had grown into a shaggy fleece, and he looked like one of those men on the covers of romance novels. "Nice hair," I said as he sat down.

"Needs a trim." He finger-combed it. "So, I guess you have just a few days left."

"Six, to be exact," I said, "but I'm just curious. Where'd you hear that?"

"Your daughter."

"Oh yeah? I didn't know you were in communication."

"We check in with each other."

"When?" I said.

"Usually at the end of the day."

"Ah," I said, picturing Sandy lying on the bed, phone in hand. While I put Tony to bed—brushing his teeth, picking out his boogers with a Q-tip, hooking up the BiPAP—Sandy was upstairs talking to Charles on the phone. How about that.

"Sounds like it's been hard for Sandy to have Mom around."

"Hard for Sandy or hard for me?"

"Everyone's trying to be decent."

"Decent," I said.

"Don't get all jammed up," he said. "It's hard to have your mom move back into your life when you're not expecting it. Makes a person feel crowded."

"For Chrissakes!"

"But everyone's making a real effort."

"Spit it out," I said.

"She doesn't know how she'll manage if you leave."

"What's it to you?"

"'Course, this is an awkward situation. I was friends with you first."

"Friends? Charles," I said. "Get real."

"Yes, friends," he said. "Now I've gotten to be friends with your daughter. I was just down at the EPA."

"Sandy allowed you to intrude on her work day?"

"We had lunch at an Italian place next door," he said. "It's the easiest place to meet."

"What is this?" I said. "She's married."

"She needs someone to talk to."

"She could talk to me."

"You're Tony's confidante."

"Confidante? I'm his butt-wiper and body servant." Trying to calm myself, I looked out the window at a couple pushing a stroller. "What's she talk to you about?"

"Everything. Her job situation, Tony, the kids. She's quite a gal, your daughter."

I felt my chair levitating. I gripped the table. Maybe Sandy saw Charles as an escape hatch, like the hatch in the roof. Like that day I'd been desperate for a breath of fresh air, maybe Sandy wanted to slip out and see the sky. Charles would be the perfect short-term lover, but he had a damn good mind, and Sandy might actually fall for him, making her life way more complicated. Not that I condoned Sandy stepping out on Tony. Far from it.

Charles tore the corner off a sugar packet and poured it onto his curled tongue. "I have great respect for Tony."

"Me, too," I said.

"I'd like to be available."

"Available for what?"

"Babysitting or taking care of Tony. He doesn't have long to live."

"Where'd you get that?"

"Sandy," he said. "Her therapist says she should think about moving on."

The mug missed my lips and coffee dribbled on my shirt. The china clinked as I returned the cup to its saucer. It was one of those two-stripe mugs that Josh had noticed, the kind he could have made.

"I wouldn't count Tony out," I said. "Maybe you should cool your jets."

"I'm talking to *Historic Preservation* about a job. The mag's here in town. I don't want to put any pressure on Sandy. Just be available."

"There's that word again," I said. "Available for what?"

"Friendship." He looked down at a blob of water on the table and rubbed it around with his finger. "I'd like to take her to dinner."

"I thought you had been."

"Well, more often."

"You don't want to be sneaking around behind my back. Is that it?"

"I told her you'd understand." He reached for my hand.

I pulled it away and grasped my mug, raising it to my lips. A tic started in my left eye. I pressed the lid to make it stop.

"She's sure got two cute kids," he said.

"That's a new one." I dug change out of my pocket and threw it on the table.

"I believe you're jealous." His face turned red and he pushed his chair back.

"You self-centered prick," I shouted.

He followed me out the door. "I'm trying to be a friend."

"Then be a friend to both of them," I said, confronting him on the sidewalk. "Be a friend to me. If you want to help row, I'll hand you an oar and you can be one of the galley slaves."

I got in my car. Slamming the door, I drove away, leaving him on the curb.

CHAPTER 21

On Wednesday, Sandy came home from work, threw her briefcase on the dining room table, sat down in Josh's chair, and put her head down on her arms. I touched her shoulder.

"What's wrong, honey?"

She raised her head. "I have to go out again."

"With anyone I know?"

"My movie group."

"Why don't you skip it?"

"I'm the movie-discussion moderator," Sandy said.

"Sean's coming over," I said. "I promised him a home-cooked meal."

Sandy managed a smile. "That's one thing I appreciate. When I come up the ramp, I smell a good dinner. I've never been much of a cook."

"Listen, Sandy, I'm going to be leaving in five more days. I need to know what plans you've made to clone me."

"I haven't had time to think about it," Sandy said.

"My mom's working on it," Tony said.

I turned around. Clicking his Saturn mouse, Tony sat at the end of the bed. In the half hour between feedings, he had gone back to the computer and worked on his book.

"Has she hired anyone?" And who could she possibly hire to do everything I did?

"There's some agency up in New Jersey she's talking to," Tony said. "I'll e-mail her and tell her when you're leaving."

"I don't have a good feeling about this," I said.

Sandy shrugged. "Insurance doesn't cover this. Since she has to pay for it, I've decided to delegate."

Sandy kissed Ben and Josh goodnight and only then did I notice the sharp pencil driving into my left eyeball. I took an Excedrin. My prescription for Imitrex had expired and my neurologist back in Evanston wouldn't renew it unless I came in. The migraine frequency had ramped up to two or three a week. The house was noisy, with kids throwing their little fits, Maria shouting, or Tony laughing at an e-mail joke. The migraines would go away once I got out of here, but I'd have to tough this one out till the end of the day.

At a quarter to seven, Sean opened the door. His tan bomber jacket gave him a swagger that he'd never had before. "Wow, dinner smells great," he said, sniffing the air. He took off his jacket and hung it over the newel post. He came into the dining room and, ducking his head so he could see me in the kitchen, he leaned on the counter.

"Hey, Mom, I found some guys to jam with."

"That's fabulous." I saw that the diamond stud was back in his ear.

"It feels good to have music back in my life."

"Is this going to be a band, or what?"

"I don't know," Sean said. He looked at Tony. "We all have day jobs. Plus, if we did get any gigs, it'd be on Friday or Saturday night."

"I see," I said.

What he was telling me was that he couldn't be coming over here once the band got going. I could leave, but he couldn't take my place. He didn't even have to say it.

"Dinner smells sensational." Tony sniffed.

"It's garlic risotto."

"Is it okay for me?" Tony said.

"Absolutely."

A good dinner usually put Tony in a better mood. I eased the cork off a bottle of Normandy cider. I'd been saving it for a special occasion: the countdown to my last day; and at this point, I was very much looking forward to seeing the little ones with their superhero lunch-pails scuff down Lincolnwood's wide, dark hall. I poured cider for Tony, stuck his straw in it, and handed it to Sean to put on the table.

Sean took the glass, swirled the cider, and held it to the light. "Good head."

"Fix yourself a plate," I said.

"Okay." Sean filled a plate and sat down, but not in the feeding chair.

I looked at Ben, rocking back and forth, inching his high chair toward Josh, who grabbed the tray. I clamped my hands on Josh's shoulders. "Don't do that, Josh."

"I want to feed Ben," Josh said.

Tony looked over, shaking his head. Not allowed.

"That's okay. I've got it under control." I found a bib, took away Ben's tiny fork, and picked up carrots the baby had pushed off the tray. "Ben's big enough to feed himself."

I settled into the chair at the head of the table. As long as I lived here, feeding Tony fell to me. "What do you want to start on first?"

Tony raised his eyebrows.

"This or this?" I pointed to risotto and carrots.

"Risotto," Tony blinked.

He opened his mouth and I put a bite in.

A half-cough turned Tony's face red. He tried to cough again, the repeat grinding of a bad ignition. Josh stopped eating, planted his hands at the sides of his plate, and stared like a hypnotist.

"Josh, relax," I said.

Food sprayed from Tony's mouth. He leaned forward and gasped. Josh, eyes wide, continued to stare.

"Sean," I said, nodding to Josh. "Intervention."

The food had gone down Tony's windpipe. He struggled for breath. Standing behind him, I pulled him upright. The wheelchair made it hard to slap his back, and he went on coughing.

Sean, looking stunned, slid Josh's chair back from the table, but even then, Josh fixed his stare on Tony's face. Eventually, Tony took a normal breath.

"Wipe Josh's mouth and take him down from the table," I said. The boy had barely touched his dinner. He looked drained.

Sean pointed down at Josh's head. "Looks worried."

"Magical thinking," I said. Whenever Tony had these coughing fits, Josh stared. He probably thought the staring stopped Tony's cough.

"Josh, why don't you show Uncle Sean your LEGO mansion?"

"Okay," Josh said. "It's in the basement."

"Can you take Ben with you?" I said.

"No problem," said Sean, sliding out the highchair's tray. "We're good buddies, aren't we little guy?"

Ben, his black eyes aglow, looked up at Sean who, with his ease and confidence around children, made me ache for Rob.

"Tony, I think you'd better not eat anymore tonight. I'm going to clear the table and then we're going to have a talk."

Tony nodded. I flicked the power switch on his wheelchair. He could check his e-mail while I rinsed dishes and loaded the dishwasher and, after that, I could brush his teeth and change him into pajamas. I swept the kitchen and emptied the garbage, then settled at the foot of his bed. In good conscience, this had to be said.

"Listen, Tony, I'm worried about the coughing. If I had to do the Heimlich maneuver, I'd have to get you out of the chair."

Tony looked at me and shrugged, opening his mouth and nodding toward the baclofen on the counter.

"What if I'm the only one here?" I said.

He shrugged again.

"What am I supposed to do, let you suffocate in front of your kids?"

Tony looked out his window at the darkness. He blinked. Like beads of water on a sliced potato, sweat broke out on his forehead. He turned pale.

"What's the matter?" Jumping up, I turned on his wheelchair, backing him into the middle of the room. "Sean, come here quick."

Sean's footsteps reverberated up the basement stairs. I grabbed Tony from behind, pulling him to a sitting position. His head slumped.

Standing in front of the wheelchair, I wrestled him to his feet. His knees buckled.

Sean squatted and took Tony's hands. "Shit. What's wrong with him?"

"He's passing out," I said.

"Should I call 911?" Sean said.

"His nurse's pager number is on a refrigerator magnet." I moved out of the way. "Hold him."

Sean slipped his hands under Tony's armpits and held him in mid-air.

I ran to the refrigerator, got the number from the magnet, and reached an answering service.

"I can't hold him much longer," Sean said. "Mom! Get over here."

Tony's face had turned mustard yellow.

"Put him back in the chair," I said. Grabbing the BiPAP's hose, I assembled the parts. "Hold his head and chest back. When he caves in, his lungs have to work too hard."

I jammed on the facemask. Tony's mouth gaped open. My forearm pressed his chin. I flipped a switch, and his chest moved, barely.

"Should I call 911?" Sean asked.

"No, we've got him back," I said. "Breathe, you SOB."

Tony fought the mask.

"Let the machine breathe for you."

He wriggled and opened his eyes.

I heard a noise. Holding up the spandex cap, the part of the BiPAP that made Tony look like an astronaut-pope, Ben toddled toward his father. Ben's eyes reminded me of children's in disasters: the thousand-mile stare. I'd worried about Josh watching Tony choke. Now, I saw the illness had affected Ben, too. I'd tried to shield the boys with an umbrella of love, but it hadn't worked.

Tony, fully conscious, straightened up. Sean massaged his shoulders. Tony's cheeks turned pink. In the kitchen, the phone rang. The ringing continued until I picked up the receiver.

"What's going on?" Eugene said.

"Tony passed out, but he's breathing now," I said.

"Have you got the morphine?" he said.

"The Roxanol? Yes, I have it."

"Then I won't bring any."

After hanging up, I returned to Tony. He raised his eyebrows and widened his eyes. Then he looked down at the mask. I removed it.

"What happened?" I said. "Was it what I was talking about?"

He stifled a cough. Food was still caught in his windpipe. Sinking down on the bed and exhaling, Sean cracked his knuckles. "Shit, man, you gave us a scare."

"Tony, maybe you're not getting enough oxygen in your lungs," I said. "You should wear the BiPAP until Eugene gets here."

"No opiates."

His voice sounded reedy.

"You passed out," I said.

"It's a good thing Mom was here," Sean said. "I wouldn't have had a clue."

Tony would have been gone. It would have been over. I looked into the dining room. Ben had climbed on the table and knocked over a vase of flowers.

Time for bed. For everyone. I turned off Tony's computer, brushed his teeth, washed his face, and helped him to the toilet. Sean changed the boys into their pajamas and tucked them in. After putting on his jacket and shaking his head, Sean gave me a hug. "Hang in there, Mom. You're a short-timer."

Pulling him close, I heard the squeak of his leather jacket, and I went back to keep Tony company until the nurse arrived. In bed, his head propped on a mound of pillows, the BiPAP pushing air into his lungs, Tony stared at the open bathroom door and the faint glow of the nightlight. I drew a chair to his bedside and took his hand. His fingers moved slowly across my thumb. Half an hour later, I surrendered my chair so that Eugene, a hospital ID still clipped to his green scrubs, could sit down.

Bending over Tony and running a stethoscope across his chest, Eugene said, "How are you feeling?"

Tony raised his eyebrows and shrugged, the only speech possible with the chin-strap and mask.

"Are you scared?" Eugene asked.

Tony blinked.

"Listen, Tony," Eugene said. "It's not your time yet."

Tony looked at me.

"It's not," I said. "Ramón's not out of the woods."

Eugene moved the stethoscope over Tony's chest. "Bring me some Roxanol."

In the medicine cabinet, I found the box of morphine. Tony turned to the wall. I loosened the chin strap and pried open Tony's jaw. Eugene squeezed an eyedropper onto Tony's tongue. My stupid directness. Suffocation. Only an idiot would have used that word with a man expecting to suffocate to death.

"Are you okay?" Eugene said.

Tony blinked, yes.

"Tomorrow," Eugene said, "we'll switch you to a hospital bed so Sandy can move you to an upright position. You'll sleep better, too."

Tony blinked his agreement.

"I'll call Dr. Stevanovic," Eugene said. "She'll want to see you."

Tony blinked again.

Finally, after all this time, I would get to meet Dr. Stevanovic, the doctor who'd confirmed Tony's original diagnosis. Tomorrow, a trained medical professional would take over and tell us what to do, and four days from this moment, the inept idiot who'd just about killed Tony could pack her clothes and tools and skulk back to Chicago. By tomorrow night, if there still wasn't a plan for my replacements, I'd call Lillian and force the issue.

***

I actually hadn't expected choking problems. I'd been more concerned about breathing. But Tony had passed out before, in the Jacuzzi at Koolfont, and I should have seen this coming. On the neurology floor at George Washington University Hospital, a nurse called Tony's name. Silently, Sandy and Tony filed into a small room with pictures of rainbows on the walls.

"Nice rainbows," I said. They reminded me of Josh's plate.

The respiratory technician, Vivian, a wavy-haired brunette with a Bronx accent, said, "Oh yeah. Rainbows are my special thing." She put on medical gloves and held up a rubber snorkel. "Who's going to help today?"

Sandy raised her hand. "I'll do it." She fit the snorkel between Tony's teeth and pinched his nostrils. Vivian turned on the machine that measured Tony's ability to breathe. At the last minute, lab coat flying, Dr. Stevanovic squeezed into the room. A beeper was hooked to the waistband of her skirt, and I wondered if it flashed for ALS patients in distress. Of course, as I'd come to know, it wasn't just ALS. People with advanced MS and Parkinson's had swallowing and breathing problems, too. They choked. They suffocated. The only difference was, they didn't go downhill so fast.

"Okay, Tony, now," Vivian shouted. "Deep, deep, deep, deep. Okay. Now exhale. Push, push, push, push." Perched on a stool next to me, the neurologist leaned forward, looping a finger through the ticker tape as it unfurled. Vivian repeated the test three times.

"The best was thirty-nine," Vivian said, taking out the mouthpiece.

"That's not as bad as I feared." With her salt-and-pepper man-cut, Dr. Stevanovic, all business, flipped back through Tony's chart.

Feared? I thought.

"He wants to go ahead with the feeding tube," Sandy said.

Feeding tube! What the heck was that?

"Has he had his swallowing test?" the doctor said.

"Not yet," Sandy said.

Dr. Stevanovic stood up abruptly. "Let's go to my office." She paused halfway down the corridor and looked back at Tony, fumbling with the control of his chair. "I wish you'd come to the clinic," she said. "You'd find a lot of support."

"What clinic?" I said.

"The support group for patients and their families," Dr. Stevanovic said. "We've told Tony about it several times and we really wish he'd participate because we have a lot of services: the speech therapist, the PT guy, the OT person, and group support that's just amazing."

"You could see Roosevelt again," I said.

"Not interested," Tony said.

I was interested. Damn right, I was. But it didn't matter. I would be out of here. Tony's parents could deal with this. Lillian could hire the illegals.

Dr. Stevanovic distributed chairs. Sandy sat on one side of Tony. I sat on the other. Across from us, the doctor hunched forward, her elbows in her lap. "So, I have to tell you, this is getting pretty close to the end, but like I say, it's not as bad as I expected. That's the good news."

Sandy and Tony looked at each other.

"The bad news," said the doctor, "is that it's probably too late to put in the feeding tube because your breathing is compromised. I'll have to talk to the G-I surgeon and ask him whether he can do it with just a local anesthetic, plus maybe some Midazolam. That's a drug that puts you in la-la land and gives you amnesia afterwards. He may not want to risk it, because, you know, he could lose you right there on the table."

"Wait a sec," Sandy said. "You told us Tony needed a feeding tube, but you said we had plenty of time to make up our minds."

"That was three months ago," the doctor said.

Sandy had known this for three months. Incredible.

Dr. Stevanovic tilted her head sideways, raising one eyebrow. "Your respiration was holding about fifty to fifty-five." She waggled her hand. "Now it's down to thirty-nine, better than I expected, but still a big dip, and we find that once respiration becomes involved, that's the surest indicator of the amount of time you have left."

"And what is that time?" Sandy asked.

Dr. Stevanovic sat back, making a circle of her fingers and coughing into it. "A few weeks to maybe two months. When I heard about the thing last night, I thought maybe just a few days. I think his breathing will fail before he loses the ability to swallow."

There was a sink in the corner. Water dripped from a tap.

Sandy took Tony's hand.

"Could you give us some idea," I said, "how long this final stage is going to last? I'm concerned that Tony will be in pain."

The doctor coughed again. Standing, she bent over the sink for a drink of water. "When Tony has trouble breathing even when he's sitting up, I'll switch him to pure morphine. I just got back from a conference, and the ALS doctors were talking about the amazing amounts of morphine they were giving patients, so I don't think you have to worry about pain. It's more like a feeling of panic." Cough, cough. "Until then, make sure you wear the BiPAP at night to give your lungs a rest, and make sure you sleep sitting up."

"I don't think I can," Tony said.

"I'm not telling you to do anything I don't do," the doctor said.

"You sleep sitting up?" Sandy said.

"I've had asthma all week. If I don't sit up, I feel like I'm suffocating."

I looked at Tony. He didn't start sweating. A blue thread at his temple pulsed. He took a breath and squared his shoulders. Maybe he wasn't thinking about the coffin lid closing down. Maybe he was numb.

"What about the kids?" I asked.

"Kids in this culture are shut off from death," Stevanovic said, "but death is a part of life. We'll keep Tony comfortable. Just don't tell the kids he's falling asleep, or they'll never sleep again."

"They don't sleep anyhow." I looked over at Sandy to see if my attempt at humor lightened things up. Despite her polite smile, she refused to look at me, and a knot worked at the corner of her jaw. Sandy let go of Tony's hand and took it again, lacing her fingers through his. She gathered his hand into her lap.

Dr. Stevanovic reached over and took Tony's other hand. "So Tony, no more solid food. I want you on a liquid diet."

"So—should we give him shakes with Ensure?" Sandy asked.

"That would be fine. Use Thick-It if he drinks water."

"What's that?" I said.

"A powder you mix in," Sandy said. "They told us about it before."

Why didn't they tell me these things?

"For solid food, Tony can only have pureed foods," the doctor said. "Think baby food."

"But I'm not having trouble swallowing," Tony said.

"Cough for me, Tony," Dr. Stevanovic said.

Tony took a deep breath, and from his throat came the sound of a worn ignition, starting, stopping, starting, stopping.

"See?" she said. "If a small piece of food got caught, you couldn't bring it up."

Sucking in his cheeks, Tony moved his jaw, and with an effort, swallowed a pebble of saliva. I thought of the food stuck in his throat last night. He might choke to death in front of the kids. They might have to watch him gasp. Suddenly, I knew I could go on. I would go on. The moment I got back to the house, I would call my principal and tell her to find a long-term substitute. Whatever it took, I would do. Anything to push back that fatal day and be there for Tony when it came.

***

Driving home from the hospital, I looked in the rear-view mirror and tried to unscramble the garbled words coming from Tony's lips. "Starting tomorrow," he repeated, "I'm going to make lemonade out of lemons." No more *Washington Post*. No more breakfast omelets. He'd begin his day at the computer, working on *Ramón*. At home I left Sandy and Tony in their bedroom and took my phone to the porch. Sitting on the railing, I girded myself for the call to school. The office staff was busy, I knew, with last minute registrations. The children's immunizations had to be checked, addresses verified, and parents who had not gotten their teacher of choice had to be convinced that their child's psyche would not be damaged by the teacher the school had assigned them. This was not a good time for me to load Dr. Hidalgo down with another task, nor did I look forward to turning over my children—this new batch of eager, squirming, little beings—to a substitute who might or might not establish the right tone on the first day. Most of all, I hated having to make these arrangements because as soon as this was over, I'd have to step back in and deal with whatever kind of classroom the kindergarten had turned into.

Dr. Hidalgo picked up the phone.

"Listen, Angie," I said, "I've got a situation here."

"A parent situation?"

"No, a family leave situation."

There was silence, then a sigh. "Is this the same deal as last year? You need a day or two?"

"More than that," I said, "and I know this is extremely bad timing, but it looks like my son-in-law only has a month to live. I can't bail on my daughter."

"I understand, and in a way, I've been expecting it."

"You have?"

"Maureen told me what's been going on. She said she'd be willing to step down and take your class."

"But wouldn't that mean disrupting two classes, hers and mine?"

"I have a good second grade substitute lined up," she said. "Maureen vouches for her. The girl's pregnant, so she can only teach one semester anyway, and when you come back Maureen can reintegrate with the second grade team."

"Maureen will have a hard time adjusting to kindergarten," I said.

"I know," Dr. Hidalgo said, "but I've spoken to Linda about this, and she says she'll step forward."

Linda, who'd been wanting to expand her unit on nutrition, could be a leader. Linda could do more with her rescue dogs. For both Linda and Maureen, arts and crafts would be the big challenge.

"I don't know if that's a workable plan," I said.

"Listen, Colleen," Dr. Hidalgo said, "you are not Atlas. You do not have to hold up the world. Maureen and Linda will do fine without you hovering over them."

In the background, I heard children's voices. I would miss the first day of school.

"Okay," I said.

"The good thing about you old warhorses is that you can handle about anything."

Old warhorse. Probably an accurate description. I certainly had been feeling like an *old* warhorse lately. Or, maybe an old battleaxe.

"Thank you."

"You'll have until January 1," the Principal said. "Do you think you could be back by then?"

"Yes," I said. "I'm sure of it."

I checked the phone battery: low. Taking a deep breath, I sat down on the porch chair and put my feet up on the recycling box. I wanted to make this call even less than I'd wanted to make the other.

Kevin's phone rang and rang. The wind broke up his hello.

"Where are you?" I said.

"Barbecuing hamburgers," he huffed. "I ran in from the porch. What do you want?"

"I have a favor to ask."

"Sure," he said. "What?"

I needed him to fly out to Chicago and deal with my tenants. If only Esmeralda had been there. He asked what needed to be done. "Make sure the apartment's clean," I said. "Duplicate keys. You know the drill."

"I don't know if I can," he said. "I'm looking for a job."

"I thought you had a job."

"I got riffed back in June. I thought for sure they'd hire me back, but I haven't gotten a new contract."

He hadn't told me. "Why don't you look in Chicago?"

"My girlfriend wouldn't like it."

His girlfriend? Should I have known about this? The fact that he'd even mentioned a girlfriend must mean it was somewhat serious. Usually, they came and went without my knowledge, leaving me with a strange, empty feeling that I wasn't privy to certain parts of my children's lives.

"You'll have to go next weekend. You can get a one-week, advance purchase on Southwest if you do it today, and as long as you're out there, you might as well look for work."

"I'm not going to move back in with my mom," he said.

"What about your old friend Jeremy? You could work on your *anime* stuff."

I heard a pause. I could just about see the smile. "Yeah, I guess I could do that."

"As for the job, I suggest you try Arlington Heights," I said. "Either that or Elk Grove Village. They pay better than Evanston."

"How's their basketball program?"

"I have no idea."

The phone went dead. Maybe I should buy him a ticket. No. I'd given him the parameters. He was a big boy. I returned to the house.

Late in the day, a delivery team from Apria toted the top half of Tony's trundle bed out to the garage. Sandy's half remained. The men brought in a hospital bed. With the same green bedspread and square bolsters, no rails because Tony didn't need them, the hospital bed looked like the old one, just six inches higher. While Josh watched cartoons, Maria put Ben down on the floor of Tony's room and ran to catch her bus. Ben discovered the electrical control and folded the bed into a pita sandwich. Later, I told Sandy, who stood at the kitchen counter sorting bills, "There must be a reason nursing homes and nursery schools aren't in the same facility."

"Mom," Sandy said and looked at Tony, "that's not funny."

It was funny. Sandy just didn't see it.

"So, Tony," I said, "what's the verdict? Are you going to get a feeding tube?"

"I don't know," he said, raising his head from his water straw. "I need to think about it some more."

This was so Tony. Instead of *Pantaleone,* Aldo and Lillian should have named him *Procrastinazione.*

CHAPTER 22

Because I planned to stay, Lillian called off her search for the illegals, but she knew I needed a break, so she and Aldo came up with the bright idea of taking Tony, Sandy, and the boys to Disney World. "He wants to do something special for her birthday," Lillian said. A hiccup of laughter escaped before I could stifle it. Tony and Disney World. Why not Fantasy Island? Act III had opened in the Theater of the Absurd. I needed a new coping strategy and convinced myself that humor would help me stick it out. If I couldn't change the situation, I could change the way I felt about it. In a macabre sort of way, life here was a laugh riot: Tony's tiny bites and the sock selection that balled up the muscles in the back of my neck. Joking with Tony made it easier to put up with his moods. "Oh, you card," I'd laugh. "Are we going to play *that* game again?" He took offense at my light-heartedness, but he was going to die soon. I didn't even nag him about the feeding tube. Every day he put off his decision brought me closer to the day I could get out of here.

Tony could have made my life easy by drinking all his meals, but no. "I'll drink breakfast," he said, "but not lunch and dinner." And, as for breakfast, he would only drink it if I could make a shake without ice cream. He didn't want to get fat. "Ah, that's my boy." I laughed to show how little his micromanaging mattered.

Then, the Tuesday before the Labor Day weekend, out of the blue, he said, "I've decided to get a feeding tube. See if you can find me a surgeon."

Slack-mouthed, I stared at him.

He could have decided this a long time ago. With a three-day weekend ahead, doctors wanted to clear their calendars. The surgeons on his Preferred Provider list didn't know Tony from Adam. Why would they do him any favors? "The surgery's risky," I reminded him. He'd thought about that. He'd take a chance. Upstairs in my bedroom, I pushed aside the wicker basket. Sandy had ten thousand in unpaid bills and more coming in every day. On top of CAT scans and co-pays for the BiPAP, this new procedure would invite another flood of window envelopes. But maybe I was needlessly concerned. No surgeon in his or her right mind would operate on a man in Tony's condition. I wrote out a script, emphasizing the risks, and talked to the surgeons' receptionists. Within ten minutes, I'd found one who agreed to perform the operation, but only if Tony could do it the next day.

Downstairs, I broke the news. As I could have predicted, Tony wanted to think about it.

"If you don't agree to this now, I'm going to call them back and cancel," I said.

"Okay," he said, sheepishly.

"Okay, what?" I said.

"Okay, it's a go," he said, rolling back from his computer.

"You are such an incorrigible procrastinator," I said. "I should make you stay in from recess."

"That's what my teachers always said, but they let me get away with murder." He smiled for the first time since Josh had left for school. "So how about a last meal?"

"Where?" I said.

"Bethesda," he said. "I know a terrific Indian restaurant."

I dressed him in slacks and a white shirt and drove him to Bethesda. In the crowded Taj Mahal a tuxedo-wearing, Indian *maître d* showed us to a window table. Maneuvering his wheelchair through the businessmen who put down their forks to stare, Tony followed me to the buffet. He wanted fish *tikka masala* and potatoes with peas. In addition to Tony's plate, I filled one for myself. Back at the table, I tied on his towel-bib and looked around, daring the men to keep making Tony the center of their attention. Conversation in the restaurant had died down to a whisper.

Tony raised his eyebrows. "Noah says he's not going to come over again."

It took me a minute to think what he meant. "But you're not done taping your music."

Tony nodded.

I put down my fork and looked at Tony, bent over his straw. "Frank will help you."

"Noah has better records," Tony said.

"Can't Frank borrow them?"

"Noah never lets them out of his possession."

"He's one of your best friends."

"He was."

"He's probably depressed," I said.

"In a month I'll be dead," Tony said. "He's depressed?"

Poor Noah. I could see his waif-like face and scraggly blond hair, his desperate, pleading eyes as Tony choked on the bite Noah had fed him. What had really upset Noah, I guessed, was Tony's comment, "One of us is dying."

"You know what people aren't prepared for, Tony?" I said.

He opened his mouth and I spooned in fish.

"They aren't prepared for the anger. In your house, there's so much anger you could cut it with a knife."

"That's naïve and stupid."

"You're saying Noah's naïve?"

He gulped down a bite. "He should have expected it." Then he began to choke. Droplets of food sprayed my face and diners turned to stare.

I wiped my cheeks with a napkin. "Nobody expects it," I said. "I didn't."

"Then that was naïve of you, too."

Yes, it was.

The waiter brought a breadbasket of *nan*. "Thank you," I said.

In truth, I hadn't known what it would take to be Tony's caregiver. The emotions were just a small part of what I hadn't anticipated. I hadn't foreseen the monotony of getting "the body" in and out of bed, washing it and brushing its teeth; the doctor's trips and special diets; the straining to understand speech; the endless translations for friends and family. I hadn't known about the infuriating delays caused by chair-back adjustments and flat tires and the missing battery charger. And I would never have guessed that pee could mysteriously spray all over the bathroom floor, even after Tony sat like a girl on the toilet. None of the caregivers' manuals mentioned the orange shit that oozed out Tony's rectum only half-way so I had to dig out the rest as I wiped his butt. And how about smearing the stuff across the backs of my hands as I held Tony's swaying dead-weight with my left arm and wiped with my uncoordinated right hand, trying to get up the crack? What about when he teetered suddenly and made me smear shit over his hairy butt-cheeks, so I had to top off the trip to the toilet with a sponge bath? I broke off a triangle of *nan*, stared at a puddle of orange-brown gravy on my plate, and covered the plate with my napkin.

One by one, the rest of the patrons slipped on their jackets. The restaurant emptied. Tony told me to hurry before they closed the buffet. He wanted eggplant and chicken. Like the burners beneath the steam trays, his body burned energy, but still, he was totally ignoring Dr. Stevanovic's instructions and risking his life, the very day before he'd risk it again under the surgeon's knife. I refilled his plate and sat down to feed him.

"Sandy says you never told her she was pretty," he said.

"What on earth made you think of that now?" I minced his chicken.

"When I met Sandy," he said, "she had zero self-esteem. She thought she was ugly and unpopular."

I thought of Esmeralda's flame-like bangs and outlined eyes, her attempt to improve her distinctive features. "But Sandy was pretty."

"It took me years to convince her of that." He opened wide. I spooned in a bite of chicken. He chewed and swallowed, but as I listened to him smack, the smell of curry began to make me sick.

"If she was such a basket case," I said, "why did you fall in love with her?"

"Sandy's face is like a mirror," he said. "I discovered that if you shine love in, love is reflected back."

"You're saying I didn't shine love in?"

"Not consistently."

"Tony, I was as consistent as a mother could be. I could have stood on my head and whistled 'Yankee Doodle Dandy,' but I could never have made up for what Rob's death took away. The kind of affirmation Sandy needed about her looks would have come from him."

"Her father's death was the biggest loss of her life."

"Of course."

"She was devastated."

"But she never told me."

"She'd rather die than tell you."

"But why?" I said.

"She doesn't trust you."

"She doesn't trust me?" I said. "Why on earth not?"

"I just told you," Tony said. "She doesn't trust you with her feelings. You weren't there for her when she needed you."

I looked at him, his mouth open and waiting for the next bite.

"Excuse me," I said.

Reeling, I pushed back from the table. In the bathroom, I splashed water on my face, telling myself he couldn't be right, but I felt my breath going down like the big vitamins Tony dry-swallowed. I blotted my face with my sleeve. Not there when Sandy needed me. Just when that could have been, I couldn't imagine because I'd been there all the time. Right there, trying my hardest to reach through the wall of silence, and, lately, anger. As I emerged from the bathroom, confronted by a waiter who demanded that we leave so the restaurant could close, I had to put my thoughts of Sandy aside, remove Tony's bib, and wipe his chin.

**

When Sandy returned from work, throwing her briefcase on the stairs and holding out her arms as the children ran to greet her, I had a funny, twisted feeling in my stomach. I wanted to pretend nothing had changed since that morning, no secret knowledge acquired, no despair.

"Sandy, can we talk privately for a minute?" I said.

"Can't it wait?" Sandy put her hand on Josh's head. "I haven't seen the kids all day."

I pointed to Tony, at work on his computer. Silently, I mouthed the word, "doctor." Sighing, Sandy picked up Ben. "Let's go upstairs." While

I spun around on the desk chair with Ben in my lap, I transmitted the news about the surgery. Sandy pulled her jeans up under her dress and shed her work clothes like a snake sheds skin.

"Can't you schedule this another day?" she said. "I have a meeting with a congressional staffer tomorrow."

"The doctor said tomorrow or not at all."

Sandy threw on a tee-shirt. "I'll have to make it work, then."

"If you're sure this is a good idea," I said. Somehow I wasn't, but arguing the point would have exhausted me. I had grown to distrust my own certainties and no longer knew what was best.

"So how shall we do this?" Sandy said.

I would drive Tony to the hospital. That would give her most of her work day. She could arrive by three. Watching her, I felt desperate to ask why she didn't trust me and if all these months I'd spent caring for her husband had convinced her otherwise. I could see that a lack of trust might have existed during her adolescence, but I had always hoped that teenage rebellion would open doors to a close mother-daughter bond. On the trip to Woods Hole, that bond had begun to form, with Sandy talking openly about her hopes and dreams. She had outgrown the shy, self-conscious coed Tony had fallen for, and if she carried any baggage from before, I wanted to know it. Right now, though, Sandy had so much to deal with I couldn't see burdening her with my insecurities.

***

Tony, whose neck had grown weak, asked to have his head velcroed to a telescoping pole on the back of his wheelchair. I strapped the wheelchair to the eyebolts on the floor of the van and as I drove, Tony rode with the stoic defiance of Marie Antoinette going to the guillotine.

Sandy arrived at four. She'd tried to find the *Sports Illustrated* swimsuit issue, but couldn't, so she brought Tony a couple of joke books. A nurse in booties and green scrubs, her hair clipped back, opened the door of the small waiting room. "You're here for a jejeunostomy tube, right?"

"What's that?" I said.

"A feeding tube in his small intestine."

"No," Sandy exploded, slamming down the legal brief she'd brought along to edit. "He's supposed to get a stomach tube. Mom, you told him the wrong thing."

"Are there different kinds?" I said.

"Obviously," Sandy said. "You should have asked Tony. He knew."

Tony glared at Sandy and Sandy glared back.

"Please, don't fight." He could die on the operating table. "It was my mistake. Let me call the doctor."

"I'll do it." Sandy phoned Dr. Stevanovic. The doctor said it was okay. Just make sure they didn't compromise Tony's breathing. "Mom, it's late. Go home and relieve Maria."

"Why don't I stay so you can see the kids?"

"No," Sandy said. "Tony wants me here. Tell Josh I'll call him before he goes to bed."

There was no point in objecting. Someone had to stay and someone had to care for the children.

At home I gave them dinner and a bath and played Chutes and Ladders with Josh until ten o'clock, when Sandy called to wish him good night. Tony had not had his operation until seven-thirty. Sandy had hammered on the anesthesiologists and residents, who wanted to put Tony into a twilight sleep; but the head anesthesiologist overruled them, saying, "No, we can do it with a local." Just to make sure, Sandy had made another call to Stevanovic, who'd agreed with the anesthesiologist that it was best not to compromise Tony's breathing. Because he'd been wide awake, Tony had wanted Sandy there to communicate in case the local didn't work. She had dressed in scrubs and sat at Tony's head with the anesthesiologist. The surgeon cut a hole in Tony's abdomen, just to the left of his navel, and pulled out a piece of small intestine. He opened it and inserted a tube into his slippery pink intestine, Sandy said. Exhausted, she had slept at Tony's bedside in a chair.

Early the next morning, I was shocked to see Sandy push Tony's wheelchair through the door. He was slumped over and could barely raise his head. Sandy showered and went to work. At two o'clock the phone rang.

"Yes?" I said, expecting Lillian.

"Mom, it's me," Sandy said. "I was wondering if you could meet me for coffee."

"Someone needs to be here with Tony."

"Maria can look after him."

"But she's never taken him to the toilet."

If Tony had to go to the bathroom, Maria would be horrified and he would be embarrassed. They'd have another hazmat situation. I very much wanted to meet Sandy somewhere outside the house where the air seemed freighted with death. Finally, we'd have a moment to talk, just the two of us. Then I looked at Tony's face, his eyes squeezed shut, his arms curled up close to his body. His cheeks were flushed.

"This is the worst possible day," I said. "Tony's in too much pain."

"Well, so am I." Sandy slammed down the phone.

I should have said tomorrow or the next day. Just not today. Once again, as I had with Esmeralda, I spoke before thinking through the implications. A well of fear opened in my chest. I had let my daughter down.

I didn't know then how important the phone call was to her, that she reached out, hoping I would clasp her hand. She was desperate for me, too, but I had made a commitment to look after her husband, and, in truth, on that particular day, it would have been grossly negligent for me to leave the house. Only the armrests of Tony's chair kept him upright. I asked if he wanted a pain pill. He refused. Codeine made him nauseated. Tylenol, then. No. The doctor hadn't prescribed it. We'd been round and round about medication before, but this was one time when painkillers were legitimate. He'd just had an operation. He shook his head and shivered.

I lifted the hem of his shirt. The surgery had implanted in Tony's abdomen a bright, pink beach ball with a blow-up tube. The incision looked nasty. I touched it and Tony winced. "Feels hot," I said. Yellow pus oozed from the stitches. I shook down a thermometer and put it under his tongue. He ran a fever of a hundred and four. Eugene needed to come take a look at this. I phoned, but the nurse was on vacation. They said a substitute would arrive within the hour. Of course. Another poor substitute.

***

"I'm Constance. I'm covering for Eugene." Carrying a briefcase and wearing a tan blazer, a gray-haired nurse, fiftyish, with an emerald scarf looped around her neck, thrust out her hand.

Shaking it, I thought of Eugene in his athletic attire. "Thanks for coming so soon."

"You're welcome," Constance said. In the dining room, she took off her blazer and hung it on the back of the feeding chair before running a stethoscope over Tony's chest. She felt his pulse and took his temperature. "I'll call the surgeon and ask him to phone in a prescription for antibiotics." She'd have the pharmacy send the pills by cab so that I didn't have to leave the house, and in the interim she insisted that Tony take Tylenol to lower his fever. He should skip eating until the medicine brought the infection under control, a day or two, and she wanted him to lie down and take a nap. I put him to bed and he fell asleep immediately.

"In a couple of weeks they're going on a trip to Orlando," I said. "Will he have his stitches out by then."

"When are they leaving?"

"The twenty-fourth," I said.

Sitting where she'd left her blazer, Constance speed-dialed for doctor's orders, then assured me he'd have his stitches out well before the trip. Until then, she wanted me to use cotton balls and rubbing alcohol to keep the sutures clean, especially after feedings. Apria would send over a mast-and-pump. A nutritionist would tell us how many calories Tony needed. He'd have to start with a dilute solution and ramp up slowly. I asked the nurse what that meant, "ramp up slowly." It meant get to the point where Tony took all his calories through the feeding tube. His intestines needed to accommodate to this method of feeding. Generally, that took three or four months.

"But he only has a month or two to live," I said.

Constance's beeper went off. She took it from her blazer pocket, checked the number, and placed the beeper on the table. She looked into the back room where Tony snored.

"Why did he get the feeding tube?" Constance said.

"Why?" I said.

"Yes, why." Leaning forward, looking at me intently, she lowered her voice. "A feeding tube is a life-extending measure. ALS is so hard on the family, it's better not to drag it out."

"The doctor recommended it," I said.

Constance shook her head. "The only reason to get a feeding tube is to prevent starvation. ALS burns up so many calories starvation is the best of all the end points. It's preferable to choking or suffocating."

"Have you had many ALS patients?"

"Fifty or sixty."

"Then why did the doctor say he should have had it months ago?"

"Because their whole mission is to prolong life." Constance nodded toward the kitchen. "I see you have a BiPAP. You know that's actually a respirator. It's just not hooked up to a trach tube. That could extend the patient's life by several years. The longer this goes on, the harder it will be."

I knew it, I knew it, I knew it. "Why is his doctor recommending these things?"

Constance slipped the loose pages of Tony's file back into the manila folder. "Because doctors love technology. Also, she doesn't have to live here. ALS patients are not the easiest people to live with. In my experience, they're the most self-centered human beings on the face of the earth."

"Are they *all* self-centered?" I said.

"Did the doctor talk about PLC?"

"I've never heard of it."

"PLC stands for Pathological Laughing Crying. Not all ALS patients have it, but many do. Did he ever have a strange laugh that sounded sadistic? Early on, maybe before he'd been diagnosed?"

I thought of Tony laughing about the pigs.

"Yes," I said, "but he hasn't done it in a while."

Constance tapped her forehead. "With PLC, there's frontal lobe involvement. They lose the capacity for empathy. Like sociopaths."

"What's a sociopath?"

"A serial killer," Constance said.

"A serial killer," I said flatly. "Like someone on death row."

She nodded. "Put that in a family and you have a disaster."

"Maybe you're burned out."

Constance snorted a laugh. "The ones who suffer are the caregivers."

"But I'm the caregiver." Sandy was suffering, giving Tony his shower. Tony was suffering, thinking about his death and his children. "I'm not suffering."

"I don't believe it," Constance said. "Who does the night shift?"

"My daughter."

"Does she have kids?"

"Yes," I said.

"Then she definitely is."

She leaned back in the feeding chair. Beneath the table, her shoes dropped. "When I started in this profession, you never would have seen equipment like that in a home. It doesn't belong here."

The door opened and Maria, pushing the stroller, came in. Nursery school had let out early. Before the babysitter created her usual coming-home ruckus, I put a finger to my lips and tiptoed across the living room, telling her that Tony had a fever. Maria spun the stroller around and took it onto the porch. "I'll go around back," she said, "but first see what Josh made."

Constance packed her papers. "Excuse me for getting on my soapbox." She put on her coat.

"I wish my daughter had been here," I said.

The nurse squeezed past the stroller. "Call me if his fever doesn't go down."

"I will," I said, watching the slim, middle-aged woman close the door.

"Look at this picture," Maria said.

"What?" I wanted to run after the nurse, yank open the passenger door, and drive away. Constance understood what was going on. I lived in a loony bin.

Maria unrolled a picture from nursery school.

"What's this?" I said.

Josh poked his head out from beneath the stroller's awning. "That's a picture of our family."

There was his name: JOSH. A small figure in dungarees and bright red shoes stood at the far left. Mom, the biggest person, in a purple dress and white, crayoned shoes, stood next to him, holding his hand. Next came a wagon wheel with a small, slumped figure. With one hand on the wheelchair, a woman with a braid like mine held the hand of a toddler in white shoes.

I looked at Maria. "Where are you?"

Maria patted Josh's head. "This little boy knows who is his family and who is not."

Josh reached back and grabbed my hand. "Come to the park, Grandma. I can go all the way across the monkey bars."

"You're a little monkey, aren't you?" I knelt and looked at his dimpled face. "I can't, sweetie. Not right now."

CHAPTER 23

Weighed down by another sleepless night, I changed Ben's diaper and carried him into my bedroom. It was five-thirty, barely dawn. Tethered to the warm ball in my arms, I closed my eyes, so tired I felt as if I were floating. The baby's body jerked. His eyes popped open and he stared at me. "Gam-ma, I hungey." Slipping feet first off the mattress, he gripped the blankets and toddled to the unlatched door. What a determined little wind-up toy.

Tiptoeing downstairs, I shushed him and put him in the highchair.

"Peeeeek-a-boo," I whisper-screamed, trying not to look into Sandy's bedroom. Over the banging of Ben's little cars and water bubbling on the stove, I heard the rat-a-tat of the shower. I made Ben's oatmeal and pushed a suction bowl onto the highchair's tray, then took out kefir, bananas, and protein power. Might as well start Tony's breakfast shake. Staccato bursts, mixed with sobs, came from the bathroom. Sandy, upset again.

Ben swiveled around. To blot out the crying, I turned on the microwave and spooned warm oatmeal into his bowl.

"Big boy," I said.

"I big." He grabbed the spoon.

The bathroom door opened and Sandy, coughing and in her slip, darted toward the stairs. Tony moved his wheelchair to face the back door. He stared into the neighbor's yard and hung his head.

"What happened?"

"She dropped me," he said.

I wiped Ben's hands with a kitchen sponge, and he screwed up his face. "Okay, big boy. Down you go."

He held his arms up. "Go cool?"

"As soon as Josh wakes up."

When Sandy came down, her face looked like a modern museum portrait: the skin tones green, cheeks daubed in orange. I felt her forehead. Warm.

"It's nothing," Sandy said.

From the back room where he had started working at the computer, Tony called, "My mom's going nuts about Winnie the Pooh pajamas."

"What did she buy now?" Sandy picked up Ben. He grabbed her breast, sucked for a second, and wriggled to get down. "I wish you hadn't fed him. I'm about to burst."

"He was hungry. You were in the shower." I held out my arms. "Let me take him."

Sandy transferred the toddler, picked up her briefcase, and looked in the back room at Tony. Rolling her eyes at the ceiling, she walked toward him, bent over, and kissed his hair.

"Give me a real kiss," Tony said.

"I don't want you to catch my cold," Sandy said.

A sneeze made her double over. Maria had come up from the basement, her hair tied in a scarf. She pulled a paper towel off the kitchen roll and gave it to Sandy, who headed for the door. "*Salúd*," Maria said. Sandy blew her nose. Maria held out her arms and I handed over Ben. Tony needed socks.

First, I wanted to say something to my daughter. "Sandy, please take the day—"

"I don't have any sick days." Sandy opened the screen. Looking back at the living room, she said, "This house is so hard to keep picked up. Could you do something about the books on my desk?"

"Sure, happy to." I'd found a bookstore next to Safeway and, hoping to lose myself in another reality, scooped up armloads of remainders.

Shivering, hugging herself, Sandy said, "I'm going to drive today."

"Why waste energy?" Tony called as Sandy closed the door. "Take public transit."

"Tony, she's sick."

"She's not dying, is she?"

I slammed the door and ran down the sidewalk. "Drive every day until you feel better. You look worn out."

Sandy pursed her lips. "Last night I told Tony I can't take this much longer. He just won't leave me alone."

"Are you sleeping?"

"No."

"What are you worried about?"

"Lillian's coming."

"Is that what the tears were about?"

"I can't take the pressure," Sandy said. "I feel so drained, taking care of Tony at night, working, taking care of the kids. I feel empty, and I need something back." Sandy got in the car, making a tube of her hand. She coughed, leaned against the steering wheel, and rolled down the window.

"Like what?" I said.

"I don't know," Sandy said. "Something that addresses my needs."

"How about if I straighten your room?" I said. "That way, when you're taking a break after dinner, it'll be tidy."

"That would be great," Sandy said.

Putting away the breakfast dishes, I smelled a poopy diaper in the kitchen trash. I carried the sack out to the alley and, across the way, saw a bookcase tilted into a parallelogram. The dovetails had loosened, the back was missing, but I ran my fingers over the tight knots and unpainted pine. The wood was in perfect condition.

I carried it upstairs, wiped off the dust with a washcloth, and thumb-tacked cardboard to the corners. I hoisted the bookcase onto Sandy's desk. Not quite square. What could I do to make it look more presentable? Dictionaries. I wedged two in the corners. *Perfecto.* When I'd finished arranging my books and journals, I tacked up my call list, the friends who'd implored me to come home. Maureen had called a couple of times to give me updates on the kindergartners, and my principal called to say Linda had everything under control. Kevin had called to let me know he'd cleaned the apartment, made keys, and typed up the house rules so the students would know what to expect.

"I love this place," he said. "It's the kind of house we should have had when we were growing up, but who are those people over the mantel. Are they relatives?"

"Oh, my pictures?" The man with the mustache and the woman with the curly bangs. They were hanging there, awaiting my return. "They're somebody's relatives, not mine. I found them at a garage sale and I couldn't stand it that the family was just, sort of, throwing them out."

"It's a good thing you don't like dogs."

But I did. I liked Bear. Actually, I'd liked him quite a lot.

"Oh, and Mom, I had an interview at Walter Payton Academy, the Math and Science Academy, and at Chicago Latin. I thought it would be sort of like Teach for America, but it's not. The schools are as academically rigorous as Chapel Hill."

"Are you doing okay for money?"

"I'd be doing better if you paid me."

Half the items on Sandy's to-do list, like that bubbled plaster in the living room, still needed to get done. "I have a lot of work out here. Why don't you see if you can switch your ticket and give me a hand?"

"Sounds great," he said.

Sandy wanted something that addressed her needs for a change. Kevin could help me complete all the items on her mental list. We could do the work while Tony and Sandy went to Orlando. Sandy would come back to find the dining room and living room painted, the ugly kitchen wallpaper ripped down, and all the other niggling little spots and blemishes brightened up. Kevin could hang out with Sean for a couple of days before flying back home.

In the bedroom, I looked around at the freshly made bed and tidy desk. I patted my new bookcase. I couldn't wait for Sandy to see the improvement. Instead of the stacks of books next to my bed, my books now had a place to live.

"Col-leen," Tony called from the foot of the stairs. "What are you doing?"

"Nothing," I said. "I'll be right there."

Downstairs, I lifted his shirt and swabbed the wound. The house smelled of rubbing alcohol and the cotton came away thick with yellow gunk. He'd been on antibiotics for five days, but the stitches that crisscrossed his incision continued to ooze. When Sandy was little, her favorite book had been one my mother had saved from my childhood: *Nurse Nancy*. The cartoon character had a white apron and nurse's hat and cared for patients in a doll hospital. Like that rosy-cheeked cartoon, like Sandy pushing baby Sean around in her doll stroller, I was playing pretend and at the limit of my ability.

I called Constance. The real nurse returned. She examined Tony and, putting away her stethoscope, said, "He doesn't have a fever, and the swelling has gone down. It's safe to feed him gastrointestinally."

"I still want to eat," Tony said.

"You be careful, hon," Constance cautioned Tony. "Even with a feeding tube, you can choke on saliva. If you're having trouble with your secretions, we can give you something to dry them out."

"No way, José," he said.

Constance looked at me and raised her eyebrows. I translated.

"I need a refresher on hooking up the feeding tube," I said.

Constance looked at her watch. "I have fifteen clients all over town."

"I don't know how to do it."

The man who'd delivered the mast-and-pump, the device that delivered food to Tony's small intestine, had been rushed, too. "These are expensive," he'd warned. I wondered if he'd noticed the toddler with the smile on his face and his arms outstretched as he lurched toward the mast, a six-foot-tall pole on casters.

Constance went over the instructions, step-by-step. At the top of the mast, a hook held a plastic baggie of Ensure. We'd dilute the Ensure with tap water. Half-way down, a pump the size of an electrical meter fed fluid through plastic tubing. If the liquid ran out, an alarm would blast. During the day, the nozzle that protruded from Tony's abdomen had to be capped off, as if Tony were a bottle of glue. At night, I would uncap it and hook him up.

"So, are you all set, now?" Constance smiled.

I couldn't do this. I'd never remember all the steps. "Good to go," I said.

Hooking up the mast-and-pump would be the last thing I had to do before I could go to bed, and I didn't see how I would manage, not just because Tony dragged out the tasks I already did, but because hooking the pump up came after the fifteen or twenty minutes it took to adjust

Tony's facemask. I felt like a soldier in a foxhole, hunkered down while incoming ordnance exploded. Besides which, instead of looking like a home, the house had turned into a medical unit. Sandy stashed boxes of Ensure under the buffet and tucked the mast-and-pump in a corner of the dining room.

An hour before dinner, Lillian and Aldo arrived, complaining that the traffic on the New Jersey Turnpike had wiped them out. They hadn't seen Tony's incision. He lifted his shirt. Lillian gasped and flew upstairs.

"I don't know what she's so freaked out about," I said. "Your stomach's a lot better than it was."

Aldo seated himself at the table. His chin on his hand, he flipped disconsolately through the paper. This was a man crushed by sorrow.

"It's my father's birthday," Tony said.

"How old are you?" I said.

"Seventy-four," Aldo said.

Six years older than his wife.

"I didn't know it was your birthday," I said. "Even so, I think you won't be disappointed in tonight's dinner." Feeling the need to perk up his spirits, I was glad to have traded my nurse hat for my chef hat. Every day I cooked three meals: a Tony meal, a kids' meal, and a Grandma and Mommy meal. Salmon and scalloped potatoes were on the menu. I'd pureed a portion for Tony, lightly browning the potato-cones to look like *timbales*. With a good dinner awaiting her, Sandy might possibly be in a better mood, especially when she saw the dust-free room and the new bookcase holding my novels and self-help books.

I began to whistle. Calling Kevin had been brilliant. With household jobs completed, I could leave the instant Tony died, and Sandy wouldn't have any reason to feel the lack of trust Tony had talked about in the restaurant. Really, I didn't even know what the hell Tony meant, and I didn't feel any obligation to find out. Everyone had baggage.

Sandy came in carrying a sack from the pharmacy and went upstairs to change. A moment later she appeared in the kitchen and hip-bumped me away from the microwave. The cold had entered a new phase, she said. Her trachea felt raw from coughing. She put her hand up over her breastbone, as if to prevent a ricochet, and heated water for Thera-Flu.

I pulled scalloped potatoes from the oven. "Hey, did you notice, I found a bookcase?"

"How could I not notice?" Sandy said. "Do you plan to paint that thing?"

"I like the natural wood," I said.

"It doesn't match."

The bookcase was a find, and finds didn't necessarily have to match. They could be anomalies. At least, I had one piece of furniture in the house to call my own, and I was determined not to let the thundercloud of Sandy's pissy mood throw a pall over Aldo's birthday celebration. Rob, in his infinite wisdom, used to make a little joke that everything you needed to know could be found in your bookcase. He was referring to his bookcase, of course, loaded down with philosophy, history, and engineering: all the books he had collected in college. His broad interests had made him a sort of book-omnivore.

I fixed Tony a plate and sat down in the feeding chair. "Help yourselves, everyone."

Aldo looked over at Lillian. "Go light on the potatoes."

Lillian slipped a spatula under the salmon. "How much fish?"

Aldo held up his fingers. A two-inch slice. Still slim at an age when most men had a paunch, he watched his diet. I had put on thirty pounds. Aldo, not an ounce.

Sandy served herself.

"So, did you hear we're bringing the kids down to our new condo in Orlando?" Lillian leaned across the table to hand Aldo his dinner.

"I heard about Disney World," I said, "but what's this about a condo?"

"It's in Orlando." Aldo spoke through a mouthful of salmon.

"Actually, it's two adjoining condos, one for us and one for them." Lillian, with her own dinner, sat down next to Josh. "We sold the place in Bermuda."

"I didn't know you had a place in Bermuda," I said.

"Oh yes, we did," Lillian said. "But Aldo thought we weren't going there enough to justify keeping it. Now that you're staying longer, we decided to try Florida. We like to spend the winter where it's warm."

"What about your apartment here?" I said.

"It felt cramped," Lillian said, "but if you want to use it, feel free. It's sitting empty over there until the lease runs out."

"Oh, thank you," I said, resenting Lillian for the Pavlovian "thank you" that had sprung automatically to my lips. The Dimasios should do more than take the kids on an expensive vacation to Florida. They were family. Tony was their son. They should be here. I looked at Lillian. "How about if you get a little practice and feed Tony?"

"Me?" Lillian said, her eyes wide behind her glasses.

"Yes, you." I picked up my plate. Until Aldo or Lillian stood up, it was musical chairs.

Aldo pushed back his chair. "I can do it if you're busy." He looked at me, but didn't stand.

"You have to sit here." I indicated the head of the table.

Aldo moved around. I squeezed past Lillian and took the empty chair.

Dipping a fork in Tony's mashed potatoes, Aldo tilted his head and opened his mouth, the way a mother does when feeding a baby. Tony opened wide. Lillian planted her elbows on the table and looked at Sandy.

Sandy said nothing.

Lillian's fixed smile appeared to cramp her cheeks.

"So how's life in New Jersey?" I said.

"Same, same," Aldo said.

"Next time, before buying clothes for the children," Sandy said, "I wish you'd ask me."

Lillian's eyebrows shot up. "But I did, and you said —"

"One pair of pajamas," Sandy said.

"I thought it couldn't hurt to have an extra."

"*An* extra," Sandy said. "There's four pair up there. I can't close the drawer in Josh's dresser."

"I'll take them back."

"Please do," Sandy said. "It's three too many."

Lillian looked at the ceiling, then lowered her eyes and fixed me in the tractor-beam of her attention. "The people in our ALS support group say groups are a tremendous benefit in helping a woman's mood swings. I wish —"

"Shut up," Tony said.

Lillian's neck turned red. She looked at the stalks of asparagus on her plate. Before dinner, she'd grazed in the refrigerator, pulling all the skin from a leftover chicken. She sliced the asparagus in little pieces. "I should like green things, but I'm more an orange-vegetable person." She scooted her chair closer to Josh and looked down at the flags on his place mat. "What's the flag of Romania?" she asked.

Fiddling with the straw in his milk, Josh pointed.

Sandy took the straw away.

"Take a bite of yummy, yummy potato." Lillian picked up his fork and sailed a bite toward his mouth. "Did you see the thingie in your father's stomach?"

"What thingie?" Josh said.

Lillian looked from Sandy to Tony. "Oh, I guess he didn't know about the operation."

"What operation?" Josh said, looking from his mom to his dad.

"An operation to help him eat," Sandy said. "Your dad's fine."

Sipping from her mug of Thera-Flu, hunched over her plate, she looked like an animal gathering strength before it bites.

Lillian brought her leather satchel to the table. It was packed for a road trip: magic markers for Josh, miniature puzzles for Ben. Without a word, Sandy took the toys away.

"Where's my dad's present?" Tony said.

"I don't need a present." Aldo lifted the spoon and dug another tiny hole in the potatoes.

Tony raised his eyebrows at Sandy. "Present?"

She scooted away from the table, her dinner half eaten. Ben had been quietly feeding himself, but when he threw food on the floor, I told Lillian to move aside so I could get past. I took Ben down from his high chair and settled him on the living room floor with his farm animals. Upstairs, I heard a drawer slam. I bounded up to the bedroom. Sandy, coughing, searched Tony's dresser. It was where he'd shoved all the dried-out ball-points, pencil stubs, letters, and business cards from his office. A volley of Lillian's laughter came from downstairs.

"Lillian totally dominates Josh." Sandy shoved Tony's detritus back in the drawer. "I can't wait till I have my kids to myself."

"Did you forget to buy Aldo's present?"

"I was hoping Tony might have something in here."

"Let me see." I ran my finger along my new-old bookcase. I stopped at a biography of Rossini and pulled it out. Aldo was a big opera lover. Everything I needed was right in my bookcase, just the way Rob had said.

I passed the book to Sandy. "Can you wrap this?"

"Sure," she said. "I have paper in the basement."

I led the way downstairs. Behind me, Sandy coughed. Lillian sat on the couch, Josh under her arm. In a stagey voice, she read him a story. Knee-high Ben grabbed the book.

"Time for your bath, Josh," Sandy said.

"I want Lillian to give me a bath." He looked up defiantly.

Sandy hesitated. "All right. That'll give me some time with Ben. I've hardly seen him all week."

Hiding the birthday book behind her back, she scooped up Ben and descended to the basement. I returned to my seat. Cold potato timbales tasted like week-old bread. On the second floor, the water came on. Josh and Lillian shrieked. I looked up at the dining room's chandelier, expecting to see a waterfall. I'd never seen a mother like Lillian, so "on" all the time. How could Aldo stand being married to someone so fake?

Sandy, passing through the dining room on her way to the second floor, dropped the wrapped present on the table, not even pausing to watch Aldo open it. Tony's eyes followed her. Aldo thanked Tony and held the book out at arm's length. "A biography of Rossini. This will be very interesting." He put it down, not even bothering to read the book jacket.

Tony looked at me and wheeled toward the bathroom.

"Excuse me a minute," I said. I put Tony on the toilet, spread the *Post* across his lap, and wondered why his father, a man, after all, didn't think to provide this small service. Birthday or not, Aldo should help when he came down, and not just with feeding. Roll up his goddamned sleeves. Otherwise, he was just another burden. Sandy would be down in Florida with no help. She'd have to do the day shift, which meant "the feeding," and she'd have to handle the kids and the whole night routine.

Aldo had turned on the living room light.

I sat down and threw an arm over the back of the couch. "Who'll take care of Tony in Orlando?"

"Sandy, I suppose," Aldo said.

"And who'll look after the kids?"

"Lillian will."

"Aldo, this is ridiculous," I said. "You've got to hire a full-time aide down there."

"Where would I find someone?" he said.

"Call a home health care agency." Trying to remain calm, I crossed my legs. "Why am I taking care of your son?"

"I have to work," he said.

"So do I," I said.

"Yes, but my work is important," he said. "I'm taking over a Florida beer distributorship. It's huge."

"My work's important, too." I leaned toward him and lowered my voice. "I'm exhausted. Please, Aldo, you and Lillian have to give me more help."

"What kind?"

"Figure out how to do something besides shop. Pay for help if you don't want to do it yourself."

"I don't know how much more we can do." Aldo leaned forward. "My wife's therapist says coming to D.C. is killing her. She's a little ..." He waggled his hand.

"Nuts?" I said.

"Unstable," he said.

"Even if she is that doesn't mean you guys get to delegate all the shit work to me."

"Col-lee-een," Tony bleated from the bathroom.

I went to get him off the toilet, threw open the window, and wiped his ass. When I came out of the bathroom, I saw Aldo holding the *Post* in front of his face, and the instant Lillian came down from reading Josh a story, Aldo said he wanted to leave.

The next afternoon while I went to a movie, Lillian and Aldo took Tony shopping for Sandy's birthday present. I was sitting on the couch staring into space when they came in, and I stood to give them a place to sit. Lillian handed me the hanger for a beige, wool suit with a mink collar and covered buttons. Jacqueline Kennedy could have worn it.

"Do you think she'll make me take it back?" Lillian said.

"You never know, do you?" I said.

"I like it," Tony said. "It's classic."

"Yeah, all it needs is a pill-box hat," I said.

"Put it someplace she won't see it," Tony said. "I want to bring it down to Florida."

A wool suit in Florida. What next? I took it up to Tony's closet and jammed it between his sports coats.

By the time Sandy came home, her face had turned the beige of the dress and the coughing had burrowed deeper into her chest. "Doesn't sound like you're shaking your cold," I said.

"It's because I haven't had a night out."

Probably not since the night Noah and Frank came over. A week in Florida's sun would help.

Aldo and Lillian said good-bye. They'd leave early in the morning before traffic got bad. I tried to give Aldo a hug but he pushed me away. Sandy left for her night out. I fed Tony and tried to convince him to stop reading e-mail. There was the usual three hours of bedlam while the children ran around, pulling off couch pillows. At eleven o'clock I was snapping Tony's pajamas when Sandy walked in, brushing against my sweater. Electricity zapped. She went into the bathroom.

"She's angry," I murmured. "I knew I should have had you in bed earlier."

"She doesn't know how to relax," Tony said.

Sandy emerged in cotton PJs with small blue flowers. "I'll take over."

"I can finish," I said.

Sandy passed by and went to arrange the papers on the counter. I had left a vase on the buffet, and Sandy put it away.

"Did you go to a movie?" I said.

"I went to a restaurant and read a book," Sandy said.

Oh sure. She probably went out with Charles.

After a knee-bend, I lifted Tony from the chair. His ankles buckled. Out of breath, I grunted, swiveled him around, and dropped him onto the bed. Half of him was in, his head flopped back, but his feet dangled on the floor. I pushed his hips sideways. "What book are you reading?" I said.

"Don't talk to me at night," Sandy screamed. "I'm trying to shut down."

"I didn't know it bothered you."

"I don't have any privacy." Coughing, Sandy leaned against the doorjamb, her arms folded. "I have people around me all the time. I am so sick of you three women and your big personalities."

"What three women?" I said.

"You, Lillian, and Maria. You're in my face from morning till night."

"You can finish getting Tony ready for bed, then."

"You should have done it already," Sandy said.

"Criminently, give me a break," I muttered.

Sandy turned around. "What did you say?"

Blot it up. Absorb it. "Here you go." I put the BiPAP's pieces next to Tony's pillow.

"I'm too tired."

"Suit yourself," I said.

***

The next morning, while I put a cup of water in the microwave, Sandy made Tony's bed. "I figured out what was putting me in such a bad mood."

"Besides your cold?" I said.

"Yes." Sandy was breathing heavily. The bad guys outnumbered the good guys in her immune system. She was coughing up an ocean. "I want one night a week when I don't have other people at the table."

Behind Sandy's back, Tony mouthed the word "chaos."

Sandy said, "I want you to go out for dinner."

"Let's see," I said, looking at the ceiling and putting a finger to my chin. "You want me to cook dinner here but not eat it?"

"Yes," Sandy said. "Your presence, yours and Lillian's, has totally disrupted our nuclear family."

"This nuclear family business is overrated," Tony said.

"I'm going to be late again, and it's all your fault," Sandy said. "You never get Tony to bed on time. You seem oblivious to the fact that I have to get up and go to work in the morning."

"What do you think what I'm doing is called?" I said. "W-O-R-K."

"You can take a nap any time you please," Sandy said, slamming the door. "I can't. I have to function."

I fixed Tony's shake and told him I was, indeed, going upstairs to take a nap. He asked me to hook up to the baby monitor. Upstairs, I lay down on the bed, wrecked from lack of sleep. At least, now, he could drink his breakfast. It saved me one feeding. I still had two others: five hours a day. More and more, I wished the feeding tube, which only operated at night and with a dilute solution of water and Ensure, could handle all of his caloric needs. The feeding. It was a killer. I groaned and rolled over, clutching my pillow. Sandy was sick and exhausted, at the end of her proverbial rope. The safest person for her to get angry at was her mother. It was totally understandable.

I stayed away from the kids, served dinner, and kept my mouth shut. After a weekend of trying to act the part of invisible servant, I grew tired of the charade. In the bathroom, I told Tony, "The other night when Sandy got on my case about having a big personality, it made me so mad, I hardly know what to do."

"Sandy has PMS," he said, "and her first period in two years. But besides that, she's losing it."

"Isn't she seeing a therapist?"

"He's a quack," Tony said. "What bugs me is the guy takes Sandy's word as God's own truth. He doesn't even know me."

"Nor me, either."

"We're wonderful people and we don't deserve this." Tony's caw-like laugh began.

I felt a chill. But whether we were good people or not wasn't important. This situation wasn't about us. It was about Sandy. For the sake of the children and for Tony's sake, too, Sandy had to keep functioning. "I don't mind eating in my room if that'll make her feel better."

"That's ridiculous," he said.

"Tony, I'm willing to do anything to help Sandy survive this, but if she keeps snapping at me, I'm not going to be able to hang in."

"Please don't go," Tony said. "I need you."

"I know that," I said, "but you're a pain in the ass."

"I try so hard not to be."

I bent and hugged him. "I know you do your best. And, just for the record, I think it's the stress of this situation that's making Sandy behave this way. She's trying to raise her children, hold down a full-time job, and deal with your needs. It's too much."

"I don't know what I can do about it." Skeletal, muscles withered, Tony shuddered. A fasciculation. I opened the bathroom door. Time to start another dinner.

Maybe the eating arrangement would work out for the best. Even on good nights, dinner made me tense. I couldn't stand the endless negotiations with Josh about whether he'd eaten enough of his dinner, and I was tired of sweeping up mixed vegetables from under the highchair. I put food on the counter, fixed Tony's plate, and took mine upstairs. Angrier than I wanted to admit, I opened a novel. The words blurred. Sandy hadn't said she wanted me to put Tony to bed, but knowing her, she would expect it. What pissed me off was that I was up in her bedroom and I couldn't even go to sleep. I picked at the spaghetti on my plate. When they left for Florida, I'd get a reprieve.

There was a knock on the door. "Yes?"

"Can I come in?" It was Sandy.

"It's your room," I said.

"Tony said I should tell you to come downstairs and eat."

"I'm perfectly happy upstairs, as you can see. I'm reading and eating dinner, and when I'm done I'll come downstairs and do the dishes and get Tony ready for bed. Then you can have time up here to call Charles or whatever it is you do."

"Your sarcasm isn't appreciated," she said.

"What's going on with you two anyway?"

"Nothing," Sandy said. "He's just a friend."

I went back to my novel and, at ten o'clock, walked down to put Tony in bed. When Maria came up to the kitchen for ice cubes, I wished her a good sleep, but quietly, so that the sound of our voices wouldn't carry up to Sandy's private sanctum.

As I brushed Tony's teeth, a heaviness came over me, a ball-and-chain feeling. Maybe Sandy truly didn't want more family than her own little nuclear foursome. The nuclear family was overrated. When he wasn't being a pain in the rear, Tony made me laugh. I gave him a kiss. Then, up in the bedroom—not my bedroom, but "the" bedroom—I informed Sandy that Tony had gone to bed. Sandy was on the phone. "Talk to you later," she said, hanging up. After Sandy left, I threw on a nightshirt, put on headphones, turned on a CD of ocean waves, and pulled up the covers.

A knock at the door caused it to creak open.

I removed the headphones. "Come in."

"I want to talk to you," Sandy said.

I looked up at the ceiling. "Go away."

Sandy closed the door and turned on the desk lamp. "You always take things personally, Mom."

"You snap at me. You tell me you're sick of women with big personalities. How do you think I'm supposed to take it if not personally?"

"You don't understand," she said. "I'm under a lot of pressure at work, and it's hard having a husband with ALS."

"Who is it that takes care of him sixteen hours a day?"

"You don't understand what it's like having all these people in your life. I was just getting to the point where I had confidence as a mother and then this happened."

"So, okay. Let's talk about your world imploding."

"I talk to my therapist. He gives me all the support I need."

Finally, I could put my cards on the table. I sat up. "Sandy, I've had a hard time hanging in. You snap at me constantly."

"Leave then, if you can't take it." Sandy hugged herself and shivered. "That's just how I handle my feelings."

"You're firing me?"

"You don't seem happy here."

I looked at Sandy's narrow jaw and sucked-in cheeks and thought of the years of orthodontia.

"I'm not happy," I said. "At home I don't have a single person in my life who heaps abuse on me like you do."

"You don't understand what it's like having your mother around all the time."

"I'd have loved it if my mother did one-tenth as much as I do for you." My face felt hot.

"You make me feel like a child," she said.

"I understand that you *feel* like a child," I said. "I don't *make* you feel like a child." I got up and pushed the desk chair in so the disorder wouldn't trigger another outburst. Then it struck me. Sandy wouldn't even notice. "I can go home and you could move upstairs," I said. "Is that what you want?"

"No," Sandy said. "Tony would have a fit."

"Who would take care of him?"

"Tony's parents would have to pay someone," she said. "But we don't need you. Sometimes, I think the trade-offs aren't worth it." She unwound her arms and turned to go.

"What trade-offs?"

"I'm not in charge of my own house."

"I see." Not looking at her, I pulled open my clothes drawers and stacked my underwear and tee-shirts into piles on the bed. "I can't be less competent than I am, and there's only one way I can make myself disappear." I snapped my fingers. Damn, I'd taken my suitcase to the basement.

Sandy turned. "If you think I'm doing bad, you should see the other ALS wives. They're a wreck. At least, I'm still employed. I'm not having a nervous breakdown." Sandy's bottom lip and the corners of her mouth turned down. Her chin looked like a dimpled orange. She put up a hand to cover her mouth.

"Is your friend at work having a nervous breakdown?" I said.

Sandy nodded. "She called me today. She lost her job. Her funding ran out. Her son is seeing a therapist three times a week and so is her daughter. She's taken out a second mortgage on her house and, Mom, her husband's had ALS for five years and he's *still not dead*. Tony's had it less than two."

I stopped packing. "She has no family support."

"It doesn't make any difference." Sandy sobbed. *"It's not enough."*

"Of course it's not enough."

"I can't do it. There's too much to do and it never stops."

"You have way too much to handle. No one could do it any better."

"You could."

"Not true," I said.

A button off her pajamas, not an extra ounce of fat on her, Sandy brushed aside her bangs. They were wild, as if she were a child who'd cut her own hair.

"Just because I'm stuck in this shitty life doesn't mean you have to be stuck, too."

"I don't feel stuck. I came here because I chose to. I didn't do this out of obligation, but because I love you."

"I can't say thank-you," she said. "I don't have anything to give. Just go home and leave us alone."

I stared at the piles of clothes on the bed. I was too tired to go down to the basement and find my suitcase. I began refolding.

"I can't," I said. "I made arrangements for Kevin to fly in and do some of the repair you need to have done."

"When?" Sandy said.

"Thursday, before you leave for Orlando."

"Not more chaos!"

"We'll get a lot done while you're away."

Sandy moved one hand to her forehead. She began to cry.

"Let's talk about this tomorrow when we're less upset," I said. "You want to meet me for coffee?"

Sandy nodded and took a handkerchief from her dresser to dry her eyes. "I can't tomorrow. I'm wrapping up a big case. But maybe Wednesday?"

"Where?" I said.

"The coffee shop next to the plate place."

"If Maria can handle Tony, I'll be there." I stuffed the last of my clothes in the drawer and kicked it shut, then moved around the corner of the bed and hugged my daughter. I was amazed that I could hold so much fury inside. I was angrier than I had ever been, at being jerked from one emotion to the next, careening between my need to be there as a mother and my desire to escape the insanity. My daughter's skin felt cold, even her neck and bare, thin arms. Her fever had broken. Sandy choked back a cough. I held her for five seconds before she pulled back.

"I don't want you to leave."

"I know that."

Sandy blew her nose and her face resumed its composure, eyes swollen, a teenage girl coming back to class after having a cry in the washroom. She left and I closed the door, taking a sobbing breath as I fit the latch. Backing toward the desk, I sank down in the chair. For a few minutes I stared at the door. Then, I swiveled around to face my books. *Motherless Daughters* and *Letters from Motherless Daughters.* I took the books out and thumbed through the pages. I'd picked these off the remainder table, but I had never found a book on fatherless daughters. What I needed was not in my bookcase and Rob was dead and rotting underground. I yanked off my necklace and threw our wedding rings in the trash. *You left us, you fucker. You abandoned me and you abandoned your daughter, and you're never coming back.*

CHAPTER 24

On Wednesday, with Maria the only one home to supervise Tony and the children, I felt anxious about being gone. I looked out the window of the coffee shop and half-expected to see Charles striding through the rain. Sandy, in line for a hot drink, squeezed water from her hair. Soaked, not even wearing a raincoat, she began coughing again and shivered as she slid back a chair.

"We should have done this months ago," I said.

"That's what my therapist said."

"You went running to your therapist about the other night?"

"I was complaining about how you acted all pouty and refused to come down to dinner and he said, 'What does that woman want?'"

"'That woman' being me. Your mother."

"I said she wants a relationship."

"That's true," I said.

Sandy snorted out a puff of air. "I told him I didn't have the energy."

The espresso grinder turned on with a roar and Sandy looked over at the counter. I tightened my hands around my cup. Tiny air bubbles clung to the circumference. Surface tension held them up.

Sandy looked at her watch. "I'm supposed to meet my movie group."

"You called me away from the house to tell me you don't have time for a relationship," I said. "That's the extent of our talk?"

"No, that's not it," she said. "My therapist said, 'You don't get something for nothing.'"

"You do have time for a relationship, then."

"He said I needed to make time for you," she said. "So this is it. You've got ten minutes. I can't wait to get down to Florida and jump in a pool. I'm going to shave my armpits. First time in months I've even thought about that."

I looked at the lettering on the window, the name of the coffee shop from inside the glass: AVAJ AMAM. For months, I had been seeing the world inside out.

"I need to go home," I said.

"You can go home at Christmas," Sandy said.

"I don't mean Christmas," I said. "As soon as I wrap up the work on your house, I'm leaving."

Sandy pursed her lips and, frowning, looked down at her hands. "I'm sorry about the other night."

"It's not just that," I said. "I have a life in Chicago."

"You're not angry?" Sandy smiled. "I mean, I thought if I asked you to leave, you'd be furious, the way you always are."

The way I *always* was. My forehead tightened. "I'm tired. This is dragging on and on. If I were you, I'd look for another solution, like moving Tony to his own apartment or shipping him off to his parents' place."

Sandy took a deep breath. "I've already been thinking in that direction." Her face beamed. "Come January, we're going to have fresh faces in the house. A hospice nurse came by the other day, and during the open enrollment period, I'm switching insurance plans."

"I've been meaning to talk to you about that," I said. "Constance, the nurse who came to check Tony's incision, told me—"

"After Tony's surgery, I wanted to send you home," Sandy said.

"Why?"

"I had the feeling you were as sick of me as I was of you."

"I wasn't sick of you."

"You had that look on your face."

"What look?"

"The look on your face now."

"I was worried about Tony." The words squeaked out.

"If you say it was Tony, I guess I have to believe you."

I scooped the dregs out of my cup, wishing I were a person who could say, Sandy, you are misreading me completely. "How will you manage Florida?"

"Let me worry about it," Sandy said.

"I asked Aldo to hire an aide."

"Tony won't allow it."

"Why is it always what Tony wants?"

"My therapist says I need to take control of my family again. That's what I'm doing. Your advice is not welcome." She looked down a long hall where the restrooms were located.

"There are three months between now and the new year. Maria can't take care of Tony," I said. "I know you're feeling stressed out, but if I leave, how will you fill in?"

"I'll call Eugene and find out how many home health aides his agency can provide. I'll make up a spreadsheet and job assignments for volunteers."

"Like who?" I said. "Frank and Mr. No-Show?"

"There's the Glover Park babysitting co-op. They can coordinate dinners," Sandy said, "and maybe some of them can volunteer. People at work are always asking if they can help, but I really don't know what happens here during the day. You need to write down a detailed list of tasks for the new caregivers. You can post it on the refrigerator. I don't have time to train them."

I moved my cup aside. There was a map of Italy on the saucer. Halfway round the world. Sandy must hardly know what was coming out of her mouth.

"The day before Tony's operation," I said, "he and I went up to Bethesda to an Indian restaurant."

"The Taj Mahal." Sandy smiled. "We used to go up there on dates."

"Tony told me you don't trust me."

"I don't," Sandy said. "I never have."

"Why?" I said.

"You know," Sandy said.

"I have no idea."

"It was because of what you did when Daddy died."

"What did I do?" I said.

"You sat in that red chair in Grandma Jean's living room and I tried and tried to get through to you. I tried to sit on your lap, but you didn't respond. It was like you were frozen. You sat there for hours, and you looked at me like I wasn't even there."

"What? Where are you getting this?"

"It's true," Sandy said, her voice rising like that of a small child tattling when the adults come home, "and everyone was all upset because Kevin broke Grandma's ashtray and glass got in the carpet."

I didn't remember any of this, not the chair, not the ashtray. If "everyone" was upset, it certainly had more to do with the auto accident than with broken glass. After the phone call from the police, I fainted. Rob's mother Jean knelt over me with a glass of water. She helped me to the living room and then she called her husband to get Rob's brothers and sisters out of school. They all assembled in the living room and Rob's dad broke the news. I couldn't place Kevin in that picture, or Sandy. Jean would have whisked them away.

Sandy, with angry hooded eyes, watched for my reaction.

"Give me a minute, please," I said. Lacing my fingers and making a tripod of my elbows, I rested my chin and closed my eyes. I took a deep breath and hunted back through my memory-album of school pictures. There: the chubby five-year-old, bangs below her eyebrows, off-kilter pigtails, a shy, sweet smile. This was the child I had to address. I opened my eyes, and against every inclination to defend myself, tried to do what Tony's sister did so well: listen.

"And what was that like for you, me being so distracted?"

"I lost two parents that day, not one." Sandy looked outside where rain was slanting down and people leaned forward, holding their umbrellas. "You never understood."

"I never understood."

"That's right," Sandy said. "You never understood how much pain I was in."

"That must have been terrible."

"It was. I decided then, I would never forgive you."

"That's right," I said. "You clung to it."

"What?" Sandy frowned.

"The memory of me not being there. That's what you had to hang onto. Pain. The connection to your father."

I felt inside my shirt for my necklace. The rings weren't there. It was amazing that Sandy could have kept her grief so well hidden. That was what Josh undoubtedly did. I thought of him staring at Tony to make him stop choking and what he'd told me in the graveyard about the picks and shovels. Magical thinking. Along with the broken ashtray, a red chair got etched into the glass of Sandy's psyche and a frozen mommy in the red chair. I could hear a child's voice say, "It's true, Mommy. It's really true." Sandy had needed a mother that particular day, and I had checked out. Probably checked out longer than I cared to admit. Sandy saw herself as a little girl that bad things happened to, and bad things did. Tony's illness had confirmed the story Sandy had been telling herself for years.

"We need to get home," I said. "Come on, I'll give you a ride."

"You're not mad?"

"No, I'm okay." I dropped her off and headed for the hardware store, knowing that this errand would take more than a few minutes and that she would prefer to be in the house and not see me. I had only a few more days. She had to stay here in her miserable life.

CHAPTER 25

After popping open an umbrella and inhaling the clean smell of the rain-slick streets, I pushed a shopping cart from the hardware store. I had splurged on a plastic chair to replace the broken one on the porch, cans of paint, joint compound, new locks, sash cord, and light switches. At home, I stacked the paint cans on the porch. Through the window, I saw the flicker of the television. Craning forward as if he were dying to get into the game, Kevin sat on the couch. A shower of relief washed over me. Sandy had her movie group tonight, but Kevin would pitch in. I opened the door. He smiled, and not just with his eyes. In the notch of his lower lip, I saw his teeth.

"The Lakers are playing the Celtics," he said.

"I think the Celtics are going to win by a wide margin," Tony said.

"You want to put money on it?" Kevin said.

"No," Tony said. "Sandy gives me an allowance, and I already spent it."

I closed the door behind me.

"Hey, Mom, I'm surprised to see this much rain." Kevin gave me a hug. "It was bright and sunny when I left Chicago. I'd forgotten how beautiful fall is."

"Fall is the nicest time of the year," I said.

"So, where do you want to start?" Kevin said.

He wasn't wasting time. I pointed at the bubbled plaster on the arch. "I think this is just a surface flaw. We shouldn't need a plasterer."

"Yeah, it's grunt work," he said.

"Grunt work, indeed," I said. "This place is nothing but."

"Speaking of grunts." Tony rolled to the bathroom.

"Would you mind watching Josh and Ben for a couple of minutes?" I pointed to the basement. Below, I heard Maria's singsong lilt. If she didn't hurry she'd miss her bus. "Remember, Kev, don't bump your head on the fan down there."

"As long as I don't have to change diapers," Kevin said.

"Ow!" he called a moment later.

After I had wiped Tony and opened the window, he backed toward the door and blocked it with the chair. "Sandy has decided not to go down with the *Titanic*."

"Let me out of here, Tony," I said. "I need to put dinner on the table."

"She says she's moving on."

"Moving on in what sense?" I said.

"Moving on with her life."

"Tony, this is none of my business. Get out of my way."

Tony stayed put. "I tried to ask her how she's feeling, and she told me she intended to marry again after I died. I told her if I were in her shoes, I'd be so devastated I'd never even think about it. She accused me of trying to make her feel guilty. She makes me feel like a burden," he said, "and I'm sick of being blamed for her coming to bed late. Then, do you know what she said? She said I'd forgotten what it was like to be a parent."

"Really?" I said.

"That's one thing I haven't forgotten," Tony screamed. "It's outrageous of Sandy to say that."

"Tony, let me out. Kevin's here, and you need to work this out with your wife."

"She's not my wife," Tony said. "The woman I loved moved out months ago."

I looked at Tony, the frail, shaking bundle in a wheelchair. This was not a man Sandy would have picked from a lineup of potential grooms. From Sandy's perspective, her husband had moved out months ago, too. I flipped the power switch on his wheelchair, pushed it aside, and opened the door.

"Hey," Tony said. "Turn this thing back on."

I stood for a moment, looking around Tony's room: the bed, the sock cupboard, and his computer with its cough-spattered screen. Sighing, I turned around and flipped the power switch on his chair.

I cooked dinner and while I fed Tony, Kevin drew dinosaurs, passing torn-off pictures to the kids. Josh ate for a change. I put the kids in bed, and Kevin did the dishes. When I came down, he sat on the end of Tony's bed, reading the jokes that scrolled in.

"Tony, would you be all right by yourself while I drive Kevin over to your mom's place?"

"What about the kids?" he said.

"Oh, right." Ben might wake up. Or Josh. Lately, Josh had been dreaming about wolves. I'd have to wait until Sandy came home, which would mean Kevin watching the night routine. He was squeamish. It didn't matter. He was here to help, not put another brick on the pile.

I took Tony to the bathroom told Kevin to follow me around like a shadow waiter. He could take notes, type them up, and Sandy would have her instructions for my replacements.

Kevin looked wide-eyed. "Are you bailing?"

"Yes, but Tony doesn't know I plan to leave." At least, he hadn't mentioned it.

While I put Tony to bed, Kevin asked questions and wrote on a notepad. I wanted to make sure I didn't forget the small, important luxuries that made Tony's life bearable: his three soaps and the baby scissors to cut his hangnails. "Got it," Kevin said when we'd finished hooking up the feeding tube's mast-and-pump. I dimmed the light in Tony's bedroom.

Sandbagged, I looked out the window and saw Sandy getting out of Charles's truck. So much for the movie group. Leaving by the back door to keep from bumping into them, I picked up Lillian's keys and found a sleeping bag in the garage. With Kevin carrying his duffel bag, I walked down the alley. Three blocks away on Calvert, the studio was in a concrete building that looked like a prison, but the building had an elevator. Lillian could have had the children and Tony over often. To my knowledge, she had invited them only once. I turned the key, opened the door, and switched on the light. Bare walls confronted me. She had left behind an end table, a lamp with a striped shade, and a broken chair. Josh's plate with the rainbow and the cabin and "Happy Birthday Grandma Lillian" hung on the wall. I gasped, crushed that Lillian did not value his gift, and turned so quickly that I bumped Kevin's chest. He put his arms around me.

The hard-boiled egg of need stuck in my throat.

At last, I tore myself away.

The next day they would leave for Orlando, and Sandy had asked me to assemble all of Tony's clothes, medicines, and soaps. I couldn't save my daughter's marriage or save her from the path she'd chosen. All I could do was save myself. This damn disease. It was going to win, and I could only let it.

***

Packing the van for its ride on the car-train to Orlando, I carried out cases of Ensure, the wheelchair's spare tire, and the tire pump. Tony reminded me not to forget the patch kit and wrenches. Suitcases came out of the garage, were packed and ferried to the curb, and prescriptions filled. Helping me with these tasks, Kevin yawned and said he hadn't enjoyed sleeping on the floor of Lillian's apartment.

I stood on the bed and took down ten pairs of socks. With a third the usual number to choose from, Tony might drive Sandy slightly less nuts. While Tony ate half-teaspoonfuls of yams, Kevin typed up the instructions for my replacements.

Tasks for Volunteers

As all of you know, especially folks in the babysitting co-op where Sandy and Tony have only been able to be passive participants, we have been dealing with a pretty bad situation here for going on two years now.

We're sending you this e-mail because you are on Tony's e-mail list and because we hope you'll become part of our new "caring circle." As the saying goes, "many hands make light work."

You may anticipate a certain feeling of gratification, a sort of "good citizen" feeling, but having lived here for the past umpteen months, I can say that it's more likely you will end up feeling worn down. It's common for caregivers to suffer sleeplessness, anxiety, and depression. If you feel that you've bitten off more than you can chew, please let Sandy know ASAP. Don't just stop coming.

6:00 to 8:00 a.m. If you have mornings free, no job, and are an early riser, this is the slot for you. You folks in the babysitting co-op will probably be getting your own kids dressed and fed, but please pass along this plea for help to your childless or retired neighbors. To minimize the revolving door, we would like volunteers to sign up for three or four days at a time. The person on duty must be able to lift a 125-pound man. It's a "dead lift." Tony can't support any of his own weight. The early morning time slot and the evening time slot, from 8:00 to 10:00 p.m., are the ones that involve the most difficult lifts and transfers. They wouldn't be good for a person with a bad back.

So what are we asking you to do?

The baby's first wake-up is usually at 6:00 a.m. when you'll just be arriving. Go upstairs and hand him his water. Flip the tape in his clown tape-recorder and press play. Tell him to go back to sleep. If he has a poop, change it first then put him back in the crib. Hopefully, he won't freak out at seeing a stranger. Most mornings he sleeps till 7:45 or 8:00, but sometimes just till the end of the tape. I'm kind of tired and I may be skipping around, but you'll get the hang of it.

In addition to putting Ben back to sleep, you will have several other tasks that must be performed simultaneously. Start by mixing Tony's orange-juice-and-water breakfast drink. Use two-thirds water, one-third orange juice, and half a packet of Thick-it. The Thick-it turns water into a more viscous fluid, and makes it less likely that Tony will choke. The packets are on top of the refrigerator. When you've finished making the juice, bring it and a flex-straw to the dining room table and lay out the sports section. Oh, and bring the paper in from the porch.

It takes two people to get Tony out of bed in the morning. You will be one of them. Tony may still be asleep when you arrive; Sandy will be up. She disconnects the feeding tube, but she will leave the BiPAP connected. It's the thing that looks like a bread machine and sits on the half-wall between the stove and Tony's bed. When Sandy calls you, you may enter their bedroom. Tony stays connected to the BiPAP while he is making the transfer from the bed to his wheelchair. Sandy will be on one side of him. You will stand on the other. You will need to be able to lift half his weight. Even though he looks small, he feels quite heavy because you're generally leaning over and twisting to get him into position. Once he is safely in his wheelchair, Sandy will take him to the bathroom for his morning shower. When he comes out, he will be dressed and ready to drink the juice you prepared, but before he gets started on that, you have to clean out his nose.

Tony's nose is a mess in the morning. He frequently has big boogers. He calls them "taffy apples" or "affey tapples" when he's speaking pig Latin. Drinking his breakfast is hard when he can't breathe. Wrap a tissue around a

Q-tip to clean out his nose. The Q-tips are in the medicine cabinet. Also spray in Na-Sal, a saline nasal moisturizer. If you don't take care of his nose, it bleeds. We've also found that frequent use of nasal spray decongestant makes his nostrils more sensitive, so this is a last resort to use if the saline and Q-tip treatment still haven't worked. You should get his nose in shape before you give him his breakfast shake. Also, give him his medication.

While he's drinking his juice and water, give Tony his pills. He does not take his medicine with water because it makes him choke. Instead, he is able to dry swallow. He will open his mouth, and you will put the pills as far back on his tongue as possible. His morning medications are two vitamin E (large vitamin pills), one vitamin C, and one baclofen. Lay out one more baclofen for him to take at lunch, but don't leave the pills on the counter by the high chair, or Ben will eat them.

"This is fantastic," I said, looking up at Kevin and holding a spoon out for Tony. "It's good to provide an orientation."

"I hope I got everything down," Kevin said. "I was having to take notes on the fly."

The task list might make the job sound more complicated than it really was, but I wouldn't be here to train the volunteers, and Tony could make life difficult if the person caring for him didn't do what he expected.

After work, Sandy came in, threw her purse on the counter, and looked around. "Where's Kevin?"

"At the hardware store."

"Good. One less person."

"Sandy, he's your brother."

"I don't care."

I took Tony to the bathroom, came out, and closed the door behind me. It would take Tony ten minutes to read the sports section and while he did, I wanted Sandy to review the five-page print-out in case I'd forgotten anything.

Sandy held the instructions at arm's length. "What's this?"

"Thank you," I said. "You're welcome."

Sandy flipped a page. "It looks like a novel."

"It's the scaffolding of Tony's day."

"Why can't you write up a business memo with bullet points?"

"I was packing," I said. "If you want it redone, you do it."

"Did you send this out already?"

"Yes, I did," I said. "Tony had the babysitting co-op's e-mail list on his computer. I sent it to his alumni list, too."

Her eyes ran down the tasks. "It's going to be a revolving door. Maybe the volunteer idea wasn't such a good one. I should have put an ad in the paper so you could hire people while I'm away."

"I'm glad you didn't," I said.

"Then you'll just have to stay until that's done," Sandy said.

I felt the whirring of a boomerang coming toward my head. "Even if you've changed your mind, I haven't changed mine," I said. "I won't be here when you come back." I sat down at the head of the table and began to eat.

"Sa-aan-dy!" Tony called. "I'm done."

"I am so sick of this." Sandy opened the bathroom door, gulped down a breath, and went in. I heard the window open. When they came out, Tony rolled over to the table. Not looking at me, Sandy put down a plate for Josh and wheeled over Ben's highchair. The children came to the table. I spooned food into Tony's mouth.

After a silence of three or four minutes, I decided to lighten things up. I smiled and turned to Sandy. "How are things at work?"

Sandy's face turned purple. The tendons on her neck stood out. "Don't ask me about work."

I tried to straighten up, but couldn't. I felt like a dog beaten with a newspaper.

Tony's mouth was full but his eyes, aimed at me, flashed with anger.

"I didn't know work was a hot button topic," I murmured.

"When I'm at work, I don't think about things here," Sandy hissed, "and when I'm here, I don't think about work."

"I thought you just didn't want me asking you questions late at night."

"No. I don't want you asking them at all. I'm so sick of you being here, I could scream."

Josh had his hands over his ears. His mouth looked like a stretched rubber band. This was no good. I hoped Kevin stayed away. I'd tried to give him money to buy dinner in a restaurant. He'd refused, saying he could afford to feed himself. Maybe he'd go back to the apartment or to a movie. Please, God, just don't let him walk in on this scene. He would think so poorly of his sister, he would never forgive her.

"If you want to go upstairs, I'll feed Tony," Sandy said.

"No." I straightened up and forced my eyes to bore right into hers. "I haven't moved out yet, and until I do, *this is my home, too*."

Sandy looked at her hands. She played with her ring, taking it off and putting it back on. "I'm sorry if I hurt your feelings."

"You didn't hurt my feelings," I said.

"I know you like to get inside my head."

"I was trying to make dinner table conversation."

I heard a knock and looked up. The front door opened.

Charles stood there. "Hey, Colleen. I hear you're heading back to Chi-town."

Tony's head turned. He looked back at me.

"Not my guest," I said.

Charles strode across the room, shaking the floor, and moved the highchair around to a different corner of the table so that he could help Ben eat. Without a word, Sandy fixed Charles a plate. I looked from Charles to Sandy. She'd been expecting him.

"Hey, Josh, do you remember the snow in Vermont?" Charles said.

"Yes," Josh said, looking at his father.

"And what rides are you going on in Disney World?"

"I don't know," Josh said.

Charles beamed at Tony. "How about the Tower of Terror? It's the scariest ride in the kingdom."

Tony's eyes looked from Charles to Josh. Blinking as if to erase the picture of them together, his eyes swung back to the spoon.

"I feel a migraine coming on," I said.

"I can finish feeding Tony and put him to bed," Charles said.

I leapt up from the feeding chair and pulled the instructions from beneath the beetle magnet on the refrigerator. "Read this," I said, handing the pages to Charles. If Kevin hadn't been here, I would have gone to sleep immediately. I had a boulder on my chest and, when I lay down on the bed, the weight crushed me. Downstairs I heard laughter, followed by footsteps heading my way. The door opened.

"May I come in?" Sandy said.

"Suit yourself." I stayed in the prone position.

"Could you come down?" Sandy said. "Charles thinks you're mad at him."

"I'm not. But I am upset."

"I'm sorry I blew up at you."

"No, you're not."

"You're refusing to accept my apology?"

"At a certain point, an apology is an empty promise."

"I don't understand."

"You have no intention of changing, so you might as well not imply you're going to by saying you're sorry."

"I have no idea what you're talking about," Sandy said.

"Why don't you go pack and not worry about me, okay?" I said.

The floor creaked. I opened my eyes. Sandy was on her way out the door. She turned. "Six boxes of shutters should arrive tomorrow. Could you and Kevin install them?"

I swung my feet off the bed. "Your mental list is a mile long. I try to keep up, but I always fail."

"What do you mean?"

"I always think, if I do this one more thing, it'll relieve the pressure on Sandy. That's why I brought Kevin back here. Knock off the list. But no sooner is one thing done than you add ten more."

"Don't bother, then," Sandy said.

"It's dawning on me that nothing I do will make you happy."

"Of course not. My husband is dying. That's the only thing that's going to make me happy."

"When he's dead?"

"Yes. When he's dead so I can get on with my life the way you got on with yours."

"What's the 'get on with' business?"

"My therapist said my needs for intimacy aren't getting met. He wants me to broaden my circle of friends."

"Broadening it to Charles."

"Not just him," she said. "I need to meet new people, men and women. I need to start my life again. The life of Sandy."

"It would be easier if you could wait until Tony were actually dead," I said. "Like, in-the-ground dead."

"But he's not, so I have to do it anyway. Move on from this stuck place. The house of death. Yuck!" Sandy made a gesture as if brushing off lint.

"Does it strike you as an odd coincidence," I said, "that the people you lean on for support are men?"

The phone rang. Sandy looked at it. "The answering machine will pick up."

"I don't have anything more to say." I reached for the phone and caught it just as the message on the machine began. It was Josh's voice. "This is the home of Josh, Ben, Tony, and Sandy. Leave a message and we'll call you back." The nuclear family. Despite Josh's picture, I wasn't part of it.

"Hello, Mom," Kevin said.

"A voice crying in the wilderness."

"I'm at a bar. Want to come down for a beer?"

"Gladly," I said.

"I have your car."

"I'll take a taxi."

He gave me an address in Georgetown. Sandy had paused at the door.

"That was Kevin," I said. "You're on your own tonight. You and Charles."

"Fine," Sandy said.

I blew my nose and put on a clean blouse. Then I thought about my underarms and washed them. My hair was knotted. I hadn't combed it in days. I found my steel comb and undid the rubber band. It would be hard to explain to an outsider what life here was like. But Kevin had seen the tension. Feeling a bit more put together, I went downstairs. Suitcases lay open on Tony's bed. Charles untangled wires from Tony's computer. Ben threw couch cushions on the floor. Sandy cursed because the battery charger for Tony's chair had disappeared.

"It's in the car," I said.

"Can I have a minute?" Charles said. "I need to touch base with you."

"Some other time." I knew what he wanted. My blessing. If Sandy wanted to start a new life, a life with Charles, I didn't want to know.

A taxi honked.

"I came to pull the oar," Charles said.

"Don't get blisters." I stepped over the toys and opened the door.

"Grand-ma, Grand-ma," Ben chanted, butting me from behind and fitting his head between my knees. The little people were the ones I was going to miss.

***

In the morning, Sandy walked back and forth across the living room, rounding up last minute items for the Auto Train. When she stopped, I helped Kevin roll the carpet.

"I don't want to find the house a dusty mess when I get home," she said.

Kevin looked at me and frowned. "Mom's just trying to—"

"Don't worry," I said. "We'll dust and vacuum."

"We're ready, then," Sandy said. "Tony?"

Tony motored over and looked at me. "Did you pack the . . . ?"

Sandy's birthday outfit. "Yes, of course." I followed Tony down the ramp. Sandy lowered the van's lift gate and buckled the kids in their car seats. "Would you mind strapping in the wheelchair?"

"Not at all." But why didn't she? She was a lot younger. The elevator raised Tony up to the same level as the van's bed. He maneuvered himself into position, facing front. I crawled in. The straps were all tangled up beneath his wheels. This killed my back. Finally, I made him secure: tight, front and back and side to side. I folded the lift and slammed the door. "You're good to go," I said.

Sandy, who'd gone around to the driver's side, snapped her seat belt and opened the window. "How late did you and Kevin stay out?"

"None of your business," I said.

"I guess I deserved that."

"You didn't deserve it," I said. "You deserve only good things."

A corner of her mouth twitched and she looked down at the gearshift. After turning on the engine, she eased away from the curb.

CHAPTER 26

With a putty knife Kevin, standing on the stepladder, dug out the bubbled plaster and smeared on joint compound. While it dried, we pushed the TV cabinet into the center of the room and stacked the couches. The mahogany piano, which no one played, moved out of harm's way beside the dining buffet. The grime-covered baseboards had to be washed, and I filled a bucket with hot water. Kneeling hurt my back, but it was better than working overhead and washing walls. My father's little stool would have come in handy. It was probably still in the storage locker. I wouldn't have thrown it away.

"Hey, Kev, did I ever show you my dad's little stool?"

"What stool?" he called from the kitchen where he was turning on the tap.

After Rob's death, I'd gone back to school to finish my teaching degree. My mom babysat as much as she was able, but she had a hard time keeping up with Sean, and often it was Dad who took Sandy, Kevin, and Sean to the park. After one of my late-night, freak-out calls, he suggested I drop by his job site for a chat.

Remembering how I'd helped him summers when I was in my teens, I'd brought a brown bag lunch; but before he'd even unbuckled his nail apron, I started in complaining that I couldn't handle all three kids and stay in school, too. I had to stay up late to do my homework. I wasn't getting enough sleep. I'd gotten a B on a mid-term, and as far as I was concerned, that was a failing grade.

His thumbs notched in the straps of his overalls, he looked at me and said, "Well, enough of that." Feeling deflated, I sat on the joist of the deck he was building. He took a sandwich from his lunch box and picked up his three-legged work stool. Job-site dirt had ground into the whorls of the pine. It was nothing to look at.

"See these legs?" he said.

They were made of wooden closet rod, thick and sturdy.

"Yes," I said.

A power saw lay nearby, and he stood up just long enough to reach it. He cut off one of the legs and sat back down. Calmly, he took a bite of his sandwich. He even rocked. The stool didn't tip.

"You ruined it," I said.

"What's a stool for?" he said.

"To sit on."

"Am I sitting?" He looked down.

He was, and not about to collapse.

"Listen, honey," he said. "Life will throw a lot of bad stuff at you."

"Don't you think I know that?"

He shook his head. "It might not just be this one thing. There might be others, things you think you can't bear, but somehow, you do."

"I can't imagine anything worse than losing your husband."

"I know," he said, taking a bite of sandwich. "But there are worse things, believe me, and everyone has their share, sometimes a big share and sometimes a sliver."

"I'm never going to marry again, if that's what you're getting at."

"I'd hate to think that," he said, "but your matrimonial plans are none of my business. Anyway, people don't plan to get married. It's more like a hole you step into on the path of life." He took another bite of sandwich. "I've been debating on whether I should tell you this."

"What?" I said.

"About why you was an only child. Why you come along so late."

I had always assumed my birth had been an accident. Mom was forty-two when she had me. "Tell me," I said.

"Well, your mom had three other children," he said.

"You mean I had siblings?"

"Two died before they were born. But the third, a sister who would have been two years older than you, she made it to the end, but come out damaged."

"Damaged?" I said.

He tapped his head. "She had half a brain. She didn't live but six weeks."

I gasped but knew it was true: my mother's staring-off-into-space look; the way she'd be in the middle of dishes and cross herself. Dad never did that. When he was home, he kept busy: cleaning the gutters, puttering in the garage, sticking glow-stars to the ceiling of my bedroom. The one thing I could never bear—it would be a million times worse than Rob's death—was the death of one of my children.

"How'd you find the courage to go on?" I said. "To start over again after having that kind of loss."

He gave a lopsided grin.

"I cut me off a leg. If the stool still held me up, I knowed we was all right."

These were the compromises life demanded, I told Kevin. The adjustments.

"Wow, Mom," Kevin said. "He was a philosopher."

"No, honey," I said. "He was a carpenter, and his trade required him to have common sense."

I might not be the most brilliant person, but I think I had that, too. Flipping up the toilet seat in the bathroom and dumping in my wash water, I counted the legs on my stool. I had no love life, but I had a job. And Kevin, scrubbing the gray corners of the room, gave me strength; Sean and the grandchildren, joy. I had plenty of legs on my stool. More than most people.

We knocked out the living room in record time and moved the dining room table, but by the next morning, as I cleared the buffet, piling its contents on the counter and lifting out the drawers, my back hurt like it had the day Esmeralda and I moved furniture from the storage locker. One day she'd show up on my doorstep with a duffel bag and a baby, because I was pretty sure she wouldn't have let her father take that baby away.

After we put the couches back where they belonged, I played sidewalk superintendent and watched Kevin scrub the dining room walls. Glancing at me, he asked if I had any more stories, but I didn't, so he turned on the radio and went back to work. I sat with my eyes closed and listened to the music. The peacefulness reminded me of sitting in my living room, a book open, Bear sleeping in my lap.

Someone nudged my foot. Kevin stood holding an empty blue pail. He put it down and joined me on the couch, then threw an arm behind me and massaged my neck.

I closed my eyes and leaned back. "My motivation disappeared," I said.

"Maybe we should take a mental health day."

"Sounds good," I said. "Let me get cleaned up."

Yesterday, I'd scraped off flaky paint and sanded joint compound. In the shower, I washed my hair, letting the grit sieve down to the drain. I turned down the cold and luxuriated in the bathroom's steam. I was over the need to serve my daughter or save my daughter or read my daughter's mind. I had paid my dues. Sandy didn't need me. Sandy resented me. Sandy misunderstood me, intentionally, it seemed. The investment of energy it took to ponder the imponderables of my daughter's pain was not yielding much fruit. I sighed and turned off the water. For the first time in months, I felt clean and unrushed.

Downstairs, Kevin was slipping a belt through his khaki pants. He looked up, beaming. "Let's head over to the National Portrait Gallery. For dinner how does Italian sound?"

"What a concept," I said. In all the months I'd lived here and the year before that when I'd ferried casseroles, I'd never once taken advantage of the capital's many attractions.

With a rotten back, a museum probably wasn't the best idea, but I liked the whisper-quiet halls and the faces staring out at me from behind the cloak of time. Kevin set off with our roadmap of the galleries. Fifteen minutes of the slow-paced museum walk turned my back into a magnet that attracted the metal filings of pain. Better not fight this, I thought. Find one thing to soak up, one thing to like. Pretend you're on a nature walk and learn to recognize one new tree.

In the Daguerreian Gallery, a tiny image stopped me: an early daguerreotype of a young boy and his sister. I recognized these people, but how? Narrow of shoulder, with a lace collar and a jacket whose gold buttons went to his throat, the boy held a bow and arrow. His thin hair was brushed to the side, exposing a high forehead and solemn eyes that looked right at me as if I'd commanded him to hold his breath. The audio guide said the children were the future painter, Thomas Eakins, and his sister Fanny.

Dressed up like a belle at a ball, she sat with one hand in her lap, the other clawing the neck of her satin dress. Her eyes aimed like misaligned headlights, and if Eakins had painted her five-year-old self, he could have drawn a line down the center of her face and had two different portraits, one cheerful, the other sullen and depressed. *When she was good, she was very, very good, but when she was bad, she was horrid.* It was Sandy.

Kevin found me sitting on the bench staring into space. The revolving door let in gusts of air along with the occasional visitor, but the staff talked quietly, and even looked my way and asked if I needed anything. A box of kleenex. A drink of water. "I'm okay," I said. In a delicious surrender of control, I passed my car keys to Kevin, and he drove to Georgetown.

At the restaurant he told me he'd started drawing again, "just for grins." We talked about what kind of classroom I'd have when I started teaching mid-year and how crushed he'd felt when his contract didn't get renewed. Fifty-nine teachers lost their jobs and only two were rehired. COBRA covered his health insurance, but cost an arm and a leg.

Our salads appeared. I told him about my friend Maureen and her involvement with the union. The teachers' federation put constant pressure on the state legislature to keep layoffs from happening. Most of the time we lived our lives as nonpolitical people. I certainly had, and it was easy to forget politics played a huge role in job security, especially for public servants: police, firefighters, and teachers. My big worry was that the legislature wouldn't chip in their share to the pension fund. They'd short-sheeted us for years.

A busboy took away our salad plates and a waiter brought our dinners. The legislature had better fund my pension because, as a single person, I didn't have a second income. "If your father had lived, we would have had it made in the shade."

Kevin raised his eyebrows, looked down at his plate, and twirled spaghetti. "I guess you probably want to know a little about my girlfriend."

"Not necessarily."

"After a while, you get tired of looking and grab what you can."

"What did you grab?"

"A roller coaster."

"She probably wants a ring," I said. "Women go kind of nuts if you tantalize them."

He smiled through his eyes. "Getting to know a person takes awhile."

"Yes, it does," I said, "and even when you think you know them, you're surprised."

Kevin leaned back and motioned to the waiter. "I'll have a decaf espresso."

"Same," I said.

A serious look came over Kevin's face. "You know, Sandy wasn't feeling well."

"She wasn't?" I said.

"Talked about some bump under her arm."

"What kind of bump?"

"A hot, red one," Kevin said. "She wanted to skip this trip and go to the hospital. Big argument about it in the bathroom before they left."

They always argued in the bathroom.

"It's probably just a cyst," I said. "Women get ingrown hairs."

I was more worried about whether Tony would survive the train. It was a long ride, twelve hours, and I couldn't imagine how Sandy would maneuver him in the toilet. When Aldo had Tony under his roof day and night, maybe he'd realize what a toll it took; and if he wasn't completely worn out himself, he'd ride back with them to D.C. But, then again, knowing Aldo, he probably wouldn't.

On the warm, fall night Kevin suggested a walk through the side streets of Georgetown. I wanted to get back to the house and hit the sack. "If we see a liquor store on the way home," I said, "remind me to stop."

"Why? Are you becoming a lush?"

"No, I need some boxes. I want to load my stuff in the trunk and be ready to go."

"I can drive you home, if you want."

"I know. You drove to the restaurant."

"I mean home to Illinois," he said. "I'm on Southwest. It's easy to change a flight."

"That's okay. I can drive. I'm not going to push it."

I felt the weight of his arm on my shoulder. "Listen, Mom. The moment I stepped in that door, I figured out what you've been up against. Sean told me, but I didn't understand. Sandy ought to thank her lucky stars for you."

"Oh, I don't know," I said. "It's pretty hard to accrue a big feeling of indebtedness. What usually happens is people come to resent it."

Being thanked had never been what I'd needed anyway. When it came right down to it, my commitment of time hadn't even been about saving their marriage or keeping Sandy from feeling regret at how she might have lived these last few months. What I had needed and had never gotten was what Sandy's therapist had so correctly surmised: a closer relationship with my daughter. Taking care of Tony had messed that up. I had to be satisfied with what I had. A job. A life. Two sons.

***

I slept until almost one o'clock and when I came downstairs, I saw that Kevin had painted half the dining room. He'd run down to Starbucks and brought me a latte. A cardboard cup sat on the counter. The coffee was cold.

The phone rang. I went to the kitchen. "Mom! Mom!" Sandy was jerk-sobbing. "You've got to come to the hospital."

"Which hospital?" I said.

"Georgetown," Sandy said. "Hurry. They're taking me in."

The phone disconnected.

Georgetown, the small, teaching hospital on Reservoir Road where Tony had his feeding tube put in? Normally, Tony went to GW. I looked at the receiver. The phone started beeping.

"What's going on?" Kevin climbed down the ladder.

"Sandy's in the hospital. But I must have heard wrong. Sandy must have said, 'Tony.' *Tony* was in the hospital."

We looked at each other. Kevin threw his sponge on the counter and I grabbed keys and ran for the car. Kevin hopped in, tying his shoes as I sped down Wisconsin Avenue. In the turnaround of the emergency room, I saw the white Ford van, its panel door slid sideways; the lift was down. I ran into the waiting room. Tony looked up. Josh ran over and clung to my legs. A woman with a toddler was looking after Ben. "What are you doing back so soon?" I said.

"Sandy made us come back early."

"Where is she?"

Tony nodded to the wide, closed doors. "Somewhere in there."

"What's the matter with her?"

"She has some stupid red line running up her arm, and she made us leave Disney World because of it."

"My mom's really sick," Josh said, looking up. "The doctor made her lie down on an ambulance bed."

I heard the drumbeat of my heart as I spoke to a receptionist. The woman made a phone call. "She's in ICU." Zigzagging with her hand she gave directions. Kevin said he'd watch Josh and Ben. With Tony following me through the door that led into the examining rooms, I hurried down a long corridor with curtained cubicles and through another door that led to the elevators. Tony maneuvered his joystick and his chair turned in a circle as he backed into the elevator. We floated up.

"Why did they take her to intensive care?" I said.

"I don't know. She was fine on the train."

"She's obviously not fine now."

The elevator doors opened. Tony sped ahead to the nurses' station. "Where's my wife?"

A nurse, sitting behind the counter, looked over the top of Tony's head at me. "Excuse me?" the nurse said. "I didn't quite get that."

"We're here for Sandy Gallagher," I said. "I'm her mother."

"Thank goodness," the nurse said. "She wouldn't let us intubate her until she spoke with you."

"Intubate her?"

"She needs to be on a respirator."

"What's wrong with her?"

"The doctors think it's either septic shock or strep. They called an infectious disease specialist."

"Where is she?" I said.

The nurse motioned to the window behind my back. Tony turned his chair. "Excuse me," the nurse said. "One at a time."

"Can I speak to the doctor?" Tony said. "Nobody's explained what's going on to my satisfaction."

I translated.

"Of course," the nurse said. "Wait here."

In bed, in a hospital gown, Sandy lay with her eyes closed. Rimmed with red, they looked as if she'd been crying. A clear plastic mask covered her nose. Her arms lay on top of the sheet, a needle from an IV was taped to her wrist, and her chest pumped as fast a bird's. A nurse pressed Sandy's pulse. "This girl needs to be on a respirator ASAP, but she decided to fight us till you came."

"You're giving her oxygen through the mask," I said. "Isn't that enough?"

"We're barely getting a pulse."

I slid a chair to the bedside. "Sandy, wake up, honey." Sandy's skin looked blue, except for a flush of red near her neck. Her hand felt cold.

Sandy's eyes fluttered open. "Mom, I don't want to be on a respirator."

"I know, but this is just temporary." I looked at the nurse.

"We need to support her breathing," the nurse said.

"See, honey? It's just till you get better."

"I want to get better," she said.

"What happened?"

"I had this thing under my arm."

The nurse pressed a button above the bed. "I'm going to have to ask you to leave. You can come back after we've finished."

"The little boys are downstairs," I said.

"Make sure they have a happy childhood," Sandy said.

"What are you talking about?"

"I love you, Mommy."

The nurse picked up the phone. "She's crashing. Let's do it."

A distant intercom summoned a doctor. Wheels squeaked. Metal rattled. A man in green pushed past me and drew a curtain around the bed. Backing from the room, I paused in the corridor: Sandy gagged and gagged and gagged again. I covered my ears.

Turning, I saw Tony wheeling toward a middle-aged woman in a white coat. The woman had short black hair and a stethoscope around her neck. Her head dropped so that she appeared to be looking at her shoes. Dr. Monique Figuer-Leblanc introduced herself as the infectious disease specialist.

"You know your daughter is very ill, yes?" the doctor said.

"Yes," I said.

"I must ask you, your daughter's color is a little flushed, no?"

"Actually, I thought her skin looked blue," I said.

"Did you not see a bit of redness around her eyes and on her neck," she pointed to the V of her throat, "the same red, almost a rash?"

"I thought she'd been crying," I said.

"Perhaps, but to me, it is a sign that she is suffering a streptococcal toxic shock syndrome."

"Strep! How would she get that?"

"This is not strep that makes one have a sore throat," Dr. Figuer-Leblanc said. "It's a virulent strain. Rare, but like the flesh-eating bacteria. Is she allergic to penicillin?"

Sandy had had scarlet fever as a child. Doctors had prescribed penicillin for ear infections. When Josh turned one, he'd come back from daycare with strep throat. It had taken two rounds of Amoxicillin before it finally cleared up. Sandy had taken it, too.

"She's had penicillin before," I said, "pretty often, in fact."

"This is not good news," the doctor said, dropping her head. "Penicillin is still the best weapon in our arsenal."

"Can't you give her antibiotics?" Tony said.

"Excuse me," the doctor said.

"He wants to know if you can give her antibiotics," I said.

"Her body is filled with a toxin that is like a bomb." She made an exploding motion with her hands. "Her organs are overwhelmed by infection and from fighting the infection."

"Which organs?" I said.

"Her kidneys, heart, and lungs."

"How do you know that?" Tony looked up, glowering.

I translated.

"She's not urinating," the doctor said.

"She didn't start to feel lousy until we hit South Carolina," Tony said. "I don't see how it could be so bad."

"I take it she managed to drive to the emergency entrance and her son ran in and summoned help," the doctor said. "Her blood pressure had already dropped." She looked at her watch. "That was approximately forty minutes ago. In these cases, every minute adds to the cascade of negative events."

"I think it'd be okay if she's on a respirator for a little while," I said, "but only for a day or two."

"Why is that?" the doctor said.

"Respirators have been an issue in our family."

"Hook her up," Tony said.

"Her husband says he thinks it'd be all right," I said, "and, anyway, I already told them to go ahead."

The doctor looked at each of us. "If she'd come in the hospital twenty-four hours ago, then she'd have had a much better chance. As it is, there's a seventy percent mortality."

"You're saying she's going to die?" Tony said.

The doctor raised her eyebrows. "It depends on her immune system."

"Can't you do anything?"

"I've ordered some intravenous immunoglobulin. It might give her a boost. And we will certainly support her breathing and do whatever we can."

"I want to see her," Tony said.

I watched him spin his wheelchair around and head toward the small, glass room. I wanted to say something to him, but what?

At the ICU counter sat a nurse with smile wrinkles and cottony hair. April, her nametag said. She looked over the top of her half-moon readers. "Ye-es?"

"Are the doctors doing everything they can?" I said.

"You can be assured of that."

"Should I call in another specialist?"

"You can if you want, but in all of D.C., I think your doctor's the best."

"What makes you think that?"

"Because she cares."

"Fat lot of good that'll do." I poked my head in the door of Sandy's room and told Tony I was going down to see about the kids. He nodded.

"Wash your hands before going out." The nurse pointed to a restroom with a stencil of a figure in a wheelchair. "If you're wearing a wedding band—"

"I'm not married for Chrissake."

The nurse raised her eyebrows. "It's normal to be upset."

Upset didn't even begin to describe it.

In the restroom, water splashed on my hands. I should not be crying when I faced Josh and Ben, so maybe it was better to let it all spill out, this Niagara. Well, go ahead, here it came, coughed-up clots. My chest ached. I dreaded the night ahead.

In the elevator, bright red numbers flashed. Seven. Six. Five. The layers of Dante's *Inferno*. Anyone who had anything to do with this should be sent there. What had Mark Twain said about liars and statisticians? Thirty percent survived. I had to hold on to that.

The doors opened. Giving my nose one last blow, I retraced my steps and entered the waiting room.

Josh ran up to me. "Is my mom okay?"

The doors of the emergency room opened. Sean rushed in. He looked at Kevin and Josh. "What's going on?"

I took Sean's hand. "I'm sorry to say, I don't have much good news."

"How is she?" Kevin said.

"Best as I understand, she has a systemic strep infection."

"Sandy?" Sean said.

"Yes," I said. "And I'm not talking strep throat. It's some kind of strep that spread throughout her body."

"So how long's she going to be here?" Kevin said.

"They don't know."

"But she is going to be okay," Sean said.

I shook my head. "The odds aren't in her favor."

"What are they?" Sean said.

"Seventy-thirty. The good news is, it's not zero."

Sean walked down the hall, slamming a fist into his palm.

Josh frowned, flaring his nostrils, and inhaled the news. "Did my mom say anything?"

"Your mom said she loves you more than anyone in the whole wide world."

"More than Ben?"

I looked around the waiting room. Ben was scattering the magazines on an end table. "She loves you for you and Ben for Ben. You boys are the center of her whole life."

Yes, of course they were. They were the center of Sandy's, just as Sandy had been the center of mine. Sandy and her nuclear family. Sandy would fight. She would be desperate to get back to her kids. I hugged Josh and felt him stiffen. I was a placeholder, on duty until Mommy came back.

"I wonder why she didn't go to the hospital in Florida?" Kevin said.

"She *did*," Josh said. "She went to urgent care."

"Oh?"

"The doctor said she had the flu."

"And when you got here, you brought the doctor for your mom," I said.

Josh nodded. "And one of the doctors took Ben out of his car seat, and he was running between the cars. The grownups couldn't catch him."

"Sounds like mayhem," Kevin said.

When minutes counted, I wondered how long it had taken to unload the van from the train. The van was still outside and in the way of ambulances. The keys were probably still in the ignition. Someone should move it.

I put Josh down. I needed to go back upstairs. Kevin could take the car seats from the van and put them in the car. He or Sean could bring me the van's keys before they took the boys home. People needed to be mustered for a prayer circle. Aldo and Lillian. Charles. Frank. Noah. The rolodex was in the TV cabinet.

"I want to stay until she's better," Josh said.

"No, honey," I said. "The hospital doesn't allow children in the room."

I would need to be here for a while, and Tony would want to be here, too.

When I went back upstairs the nurse sent Tony and me to the waiting area. They were still working on Sandy. Sean brought up the keys.

"You want to see her?" I said.

Sean shook his head. "I'd be a basket case and I think I can do more for her if I go down and deal with Josh."

"I'll go in," Tony said.

I gave Sean a hug and patted his cheek. "You're the one the boys know best."

Hands thrust in his pockets, he walked off down the corridor. I sat in the waiting room until seven o'clock. Tony motored over.

"My bladder's about to burst," he said. "Would you mind taking me?"

"How is she?" I said.

"She can't say anything with that tube in," Tony said.

"I know," I said.

I took him to the bathroom, one of those huge, accessible hospital bathrooms where it was easy to maneuver the wheelchair. After I'd washed his hands, I said, "Tony, may I spend a minute with her?"

"Sure," he said. "Anyway, I think you can relax. She's looking better."

"I hope so," I said.

At the foot of the bed, I held Sandy's toes. They were her father's toes, long and prehensile, and even through the sheet, they felt like popsicles. I squeezed and worked my thumbs along the bottoms, urging the blood, now full of lifesaving drugs, to course through her veins and revive her vital organs. Which were failing. The little bag clipped to the bed, the bag that held urine, had nothing in it.

April, the white-haired nurse, squeezed past me. At a corner sink, she washed her hands, then snapped on rubber gloves.

"Is she passing any fluids?" I asked.

"They're bringing in a dialysis machine," she said.

Sandy's eyes were closed and even the hard pressure on her feet did nothing to awaken her. "She must be in a coma."

The nurse pursed her lips. I took that for a yes.

"Is she breathing on her own at all?"

The nurse shook her head. "No."

She adjusted the mask's elastic. Two more medical people came in, a man and woman, and between them, they maneuvered a machine that looked like a robot. It was white, the size of a human. They plugged in the cord. A phlebotomist came to draw blood. He tapped the inside of Sandy's elbow, balled her limp hand into a fist, and tapped again. "Looks iffy," he said.

"Should I leave?" I said.

"Depends how you feel about needles."

"I won't faint." I took a deep breath. A needle as big as a porcupine quill emerged from its paper cover. April pushed over a chair. I sat, holding Sandy's feet as if they were the rudder of a ship. Which they were. How long had I steered my life by this girl? Ever since her father's death. I watched the man ease a needle into her vein.

"Sandy, honey," I said, "you've got to fight."

Sandy lay there, the bellows of the respirator wheezing like the BiPAP. I waited for her eyes to flutter. Nothing.

Tony came to the door. "My turn."

I rose and moved the chair aside so that Tony could take my place at the foot of the bed. "What's up?" he said.

"Dialysis."

Tony raised his eyebrows. "They didn't tell me."

"Me neither."

Out in the corridor, I saw Dr. Figuer-Leblanc. The doctor, her expression without the hint of the smile she'd had earlier in the day, motioned me over. I waited while she gathered papers and a clipboard and stopped at the room to say a word to Tony. Then she headed for the waiting area with Tony trailing behind her. We sat, the three of us, me nervous about the doctor's attention to her clipboard and the ballpoint she continued to click. Because Sandy was not urinating, the doctors knew Sandy's body had no way to expel the toxins building up in her blood. The medical team had just put their heads together about the best course of action: dialysis, support of respiration, massive fluids to try to raise her blood pressure. So far, pumping her with fluids had merely succeeded in getting medication into her system and reducing the stress, but Sandy was unresponsive.

"The nurse said she's in a coma," I said.

"It's good that she's sleeping," Tony said.

"She's not asleep," Dr. Figuer-Leblanc said. "There are some indications that her brain may have suffered irreversible damage."

"What indications?" Tony said.

"How do you know?" I said.

"An hour after we put her on the respirator, we suctioned her lungs."

An hour. Had she been here an hour already?

"Normally, patients, even those in a coma, will have a gag response. The nurse called one of our neurologists to take a look."

"Who?" Tony said.

"Dr. Hankerson."

"I don't know her," Tony said.

"He sees Dr. Stevanovic over at GW," I said.

"We have our own neurology department, and for this, they are excellent clinicians." Dr. Figuer-Leblanc's eyes were warm as she looked at Tony. "Dr. Hankerson checked her eyes. Normally, when you turn a person's head from side to side, their eyes move like a doll's eyes." She lifted her eyebrows and rolled her eyes. "Sandy's crossed."

"She's not cross-eyed," I said.

"That's a simple determinant of brain death. We're going to run some other tests."

"What you're saying is that she might not be in a coma," I said. "She might be brain-dead."

The doctor nodded. "Right now, it is very likely that her heart is going to be the next organ to fail."

"And the question is, what should you do then?"

The doctor nodded and looked at each of us. "Do you know her wishes?"

"Yes," I said.

"Isn't there such a thing as a heart-lung machine?" Tony said. "Couldn't you hook her up to that and give the medicine a chance to work?"

I translated.

The doctor dropped her head, looking at the floor. "Heart-lung machines are for cardiac patients, and the surgery is quite intrusive. Your wife would need anticoagulants. Her heart would be opened up. Her system couldn't take the insult."

"Couldn't she just be on it long enough for a transplant?" Tony said.

Tony could be so damned obtuse. "For crying out loud," I said. "A transplant takes forever. She's brain-dead."

The doctor frowned. "Maybe I'm not explaining it clearly. Heart-lung machines are designed to support life for a few hours. In the case of brain death, it's only the respirator that makes it seem that she's still living."

Heaviness settled on my shoulders. "It's not what my daughter would want."

"How do you know?" Tony said.

"She told me."

"But, you have to save her," Tony cried.

"Tony," I said. "There's nothing to save."

"You want us to sign some paper, is that it?" Tony's eyes brimmed.

"Did you bring a release?" I said.

"Yes," the doctor said. "It's a DNR order. Do not resuscitate. If she goes into cardiac arrest, at that point we will allow nature to take over."

"I can't sign anything anyway," Tony said, "so it's a moot point." He spun around and headed back to the room.

The doctor passed me the papers. I looked at the X on the signature line. "Is the neurologist sure about the . . . " I moved my eyes.

"He'll see her again tomorrow to be sure," the doctor said, "but if she were to go into cardiac arrest before then?"

I looked down the hall at the EXIT sign.

"If it would make you feel better to wait . . ."

"Doctor, before my daughter lost consciousness, she said, 'Mom, I don't want to be on a respirator.' She knew what it meant and didn't want it. She would not want us to prolong her life by artificial means."

"That sounds pretty definite."

I clicked the pen open and closed and looked at the X. People who came back from the brink of death talked about the penumbra of light. What were the odds Rob would be there, his arms outstretched? Maybe he'd spin her around and send her back, or maybe he'd decide to keep her. I wrote my name and handed back the pages.

CHAPTER 27

The ICU was quiet, the silence only broken by the hum of fans in the vents and the nurses' crepe-soled shoes. The respirator and the dialysis robot sat outside the door of Sandy's room. Good. No more equipment. Sandy had slept next to that damn BiPAP far too long. A nurse with a doughy face rolled a washcloth and tucked it under Sandy's chin.

"What a beautiful girl," she said.

"Yes," I said.

The lines of tension had bled away and Sandy looked at peace, the hopes and dreams for her own little family contained beneath her eyelids. All that was missing was her breath.

Kevin handed me a box of kleenex. The call had woken me at four-thirty, and by now my nose felt raw. Sandy's wedding ring and a heart-shaped necklace were in a paper sack. The nurse gave me Sandy's purse. The hospital social worker could help with arrangements, but she didn't start work till eight.

Kevin and I sat looking at the tent made by Sandy's toes.

"We should call Tony," Kevin said.

"Let's tell him in person."

"That was smart of you to turn off the ringer."

"It would have taken forever to get him dressed."

"I don't know about you," he said, "but I'm starving."

"I guess I should eat."

Downstairs in the cafeteria, we carried our trays to a table. "I should call Maria," I said. The babysitter was supposed to have the week off, but she would come over.

Kevin stared at a triangle of toast. "I wonder why the train guy didn't call an ambulance?"

"He would have had to do something with Tony and the kids."

"I suppose," he said, "but, still, if she was that sick, you would think he could have done something."

At eight, a young woman in her twenties, the hospital's social worker, juggling a styrofoam cup and a briefcase, unlocked her office. She put her coffee down and said it'd be a minute till she got set up.

Kevin scooted his chair next to mine and leaned forward. "Upstairs, the lady said you had a list of mortuaries."

The woman reached in a file drawer and pulled out a crookedly photocopied sheet.

"I don't want this to turn into a big research project," I said. "DeVol is the closest."

"They'll pick up the remains as soon as you call," the woman said.

"Please don't say 'remains,'" I said.

"I meant your daughter, of course." The woman closed the drawer. DeVol would bring Sandy to the mortuary, and we could stop by later and pick out a casket.

My cheeks turned numb. Going to the body dentist. That's how Sandy had felt the day Tony got his diagnosis. On the way to the parking garage, I handed the keys to Kevin. Traffic on Reservoir Road went by in a blur. We passed DeVol's. No lights on yet.

At home, Tony and Josh were eating breakfast.

I heard the patter of Ben's hard-soled shoes in my bedroom. "No, no," Sean said. "That's Grandma's."

Josh turned around in his chair. "Where did you go, Grandma?"

He must have heard Kevin and me sneaking down the stairs. "To the hospital," I said, sinking down on the couch.

"I'll go as soon as I have my shower," Tony said.

"It's too late," I said.

"It's only nine o'clock."

I looked at Josh. His face had gone white. He jumped off the chair and ran, his feet pounding up the stairs. "Mommy's dead! My mommy's dead!"

"Is that true?" Tony said. "Is Sandy ...?"

Coming downstairs, Sean held Josh's hand. Ben sat in the crook of Sean's arm. "What happened?" he said.

I told them what I knew. No details. The doctor hadn't been there to answer questions. Hands on hips, mouth twisted, Sean shook his head and put Ben down on the couch next to me. Tony spun his wheelchair around and rammed it against the table. He backed up and rammed again. The table moved.

"Hey, guy," Kevin said. "Hang on a minute."

Panting, his face red, Tony shoved and backed, shoved and backed. Kevin reached over and flipped off the power. Tony flung his body in slow motion.

"Calm down," Kevin said.

Tony threw his head back. "I'm c-c-c-alm," he bellowed. And then he panted to catch his breath.

Kevin and Sean looked at each other.

Finally, Tony's shoulders sagged. Breathing hard, but not in distress.

"Got yourself under control?" Kevin said.

Tony nodded.

"Good," Kevin said. "I'll switch on your power."

Tony backed up, turned, and came into the living room. Good for Tony. I could throw a vase with the greatest satisfaction. I could smother him with a pillow or put my hands around his neck and choke him. Instead, I was going to have to hold it together. Josh looked from his father to each of his uncles, and then to me, and Ben slid down from the couch. Forcing myself to move, I scooped Josh into a bear hug, kissed him, and put him down.

"I thought she'd pull through," Tony said.

"The probabilities weren't in our favor," I said.

In the dining room, I put the mortuary information and a credit card on the table and gave Kevin instructions. We'd need a funeral plot and DeVol could point him to a place that didn't cost too much. Ditto for the casket.

Tony rolled toward me. "I want to see her."

"Kevin, when he's finished eating, would you dress Tony?"

"I'll skip breakfast," Tony said.

"Fine," Kevin said. "I'll dress you now."

"You don't know how," Tony said.

"I'm not dressing you," I said.

"Call Charles," Tony said.

"In a few minutes," I said. "I'm busy. On second thought, there'll probably be a service tomorrow night. Maybe you could wait till then to see her."

"She might not even be at the hospital," Kevin said. "The mortuary was supposed to come get her."

"All right," Tony said, "but I want to make sure she wears her new suit."

As I explained about the suit, Kevin bit his bottom lip. Probably, the scene here was more than Kevin had bargained for, but I didn't have the energy to worry about anyone but myself and Sandy's children. Ben opened the puzzle cabinet. Looking angry, he grabbed a stack and threw them on the floor. "Ma-ma. Ma-ma."

"Hey, little guy." Sean picked up Ben. He poked his belly. "You're making a mess."

Josh looked up at Ben. "Mommy's dead."

"Mommy home," Ben insisted.

"No," Josh shouted, making a fist. "Mommy's *dead!* Mommy's *dead!*"

I picked Josh up. His legs were long and dangling. He wasn't a baby, but I forced his head down on my shoulder and rubbed his back. "There, there, honey. He's too little to understand." But Josh understood. I didn't want to leave him for an instant, to have him feel the space between himself and the infinity that separated him from the person he most loved. Josh was my anchor in a topsy-turvy world, and Ben, too. I would have to be theirs, giving them my body to lean on.

***

The viewing would be tomorrow night. We were going to have to put the house back in order before people showed up. Kevin and Sean straightened the dining room. I sent Kevin to Boston Market for dinner. At bedtime, I asked Sean to give Josh a bath. While Kevin washed dishes, I went upstairs to deal with hospital paperwork. Sitting at Sandy's desk, a mountain of bills confronting me, I heard Sean ask Josh about Disney World.

"I went on the Tower of Terror," he said.

"Was it scary?" Sean said.

"Not as scary as the train."

I rolled back from the desk. Standing in the bathroom door, arms folded, I said, "Why was the train scary?"

Josh was paddling. He looked up. "My mom had a fever. The conductor wanted to stop the train and call an ambulance, but Mommy screamed she had to get home."

"Do you know why?" I said.

"No," he said.

I didn't understand why Sandy hadn't gotten off the train, or why she had boarded in the first place. Down in Florida, she must have known she was sick. Kevin said she'd been worried about the welt before she left, and she'd even visited urgent care. Take two aspirin. Yeah, right.

I read the children *Good Night Moon*—keep life as normal as possible—and came down to find Charles and Kevin double-teaming the night routine.

Charles apologized for not coming earlier. "I was in New Hampshire."

"That's okay," Tony said, as if Charles had been speaking only to him. "There wasn't anything you could have done."

"But there was," Charles said, "and I should have."

I had no idea what he was talking about, but at least he'd been here recently enough to get what Tony said. I was sick of playing interpreter.

Charles and Kevin changed Tony into pajamas and transferred him to bed. Kevin said he'd sleep next to Tony since Sean had done it the night before. Tony raised his eyebrows. His eyes rolled toward me.

"No way," I said.

"I'll go upstairs and see if I can find some sleeping attire," Kevin said. "I don't want to be down here in my boxers."

"Good luck," I said. "But you're a lot bigger than anyone else in this house."

"I have some pajamas," Charles said. "I'll bring them in soon as I have a word with your mom."

"I don't have anything to say to you," I said.

His look of amused forbearance annoyed me.

"I'd appreciate if you'd stick with me while I adjust the BiPAP,"he said.

"Oh, all right," I said.

Charles taped and untaped the BiPAP's Velcro bands.

"No, like this," I said, giving the exact rip that would sound right to Tony. He blinked a "thank you." I hated the glow in Tony's eyes. It made me feel trapped.

Charles connected the feeding tube and hung the baggie of Ensure. He was trying to be a Good Samaritan. See how long that would last. He took my elbow. "We have to talk."

"Do we?"

"For old time's sake."

I supposed I owed him that, even though I would have much preferred to go to bed, and not with him. I grabbed a parka and opened the front door. It was dark on the porch. The bulb had burned out. One more thing to fix. But, hey. Leave it. We sat down.

Charles shivered and tucked his hands in his pockets. "It's cold."

"Is it?"

"A damp cold."

"I don't feel anything."

The house across the street had red and green lights around the windows and an illuminated snowman in the yard. People put up their Christmas decorations earlier and earlier. It was ridiculous.

"You wanted to speak to me," I said. "What about?"

"I thought we should set up a suicide watch."

"Suicide watch! Whatever for?"

"Your daughter was ready to throw herself off Memorial Bridge," he said. "That's why her therapist told her she needed new friends."

"What did friends have to do with it?"

Charles was silent for a while, wiped his eyes, then stretched out his legs and propped them on the railing. "Her old friends were sanctimonious creeps."

"I don't understand."

He leaned back, hands behind his head. "She had this one friend, a woman she used to walk with. Their kids played together. The woman cut her off."

"Why?"

"I guess Sandy was bitching about Tony. Everyone has so much sympathy for the dying man."

"But none for Sandy."

"She didn't expect pity."

"What did she expect?"

He turned, his eyes liquid light. "Deep down? What we all take for granted. Ordinary happiness."

"Ordinary happiness." I sniffed. "That's funny. I would have said something like comfort or possibly that she wanted to be cherished, not by me but by a man."

"You know the last thing she told me?" Charles said.

"No."

"'Everybody gets to escape but me.'"

"She escaped, Charles. Just not the way she wanted."

"And not the way *we* wanted," he said. "You and I."

You and me. I looked toward the corner where Tony and the woman with the mustache had appeared the time we went to Koolfont.

"Are you going back to Vermont?" I said.

"I never did move," he said.

"Did you pass on that job in D.C.?"

"Yeah."

"Then what were you doing here the other night?"

"Dropping in to pull the oar."

"Your truck was down here. I saw it."

"That's my old truck," he said. "My sister's buying it off me."

I watched his fingers flex on the armrests. He seemed to be trying to grasp something just out of reach.

"I feel bad," I said.

"Why?" he said.

"I misjudged you."

"You didn't misjudge me," he said. "If you hadn't slapped me around, I was going for it. Sandy. The boys. Get them out of here. This was an untenable situation."

"I wish you had."

"I don't see how she could have resisted my charms, overpowering as they are." He took my hand. "She was a fine, fine woman, your daughter. Much like her mother."

"Thanks, Charles, for being her friend."

"I feel like I let her down."

"Me, too."

"Don't beat yourself up," he said. "She knew she could count on you."

"How do you know?"

"She told me so *all the time*."

"Then why did she want me to leave?"

"I don't know that she did."

CHAPTER 28

Trying to figure out what the heck I was going to say to Aldo and Lillian, I sat at the dining room reading the fine print about the cemetery's perpetual care. After sleeping by Tony's side all night, Kevin had gone upstairs to take a nap. "Tony's parents are here," he called down.

A moment later, Lillian burst through the door. Lacquered hair pressed my cheek. "Poor, poor dear," she said.

I pushed her away.

"Now you know how I feel," Lillian said.

"How you feel about what?"

"Losing a child," Lillian said.

"I don't think you have any idea."

Tony was busy at his computer. "Hi, Mom. Hi, Dad. Don't interrupt me. I'm planning a Memorial Service."

"For tomorrow?" Lillian said.

"No," Tony said. "In six weeks."

"Aldo, Lillian, let's go upstairs," I said. "We need to talk." I led the way, Lillian clomping behind in her heels, Aldo doggedly trailing.

"Take a seat," I said, indicating the bed.

Kevin sat in the desk chair and pulled a leg up on his knee.

Aldo and Lillian looked at each other. "We'll stand." Aldo folded his arms across his chest.

"I took the liberty of contacting a nursing agency to arrange for Tony's care." I presented Aldo with a contract. The fax had warmed the paper. "Starting tomorrow, they'll provide three live-ins for the week. They said Tony should have two aides for weekends."

Aldo stared at the papers. "At twenty-two an hour?" He tried to hand the contract back. "You'd better keep looking."

"We're leaving after the funeral," Kevin said.

"You can't leave until you find someone to take care of Tony," Aldo said.

I sat down on the bed.

Lillian took the contract from him. "But we can't afford this."

"Do you still own your house in Camden?" I said.

"It's our primary residence," Lillian said. "The place in Florida is just our getaway."

"Here are your choices." I had to talk to them like children. They could help Tony qualify for Medicaid and move him to a nursing home, either in Florida, New Jersey, or D.C. Or they could move him into one of their spare bedrooms. Even so, he'd need caregivers. If they wanted him to stay here, they could assume the two mortgages on the townhouse, plus the other expenses, such as those that would pay for Tony's twenty-four-hour care.

"What about Sandy's life insurance?" Aldo said.

I slid open the drawer in Sandy's filing cabinet. Yesterday, I had worked nonstop to sort out her bank accounts and insurance policies. I handed Aldo a manila folder. "Sandy has a group policy worth $100,000."

"That'll be a start," Aldo said.

"I believe if you check that," I said, "you'll see that she named the children, not Tony, as beneficiaries."

"He's their guardian," Aldo said. "I'll have him sign the money over to me."

"Tony and I will share guardianship," I said, "and I won't agree to that. The money should be put aside for their education."

"Tony's their father," Aldo said. "There's no question that, legally, he'll be their guardian."

"He's incapable of being their physical guardian," I said. "The children will go home with me."

"And me," Kevin said. He twirled my car keys around his finger.

"You can't remove them without his permission." Lillian's eyes flashed.

"Whatever you make in Illinois," Aldo said, "we'll pay you," he paused and looked up at the ceiling, "two hundred more a month to stay here."

"You couldn't pay me enough," I said. "Come on, you guys. We have to divvy this up. Unless you want to put him in a nursing home, Tony needs the umbrella of your health insurance. You'll have to put him on as a dependent."

"I'd rather have the children," Lillian said.

"Well, I'm not taking Tony," I said.

Aldo looked at Lillian then back at me. "What do you recommend?"

"Except for the kitchen, the house is in good shape," I said. "Put it on the market."

"Tony loves this house," Lillian said. "He'll never move."

"Then we should sit down as a family and discuss the options with Tony," I said. "From what I know of Medicaid, they won't cover twenty-four-hour home care. Tony will have to move to a nursing home."

Lillian wrung her hands. "Tony would be upset if we even suggest that."

Aldo looked at her. "We don't want anyone upset."

"I'm actually a lot more concerned about not upsetting the kids," I said. "They need regular contact with their father, but I can't live here and raise them."

"Maybe they could come for a couple weeks in the summer," Kevin said.

"Oh, it's got to be more often than that," Lillian said.

"Then you can pay for the plane tickets," I said.

"This is going to be so terrible for Tony," Lillian said. "First his wife, then his children."

"When did you say you were leaving?" Aldo said.

"After the funeral," I said.

"Why don't you take the kids while Tony's *at* the funeral," Aldo said. "I'm afraid the shock might kill him."

"What a good idea," Lillian said. "You could tell Josh he's going for a short visit, and then it could get longer and longer."

"I won't lie to Josh," I said.

"Oh, please, please, please don't tell him before the funeral. He'll let the cat out of the bag." Lillian clasped her hands.

"I agree with Lillian," Aldo said. "It would be very hard on Josh if he sees Tony throwing a fit, which we all know he will. We'll break the news to Tony after you're gone."

Aldo was right. I could imagine Tony zipping down the wheelchair ramp. Sobbing. Crying. Without the kids he would have no reason to live, but he was too incapacitated to harm himself.

"Okay," I said. "He's your son and I'm sure you have ways of getting through to him that I don't."

Aldo took Lillian's arm and led her to the door. "Come on. We brought some toys."

"A children's book of grief," Lillian said. "That sort of thing. To keep Josh's mind off his mother."

"Lillian, Josh's mind is never going to be off his mother," I said. "It won't be for the rest of his life. Nor off his father, for that matter. I really wish you'd let me tell Josh so he can say good-bye to his dad. I don't want to kidnap him."

"It's *much* better to keep it a secret. You can just vanish like that." Lillian snapped her fingers. "The way Sandy did."

Kevin stood up abruptly. A second later the bathroom door slammed.

I stood. "There's a visitation at the funeral home tonight."

Lillian looked me up and down. "What will you wear?"

"I have no idea." I couldn't go in jeans.

"Would you like me to run out and buy you something?" she said.

"That would be very kind of you," I said.

"Do you want a dress?"

"Black slacks, a black blouse. Size twelve longs. I'll pay you back."

"No," Lillian said. "It's my pleasure."

***

I buttoned my new slacks.

Sean looked in from the hall. That afternoon he'd driven back to Maryland and packed a suitcase, including the suit he'd wear to the funeral.

"Are you sure you don't want me to go with you to the visitation?" he said.

"You, me, or Kevin needs to stay with Josh and Ben at all times," I said.

"What about tomorrow?"

"The kids are used to being with Maria during the day."

"Good," he said. "The funeral's more important than the viewing. I don't think I could stand seeing her in an open coffin. She was a second mother to me."

"That she was. That she was."

"What's the drill tonight?"

"Give the boys a bath and read them a couple of stories, as normal a night as possible."

Picturing the two children on the train with their helpless father and Sandy, feverish and disoriented, filled me with such rage that my blood effervesced like Alka-Seltzer.

"Ready?" Kevin called from downstairs.

"As I'll ever be," I said.

I went downstairs, my feet leaden.

"Do you know the Buddha's last words?" Kevin said, putting a hand on my shoulder.

"No, I don't."

"Detach. Soldier on."

In spite of myself, I smiled. "I seem to be pretty good at the second part, but I'm not good at the first. Sort of the opposite."

"I've mastered detachment," he said, "but this has me thinking I've gone too far."

At the mortuary a man in a dark suit escorted us to a small, ivory room. Bouquets of flowers had been arranged around a white casket. I didn't want to walk up the aisle and look in, but Kevin had hold of my elbow.

Sandy wore the beige suit. The mink collar looked like a curled ferret around her neck. She would never have been caught dead in that outfit. They'd given Sandy's face a somber look. Like Kevin, Sandy had a way of smiling with her eyes, especially when she looked at her boys. And how she loved to greet them at the end of her workday. She hadn't been at her best when she stood on the sidewalk and watched me strap Tony into the van. That stupid trip. Dragging all of Tony's crap: the BiPAP, the commode, and the mast-and-pump. Sandy should have left Tony down in Florida. She'd be alive, but he would have been at the mercy of two poor substitutes.

Organ music poured from the corner speakers and Kevin wiped his eyes. "That's so treacly, it makes me sick."

"It's what they always play in these places." I retreated to the front pew. The music had a way of making you cry. Kevin sobbed. I passed a packet of tissue. I wondered if it was better to have seen the body or not, if the viewing was supposed to bring me some kind of closure. I hoped it would. Except for that one cry in the hospital, my tears had gone deep inside, and I couldn't summon them.

CHAPTER 29

For the sake of the children's happiness, I tried to talk Maria into moving to Evanston, but with family in D.C., she said the best she could do was babysit when the children came to see their father. Although shocked, she'd already started looking for a new position. Now, three short Filipinas stood behind me in the kitchen. Lillian had dropped them off by the back door, and Kevin had let them in.

"Who are *they*?" Tony said.

"Three women dying to touch your privates," I said.

Tony recoiled.

"They're just helping out temporarily," I said, "until we can get all this sorted out."

"I guess that makes sense," Tony said.

Leaving the new caregivers with the sheets of instructions, I followed Maria out to the porch. The stroller's basket was full of snacks, diapers, and jackets. Josh would go to school, Ben to the park, and Maria would have them back at the house by the time Kevin and I returned.

I folded a hundred-dollar bill into Maria's hand. It was far too little.

"You brought a lot of happiness to this house," I said.

"I love the children," Maria said. "I love your daughter, too."

Kevin came up behind me. His shadow stretched down the sidewalk. "You think Tony knows what you intend to do?"

"He probably suspects, but he's 'Mr. Denial.'"

"Why do you say that?"

"Because he's been that way from the beginning. Not wanting to take drugs. Thinking the respirator would be feasible."

He shook his head. "I've been a little bit out of the loop."

"You have, but that's okay. We need your energy to make this move happen."

"Should I start packing?"

"As soon as the women have Tony in the shower, unless you want to drive around back. It might actually be easier to take things from the basement. The toys are down there."

"Will do, boss." He saluted.

I went upstairs, found Tony's suit, and dusted the shoulders. After the women had finished giving him a shower, I stood on the bed and began the sock selection. Green socks, black socks, navy blue.

"Pick one," I said. "We have to go."

"Black, then."

I climbed down from the bed. I could barely pull the socks over Tony's bloated ankles.

"All right," Tony said. "How do I look?"

Sitting up straight and in a white shirt and necktie, he looked as if he could get up from his wheelchair and walk. "You remind me of Lazarus," I said.

"You thought it would be me," he said.

"I did." I bent over and gave him a hug. "But you know what? I'm glad you're still here."

He nodded. "Me, too."

"Listen," I said. "I need to tell you something."

"We're late," he said. "Get the keys."

"They won't have the funeral without us." I lifted his hand, put it on the joystick, and opened the door. "Before we leave, I think you should know—"

"Why do you always want to talk things out? That's one thing Sandy couldn't stand about you." He rolled toward the door, bumped the screen, crossed the threshold, and maneuvered down the ramp. "Talking's not going to bring my wife back."

That was a fact. I thought about the day Sandy had met me in the coffee shop. I don't know why I clung to the notion that talking could have made a difference in the sleepless nights and tedium of Tony's care. With him buckled in the back of the van, I drove looking straight ahead.

The cemetery was out in Maryland, in the boonies, Sean had said. The boys had gone plot-shopping together. I drove slowly down the narrow lanes and was amazed at the number of cars parked with one wheel on the grass. Near the tent that had been set up to provide shade, I double-parked, unstrapped the wheelchair, and lowered the van's lift ramp to the ground. Tony sped off toward Roosevelt, the physical therapist. Dressed in a white suit, Bible in hand, he was the only person in a crowd of two hundred not wearing black. I closed the lift gate and panel door. Kevin walked toward me. "Give me the keys. I'll park it for you."

"Park so Aldo can find it."

"I'm going to make him walk," Kevin said.

"Thanks."

The delay would be good. We'd need time to get back to the house and load up the kids.

My feet sank into the damp grass. A few faces were familiar. Wide-eyed Christie Carney and her husband, Phil Krankauer, the environmental reporter for the *Washington Post*. The Huongs. Sharon wore a black silk coat, slit up the sides, and carried a single red rose. For the coffin, probably. Lowell Jaffee, the tomato grower, Noah and Frank, and Eugene, the nurse. Three brunettes and one blonde, all wearing heels, clustered together, looking around and leaning in to console one another. Sandy's movie group. I waved to Sandy's high school friend Rosemary and Penny, whose mother was a woodworker, and I looked for the woman with the mustache who'd taken care of Josh before the trip to Koolfont. I didn't see her and couldn't remember her name. She must have been the one who'd cut Sandy off.

Tony's sister Lisa, in a black cocktail dress, looked as adrift as I felt. "Thanks for flying down," I said.

"Oh, Colleen. I'm so sorry. What a horrible day."

"Yep, it is."

Someone tugged my sleeve. I turned. Aldo and Lillian.

"We just wanted to make sure," Aldo said, "there's no hard feelings."

"I mean, it wasn't our fault," Lillian said.

"I have a question," I said. "Why didn't you insist she go to the hospital? Why didn't you carry her there, bodily, if you had to?"

Lillian and Aldo looked at each other. With fresh tans and stooped shoulders, they looked like any other pair of sun-damaged, Florida retirees. I had never noticed the constant quiver of Lillian's hands.

"We didn't think we could handle Tony and the children," Aldo said.

"We had never been trained on the new machine," Lillian said.

"Tony said it'd be better if they came back here," Aldo said.

"Besides," Lillian said, "You're the only one she trusted to do it all."

"Thank you for telling me," I said. The trust thing might have made me feel the teensiest bit better if Sandy hadn't been dead.

The crowd moved toward the folding chairs. There were two empty seats in the first row next to Sean and Kevin. When I sat, Sean took my hand. I asked him for a handkerchief and turned to look for Charles. Wearing dark glasses, Charles was standing at one of the corner tent-posts. I motioned him over. He made a thumbs-down.

Tony motored slowly up the Astroturf aisle. A murmur passed through the crowd. "There's her husband." "That's him? He doesn't look as bad as I thought he'd look." "Someone told me he's totally paralyzed."

Tony glided to a stop at the end of the first row. Lillian, Aldo, and Lisa sat next to him. Family of the bride. Family of the groom.

I looked out at the flat, featureless lawn. Saplings had been planted, maples of some sort, with new mulch around them. The leaves were limp. Probably dead. Dead trees for the dead. When I'd told Kevin to keep down the price, I hadn't meant Filene's Basement. But, oh well. I couldn't do everything.

Kevin had called a friend to do the service. In his black serge suit, the fresh-faced kid at the dais looked more like a missionary Mormon than a Unitarian. His homily brought up the old saws. Some people believed and some didn't. Death tested us all. For some reason, my teeth hurt. I must be clenching them. It was weird to have the grave covered by Astroturf. I could see the Astroturf aisle and the Astroturf unrolled beneath the tent—that made it easier to set up chairs—but covering the dirt, the actual dirt, with its plant-roots and pebbles and whatever else was embedded there, as if we weren't going to think about worms, that made no sense. As Josh once said, it was still underground, wasn't it.

Above the hole, the casket hung suspended from canvas straps. It was the cheapest casket they'd had. Last night, it hadn't looked so bad, but then I'd been looking at Sandy, not the box itself. The morticians had swapped Sandy for a mannequin in a wax museum. Of all the Sandys I had ever known—strong, wounded, loving, pissed-off, private, a mother and a career woman—the little girl with the lopsided pigtails had been the one who came back at the end. *I love you, Mommy.* Those three simple words—I love you—were what I kept hearing. Small consolation. It was not the relationship I'd wanted, but the only one I'd ever have.

CHAPTER 30

I grabbed the jar of peanut butter from the fridge. The cold had turned it to concrete, and after spreading it the best I could, I licked the knife, washed it, and popped open the grape jelly. Josh would eat half a sandwich, crust and all, but not if I cut the bread diagonally. Ben ate both halves, but left the crusts.

Hurrying now, because I didn't want the boys to be late for school two days in a row, I went upstairs. Two peas in a pod, they slept together every night. Even when I made Ben promise to stay in his youth bed, he'd say, "I stay put, Gramma," and then sneak through the adjoining bathroom. In the morning I'd find him curled up like a sow bug next to his big brother. At least in his blue feet pajamas, Ben was warm enough. Not Josh. He slept in what he'd worn to school, putting his clothes back on after he'd had his bath, as if climbing back into his own familiar scent brought him comfort.

"Wake up, boys." I shook Josh's leg. "Time to get going."

Josh's eyes popped open. He blinked and looked around.

"What's the matter?" I said.

"I was having my wolf dream."

"I thought Ben kept the bad dreams away."

"He does," Josh said. "Mostly."

He put a hand on Ben and shook him. "Wake up, Ben. We have to get going."

Ben turned and yawned. He looked at Josh, then at me. "Uh-oh, Gramma."

"Hurry to the bathroom."

Ben hopped up and pitter-patted to the bathroom. The stepstool scooted across the tile. "I no have to," he said.

I felt the bed. It was wet. I'd deal with that later. Josh was standing there naked, a wren of a boy hopping from foot to foot as he slipped on white jockeys one size larger than Ben's. The drawer in Ben's room screeched open. In the bathroom, I scooped up soggy feet-pajamas.

"Hey, little naked boy," I said.

"I sowwy."

"It's okay," I said. "Let's get you dressed."

I held out his underwear and felt him shiver as he leaned against me for balance. He threw his arms around my neck and with his pipe-stem legs wriggling in the air, slipped into his jeans. I found matching socks, not so easy considering that the washer gobbled them, or maybe in my haste to pack the boys' clothes I'd left a load behind. If so, they were probably still down there moldering in Sandy's basement.

"Dressed, Josh?" I called.

"Almost," he said from his room.

"Socks on," I told Ben, sweeping him into the bathroom and onto the counter. I dampened a hairbrush and ran it through his hair. A lice warning had been sent home from nursery school. God, if the boys got lice that would just push me over the edge. Bringing lice to Tony's wouldn't do him any favors either.

Josh appeared in the bathroom for inspection. "Let's have a look at you." I held his shoulders. Both boys had their father's dimples, but when I looked at Josh, I saw a lot of Sandy in his thoughtful eyes. A skewer of pain pierced my chest.

With Rob I had told myself just take out one gumball of grief at a time. That had sort of worked, but this was different. It was always there, along with a constant worry about Tony, marooned in the house with his new attendants.

"Let's go, let's go," I said, putting Ben on my hip. Downstairs, in the kitchen, I poured cereal. "What's for breakfast, Grandma?" Josh said.

"Cheerios."

"Could we make pancakes?"

"Not on schooldays," I said.

"I don't want to go to school."

Not this again. "Hop up and eat." I patted the stool and lifted him onto it.

Josh brushed his bangs aside. His hair grew faster than grass. It was going to look like girls' hair if I didn't get him to a barbershop, one of the errands that seemed impossible to fit in.

Today, I was going over to school at lunch hour to make a transition plan. Teaching was quite possibly the last thing in the world I felt like doing but, oh well. I had to buy groceries.

From the living room came the sound of the toy box lid creaking open. Ben's favorite game was hide-and-seek. I went to get him. He had dumped all his toys on the floor.

"Ben," I said. "What am I going to do with you?"

Round-faced, he looked up and smiled. "I hide."

"I see that." I bent down and, feeling a tug in my back, decided he could walk to the kitchen. Luckily, he hadn't taken off his socks, another of his favorite tricks. Positive messages, I reminded myself. Look for anything to praise. After I put him in his highchair, I squeezed his foot.

"Good boy," I said. "You kept your socks on."

He wrinkled his nose. "Me go cool."

"You bet. Me, too."

"Don't forget to buckle him," Josh said.

"I know." I clipped the strap.

I couldn't let Josh think he was the designated adult, though I suspected he watched out for me as much as I did for him. I could feel his vigilance, and sometimes, I felt tempted to ask him if I was doing all right, if I was giving him a happy childhood. I suspected I wasn't. Not really, though I certainly tried. How elusive that word happiness was for all of us; how its meanings shifted from day to day. I poured Ben his cereal and handed him a "big boy" spoon, not the baby spoon I'd left back in D.C. After slicing the skin of a banana lengthwise, I started to cut it.

"He doesn't like bananas, Grandma," Josh said.

"Are you kidding?" I said. "He's part monkey."

Ben looked at Josh's face and at the banana in my hand. He scrunched his eyes and wrinkled his nose. "Me no like."

"Since when?" I said. "You've always liked bananas." I held out a piece.

He shook his head, trying to make himself dizzy.

I laughed. "Bananas are good for you," I said, hoping logic might prevail. It wouldn't, of course. Not with him or anyone else, because we were all creatures of our impulses, and logic had nothing to do with the urges that came from so deep in our brains, we didn't even recognize how powerful they were. I'd learned that. But now I was paying attention to feelings—my own and my grandchildren's—in a way that I had never done before, not even after years of teaching. My way of dealing with grief had always been to stay busy—obsessively, compulsively busy. My daughter had been right. There was something pollyannaish about the way I approached life, some failure to understand the depth of my daughter's pain and divided loyalties.

My loyalties were divided, too. When Kevin and I drove off with the kids, I assumed that Aldo and Lillian would want Tony closer to them, if for no other reason than the practical one: it would be hard to manage his care from so far away. In the end they decided not to, saying that Tony preferred to live in a house where he had memories, and also didn't want to leave his friends.

Not knowing when to quit, I sent an e-mail to Lisa and suggested she drop in more often, but she wrote back that she was providing enough support by sending Tony a daily joke.

There was no reason I should have felt obligated to fly back with the kids more than once a month, but, of course, I did and even inquired about getting a teaching job in Maryland or Virginia. If only my retirement would have permitted it. If only I hadn't had a house with rental income. Well, I could play the "what-if" game forever, or else I could put one foot in front of the other and get on with my life.

The kids' nursery school, in the education wing of a Methodist Church, was two blocks from the house. I dropped Ben off and walked Josh down to the pre-K room.

His teacher, Nancy, frowned. "Hey, Colleen, you look like you pulled an all-nighter."

"Yeah, I'm participating in a scientific test on sleep deprivation."

"Really?" she said.

"No, of course not."

It was pretty evident from the bags under my eyes that I hadn't slept well. Not well for months, when it came down to it.

***

I picked up the boys at four.

At the door of his classroom, Josh stood like a little soldier, hands behind his back. "I don't feel good," he said. I felt his head. Not feverish. But then he hadn't meant "sick." Not feeling good meant he felt how I felt half the time. I bundled him into his new winter togs. Holding Josh's hand and pushing the stroller that Ben was trying to wriggle out of, I began the walk home.

"Is Uncle Kevin going to eat dinner with us?" Josh said.

"I don't know," I said. For the past week-and-a-half, after he'd flown out with the kids to D.C., Kevin had been making himself scarce. I didn't blame him. "The plane ride was the longest three hours of my life," he'd said. Maria hadn't been free, so Kevin had to sleep over. One night had left him feeling trashed. Bundles of kinetic energy, Josh and Ben behaved like the birds at Koolfont. From now on, I'd have to arrange for Sean to meet Kevin at the airport, or else I'd have to go myself. I didn't think I could make myself walk back in that house, but I supposed that if push came to shove, I'd have to make myself do it.

I parked the stroller in the mudroom. Josh took off his boots and put on house slippers.

In the kitchen I made hot chocolate and Josh, sitting on the counter, drank it. I fixed Ben a peanut-butter graham cracker and put him in the high chair. He pulled the crackers apart and licked the goo. That was the kind of thing that made me crazy. I wanted it to be different from how it had been at Sandy's house, the kids eating their vegetables and sitting at the table, not kicking their chairs and throwing tantrums about zucchini. I wanted to prove to someone—God, the universe, Sandy—that I was not going to make a total mess of their little psyches.

"I'm bored," Josh said.

"Me bore, too," Ben said.

From now on, my days were going to be exactly this way: letting the yo-yo drop in the morning when I took the children to school, giving the string a flick, and letting the yo-yo return to my hand the moment school let out. I had promised to give the children happy childhoods, but I was fifty-four. Whatever groundwork I could lay had to be laid now, and that included the month I would spend every summer in D.C. As I cleaned the lunch boxes, I saw that Ben, as predicted, had eaten none of the crust and Josh had left half his sandwich untouched. I washed the lunch pails and propped them on end to dry.

"So!" I clapped my hands. "What shall we do for fun?"

"Go see fishies," Ben said.

Shedd Aquarium was too far away. We could do that on the weekend.

The front doorbell rang. "I wonder who that is?"

"Uncle Kevin," Josh said, running through the dining room.

The front door opened.

"Esmeralda?" I said, my heart pounding.

"It's me," Kevin said, stomping his feet. "I brought something for the kids."

"Me get down," Ben rocked.

"Okay, okay." I wiped his hands.

In the front hall Kevin held out a cardboard box of wood scraps: 2x2s, 2x4s, and 2x6s. "I stopped at Home Depot and got some cut-offs."

Josh looked in the box. "What're they for?"

"Constructions," Kevin said.

"Where'd you come up with this idea?" I said.

"It's something I saw once at a Special Olympics camp." He smiled with his eyes. "I thought the boys could use a little physical release."

"So what are you going to do with the wood?"

"We're going to make a city on your porch."

Josh tugged Kevin's coat. "What city?"

"You can decide what to call it," Kevin said.

"I want to make Montpelier."

"Okay, Montpelier it is."

"It's cold outside," I said. "I don't want him getting sick."

"I brought a space heater," he said. "Put your coats on. Ben can do this, too."

"Oh, all right."

Ben jumped up, trying to pull his coat from the hall tree. I put on a jacket.

"Guess what?" Kevin said.

"What?" I said.

"Chicago Latin gave me a job as a long term sub."

"Is it permanent?"

"Nothing's permanent."

Maybe it wasn't.

Warmed by the space heater and with Kevin straightening bent nails, we worked on the constructions: Ben with a toy hammer that had once been Kevin's, Josh with a finish hammer, and me with my father's old, wooden-handled Stanley. The hammers tapped away like so many woodpeckers.

Kevin stood back to admire the U-shaped, staggered blocks with towers and penthouses. "Lights," he said.

"I have some Christmas lights in the basement," I said.

"Keep working," Kevin said. "I'll find them and be back in a minute."

It took him longer than a minute, more like ten.

"Where's Uncle Kevin?" Josh said. "I want to tell him something."

"He'll be back," I said.

"I'm going to get my markers." Josh ran to the door.

"Bring the washables for Ben."

With Kevin around, that's one thing the kids didn't lack for: art supplies. They each had an easel and sheets of newsprint that Kevin bought from a print shop. He'd started teaching Josh how to cartoon. Feeding an extension cord under the door, Kevin backed onto the porch, unraveling strings of tiny, winking lights and arranging them across the buildings. Josh handed Ben his markers. Ben started to scribble.

"Is that okay?" I asked Josh.

"Sure," Josh said. "That's his end of town. Mine's going to be perfect."

Another perfectionist, I thought.

Josh sat cross-legged at the far end of the porch and began drawing windows and doors. He looked up at Kevin. "We forgot the Capitol," Josh said. "We need a dome."

"Let me think how to do that," Kevin said.

"Maybe an old basketball covered with foil?" I said.

"That'll work." He offered me a hand.

My knees had stiffened. I huffed on my fingers. Down on the concrete, I hadn't felt cold, but standing, I froze.

"Let's go inside." I opened the door. "I need to warm up."

In the living room, holding my hands to the radiator, I glanced up at the portraits over the fireplace. I had swapped the pictures I'd bought at the estate sale for a picture of my father in his Sunday suit and one of Rob, the year before he died. A generation apart, they both stared down at me with camera smiles: the angels of the house. Rob had been a sort of angel, though more an idea of a protective spirit than the man himself had ever been. If I consulted him, he might say I'd failed Sandy not just once, but twice. At least with my dad, I had some generational backup. As he had in life, he encouraged me with his gentle, approving eyes.

"I hope you don't mind," Kevin said, "but I have to fly back to North Carolina."

"Before Thanksgiving?"

"This weekend," he said. "I have to sell my girlfriend on Illinois."

"Ah, yes, the mystery woman."

"That flight I skipped to drive you home? I've been saving the credit for a special occasion."

"I see. Well, good."

"But don't worry," he said. "I'll be back in a week or so. In time to help you eat the bird."

Josh knocked on the window and pointed to the door.

I hurried to the front hall. "I can't believe I left Josh and Ben out there alone."

I turned the knob, and it fell off in my hand.

"I'll get a screwdriver," Kevin said.

"That's okay. I've got it." I took a barrette from my hair, picked up the set-screw that had fallen to the floor, and spun the knob back into position. "Come on in, boys." I grabbed their hands. Ben's little fingers felt like ice. "We'll work on Montpelier tomorrow."

EPILOGUE

Some people never recover from the death of a child, but I could not afford to be one of them. On days when the black wave crashed over me, I stripped the bedroom wallpaper. I emptied the storage locker. I memorized trees. I took in a rescue dog and named him Bear. And then, when I'd given up all hope of seeing Esmeralda again, she dropped me a postcard and signed her last name—Neidert—which turned out to be a pretty easy name to track down. She was working as a waitress and living with her aunt. Little Colleen was the cutest baby ever. The next June, when I drove the boys back to celebrate Ben's and Tony's birthdays, we stopped for a night in Ohio.

Six years after Sandy's death, Tony's hospice manager summoned us back one final time. Tony's pneumonia had not responded to antibiotics; he had slipped into a coma. Besides his parents and my sons, Maria came to the hospital and so did Frank and Noah. We sang. We laughed. We played the blues' tapes that Tony had recorded so long ago. Charles and Lisa showed up for the funeral, a very hard occasion for Josh and Ben. After that we went on with our lives. There were things to fix—meltdowns and musty lunch pails—but I never again faced life alone.

About the Author

Marylee MacDonald's fiction has won the Barry Hannah Prize, the ALR Fiction Award, the Ron Rash Award, the Jeanne Leiby Memorial Chapbook Award, the Matt Clark Prize, and two Illinois Arts Council Fellowships. Her work has appeared in the *American Literary Review, Bellevue Literary Review, Blue Moon Literary & Art Review, Briar Cliff Review, Broad River Review, Folio, North Atlantic Review, Raven Chronicles, Reunion, Ruminate, StoryQuarterly, Yalobusha Review,* and others. She lives in Tempe, AZ. (Author photo by Eric Williams).

ALL THINGS THAT MATTER PRESS

FOR MORE INFORMATION ON TITLES AVAILABLE FROM
ALL THINGS THAT MATTER PRESS, GO TO
http://allthingsthatmatterpress.com
or contact us at
allthingsthatmatterpress@gmail.com

**If you enjoyed this book, please post a review on Amazon.com and
your favorite social media sites.
Thank you!**

CPSIA information can be obtained at www.ICGtesting.com
Printed in the USA
LVOW07s1514221015

459337LV00019B/1246/P